"This is a must-read for anyone interested in the ideas shaping our world. The author delivers a thought-provoking defense of the link between Judeo-Christian values and human dignity and progress, and strongly emphasizes the importance of common sense in world affairs."
—Antonio Mora, Editor in Chief of NewandNews.com, former Good Morning America news anchor and correspondent for ABC News, and lecturer at the University of Miami School of Communication

Dr. Piedra's magnificent analysis is a classical liberal education in one volume. Surveying the philosophical history and causes of Western Civilization, it demonstrates the indispensability of a divinely-inspired natural law for a humane society based on the common good. Exposing the historical and philosophical illiteracy of today's anti-theists, Dr. Piedra shows how their materialistic scientism cannot address the elementary question of metaphysics: the origin of being. In sum, he chronicles the millennia-old struggle for civilization – the "cold war" between those who believe that there is a transcendent dignity in the human person and a transcendent, universal, objective moral order in the world, and those who don't.
—John Lenczowski, Founder and President, The Institute of World Politics

"Dr. Piedra's book is a much-needed antidote to the flawed intellectual notions that have done so much to debase our cultural standards. This is a book for politicians and policy makers as much as for philosophers and the discerning general public. It needs to be widely read and taken to heart."
—The Honorable Faith Whittlesey, United States Ambassador to Switzerland under President Ronald Reagan

"At a time when young men and women are desperately in search of reasons to believe and hope in something bigger than themselves and the material world around them, Dr. Piedra presents a wise proposal: to draw from the rich heritage of the Judeo-Christian tradition the fundamental principles that helped build the uniqueness of this nation."
—Sophia Aguirre, Catholic University of America

D1238557

NO GOD,
NO CIVILIZATION

No God, No Civilization

The New Atheism & the Fantasy of Perpetual Progress

by Alberto Martinez Piedra

Lambing Press | Pittsburgh

Lambing Press

Copyright © 2018 Alberto Martinez Piedra

Published in the United States by Lambing Press.

www.LambingPress.com

ISBN 978-0-9978215-7-4

Book design by Christina Aquilina

Cover image: Dr. Piedra attended St. Edmund's College & Prep School from 1935 – 1937. It is the oldest Catholic school in England (1568). Its Pugin Chapel (1853) provides a potent daily reminder of the glorious heritage of the Judeo-Christian civilization. Image used with permission.

This book is dedicated, in the first instance, to all men and women who are open-minded and willing to engage in a genuine and sincere discussion about the most important questions facing each one of us: Who are we? Where did we come from? And where are we going? The answer to these questions determines how we live our lives, and how we treat others and God, the one, uncreated being. May we always keep in mind that the object of all inquiry is not to know the nature of virtue but to become virtuous for the sake of others.

This book is likewise dedicated to my parents who taught me that all art and science and education, and, ultimately, all ideas are not equal. To my father for living as a true Christian gentleman who knew the importance of humility, kindness, and justice in an age of utopian ideologies, relativism (the ideology that no truth exists), voluntarism (the ideology that no rational order exists) and meaninglessness. To my mother for her Christian common sense, great wisdom, and, above all, ability to discern the link between integral human development, the dignity of the human person, and the Judeo-Christian spirit of service towards others without abandoning rationality and the natural order of being.

Abbé George Lemaître, who formulated the modern big-bang theory, with Albert Einstein in 1933. Credit and Original Drawing by Mr. Nigel Cox

ACKNOWLEDGEMENTS

While it is impossible to thank everyone, I would like to mention a number of scholars whom I have not met but whom I immensely admire for their courage, explanatory abilities, and open-mindedness: John Lennox, Professor of Mathematics (emeritus) at the University of Oxford and Fellow in Mathematics and the Philosophy of Science at Green Templeton College, Oxford; [1] David Berlinski, American writer, thinker, and raconteur; Philip Trower, English writer, whose insights into the crisis of modernity are formidable, and Francis Collins, the former Head of the Human Genome Project. I would encourage everyone to read their publications and see their presentations and lectures.

As a 92-year-old born back in the days when gold coins were still in circulation, it is possible that I have forgotten a footnote or citation in the process of trying to capture some of the key ideas that I have wished to lay out in this book. In this connection, I am indebted to innumerable academics and scholars whose names appear in the footnotes.

I am grateful for the education I received at St. Edmund's College and Prep School, Hertfordshire, United Kingdom, which I attended from 1935 to 1937 — indeed extraordinarily wonderful years. I have the fondest of memories. St. Edmund's instilled in me the basic intellectual, physical, emotional, and spiritual attributes and outlook which remain at the core of any well-rounded person; this outlook was never forced upon us but taught; it was shown to us in everyday practical ways: in the classroom, on the sports field, in the dining hall, and in the chapel. Is it not true that a proper understanding of the human and supernatural virtues lived in one's everyday life makes a real difference in the world? To say otherwise is to know nothing of human nature and history. Is not the living of these virtues day to day, which is far from easy, the process that makes great men and saints? David J. S. Kay, President Emeritus & Archivist, The Edmundian Association, graciously allowed me to use the aerial photograph on the front cover – thank you.

I am also grateful for the couple of years I spent at the École Nouvelle de Paudex in Switzerland. They gave me an excellent insight into continental thinking and France's cultural influence, especially in philosophy and literature during the crucial years of the Enlightenment, and later in the early 1930s, as reflected in the works of such writers as Jean Paul Sartre, Albert Camus, and Andre Gide.

With equal enthusiasm, I am grateful to the Jesuit Fathers who taught me in the past — at Loyola School, New York City; at Colegio de Belén, Havana, Cuba; and at Georgetown University, Washington, D.C. It is my hope that the Jesuits and all religious orders may educate students to live in ways consistent with the teaching and actions of the current Holy Father, Pope Francis.

I would like to thank Jude P. Dougherty, Alyce Ann Woroniak, Walter Jajko, Samuel Gregg, Maria Sophia Aguirre, Ralph and Maria Galliano, Enrique Pinilla, Anthony Salvia, Peter Robinson, David Carradini and Ishmael Virto for their support and endurance during the preparation of this manuscript. I must likewise recognize the outstanding scholarship of Fr. James Schall, S.J. and Robert Reilly, who have, along with the writings of Samil Khalil Samir, S.J., educated me (and I hope so many others) on the meaning and significance of Islam. Big thanks as well to Ravi Zacharias and Bishop Robert Barron whose pedagogy is towering. The vision and generosity of Dr. John Lenczowski, President of the Institute of World Politics has been monumental in my life, as that of Donald E. Bently, philanthropist and entrepreneur, who has supported the Institute for World Politics in so many ways.

I must extend a huge thanks to Ronald Neff, who edited the entire manuscript with gusto, expertise, and dedication; to Larry Kutz and Simon Wenham, both of whom provided insights and in-depth commentary which helped me hone the material; and to Warren Pledger, who edited the first iteration of the text. Their work reflects a profound understanding of the material. In a word, their pens were magical. And thanks to Jonathan Labuhn, whose attention to detail, sorted out pre-publication issues, and to Nigel Cox, who sketched Father Lemaître and Einstein in an entirely novel and interesting way.

While I vehemently disagree with their worldview, let me not forget to thank Christopher Hitchens and Stephen Hawking (may they rest in peace) who challenged me no end. I could say the same of Richard Dawkins, Peter Atkins, Sam Harris, Peter Singer, Daniel Dennett, Steven Pinker and Lawrence Krauss; they all inspired me to write this book. Pope Benedict XVI once wrote that atheism's "dismissal of God is only apparent…it represents a form of man's concern with the question of God." In that sense, the scholars and publicists here cited have done the public a service. I only wish they could see that God is not of this world but rather outside of space and time.

I also thank my family, and, in particular, my wife Edita, who, after nearly 60 years of marriage, passed away in January 2015. No words can describe her sagacity, brilliance, beauty, ability to multi-task and, well, keep me from eating too much ice cream. Our five children and 14 grandchildren are the source of my continuing inspiration and are always lovely to be with. Their presence offers constant opportunities to serve, which is the real source of happiness. Self-absorption is madness for it destroys the joy that comes from man's personal effort day in and day out to fall in love with the laws of nature, tangible and intangible. Without acknowledging those measurable and immeasurable laws, airplanes don't fly, generosity is vainglory, purpose morphs into random happenstance and voluntarism, truth is reduced to power, and the one, uncreated God becomes an enemy.

A warm thanks to my son Javier, who advised me on the original manuscript in 2013. He forced me to be a smidgen incendiary. As such, I also laced the text with some hot sauce to spice up the style while enhancing its overall quality and focus.

Alberto M. Piedra
September 2018

---

1. See http://www.johnlennox.org/

TABLE OF CONTENTS

FOREWORD

"Good" indeed means one thing, and "useful" means another; but I lay it down as a principle, which will save us a great deal of anxiety, that, though the useful is not always good, the good is always useful. Good is not only good, but reproductive of good; this is one of its attributes; nothing is excellent, beautiful, perfect, desirable for its own sake, but it overflows, and spreads the likeness of itself all around it. Good is prolific; it is not only good to the eye, but to the taste; it not only attracts us, but it communicates itself; it excites first our admiration and love, then our desire and our gratitude, and that, in proportion to its intenseness and fulness in particular instances. A great good will impart great good.
— John Henry Cardinal Newman, *The Idea of a University*

This book, while not a history or philosophy of the Judeo-Christian legacy, is designed to help people everywhere, irrespective of religion, culture, language, or nationality, to realize that humanity faces serious questions about life and living, and that the answers to such questions must not be left to the Wizards of the Enlightenment. "Wizards" is a term I shall use throughout the book that applies to a very general group of thinkers — though not to any one of them as such — holding more or less to a common body of ideas and methodologies. They tend to be militant atheists, radical agnostics, stubborn skeptics, or ideological relativists (utopian dreamers), who tenaciously oppose the claims of the Judeo-Christian worldview. In its place, they offer, to one degree or another, an illusory belief in the idea of perpetual progress and in the unstoppable powers of human ingenuity and reason. They often mock any reference to God and they advance the notion that "salvation" is attainable in this world without any help from God, who, in any case, does not exist.

The Wizards, whose numbers have increased since the onset of the 17th century, disagree with the Judeo-Christian meaning of "genuine human development,"[1] and cannot see that "though the useful is not always good, the good is always useful."[2] Often, they are anti-theists.[3] Their ideas predate the Enlightenment, but they would have us believe that the Scientific Revolution and the 18th-century Enlightenment gave us a clean break between science and God. A key element of their thinking is that real progress began only with the Enlightenment.

Over the past several years, I have come to respect the tenacity, self-confidence, and combative spirit of most of the Wizards. They are a class of people who show a dedication to a cause much larger than themselves — the discovery of the truth. While I wholeheartedly disagree with their worldview, academics such as Christopher Hitchens, Stephen Hawking, Victor Stenger, Lawrence Krauss, Sam Harris, Steven Pinker, Peter Singer, Peter Atkins, and others deserve our esteem, despite often delivering messages in brassy tones and contentious language. I admire their determination to comment on and advance discourse about the great issues of life and living. And I hope that some of the ideas contained in this book will get them and many others to rethink some of their philosophical positions and, most important, their epistemology and cosmology.

The anti-theists' intellectual heroes are Charles Darwin, David Hume, Emmanuel Kant and similar luminaries. Their religion is "perpetual progress" and "scientism," and their morality is arbitrary and based on a self-sacrificial altruistic behavior that is balanced by a touchy-feely spirit of communal cooperation geared toward human survival.

I am particularly concerned to alert people to the "Enlightenment Trap," which is a brilliantly played verbal sleight-of-hand cloaked in scientific language and sprinkled with an irresistible promise of deliverance from earthly suffering. The Enlightenment Trap appeals to the intellect and the emotions with equal vigor. It holds out the hope of liberation from the uncomfortable realities of life, including its mysteries and vexing contradictions. It even claims that it is within people's own power, *eventually*, to come up with a formula (figuratively speaking) capable of fashioning for themselves another, and presumably better, earthly condition (like a primordial earthly Garden of Eden) *before* the end of time. That is utopianism pure and simple. The Wizards' battle cry is that a belief in a personal God, and Christianity in particular, stand in the way of progress; I maintain that the Judeo-Christian worldview is the best and perhaps the only guarantee of genuine human development, and that it not only enlightens but indeed explains the emergence of the Scientific Revolution and of the Enlightenment itself.

The Wizards discard the Judeo-Christian concept of the dignity of the human person. Perhaps unknowingly, some of their ideas[4] inspired political movements including communism, National Socialism, liberation theologies, techno-scientism, radical back-to-nature sects, new world orders, and even religious-like radical ideological elements of globalism and multiculturalism. Godless materialism and relativism stand at their core.

All these movements resemble faith-based crusades, and generally cannot see the relation between philosophy and science, or the spiritual and material worlds. They use the language of Biblical salvation and transfiguration to convince people that it is possible to reach a state of perfect freedom, equality, and brotherhood. To disagree with some of them is to risk the guillotine, imprisonment, the Gulag, marginalization, the loss of religious freedom,[5] or exile to the loony bin. The threat of the last is an increasingly effective means for generating compliance or uniformity in modern society.

Put differently, the Wizards of the Enlightenment — their most articulate apostle was arguably the brilliantly lyrical Christopher Hitchens — liken the universe to a big jigsaw puzzle: Given enough time, scholars and scientists will figure out how the universe works, allowing them to eliminate all suffering and uncertainty, at which point they will have mastered the universe. They urge people to be at once useful (the productive bit of their argument), to feel good about themselves (the uplifting bit), and to minimize suffering (the essential bit). In their system, morality is self-referencing (i.e., derived only from the biological needs of the individual). It is subjective and reducible to altruism, which is little more than a survival strategy; that is the clever bit. And they claim that their approach to understanding the truths of nature, which allows them to control outcomes, lies in their unprejudiced and neutral ability to uncover the secrets of the cosmos through science, because science is the gateway to truth, and, thus, to liberation.

In their system, a person is nothing but the culmination of a process of natural selection over a long nonlinear series of evolutionary events. To advance in an otherwise haphazard world, a person must graduate from the enslavement of religious fantasy, which apparently blocks the neural transfer of chemical and electronic signals to the brain. Graduation from the slavery of belief in the supernatural signifies freedom from infantile naiveté, and describes how the Wizards win adherents to their ideology.

The Judeo-Christian worldview, on the other hand, rests on the conviction that there is one uncreated God who gives the human person insight into the meaning of life and the universe, and who loves (rather than merely tolerates and torments) humankind. He is the source of morality. In this context, life takes on meaning amidst daily uncertainty, contradictions, and suffering. Randomness becomes purpose. The "survivalist rat race" turns into an opportunity for service. Freedom becomes a means of participating in the redemptive process of salvation.[6] Despair turns to hope, enemies are seen in a different light, and economics becomes a tool for creativity and integral human development.[7] Leisure becomes the basis of culture rather than an excuse for selfishness. Just as the Wizards confuse the one uncreated God with any old run-of-the-mill made-up god, they confuse Christianity with any fabricated religious belief. Contrary to the Wizards' claims, the Judeo-Christian worldview does in fact embrace science and acknowledges that it offers opportunities for creative development.

Ideas have consequences. The causes of genuine human development cannot be explained either by chance, or man's ability to manipulate the forces of nature, nor by Nietzsche's "will to power", relativistic political philosophies or any forms of voluntarism akin to that of Islam's literalist theological tradition. The many speculative ideas (intellectually grounded in the heady days of the Enlightenment) have given us developmental models that do not fully take into account the dignity and spiritual dimension of the human person which are embedded in the Judeo-Christian worldview. These models eventually reduce any policy, domestic or foreign, to a set of calculations akin to those necessary for managing a zoological park. Furthermore, education becomes a means for training circus animals and science a quest to do a better job of it. Law becomes an instrument to override the conscience and the police a force to control outcomes, deal with the weak, and dominate the uncooperative. These transformations, and more, are always brought about, supposedly, for the good of the people.

When a country's foreign and domestic policies (and its universities) become hostage to developmental models divorced from reality, and, ultimately, from truth itself, anything goes; a defense of the basest of instincts and actions are justified in the name of futuristic utopias or mere survival. In the face of modern political thinking, has not economic policy (and the drive for genuine human development) been reduced to a plan to maintain in place a system of "happy hour" economics, often disguised as "our way of life"? The goal of "happy hour" economics, as opposed to economics in the strict sense, is ever-increasing cash flow, fitness centers around every corner, and endless flows of red wine, sex, and photo shoots down a road under a de-gendered multiculturalist umbrella. Is not such a vision a pathetic and distorted view not only of economic policy but of the meaning of entertainment and healthy living, for that matter? When common-sense economics, which is the ennobling genius of free enterprise on which the United States was founded, morphs into "happy hour" economics, a nation's foreign and military policies are increasingly used to secure resources in an endless cycle of perpetual struggle where the conscience plays no role and crony capitalism dominates.[8] In such a world, I envision an escalation of violent conflict at multiple levels, usually initiated by the strong, because their acceptance of moral relativism, which is supercharged by intellectual hubris, serves as a guide to survival.

The proponents of this ideologically motivated subset of American foreign policy often employ unnecessary threats, bullying, and ready resort to force in the name of freedom, egalitarianism, and brotherhood. Is not the real objective of these ideologically inspired elites (and globalists) obvious, e.g., to secure and control assets for purposes other than the common good and genuine human development? Does not this type of thinking reveal a dangerous indifference towards the idea of the universal recognition of the dignity of the human person (as embedded in the Judeo-Christian worldview) and expose an a priori acceptance of a "dog-eat-dog" world akin to atheistic naturalism as promoted by the Wizards of the Enlightenment?

This book is not for those with an inbred, closed-minded mentality (whose main strategy in life is to stand on the sidelines and throw grenades at any passing idea that is not in sync with their own vision). Such people live in a bubble and in the past, and fear engaging with the outside world or opposing views. They are not interested in listening to or in learning from atheists, agnostics, theists, relativists, environmentalists, multiculturalists, or globalists, and seem to live in the unenlightened era of evolutionary pre-history.

Rather, it is for common-sense free-thinkers, for free-thinking means the willingness to listen to nature, to the universe, to others, and to the voice of God who communicates the truths all around us in so many different ways. We must listen to the totality of the evidence. Free-thinking should mean maturity and the ability to see the extraordinary, even the invisible, in the ordinary realities and suffering of everyday life. It also means having the humility to accept that we are not masters of the universe.

To some of my non-ideological atheist friends, I thank them for their insightful commentary, warm hearts, and openness in discussions over the years. While I do not accept their worldview, I respect their opinions as they respect mine. Unbeknownst to them, the genesis of their selflessness is embedded in our very nature and is not the sole product of handy social behaviors formed over eons of evolutionary history. My atheist friends are wonderful people with delicate and caring souls.

To agnostics, I would merely say that to doubt is normal, but to reject the metaphysical and cosmological evidence for the existence of God and absolute truth on the basis of doubt is to stand against rationality itself, including the reasonableness of the Judeo-Christian worldview and experience.[9] It is unwise to elevate the scientific method, which is limited in scope by definition, to the status of an unassailable and universal system. It acknowledges nothing outside the material world. Unlike some dogmatic atheists, at least most agnostics are not afraid to ask the question "Why?"

As for "seekers," the mass of men and women who live each day in the presence of uncertainty and doubt and who have not made up their minds, I encourage them to keep searching for answers to the meaning of life. Listen to both sides of the atheism/theism dialogue, but don't buy the claim that the Judeo-Christian worldview is a non–evidence-based fairytale dead set against creativity, originality, discovery, and imagination.

It might be a good idea for vehement atheists to take notice, for example, of Fr. Georges Lemaître (1894–1966), a brilliant cosmologist who was ignored by many of his fellow scientists in the 1920s (and even today). A mere Catholic priest, he offered an alternative explanation, which proved to be correct, to Einstein's cosmological-constant argument about the forces in the universe. It was Father Lemaître, and not Edwin Hubble, who fathered the Big Bang theory. It is important to note such men to underscore that the Judeo-Christian worldview embraces science and the scientific method while at the same time having an answer for how "something" can come from "nothing." Lest anyone get the wrong idea, the Judeo-Christian worldview is in a profound love affair with the sciences. It has nothing to fear from evolutionary biology, physics, astronomy or, indeed, reason itself.[10]

The Wizards of the Enlightenment would have us believe that the Judeo-Christian worldview, and Christianity specifically, are nonsense. They claim that it is childish to believe in something that has not been confirmed by science. But why then do scientists *believe* that consciousness or energy exists, when scientists themselves don't know *what* consciousness is or *what* energy is? Scientists believe in them because of their explanatory power, as John Lennox, professor of mathematics at Oxford University, illustrates.[11] It is just as foolhardy to dismiss those who *believe* in the Judeo-Christian worldview on the basis of their belief in God as it is foolhardy to dismiss scientists who *believe* in consciousness and energy. In both cases, belief arises based on the *totality* of the evidence around us.

It is no accident that clever and well-trained Judeo-Christian scholars can explain the difference between magic and miracles. A physicist with a Judeo-Christian view has every advantage over a physicist who is an atheist, because the latter is only a scientist while the former is both a scientist and wise. It is wise people who see that the intangible dimension in something is more than mathematics and the physical laws of nature.

Those who reject Judeo-Christian metaphysics, cosmology, morality, and natural-law principles seem unable to deal with an uncaused God who is omniscient, omnipotent, and timeless. Perhaps, some scientists want those attributes for themselves. But those attributes are "God genes": people cannot have them, or else they would be God.

To clerics, pastors, and theists, especially those in the Biblical-literalist camp, let it be clear that there can be no conflict between science and revelation, as many Biblical-literalists seem not to get. Moreover, although you are *often* in the realm of inscrutability, it doesn't follow that you are *always* in that realm. When something or some question is unclear, your answer to inquisitive men and women should not be a frivolous "God of the Gaps" response, which usually goes as follows: "Good question, but since no one knows, God must have done it!" To give such a response with little or no reflection is unwise if not puerile and tends to undermine the explanatory power of the Judeo-Christian worldview with respect to singular events or mysterious realities.

In much of the non-English-speaking world, the "God of the Gaps" argument is overused by old-fashioned or old-school thinkers, a situation made worse by the generally top-down, "force-feed-the-natives" approach to education that has been prevalent since the time between the 12th and 19th centuries in the lands ranging from Central Asia to Iberia. Cannot this anti-Socratic, "anti-reason" mindset, which discourages creative thinking, be attributed, in part, (a) to the branch of Islamic philosophy that fathered ideas that led to the intellectual suicide of inventiveness and secular public policy in much of society in the Muslim world,[12] and (b) to the fact that many of the good ideas of the Renaissance, the Protestant Reformation, and the Enlightenment never meaningfully penetrated south of the Pyrenees or east of Constantinople until recently?

Finally, ideas indeed have consequences. Does not our idea of god make all the difference in how we behave and organize our lives? On closer inspection, is not the god of Islam different from the god of Christianity or Judaism? It is a thought worth pondering. As Fr. Schall, S.J. says, "[i]t seems ironic, in a way, that the voluntarism that came to rule the Muslim mind is almost identical with the will philosophy that grounds much of Western public life. Voluntarism is the philosophical-theological view that no rational order exists in things or in human nature. What is behind all reality is a will that can always be otherwise. It is not bound to any one truth."[13] Is not this mindset dangerous and often used to justify violence, manipulation and the use of force in the name of peace, progress, self-defense, or all sorts of utopian intellectual or theological structures? It is a question well worth asking.

There is a certain amount of repetition within the pages of this book in order to communicate my main points to the reader. Repetition for the uninitiated is often a good idea; for the learned it is often better, because the will also needs to come into play, not just the intellect, in order to see what is going on within and around us.

While there may be a number of controversial and provocative points within these pages, they are intended merely for the sake of clarity and to stimulate dialogue or to underscore the seriousness of a particular issue. Nothing said herein should be taken personally. I sincerely ask for the forgiveness of anyone whom I may have misquoted — that is not my intention. I likewise ask for the forgiveness of anyone whose ideas I have misunderstood or misstated — that also is not my intention.

In his September 2014 statement at the Italian Military Memorial of Redipuglia, Pope Francis juxtaposes the Judeo-Christian worldview with the non–Judeo-Christian (indeed anti-theist) worldview whose ideology and machinery are indifferent to God and to the dignity of the human person:

> With this "What does it matter to me?" in their hearts, the merchants of war perhaps have made a great deal of money, but their corrupted hearts have lost the capacity to cry. That "What does it matter to me?" prevents the tears. Cain did not cry. The shadow of Cain hangs over us today in this [World War I] cemetery. It is seen here. It is seen from 1914 right up to our own time. It is seen even in the present.
>
> With the heart of a son, a brother, a father, I ask each of you, indeed for all of us, to have a conversion of heart: to move on from "What does it matter to me?" to tears: for each one of the fallen of this "senseless massacre," for all the victims of the mindless wars, in every age. Humanity needs to weep, and this is the time to weep.[14]

I am thankful for having lived in the United States for nearly 70 years. Much has changed over the decades since emigrating from Cuba in 1959, but I remain confident in my adopted country's ability to move beyond its emotional exuberance in certain policy areas and intellectual malfunctions, many of which I mention. And so, as they read and listen to voices in the media and elsewhere, academics and policymakers should carefully examine their consciences and revisit the great history and literature of our Judeo-Christian legacy. Moreover, I urge a second, deeper look at President Eisenhower's January 1961 farewell speech to the citizens of the United States.[15] In retrospect, were not some of his warnings about the possible perilous direction of the country prophetic?

And so, I invite you to reflect on a line from J.R.R. Tolkien's book *The Two Towers:* "There is some good in this world, and it's worth fighting for." Let's first, however, understand the forces arrayed against reason, reality, the

Judeo-Christian understanding of the dignity of the human person, and common sense before embracing ideologies and utopian schemes that do not advance genuine human development.

---

1.   Benedict XVI (pope), "Caritas in Veritate" (encyclical letter; June 29, 2009) (http://w2.vatican.va/content/benedict-xvi/en/encyclicals/documents/hf_ben-xvi_enc_20090629_caritas-in-veritate.html).

2.   John Henry Newman, *The Idea of the University* (London: Longmans, Green, and Co., 1886); p. 164 (https://archive.org/stream/a677122900newmuoft#page/n5/mode/2up).

3.   In this book, I will generally use the word "atheist" interchangeably with "agnostic," "skeptic," or "anti-theist". The word "anti-theist" refers to an activist or, generally, a public figure who has spoken out against God, religion, or faith in one form or another.

4.   Many modern secular ideologies are utopian belief systems similar in approach and tone to religious movements. Therefore, we consider the present-day use of the word "ideology" as synonymous — in a pejorative sense — with the gods of ancient Rome and Greece.

5.   See Pope Paul VI, "Declaration on Religious Freedom, Dignitatis Humanae, On the Right of the Person and of Communities to Social and Civil Freedom in Matter Religious," December 7, 1965 (https://web.archive.org/web/20120211202206/http://www.vatican.va/archive/hist_councils/ii_vatican_council/documents/vat-ii_decl_19651207_dignitatis-humanae_en.html).

6.   See St. John Paul II (pope), "On the Value and Content of Freedom of Conscience and of Religion" (message, November 1980) (http://w2.vatican.va/content/john-paul-ii/en/speeches/1980/november/documents/hf_jp_ii_spe_19801114_atto-helsinki.html).

7.   See Bl. Paul VI, "Populorum Progressio," (encyclical letter; March 26, 1967) (http://w2.vatican.va/content/paul-vi/en/encyclicals/documents/hf_p-vi_enc_26031967_populorum.html).

8.   With such a dysfunctional and dangerous subset of foreign policy, a state's overall policies may easily devolve into a series of impersonal and aggressive economic transactions that operate under the slogan "it's nothing personal; it's just business." This attitude also extends into the business of armaments and military preparedness, even in the face of fictitious enemies. I fear such a view may represent one of today's dominant stances in government circles and think tanks around the world. Is not this type of thinking incompatible with the goal of bringing about genuine human development, since it is quick to reject statecraft and seems to pay only lip service to the dignity of the human person?

9.   John C. Lennox, *Gunning for God: Why the New Atheists Are Missing the Target* (Oxford: Lion's Head, 2011).

10.   See David Berlinski, "The Devil's Delusion: Atheism and Its Scientific Pretentions" (New York City: Lecture at the Union League Club, 2012) (https://www.youtube.com/watch?v=0XIDykeZplU).

11.   John Lennox and Daniel Lowenstein, "Christianity and the Tooth Fairy: A UCLA Law Professor Questions an Oxford Mathematician on the Claims of Jesus" (interview, April 2011) (http://www.johnlennox.org/jresources/christianity-and-the-tooth-fairy/). It

should be confessed that certain interpretations of Christianity have been (and still are) antagonistic to science, though they ae decidedly in the minority.

12.   Robert R. Reilly, *The Closing of the Muslim Mind: How Intellectual Suicide Created the Modern Islamic Crisis* (Wilmington, Del.: Intercollegiate Studies Institute, 2010).

13.   See James V. Schall, S.J., *"On Islam: A Chronological Record, 2002 - 2018,"* (San Francisco: Ignatius Press, 2018); p. 7.

14.   Francis (pope), "War Is Madness Which Brings Destruction" (homily; September 2014) (http://vaticaninsider.lastam- pa.it/en/news/detail/articolo/francesco-redipuglia-36290/).

15.   See Dwight D. Eisenhower, "Farewell Address to the Nation," 1961 (http://mcadams.posc. mu.edu/ike.htm).

A Note to Readers

A few years ago, my beloved husband, Alberto, lunched with Christopher Hitchens (1949–2011), who, until his untimely death, was one of the brightest stars in the firmament of contemporary atheism. Hitchens was blustery, arrogant, over-the-top articulate, and defiant but funny, entertaining, and sometimes right. My husband's heart sank, he told me later, when Hitchens cavalierly lambasted just about everything under the sun and in sight except that which could be traced to his own moral code and to his own orthodox world of defiance and unbelief.

As they spoke, Hitchens's cool cerulean eyes were exuberant from what appeared to be a superlative confidence in the almost-unquestionable ability of smart people to solve once and for all the problems of suffering and doubt in life. And yet, during their conversation, Alberto got the impression that Hitchens was searching for someone to level with rather than simply to preach to or blame for the psychological torture of having to answer to others. Hitchens's unwillingness to listen seemed to bespeak interior desolation. He didn't need to be slapped down. He needed to be loved. He needed a friend.

Alberto sensed across the table the agony of an experienced paratrooper who had jumped out of a plane only to realize (in midair!) that he had forgotten his parachute or even deliberately left it behind. He fluttered confidently downwards as if science or chance would come to his rescue in the nick of time. What is staggering is that there are people like Hitchens who, despite all the evidence to the contrary, adamantly deny the natural moral law as "something" independent of reason. They might as well deny the existence of the law of gravity while plummeting to the ground with no parachute.

Hitchens's prodigious mind could corner pretty much anyone in open debate. With his customary flick of the hair, he'd go in for the verbal kill. He was a superb sparring partner. A colorful Oxonian to the hilt, his barrage of shrewd and often insightful remarks during lunch was unrelenting, especially as he deployed the best of the Judeo-Christian lexicon to defend his ideological atheism and unremitting inward-looking relativism. Not unlike Sam Harris, Richard Dawkins, and Peter Atkins, Hitchens not only rejected out of hand any evidence for the existence of God and universal moral reasoning but pushed the idea that the meaning of "faith" is synonymous with the meaning of "blind faith," although in fact his own atheism was a leap of faith into total nothingness. Maybe that's why he seemed to be so angry and miserable so much of the time.

By way of example, the Wizards' theory of the existence of multiverses — a desperate attempt to get beyond the Big Bang theory — is so absurd that it shows that its adherents in the scientific community have entered the world of cosmic teapots and little green men on Mars to justify their atheism: the theory is at least great fun to mull over. As St. John of the Cross (1542–1591) said, "The mind is an idol-making machine." Or if you don't like the words of a Christian mystic, maybe Paul Steinhardt, Albert Einstein Professor in Science at Princeton University, makes a bit more sense. He describes the concept of the multiverse as the "Theory of Anything," which essentially means that some scientists have gone far beyond the realm of science.[1]

At the end of the day, Hitchens and his like-minded Wizards are die-hard anti-theists whose religious fanaticism rests on a set of self-destructive "take-it-or-leave it" premises, brash assertions, unfalsifiable theories, and blind beliefs in the kingship of science, perpetual progress, and unassailable but increasingly shaky Darwinian assertions. Hitchens himself was a high priest of the Enlightenment who worshiped the same gods as Democritus (c. 460–c. 370 BC), Denis Diderot (1713–1784), David Hume (1711–1776), Ludwig Feuerbach (1804–1872), Friedrich Nietzsche (1844–1900), Immanuel Kant (1724–1804), and Francis Bacon (1561–1626).

Hitchens awkwardly seemed to confirm that relativism is a lethal virus that destroys meaning, authenticity, and the ability to make sound judgments based on real comparisons. Ideas, persons, art, music, schools, political systems, and economies are not all equally good or bad, equally meaningless or meaningful, or equally effective or ineffective. Whether one likes it or not, there is a hierarchy of meaning based on reality, which science must recognize, or else everything is based on power alone. The inability to entertain the possibility of some form of intelligence behind the laws of physics or the beauty and complexity of living organisms compels a person to search for answers and peace of mind in utopian constructs or whiskey.

It might make sense to revisit Hitchens's debate with John Lennox on March 2009 at Birmingham, Alabama's Samford University to debate the question "Is God Great?" In closing, Lennox provides Hitchens with a brilliant response centered on the universal moral law and Jesus Christ.[2]

Hitchens understood that the Judeo-Christian worldview is *not* just a set of Euro-centric ideas that simply embody European prejudices and that have no lasting meaning to non-Europeans. What he didn't get is that the Judeo-Christian worldview is attractive because it is universally reasonable and epistemologically sound. Koreans as much as Norwegians and Brazilians and Nigerians and Canadians and Italians and Pakistanis and Eskimos and Ibos and Cherokee and Quechuas and Kalmyks and Maoris can understand its value because it has the power to explain the meaning and purpose of life and living.

Modern civilization, it would seem, is on the brink of collective suicide — especially given the predominant "culture of death," which refuses to recognize the dignity of the human person. The evidence for societal self-destruction is all around us. Just listen to the pundit scholars who are calling for the creation of "ideal" human beings through advanced cloning techniques, or the implementation of other techno-utopian drivel that is utterly dehumanizing and destructive of humanity, the biosphere, and integral human development.

Hitchens seemed not to disagree with Alberto's statement that in the coming years, as *radical militant* Islam (not cultural Islam) spreads across a flabby and intellectually defenseless formerly Judeo-Christian European landscape, Russia will hunker down and watch London, Paris, Rome, Madrid, and Berlin go up in smoke from civil disorder and clashing worldviews. (Unless Islamic scholars revisit their historical and philosophical roots, where there was minimal friction between faith and reason, radical Islam may grow in strength.[3]) Hitchens could see that the cultural disintegration of Western Europe and the Anglo-Saxon world advances because of ideological relativism, the gods of multiculturalism, and the supposedly invincibility of reason.

The Russians, on the other hand, have linked their identity and survival as a nation to the revival of their thousand-year-old Judeo-Christian traditions, which are inexorably linked to the messages of the Old and New Testament. It would seem that they are right in so doing. They understand that at the end of the day, godless utopianism, radical atheism, and scientism (all of which they experienced first-hand during the reign of Soviet communism) are dead-end ideas that lead to the destruction of nations.

It is Alberto's firm belief that there is an urgent need for a fresh group of academics to counsel modern man from going nuts. A Judeo-Christian anthropology that is off-beam will always bring about a deficient understanding of the relationship between human beings and the world.

If Hitchens were still alive, Alberto would challenge him to give us a socio-economic theory that offered more than Rousseauian egalitarianism and the promise of endless profits and abundance and that, at the same time, respected free enterprise, individual creativity, and the dignity of the human person in all its dimensions. So far, the track record of the Wizards (the masters of the universe) has been abysmal. Alberto would further challenge Hitchens to show us how his development model would give us a cultured street-wise people with communication skills and ideas more profound that those of rebellious and mesmerized high-schoolers. Alberto would challenge him to give us a people who know how to listen, who can differentiate fact from fiction, and who understand the meaning of dialogue.

Hitchens's eyes narrowed in displeasure when Alberto suggested a return to an educational system that guided people to understand the difference between physics and metaphysics and that pointed out that declarations by renowned scholars are not always declarations of scholarship; the same may be said of science and scientists. He groused when Alberto said that it was possible to passionately love the world while simultaneously working and living in it. Genuine (and sustainable) human development, Alberto continued, was possible mainly because of the Judeo-Christian worldview and its legacy and commitment to serve the good of the human person over the long haul, not in spite of it. Hitchens bellyached but seemed to recognize the wisdom of the argument when away from the limelight.

Alberto urges people to review the splendid achievements of the Judeo-Christian civilization and refrain from hammering on it because it is an easy target. The sanity of the world depends on it. C.S. Lewis said, "If you read history you will find that the Christians who did most for the present world were precisely those who thought most of the next. It is since Christians have largely ceased to think of the other world that they have become so ineffective in this." Unfortunately, Hitchens lost sight of eternity. He confused the non-contingent Judeo-Christian God of the universe (God our Father) with the man-made Greco-Roman-like contingent God-tyrant, who was akin to Prometheus or some severe un-fatherly god of radical Islam.

Moreover, Hitchens thought that the Judeo-Christian God and human freedom could not co-exist. He reasoned that since a person is free, God, who could only be a tormentor and control freak, cannot exist, for if God existed, then the human person would not be free. Since we know from experience that we are free, it follows that God does not exist. His conclusion may follow from his premise, but his major premise is pure nonsense because it is incorrect (and based on blind faith).

Hitchens just couldn't see that the Judeo-Christian worldview built the lasting, attractive, and downright decent, not to mention funny and inspiring, aspects of modern life. Without a real friend, he was blind. He needed a friend who could show him, not tell him, as Lewis puts it, that "happiness means knowing how to limit some needs which only diminish us, and being open to the many different possibilities which life can offer." Hitchens could not see that a self-referencing morality — entirely inward-looking — operating within a techno-economic paradigm was a recipe for humanity to return to the Stone Age, as history on occasion shows.

And lest anyone forget, the Stone Age was a period in the history of the world that lasted roughly 3.5 million years, and ended around 3000 BC — not much to show for a couple of million years. By way of contrast, look at what the last 2,000 years, since the Christian worldview appeared, have given the world. Alberto regularly thinks about Christopher Hitchens (and prays for him), because at the end of the day, despite his pigheadedness and protestations, he was a good man who was lost in own brilliance.

— Edita Martinez Piedra
1931–2015

PREFACE

D o we dare call them "fanatics" — scientists, politicians, whimsical judges, and other officials who seem to have abandoned common sense, good judgment, and the rule of law, if not reason itself? A fanatic whether in politics or academia is, by definition, one who thinks he is never wrong. A fanatic believes he has superior and unique knowledge, sees no limits in governing, dismisses the demands of the natural (moral) law, and challenges whoever challenges him, or, in the case of the intellectual, undermines the culture and violates the dignity of the human person. He need not be a bomb-throwing terrorist. Fanatics and terrorists have much in common.

Julian Benda, in *La trahison des clercs*[1] makes the case that the most serious form of anarchy is the treason of the intellectuals. So it is with the radical fanatics of the Enlightenment who all too often embrace the irrational in the name of rationality. Benda uses the term *clerc* to designate, as a class, writers, people of learning, artists, moralists, and the clerical set. They are by vocation the officiants of time-transcending standards relevant to their calling. They lose credibility when, abandoning objectivity, they display a special affinity for the group with which they identify and give short shrift to human dignity.

One does not have to reach far to find examples of the subjectivity condemned by Benda. Professor Alberto M. Piedra does a masterful job in linking genuine human development to the Judeo-Christian worldview, and especially to its bedrock principle of the dignity of the human person as expressed in Vatican II's Declaration *Dignitatis Humanae* (1965).

While many of the academics who are mentioned in Professor Piedra's book are scientists, they push moral relativism and a kind of voluntarism that negates the natural moral law. A compelling response to moral relativism is to be found in a recent work by Marcello Pera, former president of the Italian Senate, now professor of political philosophy at the Pontifical Lateran

University, Rome.[2] Pera takes the title of his book, *Why We Should Call Ourselves Christians,* from an essay by Benedetto Croce, a professed atheist, called "Why We Cannot But Call Ourselves Christian." Croce, in spite of his materialism, was convinced that the objective and transcendent formulation of man's dignity and freedom is to be found in Christianity. Pera is insistent: "We should call ourselves Christian if we want to maintain our liberties and preserve our civilization.... If, as Thomas Jefferson claimed, our liberties must have, or must be felt as if they had, a religious foundation in order to bind the union together, then today's secularized Europe, which rejects that foundation, can never be politically united."[3] Pera continues: "Unlike Americans, Europeans cannot adopt a constitution beginning with the words 'We the people' because 'the people' must exist as a moral and spiritual community before such a constitution could be conceived and asked for."[4] The version of the European Constitution that was finally adopted after being rejected in popular referendums by the French and the Dutch made no reference to God or to Christianity.

In addressing the moral decline that he finds on both sides of the Atlantic, Pera writes, "liberal civilization was born in defense of the negative liberties of man. When the positive liberties of citizens burgeoned forth, everything started changing. The liberal state first became democratic, next paternalistic, and finally entered the totalitarian phase of the dictatorship of the majority and the tyranny of absolute authorities. No aspect of life today, from cradle to the grave, has been left untouched by legislation, and most of all by the verdicts of judges or supreme courts, or by the decisions of supranational institutions.[5]

Pera fears that within democracies decision-making authority is today being handed over to powerful interest groups and bureaucracies. Good and evil in the absence of an authoritative moral tradition, he maintains, tend to be determined not by transcendent moral principles but by arbitrariness and the ephemeral needs of a few (often uninformed) elites more interested in power and domination than in advancing integral human development.

How part of this state of affairs came to pass is the subject of Brad S. Gregory's remarkably erudite treatise, *The Unintended Reformation.*[6] Gregory finds that modernity is failing because of the naturalistic or materialistic assumptions that pervade the academic world. Reason, he argues, has proven no more capable than "scripture alone" in devising persuasive answers to what he calls Life Questions. Professor Piedra makes a similar argument. Modernity has produced no substantive common outlook but instead has produced an open-ended welter of arbitrary assertions meant to be taken as true. Ever-expanding technological capacities afforded by scientific advance are set within an increasingly rancorous culture of moral disagreement, leaving political direction rudderless.

The failure of modern philosophy to provide convincing answers with respect to the important questions of life is, in part, due to the exclusion from the academy of alternative religious and metaphysical worldviews. Fruitful dialogue is rendered impossible in spite of the fact, as Gregory points out, "Intellectually sophisticated expressions of religious world views exist today within Western hyperpluralism," but those views have been banished from secular research universities.[7] Theology, the philosophy of God, or what Aristotle called "divine science," and nonskeptical Biblical scholarship find no place in the secular academy. As a consequence, most scholars and scientists are notably lacking in theological sophistication and even self-awareness of their own metaphysical assumptions and beliefs. Gregory is not optimistic that change is likely in the near future. "Unsecularizing the academy," he writes, "would require, of course, an intellectual openness on the part of scholars and scientists sufficient to end the long-standing modern charade in which naturalism has been assumed to be demonstrated, self-evident, ideologically neutral, or something arrived at on the basis of impartial inquiry."[8]

It is within that context that Professor Piedra articulates anew the wisdom embedded in Western culture. He brings extraordinary learning and experience to his task. Trained in both Europe and America, as a refugee from Castro's Cuba, he turns his diplomatic, academic, and business experience into a solid defense of a Judeo-Christian culture that has made much of genuine human development possible.

The author exposes the "Enlightenment Trap" of the Wizards, a line of argument designed to convince the unsuspecting of the reasonableness of godless atheism, despite its irrationality, gloom, and militancy. Their acceptance of (moral) relativism is cloaked in pseudo-science and is de-humanizing to the point of being suicidal. It is these academics' aggressive anti-theism and glorification of reason that puts them in the category of fanatical clerics who hide behind platitudes rather than objective truth. Their anti-theism demands the destruction of the Judeo-Christian legacy and worldview.

Like Pierre Manent and Brad Gregory, Piedra is well aware that Western civilization is in a period of deep existential crisis. He is convinced that only with an acknowledgment of its classical and Judeo-Christian sources will the world be able to survive as a free and open society upon which genuine human development can advance. With Thomas Carlyle and more recently in the company of Gregory, Alberto challenges the dominant secular materialism that reigns within the academy. He refuses to passively acquiesce to modern society's love affair with the utopian gods of perpetual progress, multiculturalism, scientism, egalitarianism, and globalism and the moral drift (relativism) that characterizes the present. His is a passionate plea for a transformation that partakes of the universal and eternal, and that draws upon the wisdom of Judeo-Christian scholarship and the Church. Rejecting a pessimistic outlook, he finds strength in the works of Romano Guardini, John Lennox, and Benedict XVI (Joseph Ratzinger), and other scholars.

This is a very rich book that in the end is dedicated to all men and women with an open mind. The author hopes they will increasingly become attentive to the authentic sources of their material and spiritual welfare.

— Jude P. Dougherty, The Catholic University of America

---

1. Julian Benda, *La trahison des clerc,* (Paris: B. Grasset, 1927). Trans. by Richard Aldington as *The Betrayal of the Intellectuals* (New York: Morrow & Co., 1928).\

2. Marcello Pera, *Why We Should Call Ourselves Christians* (New York: Encounter Books, 2011).

3. Pera, *Why We Should Call Ourselves,* pp. 8-9.

4. Pera, *Why We Should Call Ourselves,* p. 9.

5. Pera, *Why We Should Call Ourselves,* p. 9.

6. Brad S. Gregory, *The Unintended Reformation: How a Religious Revolution Secularized Society* (Cambridge, Mass: The Belknap Press at Harvard University, 2012).

7. Gregory, *Unintended Revolution,* p. 383.

8. Gregory, *Unintended Revolution,* p. 386.

INTRODUCTION

Keeping God in the Picture

Equality lies only in human moral dignity.... Let there be brothers first, then there will be brotherhood, and only then will there be a fair sharing of goods among brothers.
> — Fyodr Dostoevsky, *The Brothers Karamazov*

Christendom has had a series of revolutions and in each one of them Christianity has died. Christianity has died many times and risen again; for it had a God who knows the way out of the grave.
> — G.K. Chesterton, *The Everlasting Man*

I do not believe that the God who created all the universe, and who communes with His people through prayer and spiritual insight, would expect us to deny the obvious truths of the natural world that science has revealed to us, in order to prove our love for Him.
> — Francis Collins, *The Language of God: A Scientist Presents Evidence for Belief*

This book is definitely not an exhaustive or original study of European civilization or heritage. Rather, I hope that it provides a contribution to the discussion about the indispensable role that Judeo-Christian ideas have played in the process of genuine human development over the ages. The pan-European civilization of which we speak is not delimited by geography, because it is fundamentally a set of compelling ideas that transcend narrow ideological considerations.

My main purpose is to shed light on the grandeur of the Judeo-Christian heritage of our forefathers and to alert people to what may be called the Enlightenment Trap, an emotionally charged and extremely dangerous game of words launched by those I think of as the Wizards of the Enlightenment,[1] who are in the main anti-theists.[2] This trap is designed to ensnare men and women into blindly believing that the supremacy of science, the cult of moral relativism, and the clever exercise of political power will lead to peace of mind and relief from the sorrows of life at some unspecified time in the future. In order to sell this narrative, most Wizards need to knock the accomplishments of the Church Fathers, Scholastics, humanists, scientists, and, even sweep away just about everyone and everything that bears the mark of religion in the public square. They serve the gods of science and power and declare *non serviam* to any and all religions and to God.

To ensnare their victims, they assert that converts to their "liberation theology" will eventually experience a unique and thrilling personal release from the oppression of religion while moving towards an affluent, pain-free, and egalitarian society. In fact, nothing of the sort is on the horizon.

One of the Wizards' mind games is to call an "act of faith" and an "act of blind faith" one and the same. An "act of faith," which can be eminently reasonable when based on science, history, and credible authority, is completely different from an "act of blind faith," which usually is not based on science, history, or the words of credible authority. Perhaps it is the Wizards who are guilty of intellectual nescience, since their claim that atheism is backed by science stems from having made their own act of blind faith in rationalism long ago.[3]

John Lennox, University of Oxford mathematician, says this about Richard Dawkins, Oxford evolutionary biologist and premier anti-theist: "Dawkins' idiosyncratic definition of faith thus provides a striking example of the very kind of thinking he claims to abhor — thinking that is not evidence-based. For, in an exhibition of breathtaking inconsistency, evidence is the very thing he fails to supply for his claim that independence of evidence is faith's joy. And the reason why he fails to supply such evidence is not hard to find — there is none. It takes no great research effort to ascertain that no serious Biblical scholar or thinker would support Professor Dawkins' definition of faith. Francis Collins says of Professor Dawkins' definition that it 'certainly does not describe the faith of most serious believers in history, nor of most of those in my personal acquaintance.'"[4]

At this time of great intellectual confusion, a non-flippant reading of history combined with common sense, taken together, will help us to figure out what's going on in the realm of ideas. The notion that rationalism and moral relativism, so firmly held by our anti-theists can replace the conscience and the natural moral law will not work, because it reduces God to a conceptual error of evolution.

It should be obvious that the history of integral development does not correlate with the history of atheism in any holistic sense. Genuine human development does not come about by making an irrational commitment to the nonexistence of God as if the motto *scientia est potentia* alone guarantees progress and the common good. Rather, a recognition of God, moral reasoning, and human creativity is necessary for there to be integral human development. Since human beings are in the image and likeness of God, God cannot be excluded from the development equation.

Embracing the notion of human dignity (in all its objective and personal uniqueness) equips people with the vision to freely work in accordance with right reason (a concept beyond the classical notions of balance and order) and serve others for the sake of the others.

Human development, in the first instance, has come about throughout the course of history by bringing to life in the human person innate creative and unique potentialities as a means to serve others rather than self or earthly ideologies. To recognize that a person has a higher end than to constantly beaver away for the sole purpose of keeping safe, feeling good, and eliminating all competitors, real and imagined, is a first step towards sanity.

The Judeo-Christian worldview has energized the human spirit over the ages not only because its storyline is optimistic, reasonable, and respectful of human ingenuity but, most important, because it is rooted in God and tied to a real understanding of the nature of the human person and to God. In contrast, the anti-theists believe that some indefinable impersonal force with a distant ethereal connection to cosmic stardust (or some such stuff) has invaded the consciousness and set free the inner genius of human beings to perpetuate the gene pool and, ultimately, master the universe and create new world orders.

Poe Benedict XVI has some thought-provoking words concerning the meaning of genuine human development:

> God is the guarantor of man's true development, in as much as, having created him in his image, he also establishes the transcendent dignity of men and women and feeds their innate yearning to "be more." Man is not a lost atom in a random universe: he is God's creature, whom God chose to endow with an immortal soul and whom he has always loved. If man were merely the fruit of either chance or necessity, or if he had to lower his aspirations to the limited horizon of the world in which he lives, if all reality were merely history and culture, and man did not possess a nature destined to transcend itself in a supernatural life, then one could speak of growth, or evolution, but not development. When the State promotes, teaches, or actually imposes forms of practical atheism, it deprives its citizens of the moral and

spiritual strength that is indispensable for attaining integral human development and it impedes them from moving forward with renewed dynamism as they strive to offer a more generous human response to divine love. In the context of cultural, commercial, or political relations, it also sometimes happens that economically developed or emerging countries export this reductive vision of the person and his destiny to poor countries. This is the damage that "super development" causes to authentic development when it is accompanied by "moral underdevelopment.[5]

Unlike most Wizards, who are self-described ideological materialists and agnostics, the intellectual proponents of the Judeo-Christian worldview offer an evidence-based, and thus more reasonable explanation of the meaning of life. Despite all their swaggering bluster, the Wizards' dogmatic atheism and evolutionary naturalism cannot credibly explain the origin or the purpose of the universe, nor can they convincingly account for the rise of the Scientific Revolution that began in earnest in Western Europe north of the Pyrenees as of the 15th century.

The question of genuine human development, because it contains a spiritual dimension, is completely beyond the ken of the Wizards, blinded as they are by their anti-theism.

God and Science

Science can purify religion from error and superstition; religion can purify science from idolatry and false absolutes. Each can draw the other into a wider world, a world in which both faith — not blind faith — and reason flourish, and thus provide people with a better handle on truth, and the meaning of freedom. Belief in a personal God, or a Creator, as Lennox says, "upholds and makes sense of the rational intelligibility of the universe, whereas ... the reductionist thesis undermines it and dissolves it into a meaningless universe. Far from science abolishing God, it would seem that there is a substantial case for asserting that it is the existence of a Creator that gives to science its fundamental intellectual justification."[6] Chance (total unpredictability) and intelligibility are incompatible, and yet the Wizards insist that they coexist.

Science limits a person's understanding of the world because the scientific method is limited to empirical physical evidence and mathematics. Science cannot measure "nothing" nor should it pretend to do so. As a result, the materialist cannot see the link between physics and metaphysics. As Francis Collins, American biologist and former director of the Human Genome

Project, says, "Science, including the science of evolution, is limited to exploring and understanding the natural world. Therefore, to apply scientific arguments to the question of God's existence, as if this were somehow a showstopper, is committing a category error."[7]

The Wizards use the theory of evolution, in its dogmatic ideological formulation, to explain away God and bypass the Judeo-Christian mindset as a credible explanation for human development. The anti-theists' goal, a steady objective throughout history, is to "dynamite" the cathedrals of Europe and remove all religious symbols from the public square. Science, most claim, will do away with a person's reliance on mythical gods and superstitions, which create dependencies and intellectual laziness. Ironically, the Wizards' cavalier use of language, general disdain for philosophy, and frequent dismissal of historical facts expose their own faith-based crusade against rationality and the Judeo-Christian worldview.[8] John Lennox says that "there are many scientists and others who think that the New Atheism is a belief system which, ironically, provides a classic example of the blind faith it so vocally despises in others."[9] No matter what arguments the Wizards concoct to defend their worldview, science can *only* define, label, and measure the physical world; it is handcuffed by its inability to go beyond description, measurement, and secondary causes.

The Wizards claim that until there is scientific proof that God exists, there is no God. The burden of proof, they say, is on theists. That, of course, is nonsense, because the scientific method deals only with matter. Since God is immaterial, science will never prove that God exists, but that does not imply that God does not exist.

Moreover, the Wizards cannot simply dismiss intelligent design (intelligent cause) as an argument for the existence of God by classifying it as a religious argument.[10] Such classifications are childish and unscientific, because a good case can be made for the intervention of God in the universe based on evidence all around us.[11]

The Wizards work strenuously to dismiss any talk of a singular moment of creation before which nothing existed except the one uncreated God. Lennox argues that, as a scientific matter, the "evidence of a space-time singularity in the form of the discovery of the microwave background etc. confirmed the obvious prediction that the Biblical account implied. This means that the charge that notions of intelligent design are unscientific because they fail to make any testable predictions is false. Science itself has shown that the hypothesis of creation is testable."[12] When the Wizards are confronted with the question of the origin of space/time, they speak of eternity and multiverses. God must always be removed from the equation.

To have faith in someone or something is not necessarily foolish, if it stands to reason, is based on the evidence, or is placed in someone or something that is trustworthy. While faith and truth go hand in hand, their relationship is not always clear. Pope Francis provides some guidance: "Faith without truth does not provide a sure footing. It remains a beautiful story ... something capable of satisfying us to the extent that we are willing to deceive ourselves. Either that or it is reduced to a lofty sentiment which brings consolation and cheer, yet remains prey to the vagaries of our spirit and changing seasons...."[13]

Optimism and Confidence

For those who hold the Judeo-Christian worldview, there is no reason to fear the scientific claims of evolution, as a mechanism, or the findings of science. There is no need to choose between, on the one hand, science, which is limited to the truths of the material world, and, on the other hand, the core literal and nonliteral message of the Bible, because the source of both is God.[14]

Thoughtful and informed Judeo-Christian believers know that, while science has rolled back many unfounded myths, including those with a pseudo-religious genesis, science will never be dangerous to the Judeo-Christian worldview or to its legacy because all the evidence supports the view that God exists. Unless radical militant anti-theists actually take out their long knives and put them to use against innocent folk in the name of progress or messianism, as was done by the radical French revolutionaries in the late 18th century and the Marxist-Leninists in the 20th century, humanity will always have the chance to wake up from its foolish theoretical fairytales.

The Wizards offer luck and the icy laws of physics to explain the most fundamental questions about man and existence. The Judeo-Christian worldview, on the other hand, extends to man a more complete and time-tested approach to the essential questions about life to help people face the unknown and decipher the meaning and purpose of space, time, and reality.

While Lawrence M. Krauss, theoretical physicist and cosmologist, and Dawkins proffer ideas and theories packed with supposedly earth-shattering significance for popular consumption, they expose their own silliness when redefining words such as "nothingness" to suit their purpose. Do they camouflage their own beliefs to avoid being called believers themselves? Do they not in fact believe in the *uniformity of nature*, which underpins the intelligibility of the universe (and makes science possible), and in the eternal existence of "something," which by definition cannot be measured (even mathematically)? They seem to argue that "something," which came from nothing, has eternally existed even though that "something" cannot be God because God by definition cannot exist.[15]

Stephen Hawking, the eminent Cambridge University professor, seemed to believe that the law of gravity contributed to getting "something" from "nothing."[16] Had he forgotten that laws don't cause anything? They only describe. John Lennox paraphrases Hawking in explaining the absurdity of his position: "because there is a law of gravity (i.e., because there is something), the universe can and will create itself from 'nothing.'"[17] Hawking's basic philosophy is shockingly lame and his metaphysical conclusions are not based on science (testable explanations about the origins the universe), but rather on flawed logic and conjecture.

And what about his materialism, which claims that only matter exists? But if there was a time when there was nothing or "no thing," what does that do to atheism? Doesn't materialistic atheism mean that only matter has existed, and eternally? Is he playing more word games to justify atheism?

When Hawking moved beyond physics into metaphysics, did he not expose a bias that calls into question his judgment in matters nonscientific? In defending his recently proclaimed atheism, he came across a bit silly because he produced no evidence for his assertion.[18] Rather, he exposed *his belief* that the universe arose from the laws of physics, a belief that was based on a firm act of "blind faith." Hawking seemed to be stuck on his own fixed ideas.

To the vexation of the Wizards, Lennox again steps in to put so much into context: "The doctrine of creation was not only important in the rise of science because of its entailment of order in the universe. It was important for another reason.... For science to develop, thinking had to be freed from the hitherto ubiquitous Aristotelian method of deducing from fixed principles how the universe ought to be, to a methodology that allowed the universe to speak directly. That fundamental shift in perspective was made much easier by the notion of a *contingent* creation — that is, that God the Creator could have created the universe any way he liked. Hence, in order to find out what the universe is really like or how it actually works, there is no alternative to going and looking. You cannot deduce how the universe works simply by reasoning from *a priori* philosophical principles." [19]

When Hawking laid out his "Big Bumba Theory," he essentially declared that created gods are figments of the imagination (which is true).[20] Unfortunately, he lumped the one uncreated God of the universe into the pile of created man-made gods of the human mind. It is tragic that a scientist at his level simply dismissed God[21] and declared philosophy dead, while at the same time using philosophy to defend his own beliefs. "If Hawking were not so dismissive of philosophy," said Lennox, "he might have come across Wittgenstein's statement that the 'deception of modernism' is the idea that the laws of nature *explain* the world to us when all they do is to *describe* structural regularities." [22]

Another ruse of the Enlightenment Trap is the "equality of ideas principle," which, in the area of ethics, states that different ideas are morally equivalent or only as good as they are useful (utility becoming the measure of goodness). In other words, there is no evil (wrong) in holding any idea (or acting on it) as long as it doesn't hurt anyone or violate some general principle of useful altruism. Philosophical moral relativism reduces objective (not self-referencing)[23] standards such as the natural moral law to a toxic mixture of supposedly inconsequential subjective opinions and evolutionary-based core values.[24]

Christianity does not generate fanatics (though some zealots occasionally pop up), but it is easy to see why anti-theists link religion with fanaticism and violence. Pope Francis writes in his usual interesting style,

> Truth itself, the truth which would comprehensively explain our life ... is regarded with suspicion. Surely this kind of truth is what was claimed by the great totalitarian movements of the last century, a truth that imposed its own world view in order to crush the actual lives of individuals. In the end, what we are left with is relativism, in which the question of universal truth — and ultimately this means the question of God — is no longer relevant. It would be logical, from this point of view, to attempt to sever the bond between religion and truth, because it seems to lie at the root of fanaticism, which proves oppressive for anyone who does not share the same beliefs. In this regard, though, we can speak of a massive amnesia in our contemporary world.[25]

We need to look back. The Judeo-Christian worldview has embraced the idea of objective truth and understood that beauty, the laws of physics, complexity, suffering, harmony, and moral reasoning are not accidents of nature but exist for a reason. It is up to each of us to find out the significance of truth, suffering and beauty in our lives.

Some Thoughts on Islam and Christianity

Just as the Wizards do not differentiate between the one uncreated God and all other man-made gods, they do not understand the fundamental differences between the Islamic and the Judeo-Christian interpretations of natural law, freedom, and salvation. They lump all religions together. By way of example, Robert Reilly says: "In Christian anthropology, humans are created in

God's image and called to share God's life. Both of these notions are anathema to Islam, which considers them blasphemous."[26]

In the case of Islam, for example, the revered Islamic theologian Abu Hamid al-Ghazali (1058–1111) comments regarding the rite of pilgrimage to Mecca, "Blind obedience to God is the best evidence of our Islam." [27] Quite a revealing statement from one of the most esteemed Islamic theologians. The Judeo-Christian legacy, on the other hand, champions the need to interpret the sacred texts of the Bible in light of reality, truth, and common sense.

For the Christian, says Khalil Samir, S.J., in his book *111 Questions on Islam*, "the notion of *natural law* represents a common ground between the believer and the secular, and it allows the acknowledgement of universal rights." However, "the Muslim considers it inconceivable to speak of *natural law* apart from the religious law (*sharia*) given by God to man, being persuaded that there is no universal given that it is not already included in the Islamic conception of life. While in Christianity one starts from reason and arrives at revelation, in the classic Islamic conception revelation comes before reason and prevails upon it, engulfs it."[28] This difference should be broadcast so that people do not think that Islam and Christianity are fundamentally the same except in rituals and other external manifestations.

The Emotions and Ego

Whether talking about natural law or the existence of God, most Wizards roll out the argument that scientists *think for themselves*, whereas Christians are for the most part unthinking slaves chained to stultifying authority and religious sentimentalism. That may be the case with other religions and errant minority sects within Christianity, but it is definitely not the case with the majority of Christians. Scientists such as Arthur L. Schawlow, physicist, Derek Barton, organic chemist, and John Eccles, neuroscientist, to name a few, stand at the top of their professions, yet their belief in God did not reduce their science or ability to think creatively or critically to rubble.[29]

The Judeo-Christian worldview sees the universe — the solar system, the galaxies, the suns, dark matter, et cetera — as much more than one big complex riddle that smart academics will eventually figure out. There exists at the core of radical atheism a childlike belief that human intelligence, given enough time, will figure out that there is no need for God. Realizing that, the human person will be able to focus more effectively on survival and procreation — a view quite opposite to that of the Judeo-Christian tradition and of St. Augustine, for example, as expressed in his *Confessions*.

Science is much more than an instrument to describe the workings of the universe. It exists to serve others and reach into the mind of God. The universe deserves greater respect than that received from the effort of populist anti-theists trying to outfox the evolutionary imperative or reduce error rates in scientific experimentation to zero in order to bring about the conditions for an earthly utopia, and thus to get around the problem of God and suffering.

The effectiveness of science in the inner world of the person means working not only with the forces and laws of nature but with the totality of reality, which includes the spiritual. To undertake that task in a holistic fashion is what makes the search for truth at once exciting and beautiful, and an opportunity to serve others in ways consistent with the nature of the human being.

The German philosopher Ludwig Feuerbach (1804–1872) offers us pessimism and with it a window into his inability to deal with uncertainty and doubt, which he blames on Christianity:

> Christianity set itself the goal of fulfilling man's unattainable desires, but for that very reason ignored his attainable desires. By promising man eternal life, it deprived him of temporal life; by teaching him to trust in God's help it took away his trust in his own powers; by giving him faith in a better life in heaven, it destroyed his faith in a better life on Earth and his striving to attain such a life. Christianity gave man what his imagination desires, but for that very reason failed to give him what he really and truly desires.[30]

Feuerbach is not entirely wrong when such analysis is applied to timid and fool-hearty religious folk who are afraid of life and the world and who refuse to take responsibility for their decisions. The real story, however, is that Christians can (and do) participate (fully, joyfully, and confidently) in all the honest activities and creative impulses that this world offers (while believing in an afterlife) to serve others and bring about genuine personal satisfaction and human development. Feuerbach's commentary applies more generally to religious minorities who decline to engage with the world and be part of it.

Feuerbach's enticing but misleading call to grow up and graduate from what he identifies as the paternalistic claws of Judeo-Christian shallowness and indifference towards the outside world has greatly influenced contemporary society. Other scholars following his lead, including Engels and Marx, have also portrayed religion, particularly Christianity, as a psychological virus introduced into human consciousness leading to negative emotional insecurities and indifference. To achieve their objective of enticing man to accept Feuerbach's views, today's Wizards present us with a counterfeit choice between development and optimism (by rejecting God) on the one hand, and backwardness and failure (by continuing to believe in God) on the other.[31] By speaking about the Judeo-Christian worldview as stagnant and unproductive, most Wizards hope to entice more and more people to scrap belief in what they call an insensitive and vengeful God.

The Judeo-Christian worldview does not demand that people surrender their intelligence or freedom to a cold-hearted and cruel God; or that they outwit the forces of nature for the sake of survival. Life, of course, is a struggle, but it's much more than that. "Liberation," in the Judeo-Christian context, comes about when a person lives within the limits imposed by the laws of physics and nature and by the guidance of the natural moral law, i.e., in accordance with truth.

Wishful Thinking

Radical Wizards have their own "Big Bumba," which is the miracle of cold reason and a sense of personal invincibility that comes from science and an "always right" self-referencing moral code (as long as the numbers work out or no one suffers). Referring to Sam Harris's emotional harangue against religion in his *Letter to a Christian Nation* (2006), Ravi Zacharias, Christian evangelist and former atheist, insightfully comments,

> Evidently, while belief in [Harris's] atheism is worth any price, religious belief is too costly. This duplicity is only the tip of the iceberg in Harris's belabored tirade against religion. With Christopher Hitchens, Richard Dawkins, and a few others, he is calling for the banishment of religious belief. "Away with this nonsense" is their battle cry! In return, they promise a world of new hope and unlimited horizons — once we have shed this delusion of God. I have news for them — news to the contrary. The reality is that the emptiness that results from the loss of the transcendent is stark and devastating, both philosophically and existentially.[32]

It would seem that Peter Atkins, chemist, similarly, cannot distinguish wishful thinking from science, since he is so mesmerized by Darwinian philosophical determinism, mathematics, and its assumptions of materialism. Listen to Atkins, who writes with a flare more appropriate to fantasy and fiction than to science:

> I shall take your mind on a journey. It is a journey of comprehension, taking us to the edge of space, time, and understanding. On it I shall argue that there is nothing that cannot be understood, that there is nothing that cannot be explained, and that everything is extra-ordinarily simple. A great deal of the universe does not need any explanation.
>
> Elephants, for instance. Once molecules have learnt to compete and to create other molecules in their own image, elephants, and things resembling elephants, will in due course be found roaming through the countryside.[33]

Atkins's story is simplistic and delightful, but all the same pure conjecture. Isn't that the point, really? He has not even come close to explaining the origins of life or the appearance of elephants. He simply asserts, which is fine as long as everyone gets it. At the end of the day, his apparently ideologically motivated observations are not science but philosophical speculation. People must come to see that "Atkins' 'self-generation' explanation is demanded by his materialism, not his science."[34]

For the Wizards, endless "amounts of time" can explain anything, including order, disorder, cause, simplicity, and complexity. They seek to make the impossible possible, the infinite finite, and the hopelessly improbable probable through endless experimentation and in the hope that hope will make it so. Time cannot explain change; it is the measure of change.

An Observation about Science

Science has not been able to understand either the origins of life or the exact transmission mechanism itself. But even if the theory of evolution were true (and it may indeed be true as a mechanism), it would prove only how certain forms of change occur (and how God might operate in the universe).

One of the key questions in the debate about evolution is this: does inert matter itself possess intrinsic dispositions or qualities (embedded within its nature) that empower it to pass on to subsequent generations certain characteristics that result in more complex systems? Can inert matter in fact generate life from non-life (simple to complex) without any external intervention? In other words, the explicator of the ultimate source of the tendencies or powers that enable material systems to arise naturally and without external intervention would explain only that and nothing else. Answering the question "how" does not explain "who" or "what" started it all in the first place, and certainly does imply that God, the uncaused cause, does not exist.

God is a huge problem for materialism because a human being is much more than a clump of molecules and chemical interactions. Francis Collins responds with great credibility:

> At this point, godless materialists might be cheering. If humans evolved strictly by mutation and natural selection, who needs God to explain us? To this, I reply: I do. The comparison of chimp and human sequences, interesting as it is, does not tell us what it means to be human. In my view, DNA sequence alone, even if accompanied by a vast trove of data on biological function, will never explain certain special human attributes, such as the knowledge of the Moral Law and the universal search for God. Freeing God from the burden of special acts of creation does not remove Him as the source of the things that make humanity special, and of the universe itself. It merely shows us something of how He operates.[35]

Charles Darwin and St. Thomas Aquinas, the 13th-century friar who wrote the *Commentary on the Eight Books of Physics*, a follow-up of sorts to Aristotle's *Physics*, may agree on the question of change in the material world of biology. Is it not significant that Aquinas seems to agree with the Darwinian argument of intrinsic tendencies (within matter itself) as a possible transmission mechanism? That is to say, how do we explain the change within matter itself from less complexity to greater *without* the need for a miracle or external intervention? As of today, the question remains open. Even if science discovers an intrinsic generative force within matter itself, the discovery would not compel a person to deny the existence of God.[36]

The Judeo-Christian worldview holds that it is not unreasonable to believe in the existence of God and in the possibility of evolution *as an explicator for change* in the material world. The Wizards insist that we must pick between God and evolution; but there is no reason why this should be so.

Terminology

To support their ideology of relativism in the moral sphere, the Wizards speak of "brotherhood," "diversity," "multiculturalism," "equality," "freedom," and "progress." If their intentions are to promote those ideals, then it would be wise to review the historical record of their attempts to do so. In the process of moving towards new world orders, they shield themselves with political correctness and ideals such as brotherhood; their swords are rationalism and power. They skillfully convert the Judeo-Christian ideal of equality to the ideology of egalitarianism to achieve their ends. In the Anglo-American world, they seek to convert Brompton Oratory in London or St. Patrick's Cathedral in New York into all-you-can-eat multicultural eateries with vanity mirrors instead of altars serving up anything but the truths about man and the universe, while making sure that prayer is restricted to holding hands under the watchful eye of George Orwell's Big Brother. If this were a joke, it could be a smidgeon comical, but the anti-theists are playing for keeps.

Human Beings Down-Graded

The anti-theists seem to believe that there are no qualitative differences between human beings and animals. Differences boil down only to a thing's complexity, experience of pain, and usefulness. With such thinking, the Wizards have downgraded human beings to the level of sophisticated animals.

When there is no difference between *Homo sapiens* and *Culiseta longiareolata* (mosquitos) other than the number of cells and the length of DNA, why not use pesticides to minimize problems or perform lobotomies so as to create a "new man" free from suffering? Great civilizations are built on a genuine concept of man, not on a vision of man as an animal engaged in endless striving and self-assertion even at the expense of others. Nor can the avoidance of pain be made a central goal of politics and society, and yet that vision is precisely the one that prevails in so much of academia. Such a vision of man only reinforces the "culture of death" which has taken hold in many parts of the world." [37, 38]

The idea of endless scientific progress has taken on godlike qualities over the past 200 years and, yet, continues to generate new practical problems for society. What in fact do scientific achievements really mean when goodness is reduced to utility and more people are downing pain-killers like there's no tomorrow? While science continues to unlock the way the world works, it will never produce an earthly kingdom as the Wizards promise nor satisfy the deepest longings of persons. When God is not in the picture, political moralism turns to savagery and madness.

In recent years, scientists, either from misplaced zeal or arrogance, have been seeking to clone human beings. Projects to re-engineer humans with pre-determined racial, physical, and intellectual characteristics remind us of Aldous Huxley's 1931 dystopian novel, *Brave New World*. Huxley laid out the efforts of a future government to set up, by means of cloning, a scientifically planned society in which people lived happily in accordance with their pre-assigned genetic codes in class structures. He brilliantly captured the dehumanization of the human person as well as the complete loss of personal identity in a sterile and hopeless environment. *Brave New World* brings out the far-reaching dangers of scientism, which sees no need for God. [39]

If today's academics and politicians continue to regard the Judeo-Christian worldview as but a repository of private myths and demented people rather than as a source of sanity for better living and governance, it is fairly easy to predict the onset of increased social conflict and misery on a scale never seen before. It might occur, not because people are any more evil today than in the past, but rather because self-delusion and arrogance may drive humanity mad.

Malcolm Muggeridge asks a very pertinent question: Is it surprising, then, that those who have brought about these astounding developments in science, technology and politics "should see themselves, not as mere mortal men, but as very gods"? Extraordinary scientific progress, the result of human ingenuity and hard work, has developed in people a kind of dogmatic arrogance that leads them to believe that they can dispense with the transcendental and, thus, deny the relevance of God and moral reasoning. "Writers like Aldous Huxley and George Orwell," Muggeridge continues,

> have imagined the sort of scientific utopia which is coming to pass, but already their nightmare fancies are hopelessly out of date. A vast, air-conditioned, neon-lighted, glass-and-chromium broiler house begins to take shape, in which geneticists select the best stock to fertilize, and watch over the developing embryo to ensure that all possibilities of error and distortion are eliminated. Where is the need for God in such a setup? Or even for a moral law? When man is thus able to shape and control his environment and being, then surely he may be relied on to create his own earthy paradise and live happily ever after in it.[40]

Does that not describe what anti-theists and Wizards are selling? Does not that arrogance explain the self-righteousness of so many elites in modern society? Without any limits, does not the Wizards' brash belief in the near-omnipotence of science suggest that experimentation on human beings is justified in the name of progress, national security, or a better standard of living? When society allows academics and scientists to treat human beings like guinea pigs, anything is possible. No number of technological advances can assure the human person of a predictable, peaceful, and secure future. For the anti-theists, justice is reduced to revenge and mercy moves people from their homes into de-personalizing psychiatric wards in defense of the common good.

Friedrich Nietzsche

Friedrich Nietzsche, the brilliant German thinker, is among the 19th-century philosopher-historians who realized that humanity was losing its grip on the meaning of life. He predicted a rise in nihilism — the despair of meaninglessness — and saw that people were haunted by deep levels of intellectual poverty, anxiety, mediocrity, and exhaustion leading to misery and depression. According to John Hollowell, he envisioned an "excess of self-righteousness, the refusal to face the fact of evil, the condemnation of the worker to anonymous slavery, the search for money as an end in itself, the fawning sycophancy of democratic politicians, the idolatry of the state, the conception of man as a meaningless accident in a cosmic mechanism, the pawn of environmental forces, the preponderance of scholarship over creativeness, the cultivation of mediocrity in all fields of endeavor, in the realm of art the bizarre combination of charlatanism and virtuosity, brutality, and over-refinement, stimulants, and opiates, the cult of the ugly, the morbid, the exotic — in short, the pestilence of hypocrisy and self-deceit."[41] Self-deceit would seem to be an apt description of much of today's academic community and political elites currently dominating the structures of power. It is this same self-deception that compels the Wizards to continue to privatize religion, and think like Nietzsche.

In retrospect, Nietzsche's prophetic scenario of the future of humanity has proved accurate. If he was shocked by the essentially self-indulgent behavior of the elites of his age, what would he say if he were to witness the behavior of today's elites? Just turn on the television or pick up the newspaper. What do we see but an endless grasping for material things, an obsession with the body and sex, the normalization of relativism, endless wars, and manifestations of the arrogance of power wielded by utopians and anti-theists?

The Wizards hope to be the masters of the universe, i.e., they plan to remove all uncertainty and suffering in life, thus opening the door to the unremitting pursuit of happiness, and, with any luck, fun, understood as self-indulgence. Without God, they believe that human experience will be upgraded: "God, we are told — if he ever existed — has died; as a concept, he is not needed any more. We know enough now about our environment and circumstances, have sufficient control over them, to take over. Our apprenticeship is served; mankind has come of age, and the time has come for us to assume command of ourselves and our world in our own right."[42]

Have we really come of age? Haven't we heard this before? "But the snake said to the woman: 'You certainly will not die! God knows well that when you eat of it your eyes will be opened and you will be like gods, who know good and evil.'"[43]

Significantly, Nietzsche understood better than most intellectuals today the implications of the loss of belief in absolute and timeless transcendence. He claimed that man was on the brink of suicide and no amount of Christian morality could stop the inevitable collapse of civilization.[44] Nietzsche's answer to this problem was to replace the universal moral law with his idea of Superman and the drive for power. He anticipated the rise of National Socialism in Germany, Marxism-Leninism in the Soviet Union, and scientism (as an ideology) in the Anglo-American world.

Nietzsche represents the triumph of arrogance over common sense. He theorized that, since God was imaginary, the human person had no reason to adhere to a moral system based on permanent transcendent values. The solution to the human race's existential problem was to create an alternate universe with a different morality based on the supremacy of the will. A new world moral order would be directed by a handful of men and women, or the *Übermenschen* (Supermen) of the future, who would become self-reliant and thus leaders and masters of the universe. There would be no room, he said, for mediocrity or weakness; virtuous behavior had to be imposed. Nietzsche, like Machiavelli, replaced the Judeo-Christian emphasis on permanent truths, the search for truth and charity, with power, cold efficiency, and mass manipulation.

Other Considerations

Ideologically driven political action has been at the root of French revolutionary democratic thought for centuries (which is different from the American experience). French intellectuals have tended to disparage the more practical and down-to-earth approach to democracy as understood in the early years of the American Republic and as summarized by Alexis de Tocqueville (1805–1859). Unfortunately, it seems that American democratic activism in the 21st century has veered away from its foundational principles and been absorbed into the more extreme ideological elements of the French revolutionary spirit of the anti-theists and the Wizards of the Enlightenment.[45]

When politics, including the idea of democracy, seeks to exercise unhindered power to achieve utopian objectives, the human person always suffers, because human dignity is subordinated to supposedly higher, but illusory, ideals.

In view of the predominantly befuddled state of affairs in intellectual circles and given the utopians' horrendous track record, it is critical to reexamine the Judeo-Christian legacy and its role in opening a viable path to genuine human development.

Joseph Cardinal Ratzinger, in his book *The Turning Point for Europe?* outlines how modern-day elites live in an age of foolish optimism, escapism, and wishful thinking: "All this becomes so dangerous because of the decisively earthly character of the messianic hope: something unconditional is demanded of what is conditional, something infinite is demanded of what is finite. This inherent contradiction indicates the real tragedy of this phenomenon in which man's great vocation becomes the instrument of the great lie." [46] One of the most alluring aspects of the Enlightenment Trap is precisely the inability of its victims to see the fallacy in the "earthly character of the messianic hope." [47]

A Suggestion

In an effort to explain the insanity of the intellectual landscape of the age, British philosopher Alasdair MacIntyre sees a possible exit strategy for humanity from the recklessness and irrationality of moral relativism and other anti-theist socio-political philosophies that equate human beings with animals. In addressing the anti-intellectual and dysfunctional nature of society today, he sees the contemporary mind in utter disarray. Modern philosophies, he says, are unable to recognize the peril in self-referencing ethics, making it virtually impossible to find common ground with anyone on serious questions. Debates are endless, since no single position is wrong, and, therefore, no one is right. [48]

Pope Francis also sees the problem and hits upon a key characteristic of modern thinking:

> In contemporary culture, we often tend to consider the only real truth to be that of technology: truth is what we succeed in building and measuring by our scientific know-how, truth is what works and what makes life easier and more comfortable. Nowadays this appears as the only truth that is certain, the only truth that can be shared, the only truth that can serve as a basis for discussion or for common undertakings. Yet at the other end of the scale we are willing to allow for subjective truths of the individual, which consist in fidelity to his or her deepest convictions, yet these are truths valid only for the individual and not capable of being proposed to others in an effort to serve the common good. [49]

MacIntyre seems to propose a solution to man's psychological muddle and godless, relativist anxiety: "If the characteristics of our own moral arguments which I have identified — most notably the fact that we simultaneously and inconsistently treat moral argument as an exercise of our rational powers and as mere expressive assertion — are symptoms of moral disorder, *we ought to be able to construct a true historical narrative* [emphasis added] in which at an earlier stage moral argument is very different in kind. Can we?"[50] I believe it is vitally important that we make the effort to construct MacIntyre's "true historical narrative," and that we do so on the firm foundation of the Judeo-Christian worldview and legacy. But for that to succeed, we need better schools and universities than we now have.

In his encyclical "The Light of Faith," Pope Francis seems to offer a similar path through the collective amnesia and muddle of modernity: "The question of truth is really a question of memory, deep memory, for it deals with something prior to ourselves and can succeed in uniting us in a way that transcends our petty and limited individual consciousness. It is a question about the origin of all that is, in whose light we can glimpse the goal and thus the meaning of our common path."[51] This recognition that there is "something prior to ourselves" is indeed a starting point for understanding "who we are." A deeper awareness of the history of the Judeo-Christian legacy and of the central importance of selfless service towards God and others considering "who we are" must be reintroduced (in an undogmatic manner) into the public square. The Wizards' success to date in privatizing the public expression of Judeo-Christian beliefs and symbols must be peacefully reversed.

Take a Step Back

Is not the Judeo-Christian concept of the dignity of the human person the bedrock idea that keeps people from tearing each other into pieces? Selfless service is not a survivalist technique, as some Wizards would claim, but rather an act that leads to joy and happiness despite the hardships and contradictions along the way. The desire to serve is embedded in human nature and is central to Christianity, and its success as a worldview owes much to the hope it offers in the face of injustice.

People need to be reminded that the Judeo-Christian mindset is in fact a living cell that has stimulated the imagination and promoted science, art, and progress from the times of the New and Old Testaments through the Middle Ages, the Renaissance, the Protestant Reformation, the Age of Discovery, and the Enlightenment up to the present day. The Judeo-Christian worldview is not a static set of retrograde ideas encased in decaying and useless manuscripts, as the Wizards would have us believe. Rather, it is a living patrimony constantly striving to build a better and saner world.

The ideology of the Wizards of the Enlightenment is unconvincing because their gods of chance, moral relativism, and power are merciless, especially when arrogance gets the better of patience. The Wizards' better judgment is muddied in assuming that the powers of the intellect are sufficient *in themselves* to create for humanity an environment free of uncertainty and inequality. In their multiple attempts over the past 200 years to create a utopia on earth ("a new man" or "a new society," invariably without God), have they not always had to resort to enslavement, bayonets, or internment in insane asylums to get their way?

Any initiative to advance genuine human development must be preceded by a recognition of the existence of God and a respect for the fundamental dignity of the human person from which the inalienable "rights of man" flow. Sanity means becoming aware of humanity's authentic moral legacy and the origin and limits of power and science. Sanity means grasping the folly of moral relativism and the role of science in seeing the differences between magic and miracles.[52]

Sanity also means recognizing an objective order where truth and purpose are not transitory. It means being able to distinguish physics from metaphysics and an auto-body shop from a caring hospital. Sanity means seeing that the God of eternity is not just one of Feuerbach's mysterious bogeymen (gods) of the netherworld inhabiting the unenlightened minds of people in need of decontamination and de-Christianization.[53]

Genuine human development depends on moving towards God and truth and away from the desperate liberation theologies of the anti-theists, which are often camouflaged in Judeo-Christian terminology, science, and high ideals. We need to see the dynamic hand of God at the other end of a telescope or microscope, revel in the beauty of life, and discover the divine in the ordinary circumstances of everyday life. That is the program that has led to genuine human development in the past; there is no reason that it should not lead to progress in the future. History is on the side of those who believe in God and science, working together; it is not on the side of those who pick one to the exclusion of the other.

---

1.   "The Wizards of the Enlightenment" or simply "Wizards" is the term I use for radical atheists who are at the same time anti-theists. The term mainly refers to post-Enlightenment intellectuals although there are Wizards who predate the Enlightenment because of their open anti-theist stances. They are a disparate group of thinkers spanning many centuries, so when I speak of them, I cannot, of course, be referring to each and every one. They are not a monolithic group with the exact same ideas. Some would even reject being linked with the others. And it should be noted that many Wizards have made very real and valuable contributions in their respective specialized fields. For the most part, however, they see the Judeo-Christian worldview as a sort of make-believe, mind-altering, and mood-changing drug-like set of ideas that keeps otherwise normal people from thinking. For interesting debates between some Wizards and John Lennox, see the following: (a) Peter Singer and John Lennox, "Is There a God?" (debate; Big Ideas, September 2011); (https://www.youtube.com/watch?v=qA7qBtNMayQ); (b) Lawrence Krauss and John Lennox, "Lawrence Krauss vs John Lennox — Science, the Universe and the

God Question — Unbelievable?" (debate; Christian Radio, September 2013) (https://www.youtube.com/watch?v=MKt2NPbTHM0); (c) John Lennox and Michael Shermer, "The Nature of Suffering and Evil" (debate; Veritas Forum, November 2013) (https://livestream.com/pepperdineuniversity/2013-11veritas/videos/34625540).

2.   For example, see Steven Weinberg: "The world needs to wake up from its long nightmare of religious belief. And anything we scientists can do to weaken the hold of religion should be done. And may in the end be our greatest contribution to civilization." ("Religion and Science," n.d.) (https://www.youtube.com/watch?v=zYlMpvHMXO4).

3.   See John Lennox, "Does Rationality Lead Us Away from God?" (lecture; Veritas Forum, October 2012); (https://www.youtube.com/embed/AZl1LbwEb9g at the Veritas Forum).

4.   John C. Lennox, *God's Undertaker: Has Science Buried God?* (Oxford: Lion Book, 2007); p. 16.

5.   Benedict XVI (pope), *Charity in Truth* (San Francisco: Ignatius Press, 2009).

6.   John C. Lennox, *God's Undertaker* (Kindle Books, 2011); location 1304.

7.   Francis S. Collins, ed., "Introduction" in *Belief: Readings on the Reason of Faith* (New York: HarperCollins, 2010).

8.   Lawrence Krauss seems to reject the difference between "why" and "how." In discussing the planets, he says, "Not only has 'why' become 'how' but 'why' no longer has any verifiable meaning. So too when we ask 'Why is there something rather than nothing?' we really mean 'How is there something rather than nothing?'" Lawrence M. Krauss, *A Universe from Nothing: Why There Is Something Rather Than Nothing* (New York: Free Press, 2012); p. iii.

9.   "Like [me], there are many scientists and others who think that the New Atheism is a belief system which, ironically, provides a classic example of the blind faith it so vocally despises in others. I should like to make my own small contribution towards raising public awareness of this fact." John C. Lennox, *Gunning for God* (Kindle, 2011); lines 186-98.

10.   See Stephen Meyer and Michael Behe, "The Creation Conversation" (Watermark Radio, 2012) (part 1: https://www.youtube.com/watch?v=ZgsEtVe_Bis). Dr. Stephen Meyer offers an introduction to the evening's presentation and defines Intelligent Design. He is followed by Michael Behe, who, among other things, discusses the issue of irreducible complexity (part 2: https://www.youtube.com/watch?v=1mF7w_zF2DU April 19, 2009).

11.   The scientific evidence, for example, has led Michael Behe, American biochemist, to make the following statement: "Inferences to design do not require that we have a candidate for the role of designer. We can determine that a system was designed by examining the system itself, and we can hold the conviction of design much more strongly than a conviction about the identity of the designer." Michael Behe, *Darwin's Black Box: The Biochemical Challenge to Evolution* (New York, Free Press, 1996); pp. 195-96.

12.   Lennox, *God's Undertaker* (Kindle), location 1424.

13.   Francis (pope), "Lumen Fidei" (encyclical letter; June 29, 1913); pp. 30 -31 http://w2.vatican.va/content/francesco/en/encyclicals/documents/papa-francesco_20130629_enciclica-lumen-fidei.html).

14.   To get a sense of "young earth" believers, it is sufficient to read Henry Morris III, *Exploring the Evidence for Creation: Reasons to Believe the Biblical Account* (Eugene, Ore.: Harvest House, 2008/2009). It is not intellectually reasonable to subscribe to all the arguments laid out in this book.

15.   "Eternal empty void is certainly not nothing. Empty space is a boiling bubbling brew of virtual particles. In fact, we discover," Krauss says, "that nothing can weigh something ... [pause] ... nothing actually weighs something." Richard Dawkins in conversation with Lawrence Krauss at the Australian National University, Sydney, July 30, 2013.

16.   Stephen Hawking, "The Origins of the Universe" (http://www.hawking.org.uk/the-origin-of- the-universe.html). I should not be thought to be disparaging Hawking's many contributions to physics. He was a great physicist and should be honored as such; but he was not a good philosopher.

17.   John Lennox, "God and Stephen Hawking — Do the Laws of Physics Make God Unnecessary?" (lecture; Center for Science and Culture, 2011) (https://www.youtube.com/watch?v=kIZRd1NdJyg).

18.   Pablo Jáuregui, "Stephen Hawking: No hay ningún dios. Soy ateo," (interview; El Mundo, September 9, 2014) (http://www.elmundo.es/ciencia/2014/09/21/541dbc-12ca474104078b4577.html).

19.   Lennox, *God's Undertaker* (Lion), p.22; (Kindle), location 411-23.

20.   Hawking, "Origins."

21   Hawking, "Origins."

22.   Lennox, *Gunning*, lines 549-62.

23.   A self-referencing morality (i.e., one that is derived from a rejection of natural law and transcendent values) cannot serve as a basis for a sane society, as history and personal experience have demonstrated time and again. When we ignore the objective natural (moral) law and instead put our hopes on living only within the demands of the physical and biological laws of nature, integral human development is crippled, if not undermined.

24.   "Evolution provides a scientific foundation for the core values shared by most Christians and conservatives, and by accepting — and embracing — the theory of evolution, Christians and conservatives strengthen their religion, their politics, and science itself. The conflict between science and religion is senseless. It is based on fears and misunderstandings rather than on facts and moral wisdom." Michael Shermer, *Why Darwin Matters: The Case against Intelligent Design* (New York, Henry Holt and Company, LLC); p. 138

25.   Francis (pope), "Lumen Fidei," p. 32.

26   Robert R. Reilly, *The Prospects and Perils of Catholic-Muslim Dialogue* (McLean, Va.: Isaac Publishing, 2013); p. 5. Other useful books on Islam are Emmet Scott *The Impact of Islam* (Nashville, Tenn.: New English Review Press, 2014) and Ibn Warraq, *The Islam in Islamic Terrorism: The Importance of Beliefs, Ideas, and Ideology* (Nashville, Tenn.: New English Review Press, 2017).

27.   See Abu Hamid al-Ghazali, *Ihya ulum al-din* [The Revival of the Religious Sciences], vol. 1, bk 7, chap. 3, sec. 2 (Cairo, 1939)' pp. 272ff.; also (Beruit: Dar al-kutub al-ilmiyya, 1992), p. 315. As quoted in Samir Khalil, S.J., *111 Questions on Islam: Interviews conducted by Giorgio Paolucci and Camille Eid on Islam and the West* (San Francisco: Ignatius Press, 2008); p. 180.

28.   Samir Khalil, *111 Qustions*, pp. 200-201.

29.   See Meyer and Behe, "Creation," part 2.

30.   Feuerbach, *Lectures on the Essence of Religion*, lecture XXX, 1851, The same material is dealt with in Feuerbach's book, *Essence of Christianity*, Ralph Mannheim, trans. (New York: Harper & Row, Publishers, 1967) (http://www.marxists.org/reference/archive/feuerbach/works/lectures/index.htm).

31.   See Sam Harris, *The End of Faith: Religion, Terror, and the Future of Reason* (New York: W.W.Norton & Company, Inc., 2004).

32.   Ravi Zacharias, *The End of Reason: A Response to the New Atheists* (Grand Rapids, Mich. Zondervan, 2008); pp. 116 -29.

33.   P.W. Atkins, *The Creation* (MW Books, 1981); p. 3.

34. Lennox, God's Undertaker, (Kindle), location 1337-51.

35. Francis Collins, *The Language of God: A Scientist Presents Evidence for Faith* (London: Simon & Schuster UK Ltd, 2007); p. 140.

36. I'd like to thank Bobby Marsland, Ph.D. candidate at MIT, for his help in understanding some of these issues.

37. "The moral truth here is obvious: anyone who feels that the interests of a blastocyst just might supersede the interests of a child with a spinal cord injury has had his moral sense blinded by religious metaphysics." And: "Mother Teresa's compassion was very badly calibrated if the killing of first-trimester fetuses disturbed her more than the other suffering she witnessed on earth." Sam Harris, *Letter to a Christian Nation* (New York: Vintage Books, 2006); p. 12, and p. 13, respectively.

38. Peter Singer, professor of bioethics at Princeton University: "We should certainly put very strict conditions on permissible infanticide, but these conditions might owe more to the effects of infanticide on others than to the intrinsic wrongness of killing an infant." Quoted in William McGurn, "Princeton Defends Philosopher of Infanticide," *Wall Street Journal,* November 13, 1998 (https://www.wsj.com/articles/SB910930978412150500).

39. See also G.K. Chesterton, *Utopia of Usurers* (Belmont, North Carolina: Wideblood Books, 2013) for some brilliant insights into the meaning of utopianism.

40. Malcolm Muggeridge, *Jesus Rediscovered* (Wheaton, Ill.: Tyndale House Publishers, 1973); pp. 74-75.

41. John H. Hallowell, *Main Currents in Modern Political Thought* (Lanham, Md.: University Press of America, 1984); p. 551.

42. Hallowell, *Currents,* p. 73.

43, Genesis 3:4-5 (http://www.usccb.org/bible/genesis3).

44. Hollowell, *Currents,* p. 550.

45. It would seem that the American political elites in recent years have adopted the views of Thomas Paine, a largely impractical dreamer with a hint of utopian predispositions, over the more pragmatic position of Edmund Burke, who adhered to the Principle of Subsidiarity.

46. Joseph Cardinal Ratzinger, *Turning Point for Europe?* (San Francisco: Ignatius Press, 1994); pp. 27-28.

47. Collins, "Introduction," pp. 31-32.

48. Alasdair MacIntyre, *After Virtue* (Notre Dame, Ind.: University of Notre Dame Press, 1984); p. 6 (https://archive.org/stream/4.Macintyre/4.%2BMacintyre#page/n0/mode/2up).

49. Francis (pope), "Lumen Fidei," p. 25.

50. Alasdair MacIntyre, *After Virtue,* p. 11.

51. Francis (pope), "Lumen Fidei," p. 25.

52. For outstanding insight into modern thinking, see G.K. Chesterton, *Outline of Sanity* (Norfolk, Va.: IHS Press, 2001).

53. "Faith cannot move mountains (though generations of children are solemnly told the contrary and believe it). But it is capable of driving people to such dangerous folly that faith seems to me to qualify as a kind of mental illness. It leads people to believe in whatever it is so strongly that in extreme cases they are prepared to kill and to die for it without the need for further justification." Richard Dawkins, *The Selfish Gene,* new ed. (New York: Oxford University Press, 1989), p. 198.

CHAPTER 1

Towards the Enlightenment of the Heart

True law is right reason in agreement with nature, universal, consistent, everlasting, whose nature is to advocate duty by prescription and to deter wrongdoing by prohibition.

— Cicero, *De Re Publica*, III.22.33

Some believe it is only great power that can hold evil in check, but that is not what I have found. It is the small everyday deeds of ordinary folk that keep the darkness at bay. Small acts of kindness and love. Why Bilbo Baggins? Perhaps because I am afraid, and he gives me courage.

— J.R.R. Tolkien, *The Hobbit*.

Нужно иметь сердце, чтобы понять![1]

— Fyodr Dostoyevsky, *The Idiot*

Modern humanity is exhibiting many signs of mental illness combined with an unreflective stubbornness which, when left untreated, necessarily leads to making poor judgments about life and living and endangers the health, and perhaps even the very continuity of Judeo-Christian civilization. By civilization I mean the idea of a coherent but diverse Judeo-Christian culture — not bound by geography, race, rank, or class — which has been forged over millennia. The loss of this culture would be suicidal, as Judeo-Christianity represents a legacy of customs, knowledge, and beliefs that neither logic nor chance nor common commercial interests can explain. At its core, Judeo-Christianity is not just one more cultural manifestation among others; rather it has inspired men and women to serve others selflessly irrespective of their personal backgrounds, social status, appearance, or faith (if any).

My fundamental thesis is that the Judeo-Christian body of ideas is solidly anchored in the truth about man and the universe[2] and, as a result, grasps better than any other set of ideas or worldview the meaning and purpose of human existence as well as of suffering, freedom, and change. Aquinas says, "A judgment is said to be true when it conforms to the external reality." Is that not a *sine qua non* of genuine human development?

According to Pope Benedict XVI, "Integral human development presupposes the responsible freedom of the individual and of peoples: no structure can guarantee this development over and above human responsibility. The types of messianism that give promises but create illusions always build their case on a denial of the transcendent dimension of development, in the conviction that it lies entirely at their disposal. The false security they offer becomes a weakness, because it involves reducing man to subservience, to a mere means for development, while the humility of those who accept a vocation is transformed into true autonomy because it sets them free."[3]

Not only has the Judeo-Christian worldview not been unfriendly to rational thought and science, but it has been their inspiration, thus rescuing humanity's drive for progress from the irrationality of rationalism and false liberation movements, including religious cults, utopian schemes, and Orwellian anti-theism. In other words, the Judeo-Christian worldview has been the lifeblood of rational behavior, and offers the human person the opportunity to see beyond the immediate, physical laws of nature. Moreover, it maintains that the order and predictability of the material world itself stem from God, who said, "In the beginning was the *logos*," i.e., God's intervention in the universe makes rationality possible.

Christians reject the atheism of Charles Darwin, Sigmund Freud, and Julian Huxley because without God anything is permissible, and nothing is intelligible, which is a formula that leads to arbitrariness, authoritarianism, injustice, and depredation. On this matter, the historical record is clear.

We posit that where Christianity has flourished, so has reason, scientific progress, and socio-political and economic development. Moreover, without Judeo-Christian anthropology and its emphasis on self-giving, reason could not have been intelligible in its most exalted sense because it would have been detached from a) the metaphysics of God, the Creator, *Ipsum Esse*[4], and b) a creation of having *Esse*,[5] its supreme manifestation being the dignity of the human person. In this view, genuine (or integral) human development is best supported and enriched by the Judeo-Christian understanding of human nature, work (as a means to find the divine in the material), and sanctity (the finding of oneself by selflessly serving others). This approach "to dealing with the question of existence" both makes sense and works, since it goes beyond minimalist objectives of material progress or poverty reduction, and embraces the entire human person.

To be just, the Enlightenment was, in more than a few respects, a positive development in the history of Western thought. It aimed to shed light on the mysterious and the incomprehensible, to render rational what seemed to some irrational. At its best, it elevated man — a goal compatible with Judeo-Christian values. At its worst, it tended to place man on a pedestal, and in so doing failed to give God his due, thereby leading man away from — not to — the promised land. To the extent the Enlightenment degenerated into godlessness, it tended to plunge man into darkness, irrationality, and rootlessness.

Thus, although I acknowledge that which is positive in the Enlightenment, I do not hesitate to call attention to the strain of irrationality in the thought of the *radical* Wizards of the Enlightenment and their present-day followers, including the so-called New Atheists, such as the late publicists Christopher Hitchens and Victor Stenger. They represent a minority clique of scholars who seem to regularly overlook the demands of "right reason," experience, and history, often employing loud and offensive slogans to deliver their messages. They have embraced a militant anti-theism to discredit the Judeo-Christian worldview and many aspects of its cultural heritage.

Godless rationalism and moral relativism gained traction from their earliest formulations in the ancient world at the time of the split between East (Constantinople) and West (Rome) in the 11th century and took off in earnest during the Renaissance some 400 years later.[6] With the philosophy of Dun Scotus and William of Occam (both 14th-century Franciscan friars), there appeared new forms of sophisticated skepticism about "what constitutes true knowledge" in the declining Middle Ages, which morphed into militant forms of anti-theism such as hermeticism[7] and other reason-denying pantheisms down to the present. It stands to reason that one of the principle negative forces in philosophy since the early Hellenistic and late Old Testament periods is a radical militancy against God and Holy Scripture. In their turn, the Wizards believe in the idea of perpetual progress and deterministic messianisms where chance and the laws of physics must be mastered through human ingenuity and mathematics to not only survive but eliminate suffering. From the Renaissance on, these forces take the ontological form of animistic pantheisms or mechanistic materialisms.

Judeo-Christian civilization is seemingly on the ropes because of modern man's insistence on *relativizing morality* and *materializing reality*. In this sense, the philosophies of moral relativism and scientific naturalism have become dominant in modern society, signifying that truth (i.e., objective reality) is viewed as personal, situational, temporal, and limited to the material world.

In this connection, the sales pitch of the Wizards speaks of the human person as matter (that which occupies space) and promotes the idea that we are governed only by the laws of physics and biology. "As Pascal foresaw, science, like the old pagan gods, has come to belong to man's quest for power, not truth."[8] The most radical form of atheism — the militant — even touts "freedom" over physics and peddles biology over the human person, body and soul. As a result, the spiritual side of the person is ignored, intruded upon, or locked up, so to speak. Facts are swept under the rug to maintain the illusion of objectivity in the face of a subjective moral disorder.

For the Wizards, suffering and uncertainty become the measure of good and evil, of progress and retrogression. As writers Ravi Zacharias and Vincent Vitale point out, the reality of suffering is something atheists have a hard time with philosophically. They ask, "Here's the main point; one of the assumptions smuggled into the thought that suffering disproves the existence of God is this: 'If God does have good reasons for allowing the suffering that He allows, we should know what those reasons are.' But why think that? God might have many reasons for allowing suffering. And we shouldn't be at all taken aback if we aren't able to grasp them in full."[9]

The Wizards believe that God is a harmful figment of the imagination that must be gotten rid of for real progress to be possible. To believe in God is de-humanizing because it is anti-intellectual and contrary to freedom. In pursuing utopian dreams, some of the Wizards even suggest that a biblical-like salvation and redemption are possible in this life, when a person makes an "act of unfaith" in the nonexistence of God. As a result, the human mind and science are freed up from being subordinated to Judeo-Christian religious nonsense, thus permitting politics, economics, and sociology to create the conditions for an earthly utopia.

In contrast, the Judeo-Christian worldview sees human development as a by-product of recognition of God, the dignity of the human person, and personal service, and is linked to them. Although Europe's formerly God-centered Judeo-Christian civilization is (or appears to be) on life-support, and it looks as though many of its intellectual, cultural, and artistic achievements are destined to be consigned to museums and libraries, there is hope for its cultural and spiritual revival if one takes the time and energy to think through and explain the link between genuine human development, on the one hand, and fundamental principles, common sense, purpose, the human person, and the Judeo-Christian legacy itself, on the other.

Has not this unique and innovative set of ideas energized people over time to look beyond themselves, and serve others (by making great music, carrying out research, inspiring charitable acts, caring for the environment, innovating, and much more)?[10] Integral human development does not come about exclusively through economic development, which is the ideology of materialists, or just because a less-developed country has economic, trade, or defense ties with a more affluent one, as some suggest. The inspiration for development goes much deeper than some innate instinct to survive or even to prosper, which is at the core of most of the Wizards' messianic ideology of material progress

Natural Law

As distinct from the physical laws of nature, the natural moral law is the naturally[11] intelligible ordering and normativity of man and the cosmos. It takes account of the physical laws of nature, which must be respected, and corresponds to the existence and consciousness of living beings, and to God's purpose for them.[12] Scholars who held the Judeo-Christian worldview in the first centuries of the Christian era refined many ideas of the Ancients (for example, the truth of immortality and the inviolability of the individual human being) in the light of the truths of reality and revelation. They laid the basis for a true natural-law ethic as contrasted with that of the pantheistic systems of the Ancients and any of the shifting and unstable socio-cultural evolutionary, individualistic, utilitarian, multicultural, or relativistic ethical systems of today.[13] I agree with Flannery O'Connor, who said, "The truth does not change according to our ability to stomach it."[14]

While the main intellectual effort within early Christianity was the transmission of the full moral message of revelation (at a time when the main focus of theology was dogmatic and moral), the very effort to understand purpose (the *raison d'être* for a person's existence) and make the message of the Gospel intelligible led to the assimilation of many valid insights of ancient thinkers and scholars down the ages.

Some worldviews and religions are deficient in explaining the role of freedom in human development, in part because of their inherent failure to grasp not only the significance but the relationship of God to intelligibility, rational behavior, ethics, and progress over time. Zacharias sums it up nicely: "For the Muslim, submission is the supreme ethic from beginning to end until your endurance removes any present value from you as a person except as a ledger for good and bad. For the pantheist, total detachment from life and from relationships is the only way to avoid pain and suffering, similar to Islam but for a different reason. For the Muslim, it is because God is totally sovereign; for the pantheist, it is because the law of cause and effect is totally sovereign. For the naturalist, cause and effect is all material, and each of us just has to come in line with that. In all three there is, in the end, the loss of individual value and the stifling of the deepest longing of the human heart for love."[15]

By the end of this book, there should be no doubt that the philosophy of the godless anti-theists represents a dangerous vision — a survival-of-the-fittest enterprise in a godless universe — based on subjective and shifting criteria and on a politics of dominance, which, taken together, do not lead to genuine human development, especially when chance plays such a prominent role in explaining change. As Chesterton so succinctly stated, "The Darwinian movement has made no difference to mankind, except that, instead of talking unphilosophically about philosophy, they now talk unscientifically about science."[16] Tragically, the Wizards' insistence that the laws of physics and mathematics underpin existence leads to a nihilism that annihilates freedom and individual personality.

The Wizards' ontologically hazardous and downright dehumanizing message dates back to Genesis. Sam Harris, the American author and scientist, for example, could not be any clearer about his present day *non serviam* ("I will not serve") and rejection of the natural moral law: "If I could wave a magic wand and get rid of either rape or religion, I would not hesitate to get rid of religion."[17]

In extolling the power of reason, Harris denigrates religious faith, especially belief in the Christian God of love, and seems to reveal an indifference to the sanctity of individual personality and the dignity of the human person as understood throughout Judeo-Christian history: "When we find reliable ways to make human beings more loving, less fearful, and genuinely enraptured by the fact of our appearance in the cosmos, we will have no need for divisive religious myths."[18] In other words, Harris seems to endorse a kind of robotics or scientism — how otherwise does one "make human beings more loving" or "less fearful"? Does not such thinking reveal an animal trainer's confidence in his ability to elicit the desired response from a beast? That kind of thinking is at the very core of the Wizards' anti-theistic philosophies of technologism, solipsism (a form of narcissism), and naturalism and does not represent the Enlightenment's better side. In the final analysis, it would seem that Harris wants to make human beings in his own image and likeness rather than in the image and likeness of God. In order to perform that trick, he must reject *a priori* any evidence pointing to the existence of God and a natural moral law.

Rationalist Insanity

French philosopher René Descartes — often called the greatest rationalist in the history of thought — is erroneously known for having turned the entirety of reality inwards to the exclusion of reality itself. He was not, however, a rationalist in the sense of simply imposing abstract ideas and ideological constructs on reality. (See Appendix II.) That type of thinking, mistakenly attributed to Descartes, tends to isolate the true sources and scope of knowledge (how do we know what we know), and leads people to embrace utopian or deterministic philosophies. While his mathematical and logical approach to knowledge rightly remains a pillar of academic life, his epistemology should not be confused with an ideological rationalism that reduces reality to ideas to the exclusion of everything else; such reductionism, when whittled down to concepts divorced from reality, is the definition of irrationality.

Descartes' dictum *cogito ergo sum* ("I think, therefore I am"), when taken literally, can undermine a person's understanding of true knowledge, reality, and transcendent values. In the world of strict rationalism, if a person does not see the difference between "the inner world of ideas" and "the exterior world," then thought is all that exists. Reason defines truth; it does not seek it, much less find it. And power is used to realize an idea that can very easily be detrimental to genuine human development. In extreme cases, an unfettered "will to power" becomes "reality," with all its invariably heinous consequences.

Heinrich A. Rommen, philosopher of natural law, points out how destructive a hyperbolic interpretation of rationalism, mislabeled as Cartesian, can be, and indeed, has been to universal moral ethics: "All that man needs to do is constructively to develop what is in human reason; that is the innate idea. The individual intellect or reason thus becomes self-sufficient. It does not need the educative cooperation of other minds. Thus, the very spiritual root of sociability is denied. Through his 'angelism,' therefore, Descartes became the father of the individualist conception of human nature."[19] Using Descartes and others, some Wizards have turned modern man into a Cyclops, the one-eyed giant of Greek mythology, who had no depth perception and was stubborn, impossibly vain, and ultimately doomed to fall to his death. Rationalism has helped to upend the rationality underpinning the objective moral order by using reason "to create reality." As a result, moral ethics, which should be a guide to and not a strait jacket for human behavior, degenerates into a detached chaotic clash of contradictory ideas and random values that cannot possibly explain how great civilizations were built.

The Deity of Multiculturalism

Many Wizards seek to create an unassailable political position based on a politics of consensus through force in a Hobbesian world of endless confrontation — which is, incidentally, at the core of much of today's geo-political thinking. In doing so, they often appropriate Judeo-Christian terminology to make one of their main hobby-horses — atheistic, ideological multiculturalism — acceptable to ordinary people. The aim is to facilitate the exercise of power by the ruling elites as they attempt to "straighten out the world," i.e. bring about an egalitarian society according to the principle of the greatest good for the greatest number in which equality, fraternity, and moral relativism reign. History has shown that this vision does not work, particularly when it takes on messianic overtones.

By way of illustration, the Judeo-Christian concept of *ius gentium*,[20] which stands above all individual ethnic groups and races, is problematic for today's agnostic multiculturalists because it recognizes that genuine rights and obligations flow ultimately from God and a person's inherent dignity, and *not* from being a member of a tribe or race. *Ius gentium* is compatible with the concepts of pluralism, solidarity, subsidiarity, personhood, and the common good, and has little to do with utopian concepts of freedom and progress. Zacharias warns, "Pluralism is a good thing but if pluralism is taken to mean ethical relativism, that's when the danger signs will begin to appear and that's where you will see how evil almost becomes indefinable."[21] Does not ideological multiculturalism break down entirely as a model for progress when it holds that ethics flows from chance, passing cultural mores, and an idealism divorced from reality rather than coming from God, right reason, and the Judeo-Christian understanding of liberation, perfection, and salvation?

One Uncreated God

Dump God and everything is possible — that is what many Wizards would have us believe. They have many ways to reduce God to insignificance so as to turn people into believers in their own make-believe world of unbelief. Perhaps one of the more commonly used arguments is that articulated by Peter Millican, who stated recently at the Oxford Union in debate with Lane Craig, "Since [Professor Craig] has cited the alleged resurrection of Jesus as one of his arguments, I take it that we are concerned quite specifically with the traditional God of Christian philosophy, not any other. As you can check out for yourself on Wikipedia, there are plenty of other gods to consider even if we confine ourselves to the Near East and North Africa.... Clearly, we are amazingly prone to believing in gods."[22] No doubt Millican is right, but only up to a point. The Wizards insist that any deity is but a concept, a ghost of the past, present, or future, which springs from the consciousness of a human person and, therefore, cannot be real or lead to anything truly productive. For that reason, most Wizards seek to privatize all religions so that the idea of God can no longer "terrorize" communities or place limits on personal behavior and progress.

Anti-theists insist that all gods are equal because, according to them, all gods are equally man-made, equally illusions of the imagination, and equally of this world. Not unlike Hume, Millican seems to scoff at those who believe in God, despite the evidence that God exists. But consider the stunning change of view by the erstwhile British atheist Antony Flew: "Science spotlights three dimensions of nature that point to God. The first is the fact that nature obeys laws. The second is the dimension of life, of intelligently organized and purpose-driven beings, which arose from matter. The third is the very existence of nature. But it is not science alone that guided me. I have also been helped by a renewed study of the classical philosophical arguments."[23]

David Berlinski, an American academic, explains why most Wizards cannot elevate their philosophy above physics and the limitations of the scientific method: "If moral statements are about something, then the universe is not quite as science suggests it is, since physical theories, having said nothing about God, say nothing about right or wrong, good or bad. To admit this would force philosophers to confront the possibility that the physical sciences offer a grossly inadequate view of reality. And since philosophers very much wish to think of themselves as scientists, this would offer them an unattractive choice between changing their allegiances and accepting their irrelevance."[24] No one wants to risk looking stupid.

Physics Is Not Metaphysics

Metaphysics does not represent the fictional side of physics. Metaphysics asks questions that are alien to the natural sciences and tackles subjects related to existence, time, space, and purpose (at the ontological and cosmological levels). It is important to understand that most Wizards elevate physics to the level of metaphysics (or reduce metaphysics to physics), often without even knowing it. In any event, many physicists, despite disparaging philosophy, employ philosophy to delegitimize natural-law ethics and the evidence-based beliefs of believers. These same physicists cannot get beyond the fact that science only describes and cannot answer "why" questions, which is the realm of philosophy, not physics.

A sober, nonideological view of the physical and nonphysical evidence shows that there can be only one uncreated God and that that one uncreated God is also the God of science, mathematics, and the cosmos. Arno Penzias, discoverer of cosmic microwave background radiation, sees through the gobbledygook of the anti-theists, who can't distinguish the one uncreated God from all other made-man gods. His biographer, Jerry Bergman, says, "Specifically, Penzias' research into cosmology has caused him to see 'evidence of a plan of divine creation.' He says that 'the best data we have are exactly what I would have predicted, had I had nothing to go on but the five books of Moses, the Psalms, the Bible as a whole.'"[25] What is even more startling to the Wizards, surely, is the likelihood that a bunch of "religious folk" — Old

Testament prophets — knew more cosmology a couple of thousand years ago than many modern scientists do today.

Civilizations Do Not Spring from Laws, Chance, or Economics

The Judeo-Christian approach to education aims to support the human conditions for genuine human development and the common good. It aims to present human beings with the enriched opportunity to bring to life a person's everyday existence beyond survival. The Judeo-Christian mindset taps into the human soul and liberates it from its own selfishness. A cultured person aims to be virtuous (in possession of the intellectual and moral virtues) and live in accordance with right reason. The Judeo-Christian mindset recognizes and engages the truths of reason and revelation because both belong to a comprehensible and rational whole that makes sense.

In that sense, the meaning of education within a Judeo-Christian intellectual context is captured most clearly by John Henry Cardinal Newman in his book *The Idea of a University:* "If then a practical end must be assigned to a University course, I say it is that of training good members of society.... It is the education which gives a man a clear, conscious view of his own opinions and judgments, a truth in developing them, an eloquence in expressing them, and a force in urging them. It teaches him to see things as they are, to go right to the point, to disentangle a skein of thought to detect what is sophistical and to discard what is irrelevant."[26] In other words, education in the Judeo-Christian humanist tradition embraces the Biblical proposition, "And ye shall know the truth, and the truth shall make you free."[27]

I encourage the Wizards to make the effort to surface from the depths of the material world, and ascend to the heights of supernatural truths — including the truth of man's freedom as sons and daughters of the Creator.[28] How can it be that radical utopians, who love to extol human freedom, don't seem to believe in free will,[29] despite certain levels of uncertainty and unpredictability,[30] as understood in the Judeo-Christian tradition? Maybe it's because determinists think that "we are governed not by free will but by the processes of the body"[31] or that "consciousness is a collection of mundane tricks in the brain,"[32] which can't escape from the evolutionary forces of ideological materialism.[33]

The Wizards' worldview, when radicalized, exposes the irrationality of their thinking and a deep-seated suspicion of freedom itself. Such thinking is antithetical to the Judeo-Christian worldview and legacy. Chesterton sheds some light on the Wizards' irrationality when referring to evolution, making the distinction between evolution as an ideology and as a mechanism.

Evolution is a good example of that modern intelligence which, if it destroys anything, destroys itself. Evolution is either an innocent scientific description of how certain earthly things came about; or, if it is anything more than this, it is an attack upon thought itself. If evolution destroys anything, it does not destroy religion but rationalism. If evolution simply means that a positive thing called an ape turned very slowly into a positive thing called a man, then it is stingless for the most orthodox; for a personal God might just as well do things slowly as quickly, especially if, like the Christian God, he were outside time. But if it means anything more, it means that there is no such thing as an ape to change, and no such thing as a man for him to change into. It means that there is no such thing as a thing. At best, there is only one thing, and that is a flux of everything and anything. This is an attack not upon the faith, but upon the mind; you cannot think if there are no things to think about. You cannot think if you are not separate from the subject of thought. Descartes said, 'I think; therefore I am.' The philosophic evolutionist reverses and negatives the epigram. He says, 'I am not; therefore, I cannot think.'

Then there is the opposite attack on thought: that urged by Mr. H.G. Wells when he insists that every separate thing is 'unique,' and there are no categories at all. This also is merely destructive. Thinking means connecting things, and stops if they cannot be connected. It need hardly be said that this skepticism forbidding thought necessarily forbids speech; a man cannot open his mouth without contradicting it. Thus when Mr. Wells says (as he did somewhere), 'All chairs are quite different,' he utters not merely a misstatement, but a contradiction in terms. If all chairs were quite different, you could not call them 'all chairs.'"[34]

The Psychiatric Ward

If history is any indication of what is to come, unless new countervailing forces appear on the intellectual landscape, anyone who does not agree with the godless worldview of the most aggressive anti-theists should expect to be severely pilloried or even exiled to some equivalent of the Soviet "Psikhushka" ("Психушка") — a psychiatric hospital where the politically and socially non-conformist were reeducated or simply put to sleep. The Soviets used the psychiatric hospitals as jails to cut off inmates from friends and society, disgrace their beliefs, and undermine them mentally and physically. The official Soviet line explaining the existence of mental hospitals was that no sane person could possibly be against Sovietism or the regime's utopian ideals. If someone contradicted the party line, then that person must be insane and, therefore, a danger to society and the common good. As St. Anthony the abbot, the venerable founder of monasticism in the 3rd century AD, warned us long ago, "A time is coming when men will go mad, and when they see someone who is not mad, they will attack him, saying, 'You are not like us — you must be mad.'"[35] We may be approaching such a situation today. In fact, we may be there already.

Humanity needs to continue to search for ways to return to a more sane, thoughtful, and modest way of living, which includes a proper stewardship of the natural resources of Earth, and a reconsideration of our modern throwaway mentality. Given the problem of man's inability to see God (especially as a loving God), the dominance of a culture of death and the supremacy of moral relativism in the world today, it will be difficult (but not impossible) for humanity to deviate from its current morbid trajectory to self-immolation. Joseph Cardinal Ratzinger (later Pope Benedict XVI) proposed how we might regain our footing and sense of inner balance. His words are worth pondering: "I would like to make a proposal to the secularists. At the time of the Enlightenment, there was an attempt to understand and define the essential moral norms, saying that they would be valid '*etsi Deus non daretur*,' even in the case that God did not exist. In the opposition of the confessions and in the pending crisis of the image of God, an attempt was made to keep the essential values of morality outside the contradictions and to seek for them evidence that would render them independent of the many divisions and uncertainties of the different philosophies and confessions. In this way, they wanted to ensure the basis of coexistence and, in general, the foundations of humanity. At that time, it was thought to be possible, as the great deep convictions created by Christianity to a large extent remained. But this is no longer the case. The search for such a reassuring certainty, which could remain uncontested beyond all differences, failed." Ratzinger continues: "The attempt, carried to the extreme, to manage human affairs disdaining God completely leads us increasingly to the edge of the abyss, to man's ever greater isolation from reality. We must reverse the axiom of the Enlightenment and say: even one who does not succeed in finding the way of accepting God, should, nevertheless, seek to live and to direct his life '*veluti si Deus daretur*,' as if God existed. This is the advice Pascal gave to his friends who did not believe. In this way, no one is limited in his freedom, but all our affairs find the support and criterion of which they are in urgent need."[36]

Anti-theists, atheists and skeptics alike need to reassess questions pertaining to God and the meaning of work and genuine human development in light of Judeo-Christian anthropology. A person must always bear in mind that sanity is a matter of knowing "who we are," "where we came from," and "where we are going." Toward this end, I invite artists, scientists, statesmen, and students to travel beyond the beautiful and exciting, but narrow, worlds of physics and mathematics, and read the works of Judeo-Christian scholars or the Gospels themselves. In time, the Wizards, it is hoped, will see, as so many others have over the course of history, that chance, voluntarism, and the itch to master a godless universe do not and cannot answer the great question of life and living

I remain hopeful that humanity possesses the sanity to see the folly of its hapless embrace of utopianism, wrapped in moral relativism and ideological materialism. Only time will tell if Josef Pieper was right when he said: "Finally, it is no longer completely fantastic to think that a day may come when not the executioners alone will deny the inalienable rights of men, but when even the victims will not be able to say why it is that they are suffering injustice."[37] But we can be sanguine about the future because men and women are capable of great awakenings. In time, they will no doubt find the extraordinary in the ordinary, experience the liberating force of selfless giving and science, see the foolhardiness of a self-referencing morality, recognize the full dignity of the human person, and understand that mathematics is indeed the language of the one uncreated God of the universe who is outside of time and space. That is the Judeo-Christian legacy.

---

1.   "To understand, you must have a heart."

2.   As Aristotle says, "To say of what is that it is not, or of what is not that it is, is false, while to say of what is that it is, and of what is not that it is not, is true". St. Thomas Aquinas puts it thus: "Truth is the equation of thing and intellect" ("Veritas est adequatio rei et intellectus.").

3.   Benedict XVI (pope), *Charity in Truth* (San Francisco: Ignatius Press, 2009); p. 31.

4.   "Hence from the knowledge of sensible things the whole power of God cannot be known; nor therefore can His essence be seen. But because they are His effects and depend on their cause, we can be led from them so far as to know of God whether He exists, and on to know of Him what must necessarily belong to Him, as the first cause of all things, exceeding all things caused by Him" (St. Thomas Aquinas, *Summa Theologiae*, Ia, 12,12).

5.   The act of being.

6.   I recommend a close reading of Fathers of the Eastern Church and orthodox scholarship to better grasp the idea of personhood, which is the identification of the human person — body and soul — with the person of Christ, other people, and the

environment.

7.   Hermeticism, broadly speaking, describes a set of pantheistic-like beliefs — usually radical and militant — which considers the entire universe — material and immaterial — as one, irrespective of the evidence to the contrary. Its beliefs have had an enormous effect on magic and occult traditions over the centuries, particularly since the Renaissance. It reduces the one uncreated God, who is outside of this universe, to one more god within it. The aim of hermeticism is to unite in a comprehensive, harmonious manner everyone with everything in an effort to bring about peace and harmony.

8.   Malcolm Muggeridge, *A Third Testament: A Modern Pilgrim Explores the Spiritual Wanderings of Augustine, Blake, Pascal, Kierkegaard, Tolstoy, Bonhoeffer, and Dostoevsky* (New York: Ballantine Books, 1983); p. 47

9.   Ravi Zacharias and Vince Vitale, *Why Suffering? Finding Meaning and Comfort When Life Doesn't Make Sense* (electronic version; Amazon Kindle, location 23-33).

10.   See Francis (pope), Address Marking the Fiftieth Anniversary of *Populorum Progressio* (April 2017) (https://w2.vatican.va/content/francesco/en/speeches/2017/april/documents/papa-francesco_20170404_convegno-populorum-progressio.html).

11.   Synonyms might include "innately" or "intuitively" which give the idea of being embedded in one's nature irrespective of race, religion, intelligence, environment, economic well-being, customs, or personal habits.

12.   St. Paul provides the following interesting observation about natural law in his Epistle to the Romans (2:14-16): "For when the Gentiles who do not have the law by nature observe the prescriptions of the law, they are a law for themselves even though they do not have the law. They show that the demands of the law are written in their hearts, while their conscience also bears witness and their conflicting thoughts accuse or even defend them on the day when, according to my gospel, God will judge peoples' hidden works through Christ Jesus" (http://www.usccb.org/bible/romans/2).

13.   The good "is established, as the eternal law, by Divine Wisdom which orders every being towards its end: this eternal law is known both by man's natural reason (hence it is 'natural law') and — in an integral and perfect way — by God's supernatural revelation (hence it is called 'divine law') when the choices of freedom are in conformity with man's true good and thus express the voluntary ordering of the person towards his ultimate end: God himself, the supreme good in whom man finds his full and perfect happiness." St. John Paul II (pope), *Veritatis Splendor* (address to bishops of the Church, 2007); (http://w2.vatican.va/content/john-paul-ii/en/encyclicals/documents/hf_jp-ii_enc_06081993_veritatis-splendor.html).

14.   Flannery O'Connor, letter to Betty Hester in *The Habit of Being: Letters of Flannery O'Connor*, ed. by Sally Fitzgerald (New York: Farrar, Straus, Giroux, 1988); p. 100 (http://theamericanreader.com/6-september-1955-flannery-oconnor/).

15.   Zacharias and Vitale, *Why Suffering?* location 1626-36.

16.   G.K. Chesterton, *The Club of Queer Trades* (New York: Harper 1903, 1905); p. 241.

17.   See Bethany Saltman, "The Temple of Reason: Sam Harris on How Religion Puts the World at Risk," *Sun Magazine*, September 2006 (http://thesunmagazine.org/issues/369/the_temple_of_reason?page=2).

18.   Italics added. Sam Harris, "Science Must Destroy Religion, " *Huffington Post*, January 2, 2006 (http://www.huffingtonpost.com/sam-harris/science-must-destroy-reli_b_13153.html).

19.   Cf. Jacques Maritain, *The Three Reformers: Luther, Descartes, Rousseau* (London: Sheed & Ward, 1944); pp. 54ff.

20.   The word "gentes" also carries the association of "pagans" or "non-Christians." Joseph Cardinal Ratzinger, *Europe, Today and Tomorrow* (San Francisco: Ignatius Press, 2005); p. 75.

21. Ravi Zacharias, "Deliver Us from Evil: Restoring the Soul in a Disintegrating Culture" (Lecture at the Veritas Forum, December 1997).

22. William Lane Craig vs. Peter Millican, "Does God Exist?" (Birmingham, England: Debate, October 2011) (https://www.youtube.com/watch?v=9JVRy7bR7zI).

23. Antony Flew and Roy Abraham Varghese, *There Is No a God: How the World's Most Notorious Atheist Changed His Mind* (New York: HarperCollins, 2008); pp. 88-89.

24. See David Berlinski, *The Devil's Delusion: Atheism and Its Scientific Pretensions* (New York: Basic Books, 2009).

25. Jerry Bergman, "Arno A. Penzias: Astrophysicist, Nobel Laureate," American Scientific Affiliation: Astronomy/Cosmology, 1994 (http://www.asa3.org/ ASA/PSCF/1994/PSCF9-94Bergman.html). Also see Arno A. Penzias, "Forum: The Key Challenges," *New York Times,* January 2, 1979 (https://www.nytimes.com/1979/01/02/archives/forum-the-key-challenges-arno-a-penzias-donald-kennedy-edward-e.html).

26. The rest of the quotation follows: "It prepares him to fill any post with credit, and to master any subject with facility. It shows him how to accommodate himself to others, how to throw himself into their state of mind, how to bring before them his own, how to influence them, how to come to an understanding with them, how to bear with them. He is at home in any society, he has common ground with every class; he knows when to speak and when to be silent; he is able to converse, he is able to listen; he can ask a question pertinently, and gain a lesson seasonably, when he has nothing to impart himself; he is ever ready, yet never in the way; he is a pleasant companion, and a comrade you can depend upon; he knows when to be serious and when to trifle, and he has a sure tact which enables him to trifle with gracefulness and to be serious with effect. He has the repose of a mind which lives in itself, while it lives in the world, and which has resources for its happiness at home when it cannot go abroad. He has a gift which serves him in public, and supports him in retirement, without which good fortune is but vulgar, and with which failure and disappointment have a charm." John Henry Newman, *The Idea of the University* (London: Longmans, Green, and Co., 1886); p. 178 (https://archive.org/stream/a677122900newmuoft#page/n5/mode/2up).

27. John 8:32-36 (http://www.usccb.org/bible/john/8).

28. For some excellent ideas concerning education, see Paul Shrimpton, *The Making of Men: The* Idea *and Reality of Newman's University in Oxford and Dublin* (Leominster, England: Gracewing Publishing, 2014). I also suggest a close reading of Christopher Dawson's 1961 masterpiece, *The Crisis of Western Education* (New York: Sheed and Ward, 1961).

29. Lawrence Krauss and Richard Dawkins, "Something from Nothing?" (Conversation, February 2012) (https://www.youtube.com/watch?v=YUe0_4rdj0U)(https://www.youtube.com/ watch?v=anBxaOcZnGk). The question of free will comes up at the very end of the Q&A period.

30. Michio Kaku, "Why Physics Ends the Free Will Debate" (Big Think, 2011) (https://www.youtube.com/watch?v=Jint5kjoy6I).

31. Dale DeBaksey, "Do We Have Free Will? The Atheist Case for Determinism," *New Humanist,* (June 23, 2015): "Accepting that we are governed not by free will but by the processes of the body could provide a positive vision for society. Free will was a necessary idea, once upon a time. For the religious, it was the plaster over the holes in their god's benevolence. For the wronged, it made revenge feel like justice. It bolstered the pride of the great and nursed the resentment of the foiled. It was a useful lie. And it thrived, so long as there was metaphysical wiggle room for it to inhabit – some cunning dualism that shunted decision making away from the body and towards ethereal incorporeality. Yes, thirst and hunger and sex are grounded in the mechanisms of the body, we were told, but there is real, tangible freedom tucked away deep within us all, rescuing us from our clockwork natures. There's a desperate charm to that idea, but we're quite beyond it now. The mechanisms of decision making, the chemistry of empathy, the physics of neural plasticity, each gnaws away every day at the few remaining supports of a free

will model of individuality. We are forced to either redefine free will to something existent but meaningless, or chuck the idea altogether and make peace with finding the subtle joys of our exquisite programmability." (https://newhumanist.org.uk/articles/4888/do-we-have-free-will-the-atheist- case-for-determinism).

32.   Daniel Dennett, "Daniel Dennett Explains Consciousness and Free Will" (Big Think, April 2012) (https://www.youtube.com/watch?v=R-Nj_rEqkyQ).

33.   See Steven Pinker, "On Free Will" (Big Think, 2011): "I don't believe there's such a thing as free will in the sense of a ghost in a machine, a spirit or a soul that somehow reads the TV screen of the senses and pushes buttons and pulls the levers of behavior" (https://www.youtube.com/watch?v=VQxJi0COTBo).

34.   G.K. Chesterton, *Orthodoxy* ((New York: Dodd, Mead & Co., 1908); p. 63 (http://www.ccel.org/ccel/chesterton/orthodoxy.html).

35.   A free translation. See St. Anthony the Great in Benedicta Ward, ed. and trans., *The Desert Christian: Sayings of the Desert Fathers* (New York: Macmillan Publishing Co., Inc., 1975), no. 25.

36.   Joseph Cardinal Ratzinger, "On Europe's Crisis of Culture" (homily, April 1, 2005) (https://www.catholiceducation.org/en/culture/catholic-contributions/cardinal-ratzinger-on-europe-s-crisis-of-culture.html).

37.   Josef Pieper, *The Four Cardinal Virtues* (New York: Harcourt, Brace & World, Inc., 1965), pp. 51-52 (https://archive.org/details/fourcardinalvirt012953mbp).

CHAPTER 2

Classical Antiquity and Some of Its Giants

I am the wisest man alive, for I know one thing, and that is that I know nothing.

— Socrates

It is idle to talk always of the alternative of reason and faith. Reason is itself a matter of faith. It is an act of faith to assert that our thoughts have any relation to reality at all. If you are merely a skeptic, you must sooner or later ask yourself the question, "Why should ANYTHING go right; even observation and deduction? Why should not good logic be as misleading as bad logic? They are both movements in the brain of a bewildered ape?" The young skeptic says, "I have a right to think for myself." But the old skeptic, the complete skeptic, says, "I have no right to think for myself. I have no right to think at all."

— G.K. Chesterton, *Orthodoxy*

The leading scholars of the Greco-Roman world, the Ancients, debated the sources of truth and the origins of life as well as the meaning of morality, knowledge, and statecraft. At the root of the debate lay questions concerning good and evil (and certainty and uncertainty) as related to human behavior, change, goodness, and the universe. In the process of wondering about those issues, the Ancients, not unlike people today, sought to explain what constituted genuine human development and happiness. Brilliant as they were, however, the Ancients' understanding of the nature and purpose of existence was deficient. Why? Because, without the combined insights from revelation and reason, they had no way of knowing the significance of what it means to be in the image, likeness, and presence of the one, uncreated God of everything.[1]

From the Judeo-Christian idea of the special dignity of the human person (which makes us stewards not abusers of the earth) and the Ancients' understanding of dignity, flowed the notions of equality, brotherhood, liberty, justice, charity, and so much more which academics since antiquity have tried to explain. Efforts to produce a body of knowledge that enshrined and protected the inalienable and immutable rights of men and women developed slowly during the Roman Empire. "As such, the first historical text in which *dignitas* is used in conjunction with 'human dignity' is Cicero's theory of the various personae in *De officiis*. One of the personae is the persona of reason, which all human beings share and which sets us apart from animals. However, the dignity people should embrace, according to Cicero, is not something that is to be protected against outside interference or violations, but rather consists of living properly in the Stoic sense, that is, in moderation and abstaining from all manner of luxury and overindulgence."[2]

While it is evident that the Ancients grasped a great deal about the natural moral law and something about the idea that truth is the key to freedom, they could not see that human beings enjoy a God-given dignity transcending time and space. Moreover, this special dignity is only discernible as a person moves closer to his end,[3] i.e., as a person struggles to live virtue, experiences the meaning of divine filiation, and strives to serve others in the midst of uncertainty and suffering.

St. Paul (c. AD 5–67), a scholar of the ancient world, succinctly connects the Greco-Roman principle of right reason, common sense, restraint, the spiritual nature of a human being, and the universal moral vision of the Stoics with the Judeo-Christian understanding of purpose, dignity, freedom, virtue, and happiness: "[those] essential demands of the one God upon human life that have been illuminated by the Christian faith, are identical with what is written in the heart of man, of every man, so that he can recognize the good when he meets it. It is identical with 'what is good in nature.'"[4] St. Paul, thus, laid out the basis for moral ethics, right reason, responsible behavior, and good governance.

Guidance, Not Limitation

The discipline of moral philosophy aims to assist a person to exercise right judgment, i.e., to make choices consistent with human nature, and thus live in the best possible manner. Towards this end, each person must discover and interiorly embrace his purpose or divine calling, which serves as a compass to guide one's decisions throughout life. As a result, moral ethics serves as a way to facilitate and improve personal development and self-realization as opposed to a way of limiting it. The Ancients, while not able to see this dynamic in its full splendor, laid some of the intellectual groundwork for it, unlike the Wizards, who remain tied to the atomism and pantheism of the lesser ancient scholars to this day.

One of the premises of this book is that a recognition of another person's human dignity in all its original fullness (*Imago Dei*) arouses in people a spirit of service towards others that has had a greater impact on genuine human development than that associated with naturalistic explanations such as chance, altruism, and empathy (whether emotional or cognitive). Judeo-Christian scholarship, aided by the moral philosophy of the Ancients, has offered ideas which explain that human development is much more than the material improvement of a person's earthly conditions, and that the ultimate purpose of existence is much more than survival and progeny in the exclusively biological sense. In fact, empathy and altruism are most effective when "deployed" in a free act of selfless service, which is not a trait of either survival-of-the-fittest ideologies or chance.

Over the centuries, the recognition of human dignity fortified by charity (and directed by right reason) as well as a desire for others to share in the life of God have better explained human progress than the evolutionary mandate, and the applied use of reason and power devoid of God and permanent truths. At the practical level, genuine development means transforming the idea of a hospital from a place that not only cures but genuinely cares for the physical, emotional, cognitive, and spiritual needs of patients in light of eternity. In other words, to cure is one thing, but to care for and cure *at the same time* represents the difference between running a zoo and running a hospital. The Judeo-Christian vision stands out from the limited views of the Ancients, because the philosophy of the Ancients and their understanding of human nature was limited to notions of utility, balance, order, power, altruism, moderation, and fairness in human relations within a cold pantheistic philosophical tradition. And so, the Ancients' measure of excellence was wrapped around the notions of effectiveness and efficiency in dealing with suffering and comfort, while virtue was reduced to a balancing act between competing forces to enhance predictability or reduce uncertainty.

Is there not something desperately wrong with a worldview that is indifferent to or even justifies for the sake of progress a violent, dog-eat-dog, manipulative, wanton, sycophant, and dissolute world as depicted in the TV series *Game of Thrones*? To be sure, the theories of moral ethics developed by Socrates (469–399 BC), Plato (428–348 BC), and other Ancients represented the most insightful thinking about human nature and morality up to their time. Their ideas still reverberate today, as reflected in the *Nicomachean Ethics* (published 349 BC) of Aristotle (384–322 BC) and other works. These scholars, among others, envisaged that a civilization cannot long flourish without a moral code anchored in unchanging principles and in socio-political structures that reflect permanent values and that are reasonable, i.e., consistent with the nature and purpose of the existence of a human person.

Classical Philosophy So Much Drivel?

The Ancients considered reason to be an internal and immaterial power of the mind that processes data, ponders, comprehends, forms judgments, and makes decisions. But while philosophers such as Socrates and Zeno of Citium (340–265 BC) saw the human person as more than physical matter, Wizards such as Hitchens and Victor Stenger, an American particle physicist, reduced the mind to a material substance called the brain (governed exclusively by laws of nature and mathematics in a world of chance). Worst of all, most anti-theists undermine freedom, since they claim that human actions are reduced to highly sophisticated mechanistic functions stirred by an instinct evolved for the purpose of survival. Even the Ancients saw that human beings are much more than clever animals or complex machines at the top of the food chain.

While, on the one hand, some Wizards regularly appeal to the Ancients to justify their own anti-theistic cosmic worldview, others lampoon much of Greco-Roman philosophy as if it were idle and unproductive drivel. Moreover, the Wizards disparage the Ancients insofar as classical philosophy supports the Judeo-Christian worldview's insistence on the existence of a non-arbitrary and binding moral ethics that guides rather than imposes.

Animosity towards Philosophy

Though they often harken back to a golden age of reason at the time of the Ancients, it is tragic and silly that many of today's Wizards seem to scorn philosophy. As materialists and sophists, most Wizards have been enslaved not only by time, space, and mathematics, but by the incomprehensibility of suffering and pain. Philosophy as a discipline, therefore, is largely meaningless for the Wizards, since it provides little that is concrete, and does not improve personal security or physical well-being.

Why is it that many Wizards curse philosophy and even publicly demean those who intelligently disagree with their worldview? Is it not because the "philosophy-cursing" anti-theists are stuck in the materialist rut of trivial pursuits? Or is it because they find it extremely difficult to defend themselves against the credible arguments of smart philosophers who are also theists? In other words, do good ideas — does good philosophy — get in the way of anti-theists' conception of progress?

Peter Atkins, a superb English chemist and leading Wizard, says the following about philosophy: "Look where [philosophy] got [the Greeks].... [It] got them into the history books, it didn't get them into the science books."[5] While Atkins seems to have little use for philosophy, it is undeniable that great philosophical insights have moved the world. Is his commentary designed so that we believe that ideas are of little consequence in everyday life, whereas science, which supposedly is free from the constraints of bias, is what fuels and builds civilizations? Surely philosophy does more than get in the way of progress, satisfy curiosities, and gratify personal interests like some parlor card games do. As a general observation, for anyone to suggest that philosophy is mostly useless because it cannot produce tangible results misses the transformative power of ideas.[6]

In line with Atkins's observations, the world-renowned Stephen Hawking and Leonard Mlodivow, professor of mathematical physics, state that "philosophy is dead."[7] By so stating, it seems clear that they have also fallen into the Enlightenment Trap, which sucks people into believing that philosophy is exclusively a form of unsubstantiated gibberish and an unreliable form of entertainment that encourages idleness and promotes intellectual sterility, whereas science is the exclusive fount of truth, and, therefore, development. The Wizards' aim would seem to be to neutralize the power of philosophy, since it poses a serious threat to their claims and assumptions (embedded in their scientific atheism).[8] While it may be relatively easy for the Wizards to rail against philosophy, it is more difficult for them to discredit logic as developed by Greek logicians such as Pythagoras (c. 570–c. 495 BC), Aristotle, and Plato.[9]

Aristotle reminds us that "the educated differ from the uneducated as much as the living differ from the dead." And so it is with some of the anti-theists who enclose themselves in the coffin of materialism and mathematics to the detriment of science and mathematics. In contrast, the Ancients, who were able to get beyond the here and now, bequeathed to humanity without scripture a sense of transcendence based on a recognition of the fundamental immutability of eternal truths. I share their confidence that reason can deliver a potent (but not conclusive) explanation for the purpose and the meaning of moral behavior, the universe, and the purpose of life.[10] But reason alone, as the more perceptive Ancients knew, cannot provide satisfactory answers to the profoundest of the "why" questions in life, since they cannot be answered by simply unraveling the natural mysteries of the physical world.

To dismiss philosophy as not keeping up with science is as nonsensical as saying that literature has not kept up with mathematics: two completely different fields. Are not answers to "how" and "why" questions very different? Is it not the height of defective thinking to reduce everything (visible and invisible) to mathematics, quantum physics, empty space, or whatever else might suit the worldview of the anti-theists?

Take, for example, the question "Why do airplanes fly?". Do they fly because the Wright Brothers got a brilliant idea or because of the Bernoulli Principle, which explains lift? Are not both answers correct? Great ideas and human creativity support great science. The Wizards, however, urge us to choose between philosophy and science, when in fact there is no reason to do so. Both philosophy and science are important and play a role in understanding human freedom and how the world works.

Science of the Gaps

Unlike many of the Wizards, the Greek Sophists, such as Gorgias (483–375 BC), Hippias (c. 460–c. 490 BC), and Protagoras (c. 481–c. 411 BC), would *not* have invoked a "Science of the Gaps" argument, which states that if the scientific method has not yet spoken about "something" that is under consideration, then that "something" cannot be true. In this connection, the "Science of the Gaps" argument claims that God cannot possibly exist because science has not "found" God. The lesson here is that just as believers should take pains not to invoke the "God of the Gaps" argument, so materialists should take pains not to invoke the "Science of the Gaps" argument.

Just because science cannot verify that God exists does not mean that God, who is immaterial, does not.[11] Science is not equipped to confirm or deny the existence of that which cannot be measured (immateriality). It is important to recognize that the absence of evidence does not mean that science can prove the nonexistence of spirit, even though most of the Wizards try to get away with such an argument.

David Berlinski, an American philosopher and educator, writes of those Wizards who believe in the "Science of the Gaps" argument: "Whatever the gaps, they will in the course of scientific research be filled. It is an assumption both intellectually primitive and morally abhorrent — primitive because it reflects a phlegmatic absence of curiosity, and abhorrent because it assigns to our intellectual future a degree of authority alien to human experience. Western science has proceeded by filling gaps, but in filling them, it has created gaps all over again. The process is inexhaustible.... Understanding has improved, but within the physical sciences, anomalies have grown great, and what is more, anomalies have grown great *because* understanding has improved."[12] Aristotle and Cicero (106–43 BC), unlike most Wizards, would have understood Berlinski, because they also saw beyond the sensible world. The Ancients respected the limitations of science because they understood its limits. They would never have fallen into the trap of thinking that science will eventually provide an explanation for everything.

What is even more astounding is that many Wizards, unlike the Ancients, cannot see that the laws of nature themselves do not have the power to create anything. Rather, laws are descriptions of physical reality with impressive powers of prediction. But to attribute causality to laws is also to fall for the false reasoning of some of the Wizards.[13] Is it really that difficult to understand that laws do not have the inherent ability to cause anything? The Ancients would never have confused the difference between that which *causes,* and that which *is.*

While some pamphleteers may suggest that the discovery last century of the Higgs boson, an elementary particle in physics (sometimes referred to as the "God Particle"),[14] is one more giant step towards confirming the godless atomism of Epicurus (341–270 BC) or Lucretius (99–55 BC), physics is not in the business of "hoping" nor is it equipped to cross into the realm of metaphysics. The Higgs boson is a brilliant and beautiful fact uncovered by great science, but that is all it is. Its existence (and mathematical formulation) cannot show that God does not exist or that God is irrelevant, or that moral laws of nature can be reduced to the laws of physics. But do not some academics try to convince us otherwise?

Is it not surprising that Wizards so often do not fully grasp the philosophy of many Judeo-Christian scholars of the early Christian era or of the Middle Ages because of their narrow epistemology? "In the thirteenth century," Hawking writes, "the early [sic] Christian philosopher Thomas Aquinas (c. 1223–1274) adopted this [classical philosophical] view and used it to argue for the existence of God, writing, 'It is clear that [inanimate objects] reach their end not by chance but by intention.... There is, therefore, an intelligent personal being by whom everything in nature is ordered to its end.'"[15] Did Hawking feel the need to single out Aquinas because he was one of the most prominent philosopher-theologians of all time, who, not incidentally, believed in God not because tradition so mandated but because it made sense to believe in God? Aquinas presents huge problems for the Wizards just as some of the earliest of the Judeo-Christian scholars do.

Stoics and Lesser Ancients

The Wizards tend to consider Stoicism, a school of Greek and Roman philosophy that flourished until the death of Marcus Aurelius, (AD 121–180), as one of their literary antecedents.[16] The reason for this, of course, is that they approve of the Stoics' materialism.

The Stoics viewed matter as representing the totality of reality, which is in a passive and active state, and that it was given a sort of animation by reason. For them, the natural world was all-pervasive, with everything causally connected and permeated by cosmic forces.[17] The key point to grasp is that they thought that God is a part of the world, and was described as the "Fiery Reason of the Cosmos" or the universal law of reason, the "Mind in Matter." A person's constitution was similar to that of the universe in that both a human being and the universe were held together and governed by an animating cosmic force — a Logos — coincident and parallel with matter. Reason, moreover, served as the tool by which the spirit and the passions were to be managed. Only when the passions were under control could a person make right judgments and reach a state of inner peace.

Marcus Aurelius, a Roman emperor and apparently a devout Stoic, wrote in his *Meditations* (AD 167) that "the qualities of the rational soul include love of neighbor, truthfulness, modesty, and a reverence for herself before all else; and since this last is one of the qualities of law also, it follows that the principle of rationality is one and the same as the principle of justice." [18] The Wizards' worldview is in line with Aurelius's, especially when it concerns the almost salvific power of reason, and its role in bringing about effective altruism and improved empathy. Selfless service in the Judeo-Christian sense of selfless charity is not considered a part of Stoicism. When logic and utility define what is morally good or bad, or useful or harmful, right reason is reduced to either mathematics or measurable outcomes. Let us not forget that that which is logical does not necessarily equate to that which is reasonable or good.

Brotherhood and Sisterhood

In early ancient Greece, the idea of brotherhood, a concept historically limited by the isolation and self-sufficiency of the city-states at the time, took on a wider meaning after the 4th century BC because of the Greeks' outward expansion and contact with different peoples, languages, and cultures. It was during Alexander the Great's reign (356–323 BC) that state borders significantly expanded, and the idea of the *polis* morphed into *cosmopolis*. As a result, the Greeks began to develop the concept of universal brotherhood, which, of course, also required the exercise of good governance and statecraft.

Contact with foreigners forced the Greeks to recognize that the universality of reason was a key criterion for universal brotherhood, thus going beyond the criteria of blood and locality. As a result, the community could bestow the title of brother or sister on non-kin, irrespective of racial or behavioral characteristics because of the common trait of rationality.

During the later Greco-Roman period, the idea of belonging to a wider human family further merged with the Abrahamic tradition (brotherhood with a common Father). The Ancients' idea of brotherhood was enriched, therefore, by the Judeo-Christian Biblical understanding that human beings are sons and daughters (*Imago Dei*) of a loving and personal God who is Father, and even approachable (a concept unimaginable in Islam and other religions and in deistic and pantheistic philosophies).

Over the centuries, the increasingly universal acceptance of the idea of a common human dignity has advanced more than any other concept the desire for human development through service (not limited to material progress) and the rise of political and educational structures designed to serve (at least in theory) the community and common good.

Sophists

The Sophists rejected the usefulness or relevance of most philosophical speculation; expediency served as a guide to "proper" behavior. Protagoras, the most prominent of Sophists, was among the first of the relativists or agnostics. He believed that there were no absolute moral principles in a world dominated by social conventions. A general consciousness was germane to decision-making and to mastering both sides of an argument. Education served to get the better of the other guy, and supposedly gain the upper hand.

Like the moral relativism of the Wizards, the Sophists held that since everything is in a constant state of motion and only that which can be measured exists, then everything, including God and human consciousness, is transient. As a result, moral ethics are situational and transitory. Such a worldview, in practice, permits the use of intimidation, power, flattery, or utility for any reason to preserve one's own way of life or advance selfish interests, often at the expense of others, in a transient and dangerous world. Most Wizards are sophists.

The Cyrenaic and Epicurean Schools of Philosophy

Despite their general abhorrence of philosophy, many Wizards endorse the philosophy of the Atomists, Epicureans, and the Cyrenaics, founded by Aristippus (c. 435–356 BC), for whom pleasure in all its dimensions is the highest good. Having said that, they would reject Epicurus' refusal to accept certain forms of materialism because he believed the mind of the gods was superior to natural philosophy.

Along with Democritus, Epicurus also believed that the purpose of universal moral ethics was to facilitate the enjoyment of life — fun and games, intellectual pleasures, wine and sex. It is no wonder that narcissism came to be celebrated. And why not? How else gain the favor of others? There was no life after death. Suffering, or its absence, represented the main criterion for evil or good. Frederick Copleston, a philosopher of great stature in the 20th century, described the Greek materialists thus: "[P]leasure is the beginning and end of living happily; for we have recognized this as the first good, being connate with us; and it is with reference to it that we begin every choice and avoidance; and to this we come as if we judged of all good by passion as the standard."[19] These ideas are in line with those of most Wizards, who would agree that all forms of suffering are evil, unless accepted voluntarily.

Some of today's Wizards, not dissimilarly to Democritus, imagine that all of reality is essentially made up of atoms and molecules (complexity and further division notwithstanding), with real ontological differences (between beings) reduced to a single expression of matter. As detectives, the Wizards hunt skillfully for means to unravel the remaining mysteries of the mind — a good thing. They are confident they will eventually discover (so they argue) the keys to personal liberation, and even "salvation," and liberate humanity from the shackles of ignorance, uncertainty, and convention.

All that sounds great but since the Wizards are operating within a materialist framework, where life beyond the physical world is fictional, I caution against jumping into their court. When the Wizards argue that God is dying or dead, it is not because of science but rather because they have reduced the human person to automation made up only of matter. They end up lost in their own mythical and materialistic world of make-believe, like that of the Roman poet Lucretius, or Democritus.[20]

Fear of God

Most Wizards believe that fear is one of the main causes of the Ancients' belief in deities and "supernatural phenomena." They are in part right to make such a claim because fear explains the reason that so many "gods" have appeared throughout history. While fear, no doubt, contributes to the list of "thunder gods," and while the absence of fear may eliminate the bulk of man-made gods, no amount of courage or knowledge can prove that God does not exist, because the fact that God exists is not dependent on the human person (or anything else for that matter). In like manner, while fear may intensify a person's belief in God, it also has nothing to do with the existence of the one, uncreated God of the universe. Just as lightning exists, so does God, irrespective of a person's state of mind.

The evidence is overwhelming that the one uncreated God of the universe exists, whereas man-made gods are a dime a dozen. It is critically important, therefore, to keep straight in one's head the difference between the use of the words "God," and "god" or "gods," since the Ancients really did not, and today's Wizards definitely do not. For the Wizards, the one uncreated God of the universe is just another fictitious man-made god of a multitude of others.

Some Wizards suggest that once they master the universe at some distant, theoretical moment in the future), there will be no need for any gods. They are right when referring to all the fictitious gods out there, which are indeed figments of the imagination. Once fear is overcome, they argue, personal liberation and self-confidence will follow, bringing into existence a kind of fearless age of independent and productive thinking. Such ideas are nothing but wishful thinking.

If Plato and Aristotle had lived in the 21st century, they would have challenged the methodological approaches and storyline of most of today's Wizards, whose materialistic framework defines the limitations and complications of their thinking. Consider this statement by Steven Pinker, professor of cognitive psychology and linguist, which seems to reduce the Judeo-Christian worldview (and revelation) to a nasty bump in the evolutionary road: "Most of the traditional causes of belief — faith, revelation, dogma, authority, charisma, conventional wisdom, the invigorating glow of subjective certainty — are generators of error and should be dismissed as sources of knowledge. To understand the world, we must cultivate work-arounds for our cognitive limitations, including skepticism, open debate, formal precision, and empirical tests, often requiring feats of ingenuity. Any movement that calls itself 'scientific' but fails to nurture opportunities for the falsification of its own beliefs (most obviously when it murders or imprisons the people who disagree with it) is not a scientific movement." [21] In other words, without the serenity of science, most people would be blinded by their past and their prejudices, thus hampering clear thinking and human progress? Or is he saying that "work-arounds" to humanity's "cognitive limitations" can occur only by getting rid of the sources of irrationality, which is synonymous with God, faith and religion?

Eternity and More

Just as pagan Greek cosmologists believed in an eternal universe, so do most Wizards. This poses two problems. The idea of eternity enables anyone to explain away any question concerning "when it all started," because an eternity of time can apparently justify the existence of any dependent being. The second more problematic issue relates to the question of "who or what created the creator?" The Wizards have gone to great lengths to answer the latter question, and can only come up with the existence of "multiverses," "parallel universes," or the redefinition of terminology such as how "something" can come from "nothing." Greek philosophers would have laughed at the "something from nothing" argument. Belief in multiverses, let us be clear, is an act of "blind faith," and, we might add, a product of fear. Moreover, as Chesterton reminds us, "Reason is itself a matter of faith. It is an act of faith to assert that our thoughts have any relation to reality at all." [22]

It is not helpful to ignore the findings of modern science, because modern science supports the Biblical account of the origin of the Earth in time and space. The idea of an eternal material world is inconsistent not only with the current scientific consensus that sets the origin of space-time some 13.8 billion years ago, but with the Genesis account in the Bible. Unfortunately, most

Wizards, despite the science, continue to apply their own version of Aristotelian *apriorism* to much of their work, i.e., it is a fixed article of their faith that the universe is eternal. For the Wizards, therefore, matter cannot have had a beginning because a beginning implies a first cause, a first unmoved mover (a monotheistic concept), which would torpedo their worldview.

The Problem of Uncertainty

Most Wizards, unfortunately, have a hard time coming to grips with uncertainty and the idea of "universals" or "permanent forms." According to Hawking, for example, "the Ionians' view of nature — that it can be explained through general laws and reduced to a simple set of principles — exerted a powerful influence for only a few centuries. One reason is that Ionian theories often seemed to have no place for the notion of free will or purpose, or the concept that gods intervene in the workings of the world. These are startling omissions, as profoundly unsettling to many Greek thinkers as they are to many people today."[23] If I understand Hawking correctly, the material world is all that exists, free will is fundamentally a fiction, and the idea of a deity is a nuisance that leads humanity away from good ideas and progress. He seems to regret that the Ionian view of nature did not take lasting root. The world, he would surely argue, had to wait for the radical scholars of the Enlightenment to undermine the deleterious effects of religious prejudices and the fiction of personal freedom. Not inconsistent with the materialists of Antiquity, the Wizards believe that science and mathematics can eventually wean people away from the slavery of God and religion. Hitchens, for example, could not (or did not want to) distinguish between God, the unmoved mover, and the multiplicity of fairytale gods.

Some of Plato's Republic

Plato's *Republic* (c. 380 BC), probably his greatest work, delves into the nature of politics, knowledge, order, and truth. How did his metaphysics assist Judeo-Christian scholars to explain the meaning of "good" and "evil" or differentiate between a "good friend," a "friend," and an "enemy?" What is his "principle of forms?"

Plato observes that human beings and things (and the entire observable world) are in a state of flux or "becoming" (changing). For that reason, it is not possible to grasp or know something perfectly at any point in time. Nevertheless, do we not perceive that the visible world has a measure of order, intelligibility, or rationality? Clearly, we know more than what is immediately around us, and that is much more than purposeless chaos. Besides, our conscience is alive.[24]

Plato sought to understand the universal sense of morality. He advanced the idea of the existence of permanent forms (ideals or archetypes) that have always existed and do not change. The material world participates (or shares) in the world of eternal forms. In the moral order, there is one supreme form of the good, which is the ultimate object of knowledge, the enduring source of justice and all that is useful and valuable. It is that framework which the anti-theists reject and urge others to reject.

Plato held that things share in a universal world of forms (making "things" identifiable, intelligible, and comparable, physically and morally). Such a framework allows a person to distinguish, for example, "bird" from "frog," and "friend" from "enemy," and "goodness" from "badness" or "what ought to be" from "what ought not to be." This Hellenistic pre-Christian structure gave Christian thinkers a sound platform to clarify better the relationship between God and the Genesis account of creation and to defend objective (rather than self-referencing) moral ethics.

The Judeo-Christian worldview, building on Plato, posits a realm of eternal forms (the origin of which is outside the human mind and is not subjective) that is stable and unchanging (beyond time and space) because God (omniscient and unchanging) is just, and would have it no other way (although God could have had it in some other way). In Judeo-Christian terminology, God is *Ipsum Esse* (what many Wizards seem to think is mathematics or the laws of physics)[25] rather than *Ens summum* (the highest being amongst others in the same universe).[26] In other words, God is not just one more being (or thing) among many others. Rather God is "being" or simply "the act of being."

Judeo-Christian philosophy, taking from the insights and methodology of the Ancients, not only sees "things" as a sign of God "in the world" but views each being as participating in God's eternal wisdom and nature, giving purpose to existence beyond the immediate needs of men and women. Since God (not the distant clockmaker of the deists) is the source of the eternal forms (the basis of universals standards, order, and right and wrong), Christian philosophers have been able to articulate the meaning of "good" and "evil" in ways that make naysayers uncomfortable, and even belligerent.

Those Wizards who reject Plato's common-sense metaphysics reveal their inability to distinguish the physical laws of nature and the natural (moral) law: "[The] Stoics, a school of Greek philosophers that arose around the third century BC, did make a distinction between statutes and natural laws, but they included rules of human conduct they considered universal — such as veneration of God and obedience to parents — in the category of natural laws.... The notion that the laws of nature had to be intentionally obeyed reflects the Ancients' focus on why nature behaves as it does, rather than on how it behaves."[27] Hawking and Mlodivow rightfully point out the difference between "how" and "why," but don't seem to realize that asking the question "why" is legitimate because there is more to this world than matter, mathematics, magic, and mechanics.

Apriorism

Apriorism means turning *a priori* principles into definitive conclusions about reality whereby knowledge rests upon concepts that supposedly are evident to reason or that exist prior to experience and are presupposed by it. *Apriorism* has rightly evoked animated protest from materialists and scientists alike because hypotheses and assumptions cannot be properly measured or tested. That certain Aristotelian methodological approaches to knowledge — *apriorism* — dominated the thinking of the scientific community up to the 15th century is an unhappy fact. We now know that to have followed Aristotle's approach to discover the nature of knowledge (epistemology) proved to be ill advised. The fact that Aristotle was wrong does not mean that God is dead or that there is no purpose to life other than survival and procreating. Being wrong simply means that Aristotle and his disciples were wrong. His error had nothing to do with religion, and certainly nothing to do with Judeo-Christian epistemology in the natural sciences.

Let us explore this a bit more. Leslie J. Walker, S.J., suggests, "*Apriorism* asserts that thought and cognition generally have a definite structure, which is the necessary and immutable condition of all experience. It maintains that the forms, categories, principles of analysis and synthesis which characterize human cognition are not due to the circumstances in which we find ourselves, nor yet built up by the constructive activity of thought, but belong to the a priori nature of mind itself. Forms, categories and principles are all arranged or systematized a priori according to a plan or schema, which everyone carries about with him, and which conditions all his thought-activity."[28]

In retrospect, it is now clear that Aristotle couldn't see that physics and metaphysics are very different disciplines. Physics tries to describe how the universe works always and everywhere under certain conditions. As such, *apriorism* and the scientific method are incompatible.

In this connection, Hawking and Mlodivow rightly claim, "Aristotle built his physics upon principles that appealed to him intellectually."[29] I agree. But they should be careful in their proclamations, since atheism also builds upon principles that appeal to atheists. To say that God does not exist is *apriorism* at its shining best, because the basis for atheism is blind belief itself (not science) in the nonexistence of God.

Aristotle indeed got his science wrong because his science rested on the assumption that "a thing seeks what is best for it," which of course is inconsistent with the scientific method and the study of the universe. Where did Aristotle go wrong? One reason is that he assumed that the world was eternal, and that, therefore, celestial objects, for example, "had had enough time" (an eternity) to be in a pure state of "act." They did not possess the potential of being other than what they already are. Eternity, therefore, implied that no more change can take place in celestial bodies or the heavens. The upshot is that atheists as well as theists (everybody), as Stanley L. Jaki indicates, assumed Aristotle's approach to science "to be necessarily true, whatever the evidence to the contrary.... The sense of purpose, which is immediately evidenced through introspection, became, through its unwarranted generalization by Socrates, an invitation to reach truth through introspective mentation, the gist of *apriorism* and the worst pitfall offered by logic."[30] That is how Aristotle, for example, could justify "twice the weight, twice the rate of fall," which, of course, exposes the folly of his assumption.[31]

Apriorism represents a misstep in thinking that took centuries to notice and a few more to reject. The lesson here is that no one should accept as universally true theories about the physical world that have not been repeatedly tested, counter-tested, and verified, because theories must be subjected to the rigors of the scientific method. Jaki: "Prior to [Jean] Buridan" (AD 1295–1363), a priest-academic who laid the groundwork for the Copernican revolution, "not a few Christian thinkers were willing to see angels (which they took for the Christian version of Aristotelian and Plotinian intelligences) as motors behind celestial motions."[32] Buridan's commentaries on Aristotle's *Physics* and *On the Heavens* "may rightly be seen as the birth-register of Newtonian and modern science. [According to Buridan], Aristotle, as befits a genuine Greek pagan, asserts the eternity of the universe as a self-evident truth."[33] Does not this same idea permeate modern thinking as well?

While Aristotle and many others got their science wrong, their error in thinking should not be used to dismiss the Judeo-Christian worldview, its legacy, or its representatives. Let us not forget that educated clerics during the Middle Ages stopped 1500 years of Socratic/Aristotelian *apriorism* dead in its tracks, quite a feat for silly and delusional old monks. It would not be outrageous to say that, without Buridan, who understood both Genesis and the purpose of science, the Industrial Revolution may not have appeared when it did in history. So, if ever the Wizards suggest that *apriorism* is a concoction dreamed up by religious folk and reserved for them, let us be clear that they are wrong. Rather it is religious folk who exposed Aristotle and his *apriorism*, and thus contributed to the liberation and creativity of the human mind in order to serve others better.

Moral Ethics

In the realm of moral ethics, general principles are necessary and refer necessarily to external standards, which ultimately rest on the mind of God (just like mathematics) and not on ephemeral changing codes of behavioral norms of conduct. Aristotle and Plato got that bit mostly right. Moreover, it is a mistake to apply the scientific methodology as the guiding method in the area of moral ethics, because one would be making the kind of mistake that Aristotle made in connection with the truths of the natural world. Just as science can say little about love or hate, philosophy can say little about Archimedes' principle.

From a slightly different perspective, C.S. Lewis's powerful observations about existence and human insightfulness may be instructive: "My argument against God was that the universe seemed so cruel and unjust. But how had I got this idea of just and unjust? A man does not call a line crooked unless he has some idea of a straight line. What was I comparing this universe with when I called it unjust?"[34] Without universal and permanent principles, which serve as benchmarks or targets to guide human behavior, nothing can be reasonably judged to be objectively good or bad. The consequences of such thinking are that virtually anything is permissible (as long as it "works"), a vision that indeed seems to run at the core of the anti-theists' ideological agenda. Buridan, Sir Isaac Newton (1643–1727), Fr. Georges Lemaître, and Francis Collins would beg to differ with the anti-theists.[35]

Statecraft

Aristotle understood the meaning of "good" as (a) goods in the soul (wisdom, virtue, and pleasure), (b) goods in the body (health and beauty), and (c) external goods (wealth, office, and honor).[36] A good leader not only recognizes the meaning of goodness in a Platonic sense but acts in accordance with a hierarchy of goods with the guidance of a minimum of just laws to bring about goodness (without coercion) in the public square.

Aristotle's *Politics* discusses political theory considering a need for unity of life that should exist among individual, family, clan, and the city-state, the highest form of political community. He rightly rejects the practice of statecraft that rests exclusively on principles of power and fear, and mostly recognizes the centrality of the idea that society has its own "telos" or purpose beyond the enrichment of elites or corrupt politicians. Most important, he recognizes the principle that Frank Sheed, a Christian apologist, articulated so eloquently: "Our treatment of anything must depend, in the last resort, on what we think it is: for instance, we treat people one way and cats another, because of our idea of what a man is and what a cat is."[37] Does not modern society need to reassess its understanding of the human person? Because of the importance of Sheed's observation, I cite the rest of the passage in his book *Society and Sanity*:

> All our institutions — family, school, trade union, government, laws, customs, anything you please — grew out of what those who made them thought a man was. If you want to understand them profoundly, you must get at the idea of man [a human person] that they express. There are periods of human history when it is not immediately and obviously necessary to make this sort of profound enquiry. When institutions are long-established, functioning healthily, serving happiness, the mass of men may very well decide simply to live by them and ask no questions. But when anything goes wrong with an institution — so that we have to decide whether to mend it (and if so, how) or to scrap it (and if so, what to put in its place) — then the question what man is immediately becomes not only practical, but of the first practicality.
>
> This is so for two reasons, one of them vital but in our day widely denied, the other vital and not in any day deniable. The first reason is that all social orders are made of men and must be tested by their aptitude to men. There are those who would smile at this, and for the moment I shall not argue with them, but go on to the second reason, which nobody can deny, that all social orders are made *of* men. People making engines study steel, people making statues study marble, people making social systems should study man, for man is as much the raw material of social systems as steel is of engines, or marble of statues. And whereas we are not all making engines or statues, we are all involved in the making of social systems, from small ones like the family, up to the largest, the State to which we belong.[38]

That passage on its own should get some of my readers to think through their worldview and ideas about governance.

It should be obvious, therefore, that good and just governance does not necessarily mean efficient, productive, and stress-free governance. In this sense, Aristotle recognizes the difference between human beings and animals, whose differences are not simply anatomical and taxonomic.

Human Beings Are Special — Sorry

Certain Wizards tend to praise Ionian scientists for their innovative ideas in the 4th century BC. Their praise stems from the claim that there is nothing special about human beings, because human beings are made of stardust or out of some such material, and, therefore, are just another "thing" in the universe. Hawking's views seem to be representative of the Wizards: "The revolutionary idea that we are but ordinary inhabitants of the universe, not special beings distinguished by existing at the center, was first championed by Aristarchus (c. 310–c. 230 BC)."[39] In other words, is not the idea that human beings are essentially no different from animals except in their respective levels of material sophistication and cognitive complexity precisely what many of the Wizards want us to believe? Careful reflection is necessary here, since the Wizards' narrative is not only hackneyed but dangerous, especially when it falls into the hands of people in positions of power who fundamentally see no ontological difference between human beings and animals. As a matter of fact, human beings *are* special, which does not in any way mean that they may despoil the earth, dominate the weak, or hoard resources at the expense of others. (So that we are clear, protection of biodiversity and bio-resources at this time, as always. is paramount and should not be subjugated to the vices of human beings or any utopian ideas entirely divorced from reality.)

The Dogmatism of the Wizards

The world needs to recognize the folly of those who nonchalantly condemn all the belief systems of traditional religions and cultures in the world at a single go. Besides being offensive, is it not irresponsible to argue that science supports atheism and not theism? I bring to your attention just one example of such thinking, as outlined in *Scientism: The New Orthodoxy:* "To begin with, the findings of science entail that the belief systems of all the world's traditional religions and cultures — their theories of the origins of life, humans, and societies — are factually mistaken."[40] What findings? Do we *scientifically* know that all the belief systems of all cultures are factually wrong? Where is the evidence? With such unscientific claims, Plato and Socrates would have had a field day debating today's anti-theists, because science does not back up their claims.

Is not Pinker being dogmatic when he proclaims, "*We know* that our species is a tiny twig of a genealogical tree that embraces all living things and that emerged from prebiotic chemicals almost four billion years ago"?[41] Doesn't Pinker succumb to the malady of *apriorism* that the Wizards themselves violently condemn in Aristotle? We think that Aristotle, if shown his error, would have back-tracked on his flawed *a priori* principles idea. We are not so sure the anti-theists would do the same, but given the experience, seriousness, and raw brilliance of many of the Wizards, they just might come to understand Plato's Allegory of the Cave.[42]

The Wizards should show us the actual evidence that a human being "emerged from prebiotic chemicals," given the implications of making such a statement, the massively incomplete fossil record, and the irreducible complexity of nature (except in a mathematical sense). And even if the evidence were produced, the one uncreated God of the universe would still exist because the existence of God is compatible with biological change and the claims of evolution at the level of science. Science has not made (nor will it ever make) God irrelevant; it is the anti-theists who are trying to make God irrelevant.

Unfortunately, Pinker sounds a bit like a preacher when he intones that "We know that the laws governing the physical world (including accidents, disease, and other misfortunes) have no goals that pertain to human well-being. There is no such thing as fate, providence, karma, spells, curses, augury, divine retribution, or answered prayers — though the discrepancy between the laws of probability and the workings of cognition may explain why people believe there are."[43] How does Pinker know that there is no such thing as providence or answered prayers? Is not the "we know" of the Wizards nothing more than a cool "we blindly believe" that God does not exist? It is unlikely that any of the Wizards would ever agree with Euclid, who said that "the laws of nature are but the mathematical thoughts of God."

Nor would most of the Wizards agree with Cicero. In his book *On the Republic*, Cicero writes that true law, everlasting and immutable, is "right reason" *in agreement with the nature and purpose of being*. He reflects on natural law and governance: "There is indeed a law, right reason, which is in accordance with nature; existing in all, unchangeable, eternal, commanding us to do what is right, forbidding us to do what is wrong. It has dominion over good men, but possesses no influence over bad ones. No other law can be substituted for it; no part of it can be taken away, nor can it be abrogated altogether. Neither the people nor the senate can absolve us from it. It wants no commentator or interpreter. It is not one thing at Rome, and another thing at Athens: one thing to-day, and another thing to-morrow; but it is a law eternal and immutable for all nations and for all time. God, the sole Ruler, and universal Lord, has framed and proclaimed this law. He who does not obey it, renounces himself, and is false to his own nature: he brings upon himself the direst tortures, even when he escapes human punishments."[44]

Ideology Run Riot

Some Wizards can be no clearer in their opposition to Judeo-Christian and Ciceronian ideas and values concerning the human person, human nature, unchangeable principles, and purpose. Again we cite Pinker, who eloquently expresses the agenda of most anti-theists:

> "[The] worldview that guides the moral and spiritual values of an educated person today is the worldview given to us by science. Though the scientific facts do not by themselves dictate values, they certainly hem in the possibilities. By stripping ecclesiastical authority of its credibility on factual matters, they cast doubt on its claims to certitude in matters of morality. The scientific refutation of the theory of vengeful gods and occult forces undermines practices such as human sacrifice, witch-hunts, faith healing, trial by ordeal, and the persecution of heretics. The facts of science, by exposing the absence of purpose in the laws governing the universe, force us to take responsibility for the welfare of ourselves, our species, and our planet. For the same reason, they undercut any moral or political system based on mystical forces, quests, destinies, dialectics, struggles, or messianic ages."[45]

The Wizards' own worship of science tends to be messianic because liberation from uncertainty and the acceptance of personal ethics is their endgame. Their god is science, which will eventually be able to penetrate the mysteries of consciousness, intuition, love, hate, and pain without destroying but saving human nature from its self-induced mental disease of belief in one God and other similar nonsense. And most Wizards reduce the spiritual dimension of the human person to energy and impulses; there is no consideration of the *Imago Dei*. I maintain that the fact that humans are in *Imago Dei*" is precisely what has made genuine human development possible.

Extrapolating from similar statements of other Wizards, is it not naive to think that science can bring peace of mind to a person, when human nature is so misunderstood? Science cannot serve as the only bridge between life and death or comfort and suffering. Even Democritus, the Sophists, and pantheists of the Greco-Roman period would have found it difficult to accept the anti-theists' ideology of scientism, i.e., the application of scientific methods when inappropriate and the belief that human beings can eventually figure out the mystery of the human person without understanding the nature and purpose of human existence itself. The Wizards, academics, politicians, and students should consider Chesterton's keen observation, "Science must not impose any philosophy, any more than the telephone must tell us what to say." The facts of science, as the Wizards suggest, do not force us to take responsibility for the well-being of others; rather when atheism becomes enamored with the ideas of perpetual progress and moral relativism, it unmistakably undermines the foundations of a just and orderly socio-political system. Ideologies such as scientism and naturalism are dead ends in search of meaning.

Thucydides — Another Word of Caution

Thucydides (c. 460 BC–c. 395 BC) can be considered one of the founders of political realism, where good moral ethics and the effective use of power are really one and the same. He articulated a vision which most of today's power elites — as well as Thomas Hobbes (AD 1588–1679) and Nicolò Machiavelli (AD 1469–1527) — have surely embraced. As a pessimist, Thucydides preferred confrontation to engagement, and force to diplomacy, since human nature and human relations are by definition unremittingly destructive and do not admit of selfless service. "It is a general rule of human nature that people despise those who treat them well, and look up to those who make no concessions."[46] It is my view that Thucydides got the bulk of his anthropology and theory of governance wrong and looked only at the dark side of human nature. He saw brute force and technical sagacity as the primary effective means to get one's way or achieve immediate political objectives — a kind of rudimentary wolf-pack approach to social relations and governance. Such thinking makes sense only to those who see darkness, competition, and violence at the core of human existence.

In Thucydides' mind, the application of power to achieve some end that is perceived as good can be limitless, irrespective of the consequences to innocent people. Without a moral compass, politicians would be justified in putting down any perceived adversary or promoting political philosophies such as those that led in the 20th century to the murder of tens of millions of people in the name of "progress." Christopher Dawson exposes the danger of such thinking: "As soon as human beings decide that all means are permitted to fight an evil, then their good becomes indistinguishable from the evil that they set out to destroy."[47] Statecraft in the first instance means recognizing the dignity of the human person and putting in place a legal system with a minimum of constraints that is attuned to the common good and that leads to genuine human development. Let us not forget that unsuccessful nations never share security with others but only act to guarantee their own security (through belligerence and threats). Such an approach to statecraft always tends to generate even more insecurity, bloodshed, and irrational behavior.

On the Road towards Genuine Human Development

The Wizards, almost without exception, would like us to think that the great art, literature, music, architecture, and science of the Judeo-Christian civilization over the past 2500 years has been mostly the by-product of the merger of the profane and pragmatic strains of Greco-Roman erudition (enlightened reason) with the irrational forces of evolution and the creative energies of science (which unlocked the secrets of the universe). They would also like us to believe that religion, and particularly the Judeo-Christian mindset, has not only been a nuisance but a harmful add-on and, in the minds of some, a blood-sucking parasite draining humanity of creativity. But as John Lennox has convincingly said in one of his many lectures, he doesn't have enough faith to buy into the atheist narrative.[48]

In contrast, and against the backdrop of history, there should be no doubt in anyone's mind that genuine human development is best explained by peoples' living in accordance with their true nature and in love with science and the universe. Moreover, it is possible to possess a genuine spirit of selfless service that leads to personal human development, greater societal sanity, and material progress.

There is no doubt that the great ideas of the Greco-Roman world helped change conventional ways of thinking about the universe, life, education, science, and economic development.[49] We owe much to the Ancients, who, despite their elitism and inability to recognize the full dignity of the human person, grasped (at least the non-profane amongst them) fundamental and reasonable ideas, such as the immortality of the soul, the existence of immutable principles, the importance of teleology, the non-arbitrary nature of moral ethics, and the existence of an eternal being.

Would it not behoove all of us to take the philosophy of the Ancients more seriously, and read insightful commentaries on their writings rather than any old book? Seneca (4 BC–AD 65) has something to say about this: "It does not matter how many books you have, but how good the books are which you have."[50] To make the transition back to the classics, educators must acknowledge that God, reason, science, and purposefulness (that things have a purpose beyond pleasure and survival) are compatible and that some ideas are better and truer than others. Aristotle and Plato were correct to call out the ideology of moral relativism as harmful for personal and societal development.

The Ancients jolted scholars into seeing reality beyond the fuzzy images on the wall of Plato's Allegory of the Cave. They pushed scholars to recognize right from wrong and see the value of service over violence. The best philosophy of the Ancients has helped humankind to articulate a worldview in a language that is not only accessible but clear to anyone who wants to listen.

Philosophy is not dead; neither is God, despite the narrative of the anti-theists. It is fitting to end this chapter by quoting Antony Flew, the English philosopher, who shocked the world when he rejected his erstwhile atheism: "Why do I believe [in God], given that I expounded and defended atheism for more than half a century? The short answer is this: this is the world picture, as I see it, that has emerged from modern science. Science spotlights three dimensions of nature that point to God. The first is the fact that nature obeys laws. The second is the dimension of life, of intelligently organized and purpose-driven beings, which arose from matter. The third is the very existence of nature. But it is not science alone that guided me. I have also been helped by a renewed study of the classical philosophical arguments."[51]

---

1.   See John Lennox, "Has Science Buried God?" (http://www.johnlennox.org/jresources/has-science-buried-god-rice-university/). He answers the question "What of the discovery of water on Mars?" during the Question-and-Answer period (https://www.youtube.com/watch?v=IloVR-zgDNk).

2·   Jacob Giltaij, "Existimatio as 'Human Dignity' in Late-classical Roman Law," *Fundamina: A Journal of Legal History*, 22, no. 2 (2016): pp. 233. Despite falling short in practice, it "was only in the late fifteenth century that would obtain the meaning of 'dignity' in this latter sense [as "man as such"]. The literature then refers to works by Pico della Mirandola (1486) and Von Pufendorf (1672), still undoubtedly building on Cicero and other ancient sources." Giltaij, pp. 233-34 (www.scielo.org.za/pdf/funda/v22n2/03.pdf).

3.   See Bl. Paul VI (pope), "Dignitatus Humanae" (Declaration of Vatican II; December 7, 1965) for an understanding of the Catholic Church's voice in defense of the dignity of the human person (http://www.vatican.va/archive/hist_councils/ii_vatican_council/documents/vat-ii_decl_19651207_dignitatis-humanae_en.html).

4.   Joseph Cardinal Ratzinger, *Truth and Tolerance: Christian Belief and World Religions* (San Francisco: Ignatius Press, 2004); p. 173.

5.   John Lennox and Peter Atkins, "Duelling Professors" (debate; Big Questions, 2011) (https://www.youtube.com/watch?v=ZS5s-oVNsRo).

6.   See Neil Ormerod, "The Metaphysical Muddle of Lawrence Krauss: Why Science Can't Get Rid of God," ABC Religion and Ethics, February 18, 2013 (http://www.abc.net.au/religion/articles/2013/02/18/3692765.htm).

7.   "… philosophy is dead. Philosophy has not kept up with modern developments in science, particularly physics. Scientists have become the bearers of the torch of discovery in our quest for knowledge." Stephen W. Hawking and Leonard Mlodivow, *The Grand Design*, (New York: Bantam Books, 2010); p. 5.

8.   See William Lane Craig, "Navigating Sam Harris' *The Moral Landscape*," Reasonable Faith, n.d.) (https://www.reasonablefaith.org/writings/popular-writings/existence-nature-of-god/navigating-sam-harris-the-moral-landscape/).

9.   For example, the principle of non-contradiction must always be true, i.e., "something" can never be "nothing" at the same time and in the same respect.

10.   For a brilliant commentary on this question, see John Lennox, *God and Stephen Hawking: Whose Design Is It Anyway?* (Oxford: Lion Hudson, 2011).

11.   See Francis Collins, "Why It's So Hard for Scientists to Believe in God" (BigThink, 2011) (https://www.youtube.com/watch?v=pINptKQYviQ).

12.   See David Berlinski, "The Devil's Delusion: Atheism and Its Scientific Pretentions" (New York City: Lecture at the Union League Club, 2012) (https://www.youtube.com/watch?v=0XIDykeZplU); p. 183-84.

13.   See John Lennox's material on Hawking and his ideas: https://www.youtube.com/watch?v=If4XisIJNA4

14.   The particle that some hope will give "mass to matter."

15.   Hawking and Mlodivow, *Grand Design,* p. 23.

16.   See John H. Hallowell, *Main Currents in Modern Political Thought* (Lanham, Md.: University Press of America, 1984); p. 17.

17.   Hallowell, pp. 16-17.

18.   Marcus Aurelius, *Meditations,* Book 11; Maxwell Staniforth, trans. (Harmondsworth, Middlesex: Penguin Books, 1984); p. 165.

19.   See Frederick C. Copleston, *A History of Philosophy,* new rev. ed., vol. 2, "Greece & Rome," pt. 2 (New York: Image Books, 1962); p. 151.

20.   For greater clarity, see John Lennox and Michael Shermer, "Does God Exist?" (debate, August 2008) (https://www.youtube.com/watch?v=EEh1rOg6o9o at minute 1:21:00).

21.   Steven Pinker, "Science Is Not Your Enemy," *New Republic,* August 6, 2013 (https://newrepublic.com/article/114127/science-not-enemy-humanities).

22.   G.K. Chesterton, *Orthodoxy* (New York: Dodd, Mead & Co., 1908), p. 20. See http://www.ccel.org/ccel/chesterton/orthodoxy.html.

23.   Hawking and Mlodivow, pp. 21-22.

24.   "Feeling" is a word traditionalists would never apply to the conscience.

25.   "The sheer act of being in itself."

26.   Highest being (among many others in the same universe). See Flannery O'Connor, letter to Betty Hester in *The Habit of Being: Letters of Flannery O'Connor,* ed. by Sally Fitzgerald (New York: Farrar, Straus, Giroux, 1988), pp.99-101 (http://theamericanreader.com/6-september-1955-flannery-oconnor/).

27.   Hawking and Mlodivow, *Grand Design,* p. 23.

28.   Leslie J. Walker, S.J., "Criticism of Apriorism," chapter IX in *Theories of Knowledge, Absolutism, Pragmatism, Realism* (New York: Longmans, Green & Co., 1910), p. 160 (https://maritain.nd.edu/jmc/etext/walker09.htm).

29.   Hawking and Mlodivow, p. 24.

30.   Stanley L. Jaki, *The Savior of Science* (Edinburgh: Scottish Academic Press, 1990); p.41. Jaki is particularly good in developing the idea that metaphysics and physics are different disciplines and that neither can do the job of the other.

31. Jaki, *Savior of Science,* p. 53. The rates at which two similar objects fall are proportional to their respective weights.

32. Jaki, *Savior of Science,* p. 67.

33. Jaki, *Savior of Science,* p. 50.

34. C.S. Lewis, *Mere Christianity* (New York: Macmillan Company, 1952); p. 25 (https://canavox.com/wp-content/uploads/2017/06/Mere-Christianity-Lewis.pdf). Also relevant to this discussion is his *Abolition of Man: Reflections on Education with Special Reference to the Teaching of English in the Upper Forms of Schools* (Oxford: Oxford University Press, 1943) (https://archive.org/stream/TheAbolitionOfMan_229/C.s.Lewis-TheAbolitionOfMan_djvu.txt).

35. See Francis Collins, "The Language of God: A Scientist Presents Evidence of Belief" (Veritas Forum, 2010) (https://www.youtube.com/watch?v=EGu_VtbpWhE).

36. Aristotle, *Nichomachaean Ethics,* Book I, chapter 8. Plato classified the importance of goods the following way: (1) divine goods: (a) wisdom, (b) temperance (c) justice and (d) courage; and (2) lesser or human goods: (a) health (b) beauty (c) strength and (d) wealth.

37. F.J. Sheed, "Sanity Is the Point," chapter 1 in *Society and Sanity: Understanding How to Live Well Together* (San Francisco: Ignatius Press, 2013) (https://books.google.vg/books?id=5eIrZPANPRIC&printsec=copyright&source=gbs_pub_info_r#v=onepage&q&f=false).

38. Sheed, "Sanity Is the Point."

39. Hawking and Mlodivow, p. 21.

40. Richard William and Daniel Robinson, eds., *Scientism, the New Orthodoxy* (New York: Bloomsbury Academic, 2015); p. 14.

41. Pinker, "Not Your Enemy" (my emphasis added).

42. Plato, *The Republic,* 514a-520a.

43. Pinker, "Not Your Enemy."

44. Marcus Tullius Cicero, *The Republic,* George William Featherstonhaugh, trans. (http://www.gutenberg.org/ebooks/54161).

45. Pinker, "Not Your Enemy."

46. Thucydides, *The History of the Peloponnesian War,* chapter 2. Alternatively, Richard Crawley, trans.: "Concessions to adversaries only end in self-reproach, and the more strictly they are avoided the greater will be the chance of security" (http://www.gutenberg.org/ebooks/7142).

47. Christopher Dawson, *The Judgement of the Nations* (New York: Sheed and Ward, 1942); p. 13.

48. John Lennox, "I Don't Have Enough Faith to Be an Atheist" (2014) (http://www.johnlennox.org/jresources/i-dont-have-enough-faith-to-be-an-atheist/).

49. Education as understood in John Henry Newman, *The Idea of the University* (London: Longmans, Green, and Co., 1886); p. ix (https://archive.org/stream/a677122900newmuoft#page/n5/mode/2up). Also see Paul Shrimpton, *The Making of Men: The Idea and Reality of Newman's University in Oxford and Dublin* (Leominster, England: Gracewing Publishing, 2014).

50. Lucius Annaeus Seneca, *Moral Letters to Lucilius.*

51.   Antony Flew and Roy Abraham Varghese, *There Is ~~No~~ a God: How the World's Most Notorious Atheist Changed His Mind* (New York: HarperCollins, 2008); pp. 88-89.

CHAPTER 3

Rome, Early Christianity, and Sagacity

As it is impossible to verbally describe the sweetness of honey to one who has never tasted honey, so the goodness of God cannot be clearly communicated by way of teaching if we ourselves are not able to penetrate into the goodness of the Lord by our own experience.
— St. Basil the Great (AD 330–379), *Conversations on the Psalms, 29*

All human nature vigorously resists grace because grace changes us and the change is painful."
— Flannery O'Connor, *The Habit of Being: Letters of Flannery O'Connor*

The fatal metaphor of progress, which means leaving things behind us, has utterly obscured the real idea of growth, which means leaving things inside us.
— Gilbert K. Chesterton, "The Romance of Rhyme"

The acquisition of holiness is not the exclusive business of monks, as certain people think. People with families are also called to holiness, as are those in all kinds of professions who live in the world, since the commandment about perfection and holiness is given not only to monks, but to all people.
— Hieromartyr Onuphry Gagaluk

The fall of the western Roman Empire in the 5th century AD was probably unavoidable, for no human endeavor is everlasting, but even so its collapse was dramatic. There is little ambiguity when it comes to identifying the primary reasons for the disintegration of the Greco-Roman world, but it was not, as some claim and others insinuate, the result of embracing Christianity, in particular. Rather, the reasons for its crack-up and subsequent collapse were primarily linked to a growing alienation of the citizenry from first principles, an unwarranted and regular use of force over the exercise of good judgment to stamp out opposing views, a loss of purpose beyond the immediate, and the abandonment of policies that promoted virtuous living in the public square. Outer grandeur was not matched by good sense, balanced statecraft, and inner purpose. External threats were a secondary cause. An arrogance of power swamped right reason in governance.[1]

It is not our intention to demonstrate in a rigorous fashion (with yet another exhaustive study chock-full of irrefutable data) that the Judeo-Christian worldview introduced into the Roman spirit a deeper awareness of the dignity of the human person and the beauty of service to neighbor. The natural consequence of accepting such views, i.e., that the human person is capable of great feats of selfless generosity and charity, led to the emergence of Western civilization in its deepest sense.

The Judeo-Christian worldview recognized the important role that transcendent moral standards play in private and public life, and held that a recognition of human dignity drove material progress and preserved the common good. And that without moral reasoning and God (who is beyond space and time), human existence eventually becomes unbearable, hopelessness abounds, and power supplants charity. Selfishness eventually destroys the innate spirit of service in human nature without which there is no way to balance freedom and equality; That message was at the center of the young Judeo-Christian narrative at the time, and remains the same today.

Christianity did not cause the collapse of the Roman Empire and, eventually, plunge the known world into the so-called Dark Ages. That is the false narrative of many of the anti-theists who aim to undermine the Judeo-Christian legacy and discredit Christian scholarship, even to this day.

The deterioration of imperial Roman society occurred over a long period, and a few scholars at the time did what they could with their writings and influence to try to stop it. Judeo-Christian scholars toiled to share their wise council (about the meaning, origin, and purpose of life and statecraft) with anyone who wished to listen. Their efforts were undertaken not only to enhance our knowledge of ourselves and the universe but to address the wrong-headed ideas storming the intellectual parapets of the Roman Empire. In the process, early Christian scholars helped preserve for future generations the accumulated erudition and art of the Greco-Roman world, and "Hellenized" Christian philosophy and theology (which is what Islam failed to do in later centuries).

On one level, despite their love for Rome, the early Judeo-Christian scholars failed to save it from an internal (non-random) process of decay that ended in societal fragmentation and mostly self-destruction. On another level, however, simultaneous with the dissolution of Rome, Judeo-Christian scholars from Constantinople to Dublin succeeded in safeguarding the valuable ideas (and some of the not-so-valuable ones) generated by classical Greco-Roman learning. More important, they not only built up and reinforced the body of classical ideas but brought to life Judeo-Christian thought as a result of its encounter with Greek philosophy to produce a fuller understanding of God, human freedom, dignity, and suffering.

Contrary to the claims of some of the Wizards of the Enlightenment, Judeo-Christian scholarship at the time was much more than a sophisticated version of pagan fables and transient symbolism. Indeed, the Wizards' implied storyline suggests that the Judeo-Christian worldview was dreamt up to further the interests of a warped priestly class of sexist clergymen interested in maintaining control and privileges over a half-brainwashed population at a time of crisis in the first centuries *anno Domini*. In their ongoing quest to smother Christianity, some of the Wizards deploy smear tactics against reasonable arguments in furtherance of their anti-theist agenda.

Today, the anti-theist radical atheists[2] have not only largely rejected much of the wisdom of the early Christian classics and their legacy but have as an axiom blamed Judeo-Christian thinking for the fall of the Roman Empire and the so-called Dark Ages that followed. One of the themes of this book is that people must remain on high alert against most of the messages of the anti-theists, or Wizards.

Just as today, in the first centuries after the birth of Jesus Christ, Christian scholars tried to instill the idea that happiness meant much more than a full belly, victories over opponents, or balance between extremes in the classical philosophical sense. New ideas were introduced into philosophy and provided, for example, new perspectives about the significance of time and cosmology, in light of the one, uncreated Judeo-Christian God of the universe, with whom establishing a relationship is possible. In the words of Saint Augustine:

> Nor dost Thou [God] by time precede time; else wouldest not Thou precede all times. But in the excellency of an ever-present eternity, Thou precedest all times past, and survivest all future times, because they are future, and when they have come they will be past; but 'Thou art the same, and Thy years shall have no end.' Thy years neither go nor come; but ours both go and come, that all may come. All Thy years stand at once, since they do stand; nor were they when departing excluded by coming years, because they pass not away; but all these of ours shall be when all shall cease to be. Thy years are one day, and Thy day is not daily, but to-day; because Thy to-day yields not with tomorrow, for neither

doth it follow yesterday. Thy to-day is eternity; therefore didst
Thou beget the Co-eternal, to whom Thou saidst, 'This day
have I begotten Thee.' Thou hast made all time; and before
all times Thou art, nor in any time was there not time.[3]

Roman citizens by the fourth century began to see the importance of permanent moral values at the ontological level. The early Judeo-Christian philosophers, in dialogue with academics and theologians, accepted monotheism as
their worldview more and more rather than the multiplicity of so-called gods
and other figments of the imagination (that the Wizards rightly disparage). It
was increasingly understood by men and women of the age that the meaning
of liberation was linked to truth, as reflected in the phrase "and the truth shall
make you free."[4] Moreover, there could be no contradiction between the visible and the invisible worlds or between the natural and the supernatural, which
explains the significance of the encounter between philosophy and theology.

Most Christian theologians believed that humans are beings whose unique
faculties of intellect and will — the marks of spirituality — were created by
God (which does not contradict the notion that people vary according to environmental, climatic, or genetic changes). They believed that we exist for a
reason and are endowed with an ability to come to grips with (and not remain
passive about) matters such as injustice, love, emotions, and suffering. Respect
for the dignity of each person was and remains a distinguishing idea of the
Christian mindset.[5]

Judeo-Christian scholars since the days of the Gospels have tried to answer the question "what does it mean to be a person of faith?" and to articulate a position that went beyond the Aristotelian definition of "*homo est animal
rationale,* [where] the human being was mainly an object, one of the objects in
the world to which the human being visibly and physically belonged."[6] The human person is not simply made of matter, and the mind is not a collection of
neurons and synapses. Such a reductionist view turns the human person into a
sophisticated robot or computer, thus opening the door for manipulation and
experimentation as long as pain is managed.

Not understanding the spiritual side of the human person, many of the
Wizards mock Christian scholarship that claims that the physical laws of nature and the natural moral law are compatible because their source is one and
the same, i.e., God. Ironically, some of the Wizards seem to accept the idea
of the irreducibility of a person's subjective potentialities such as freedom
while at the same time being materialists. What materialists forget or ignore
is that irreducibility pertains to spiritual beings, which contradicts their claim
that the human person is a nonspiritual being, i.e., material and, therefore, like

everything else, infinitely divisible or reducible, which are properties of matter.

Christian scholars such as St. Irenaeus of Lyons (c. 130–202), St. Ephraim the Syrian (306–373), St. Ambrose (337–397), St. Jerome (347–420), Lucius Lactantius (c. 250–325), and Moses of Chorene (c. 410–490) believed that Holy Scripture was the Word of God and was not to be interpreted in a literal sense but historically in light of reason.[7] During the first centuries, the moral teaching of the Holy Scriptures remained as salvific preaching (*kerygma*) and as simple catechesis (*didache*) or exhortation, concrete, authoritative, and binding in conscience for all the faithful. More than speculative elaborations, the emphasis was on transmitting the full living truth based on the living word of Scripture. They tried to live the experience of union with Christ, showing the richness of life demanded by redemption in Christ and the call to be children of God. This vision contrasted with Greco-Roman paganism, a form of polytheism (religious worship) from which modern strains of ideological neo-paganism borrow ideas.

Contrary to claims of some of the Wizards, Christianity in principle does not promote violence, political mayhem, or disunity in any form, although disunity among Christians is visible and scandalous. Anyone who would make the case that Christianity destabilized and brought about the collapse of the Roman Empire should be challenged. Rome collapsed from its own internal socio-political moral decay and from the early clamor of the right of nationalities (later referred to as nation-states) to live independent of central authority, and not, as English historian Edward Gibbon (1737–1794) claims, from the negative influence of Christianity.[8]

The most reasonable explanation for the collapse of Rome in the 5th century was a non-Judeo-Christian and spiritual moral dysfunction, together with an identity crisis that prevented the application of practical socio-political and economic countermeasures. The result of this moral drift was an inability to strive for objectives outside narrow personal and parochial interests and confirmed Rome's disinterest in the growing self-awareness of independent peoples. No society or civilization will stand long when statesmen and politicians do not see the centrality of common and universal principles that have always guided human behavior. In contrast, a self-referencing morality supported by authoritarian tactics that are blind to the needs of others leads to personal suffering, injustice, and societal collapse.

Nor did Rome fall because it lost its technological edge against external heathen invaders or because of an institutional church that depleted the fighting spirit of Roman warriors. Rome simply lost its ability for prudential moral reasoning, and the nerve to face its own decadence, and, ultimately, its reasons to exist and carry on as a homogeneous entity. The same symptoms are evident in modern society today.

In explaining the fall of Rome, we should heed the English historian Arnold J. Toynbee, who rejected the thesis that Christianity was the root cause of the decline of Rome. Toynbee attributes the demise of Rome to factors that began long before the arrival of Christianity:

> It never occurred to Gibbon that the Age of the Antonines[9] was not the summer but the 'Indian summer' of Hellenic history. The degree of his hallucination is betrayed by the very title of his work. The decline and fall of the Roman Empire! The author of a history that bears that name and that starts in the 2nd century of the Christian era is surely beginning his narrative at a point that is very near the end of the actual story. For the 'intelligible field of historical study' with which Gibbon is concerned is not the Roman Empire but the Hellenic civilization, of whose far-advanced disintegration the Roman Empire itself was a monumental symptom."[10]

Can anyone doubt that atheism, polytheism, and hedonism, all friends of moral relativism, ultimately crushed the willingness of Romans to defend their identity and purpose? The French historian Henri Daniel-Rops (1901–1965), and Pitirim A. Sorokin (1889–1968), the Russian-American sociologist at Harvard University, seconded the major conclusions of Toynbee.[11]

Christopher Dawson (1889–1970) of Harvard University, also dismissed the widely held view that Christianity ruined Rome and, thus, thrust Europe into the arms of clerics and other clueless religious folk. He says, "It was only the Church and, particularly, by the monks that the tradition of classical culture and the writings of classical authors, 'the Latin classics,' were preserved.... [Monastic] schools and libraries and scriptoria became the chief organs of higher intellectual culture in Western Europe."[12] Other world-class historians, such as Frederick Copleston[13] also fundamentally agree with Dawson. Historians such as Gibbon have distorted the positive impact of the Judeo-Christian legacy on the development of European civilizations.[14]

Christian scholars writing in the 5th century likewise consider Rome to have collapsed from its own weight and unwillingness to fight against its own hubris and "collective sin." In *The City of God*, St. Augustine (354–430) rejected the theory that the Roman Empire was collapsing because Rome had abandoned the pagan gods and embraced Christianity. He points to moral decay and to the absence of unity in the Empire: "The only possible source of future unity lies not in multiplicity, but above it. One World is impossible without One God and One Church."[15] The majority of today's anti-theists have a very difficult time accepting that unity is possible because, in their world, there can be no unity, when deadly competition and blind evolution are the main drivers of history. St. Augustine understood that societal peace (not in any utopian sense) depended on understanding the difference between unity that comes about from good ideas and good doses of self-giving, generosity, patience, and humility, and unity that is imposed and forced upon people. While the former approach to unity more or less works, the latter never does.

The pagan world's regular use of military power against perceived threats contributed to socio-political and institutional weaknesses. Such actions, especially in victory, generated a sense of self-importance among politicians that led to a deleterious concentration of power and resources in the hands of fewer and fewer people. Virtuous leadership disappeared. Statecraft was reduced to a balancing act between competing interests. Rome developed a de-humanizing intellectual virus that undercut good governance and seemed to embrace confrontation over engagement. As St. Augustine observed, "It is a higher glory ... to stay war itself with a word, than to slay men with the sword, and to procure or maintain peace by peace, not by war."[16] Having rejected Augustine's advice, Roman leadership duped itself into thinking that global hegemony, the pursuit of pleasure, and personal grandeur brought peace and security.

Whenever power and the use of authoritarian tactics replace common-sense governance and virtuous leadership,[17] citizens ignore the calls to defend the nation and most people run for the hills. In this sense, the idea of Roman citizenship was critical to maintaining the unity and viability of the Roman Republic. Since imperial Rome overextended itself, it could not manage the influx of peoples. As Rome encountered North Africa, Iberia, the Middle East, and Northern Europe, it needed to make greater efforts to hold on to its identity and language, without which there is no real unifying element other than interesting cultural traits such as dress and cuisine — hardly sufficient to keep a people together. It would have been wise at the time for Rome to have reexamined its policies regarding the education and integration of noncitizens.[18]

The relative decline of Rome's native population through uncontrolled immigration was a challenge to old ways of thinking and governance. Social cohesiveness suffers when populations experience a crisis of identity. As a nation's wealth increases and birthrates decline, potentially unmanageable tensions tend to appear between the native population, new arrivals, and the poorer inhabitants within a territory. Rome failed to handle its population issues properly, thus generating otherwise avoidable clashes between different nations and peoples. Tensions are always heightened when new languages and wildly different ideologies overwhelm central authority. (It is in part for this reason that the European Union will eventually fail for tribe and nation, it seems increasingly apparent today, are more important to most peoples than foreign flag and artificial political union.)

Moreover, the Roman system of *latifundia* seemed to exacerbate problems of governance, encouraging the further concentration of power and privilege, and compounding the vulnerability of the defenseless and the poor. Christian social teaching was not as developed as it later became so the Church was hardly able to give useful guidance to Rome's leadership in matters of social justice at the time.[19]

Some Societal Issues

The breakdown of the traditional family and a rising ethos of radical individualism accelerated the demise of the Roman Empire. Daniel-Rops describes the situation in Rome as follows: "Men shirked marriage and its obligation.... [Slavery] provided him with bed companions who were more docile than any legal wife, and who, moreover, could be exchanged whenever he wanted! Abortion and the 'exposing' of new-born babies (in other words, their wanton abandonment) acquired terrifying proportions.... As for divorce, it became so commonplace that no one attempted to provide reasonable justification for it any more: the simple desire for a change sufficed."[20] It is unclear whether the pagan Romans understood the consequences arising from the collapse of the family; it is, however, clear that the Christian Romans did, and their minority status and regular persecution didn't seem to prevent them from promoting the family, the basic building-block of society.

It would behoove moderns to take the appropriate measures needed to maintain the traditional family and to better understand its vital role in preserving the sanity and well-being of society. While historical records are not voluminous, we know that as the family unit came under so much pressure that its very health and survival were in question, social cohesiveness and solidarity in Rome suffered – a state of affairs reminiscent of what we are seeing today in the Anglo-Saxon world and the European Union. In the early days of the Roman Empire, unfortunately, the Judeo-Christian vision of the family had not yet penetrated the consciousness of the citizenry, despite the efforts of the Church Fathers and informed laypersons at the time.

To arrest the decline of Rome, Christian scholars tried to reverse societal decay through education, philosophy, and the spread of the Gospel messages. This passage from Saint John remains as valid today as the day it was written:

Beloved, let us love one another, for love is from God, and whoever loves has been born of God and knows God. Anyone who does not love does not know God, because God is love. In this the love of God was made manifest among us, that God sent his only Son into the world, so that we might live through him. In this is love, not that we have loved God but that he loved us and sent his Son to be the propitiation for our sins. Beloved, if God so loved us, we also ought to love one another. No one has ever seen God; if we love one another, God abides in us and his love is perfected in us (1 John 4: 7-16).

Against the backdrop of a disintegrating Roman Empire, many Christian intellectuals emerged in the first eight centuries after the birth of Christ and made a profound impact on the intellectual history of the world. They warned their fellow citizens of the socio-political dangers facing Rome and Constantinople in light of poor governance, ignorance of God, and an inability to discern the divine in the ordinary. These academics pointed out that healthy moral reasoning requires the acknowledgement of transcendent rather than self-referencing principles, and tried to develop an accurate understanding of human nature in light of reality. They recognized that a moral ethics of "all for themselves" leads to societal chaos and irremediable personal suffering, as history and experience have repeatedly shown. In such situations, governance is reduced to manipulation of information and the use of power at the expense of human dignity and freedom. St. Paul, a precursor of the Church Fathers, put the matter succinctly: "For you were called for freedom, brothers. But do not use this freedom as an opportunity for the flesh; rather, serve one another through love."[21]

Scholarship

Christian scholars during the Roman Empire are referred to by various names including "the Apologists," "the Patristic Fathers," "Defenders of the Faith," and the "Church Fathers." Their insights shed light on the reasonableness of the Judeo-Christian worldview compared with competing worldviews. They tried to elaborate on the meaning of the dignity of the human person and laid out ideas that helped later scholars explain the significance of genuine human development and the link between good governance and virtuous leadership, above and beyond that understood by the Ancients. Most importantly, they embraced philosophy and saw it as a means to reinforce revelation.

It was the Church Fathers more than any other group of scholars who developed the notion that culture meant much more than the orderly use of reason, the perpetuation of traditional customs, and socio-political stability. Unlike the Church Fathers, the Ancients didn't fully grasp that good governance (in moral ethics) and personal happiness rested on non-arbitrary first principles anchored in the knowledge of an omnipotent and loving God and the dignity of the human person in the first instance.

During the Greco-Roman period, the endeavors of learned men to formulate a true "science of morality" were largely conceptual and formal. While most of their initial attempts were mixed with religious mythologies, they drew out a core of human conceptions and reasoning that were common to all persons (always) because they were grounded in the transcendent. Humanity's understanding of moral ethics was fundamentally incomplete prior to Genesis and the New Testament, which are records (not literal) of God speaking to humanity through words. The Church Fathers, among others, took up the challenge of interpreting Holy Scripture against the backdrop of Hellenistic scholarship (which Islam does not do because Greek philosophy and moral reasoning are seen to threaten the dominant literal interpretation of the sources of Islamic revelation.).

The early Christian Fathers integrated this Greco-Roman scholarship into their apologetics and philosophy, always trying to avoid all forms of reductionism — the tendency to reduce the spiritual to the material — all while exposing the ideological errors of their day. Besides Aristotle and Plato, Christian academics gained much knowledge and wisdom from scholars such as Cicero and Virgil.[22]

In Virgil's *Aeneid* (19 BC), for example, the notion of *labor* (work) was viewed as good and seemed to be linked to prayer and contemplation. *Pietas* meant humility before the gods, a love of one's country, and a sense of duty, qualities that are in sharp contrast to philosophies encouraging self-absorption, infidelity to commitments, and an adulation of "success at all costs." *Factum* signified Rome's imperial destiny, the duty or mission "to bring peace to the world, to maintain the cause of order and justice and freedom, to withstand barbarism."[23] Those are good ideals, but when any nation's policies morph into an instrument that encourages narcissistic tendencies or is designed to bring about some kind of utopian world order to secure resources at the expense of others, it is time to reassess the meaning of life and governance. Augustine and others tried to enlighten Roman leadership into grasping that, while the goal of the earthly city is peace, fraternity, and justice, it is de-humanizing to use force or other unjust measures against the common good to realize those ideals.

The Church Fathers understood that cold reason alone was insufficient to satisfy a person's inherent desire for peace, truth, security, power, and love. As teachers, they addressed a myriad of questions that have concerned thinking men and women since the beginning of time. What did St. Paul (c. AD 5–67), for example, mean in his Letter to the Colossians when he said, "Here there is not Greek and Jew, circumcision and uncircumcision, barbarian, Scythian, slave, free; but Christ is all and in all"?[24] With such statements, was Christianity to be viewed as the mortal enemy of paganism, with its hierarchical structures and many gods? Considering scripture and the growing acceptance of Judeo-Christian ideas in Rome, time, suffering, life, truth, and death took on different meanings.

The Church Fathers

Christianity always seems to challenge the status quo because it is in the business of guiding people through life – it sets a high bar. To that end, it is common knowledge that the Early Church Fathers, from the 1st to the 8th century AD, made significant contributions to the history of thought and its development. While generally united in spirit, there were eight Church Fathers who exerted considerable influence on society at the time; four of whom came from the East and four from the West. The Syriac, Armenian, and Coptic (Eastern) scholars wrote in their respective tongues (and translated into Greek), while the Western Fathers wrote in Latin. Officially, there was no geographical demarcation between East and West until the 11th century, when the Christian Church experienced one of the most tumultuous events in its history, now referred to as the "Greek Schism" (1054).

Besides St. Irenaeus and Tertullian (160–220), distinguished Fathers included St. Ambrose (340–397), St. Jerome, St. Augustine, and St. Gregory the Great (540–604); the Eastern Fathers included St. Basil of Caesarea (330–379), St. Athanasius (296–373), St. Gregory of Nazianzus (329–390), and St. John Chrysostom (347–407). While the nature of the Church and salvation history were central to ecclesial studies at the time, these scholars scrutinized the human person and the universe in relation to the Creator, God, to better understand the meaning of existence. Considering both past and present, they tried to explain the meaning of life and death in light of the problems of contemporary society, and to defend the body of Judeo-Christian thought.

While searching for truth and for better ways to explain the mysteries of the universe and faith, the Church Fathers combined the acumen of the Ancients with the profundity of the earliest of Christian thinkers to produce new insights into education, linguistics, literature, communications, governance, philosophy, theology, and science. In the process, the Fathers never lost sight of St. Ignatius of Antioch's recommendation: "Christianity is not a matter of persuading people of particular ideas, but of inviting them to share in the greatness of Christ. So pray that I may never fall into the trap of impressing people with clever speech, but instead I may learn to speak with humility, desiring only to impress people with Christ himself."[25]

The writings and sermons of early scholars serve to highlight some of Christianity's contributions to good living. The Church Fathers knew that there was more to life than self-absorption, fun, and survival. They believed that to better understand humanity's place in the universe, they needed to come to terms with Scripture, nature, and tradition (with the help of science). True freedom always rests on a complete understanding of reality, both material and immaterial.

St. Justin Martyr

St. Justin Martyr (100–165), a layman and loyal Roman citizen, is considered the first Christian philosopher.[26] He argued convincingly that reason stood to gain from faith and faith from reason, an idea that Pope Benedict XVI develops further: "These two realities, *the Old Testament and Greek philosophy*, are like two paths that lead to Christ, to the Logos. This is why Greek philosophy cannot be opposed to Gospel truth, and Christians can draw from it confidently as from a good of their own."[27] Since St. Justin was a man in and of the world, he appealed to Roman law when unjustly attacked, using evidence and legal precedent to defend himself to demonstrate the inherent dignity and equality of all persons under the law and in the eyes of God. In his defense of innocent Christians during the persecutions, he demanded fairness and dignity for all in light of fundamental unchanging transcendental principles.

St. Justin's *Discourse to the Greeks* is a brief but insightful commentary on Hellenic customs, mythical gods, and lifestyle. He appeals to the underlying goodness of all Greeks and of anyone else willing to listen. While instructing them on the human virtues, in his final appeal before his execution (165), St. Justin invites the Greeks to be open to the Word of the one, uncreated God of the universe:

> Henceforth, ye Greeks, come and partake of incomparable wisdom, and be instructed by the Divine Word, and acquaint yourselves with the King immortal; and do not recognize those men as heroes who slaughter whole nations. For our own Ruler, the Divine Word, who even now constantly aids us, does not desire strength of body and beauty of feature, nor yet the high spirit of earth's nobility, but a pure soul,

fortified by holiness....[28]

St. Justin's words are expressed in the form of an invitation to the pagans, and to all men and women of good will, to come and see the goodness and reasonableness of God's message. It is not a declaration delivered to intimidate or to force acceptance, as is sometimes stupidly done from the pulpit. St. Justin expresses the centrality of personal freedom that is to be found in the Judeo-Christian message, an idea that began, over time, to make a positive impression on Roman jurists and academics.

One of Pope Benedict XVI's statements concerning St. Justin further reflects the work and insights of the Church Fathers and of early Christianity:

> Justin in particular, especially in his first Apology, mercilessly criticized the pagan religion and its myths, which he considered to be diabolically misleading on the path of truth.
>
> Philosophy, on the other hand, represented the privileged area of the encounter between paganism, Judaism and Christianity, precisely at the level of the criticism of pagan religion and its false myths. "Our philosophy ..." this is how another apologist, Bishop Melito of Sardis, a contemporary of Justin, came to define the new religion in a more explicit way (*Ap. Hist. Eccl.* 4, 26, 7).
>
> In fact, the pagan religion did not follow the ways of the Logos, but clung to myth, even if Greek philosophy recognized that mythology was devoid of consistency with the truth.
>
> Therefore, the decline of the pagan religion was inevitable: it was a logical consequence of the detachment of religion — reduced to an artificial collection of ceremonies, conventions and customs — from the truth of being.
>
> Justin, and with him other apologists, adopted the clear stance taken by the Christian faith for the God of the philosophers against the false gods of the pagan religion.
>
> It was the choice of the *truth* of being against the myth of *custom*. Several decades after Justin, Tertullian defined the same option of Christians with a lapidary sentence that still applies: "*Dominus noster Christus veritatem se, non consuetudinem, cognominavit* — Christ has said that he is truth not fashion" (*De Virgin.* Vel. 1, 1).
>
> It should be noted in this regard that the term *consuetu-*

do, used here by Tertullian in reference to the pagan religion, can be translated into modern languages with the expressions "cultural fashion" and "current fads."

In a time like ours, marked by relativism in the discussion on values and on religion — as well as in interreligious dialogue — this is a lesson that should not be forgotten.

To this end, I suggest to you once again — and thus I conclude — the last words of the mysterious old man whom Justin the Philosopher met on the seashore: "Pray that, above all things, the gates of light may be opened to you; for these things cannot be perceived or understood by all, but only by the man to whom God and his Christ have imparted wisdom (*Dial.* 7: 3).[29]

Genuine Pedagogy

Let us be clear that those who criticize Christian pedagogy are not always wrong. Over the centuries, some Christian educators have deployed overly enthusiastic, even draconian, methods to try to secure belief in God and allegiance to the Church. That approach to apologetics or catechesis is wrong, counterproductive, and ineffectual. If someone tries to defend such an approach, then it is fairly safe to say that that person should not be teaching, especially in today's environment. Apologists must get used to the risk of human freedom.

Judeo-Christian pedagogy must never "force-feed" instruction if it is to respect a person's humanity and dignity. The Wizards rightly lash out at such pedagogy. Casuistry, rules-based reasoning in moral ethics, is counterproductive as a means to foment genuine human development. Fortunately, St. Justin's teaching style was clear and insightful, and can serve as a model for teachers in the field of apologetics.

Ideas Make a Difference

It is true that many Judeo-Christian scholars over the centuries have held some erroneous positions on cosmology, e.g., thinking that the universe is eternal or that it exists in an unchanged and stable form; whereas the distinctiveness of the Judeo-Christian view of origins is creation *ex nihilo* – and has been, since the beginnings of the doctrine. Moreover, early Christian scholars accepted Aristotelian *apriorism* — a kind of supremacy of universals — which represented a fundamental error in human thought and epistemology for centuries. It is terribly important to realize, however, that this error did not arise because of their belief in God but from inexperience and an inability to test the speculative theories of the Ancients.[30] Moreover, this error was universally held — by religious, irreligious, and nonreligious — and is pre-Christian in its origins, a fact that some of the Wizards and anti-theists conveniently forget to mention in their diatribes against the Judeo-Christian worldview.[31]

St. Irenaeus of Lyon attempted to set out in a systematic manner the reasons for God's divine plan for humanity as revealed and partially explained in Sacred Scripture. He also grasped the reality of suffering in the world, and understood that this reality, although seemingly incongruent with God's goodness and omnipotence, does not mean that God does not exist.[32]

Judeo-Christian apologetics stresses that God and humans, the crown of creation, must *work together* to find answers to the most interesting and disturbing questions about life, the cosmos, and existence. St. Irenaeus recognized that God and work are always in harmony. He would defend the proposition that there can be no contradiction between the eternal law, the natural moral law, and the laws of nature.

St. Clement of Alexandria (c. 150–215) was one of the first Church Fathers to Hellenize Judeo-Christian ideas. Moreover, he rejected magic, materialism, moralism, Gnosticism, and fairytales. For that reason, as Daniel-Rops says, "[Philosophy] is not Stoicism, nor Platonism, nor Epicureanism, nor Aristotelianism, but the sum total of all the good things said by these schools in the teaching of justice and truth."[33] St. Clement's manuscript, the *Paedogogus* (182–202), is an early attempt to better understand moral ethics in light of the New Testament and natural law, Platonic universals, and Aristotelian ethics. It served in some ways as a guide to moral living. The book is instructive and far-reaching and offers deep insights to anyone who wishes to delve into early Judeo-Christian apologetics.

Origen (185–254), a pupil of St. Clement of Alexandria, was not only a theologian but a philosopher, exegete, moralist, jurist, and lyric poet of the highest caliber. When he wrote *On First Principles*[34] in the early third century, despite some of his apparently unorthodox theological positions, he was perhaps the first theologian to present a comprehensive theory of humanity, God, and the world. He emphasized that a vulgar and uninformed faith was insufficient for a thinking person and, particularly, for a Christian. Greek philosophy, he urged, had to serve as a medium through which to better understand the universe. At the same time, Scripture had to serve as an essential tool to go beyond a one-dimensional rationalist interpretation of the world. He defended the harmony between faith and reason, which is consistent with the Judeo-Christian view concerning the sources and nature of knowledge.

The aim of Christian education is to teach men and women to use their freedom in accordance with right reason. Origen saw theology "as a religious science in its own right, founded upon articles of faith but drawing from the intellectual sphere conclusions that would enable souls in search of God to reach intellectual understanding through Christ."[35] He would have scolded any religious leader or teacher who invoked the "God of the Gaps" argument to explain the cause of some phenomenon or occurrence before all the evidence was in. He surely would have run circles around Christopher Hitchens in debate on questions concerning the universality of moral ethics and the existence of God. Origen would have made clear that ideas and beliefs are not just products of the brain but rather the primary means of moral reasoning, and, with the help of grace, to identify one's will with the will of God, i.e., to discover the will of God in this life. For this reason, the *"homo est animal rationale"* is a poor descriptor for the human person.

Tertullian, the son of a pagan centurion, embraced the Judeo-Christian worldview, and subsequently Christianity, when he was approximately 30 years old. Despite his brilliance and passion for knowledge, he emphasized a religious romanticism that led him to envisage a world with perfect souls and ascetic heroes. His teachings have been the subject of debate for centuries. For Tertullian, asceticism, or voluntary self-denial that possesses a redemptive value, is central to Christian life and does not mean isolation from family, friends, or the workplace.

As a scholar, Tertullian was a founder of non-speculative theology. In his major work, *Apology,* he defended Christianity with arguments in the face of attacks from 2nd- and 3rd-century anti-theists and polytheists. He didn't just throw dogma at his opponents, but explained to the best of his abilities the meaning of the truths of life. Broadly speaking, *Apology* is a reasonable response to those who claimed that (a) Judeo-Christianity is superstition that engages in treachery and inhuman acts of debauchery, and (b) Christianity is disloyal and contemptuous towards the state and unpatriotic in its sentiments. Today's skeptics and pantheists might learn something from one of his writings.

St. Cyprian (200–258), a martyr, was bishop of Carthage during one of the many persecutions of Christians before the fourth century. In response to controversies within the Church, he wrote *De Unitate Ecclesiae,* which underscored the essential role of the Church in the world. In *Ad Donatum,* he spoke about the dignity of the human person and lambasted the gladiatorial fighting of the day as senseless and undignified, not dissimilar to "cage fighting" today.

St. John Chrysostom, bishop of Constantinople, preached eloquently and wrote *Against Those Who Oppose the Monastic Life, On the Incomprehensible Nature of God,* and *On the Priesthood.* He highlighted the responsibility that the privileged classes in society have before their neighbors. He often chided the upper classes for their self-centeredness and indifference to others.

Because of his communication skills, Chrysostom, if alive today, would do well to debate the modern-day proponents of the "culture of death." Chrysostom knew that unselfish charity and the effort to develop a personal relationship with God (a nonsensical idea to anti-theists) was a *sine qua non* for right living. Moreover, he preached that forgiveness and reconciliation should feature prominently in any human endeavor.

For Chrysostom, there was nothing more important than the education of children.

> Seek not how [a child] shall enjoy a long life here, but how he shall enjoy a boundless and endless life hereafter. Give him the great things, not the little things. Hear what Paul saith, "Bring them up in the chastening and admonition of the Lord"; study not to make him an orator, but train him up to be a philosopher. In the want of the one there will be no harm whatever; in the absence of the other, all the rhetoric in the world will be of no advantage. Tempers are wanted, not talking; character, not cleverness; deeds, not words. These gain a man the kingdom. These confer what are benefits indeed. Whet not his tongue, but cleanse his soul. I do not say this to prevent your teaching him these things, but to prevent your attending to them exclusively. Do not imagine that the monk alone stands in need of these lessons from Scripture. Of all others, the children just about to enter into the world specially need them. For just in the same way as the man who is always at anchor in harbor, is not the man who requires his ship to be fitted out and who needs a pilot and a crew, but he who is always out at sea; so is it with the man of the world and the monk. The one is entered as it were into a waveless harbor, and lives an untroubled life, and far removed from every storm; whilst the other is ever on the ocean, and lives out at sea in the very midst of the ocean, battling with billows without number."[36]

Scholars such as Chrysostom laid the groundwork for the educational approaches that built Christendom and its great universities such as Oxford, Cambridge, Bologna, Paris, and Salamanca.

St. Augustine of Hippo

St. Augustine was the first philosopher-theologian to produce a doctrinal synthesis of the moral message of the New Testament. He also submitted revelation to systematic philosophical thought and enquiry – which any literalist theological tradition, whether Christian or Muslim, does not do. Without reducing revelation to a philosophy of life, he provided systematic structure to the great moral questions facing the men and women of his time. St. Augustine is the unspoken nemesis of most anti-theists because of his ability to explain with logic, good humor, and charity the significance of life, aesthetics, governance, and suffering, among much else.

Typical of early Christian scholarship, Augustine provides innumerable insights about the compatibility of Scripture and science and the responsibility of Christians to speak the truth about nature and the universe:

> On interpreting the mind of the sacred writer, Christians should not talk nonsense to unbelievers....
>
> Usually, even a non-Christian knows something about the earth, the heavens, and the other of this world, about the motions and orbits of the stars and even their size and relative positions, about the predictable eclipses of the sun and moon, the cycles of the years and the seasons, about the kinds of animals, shrubs, stones and so forth, and this knowledge he holds to as being from reason and experience
>
> Now, it is a disgraceful and dangerous thing for an unbeliever to hear a Christian ... talking nonsense on these topics; and we should take all means to prevent such an embarrassing situation, in which people show up vast ignorance in a Christian and laugh it to scorn.
>
> The shame is not so much that an ignorant individual is derided, but rather that people outside the faith think our sacred writers held such opinions.... If they find a Christian mistaken in a field which they themselves know well and hear him maintaining his foolish opinions about our books, how are they going to believe those books in matters concerning the resurrection of the dead, the hope of eternal life, and the kingdom of heaven, when they think their pages are full of falsehoods on facts which they themselves have learnt from experience and the light of reason?"[37]

Augustine also recognized, as so many others, the folly of invoking the

"God of the Gaps." If only the anti-theists would take note.

Augustine worked to build a lasting library of great ideas which could stand on their own as well as defend revelation. From the Christian perspective, people's weaknesses represented opportunities to get to know themselves in order to love God and serve others better. His main books, *The City of God*, *The Confessions*, *On the Trinity*, and *On Free Choice of the Will*, are remarkable in their ability to convey the beauty of life, the purpose of freedom, and the grandeur and love of God towards humanity. Those Wizards who have not yet read these books carefully, especially *The Confessions*, should do so rather than dismiss them as colorful examples of impractical romantic poetry. Augustine's writings reflect his concern that people not miss out on the secret of Christianity, i.e., that God loves each and every person beyond measure, despite the mysterious existence of suffering, uncertainty, and dependence.

The Confessions is his personal story about his conversion from being a dyed-in-the-wool skeptic. Daniel-Rops writes that *The Confessions* "is one of five or six great works which will, one hopes, survive all the disasters of history in order to show future generations what sort of man Western civilization — now threatened with disappearance — could produce at its best; from the literary standpoint alone, it is a masterpiece which can be imitated, but not surpassed, and from the Christian point of view it is one of the works in which mystical enthusiasm reaches its highest peaks."[38]

The City of God is essentially a call to hope in the face of great loss and dejection. It embodies a philosophy of history and a theory of the state and society that has served as a cornerstone of political thought for centuries. It represents a commentary on the relationship between the spiritual and temporal orders and reflects the idea that to be a Roman meant more than military victories, and bread and circuses. *The City of God* is a guide to the art of living in times of trouble as well as a book of consolation.

As the philosopher of freedom, St. Augustine believed that a person, with the help of reason, God, and the Church, could be virtuous and strive for the "[supreme good] by reference to which all our actions are directed. It is the good we seek for itself and not because of something else and, once it is attained, we seek nothing further to make us happy. This, in fact, is why we call it our end, because other things are desired on account of this *summum bonum*, while it is desired purely for itself."[439] This idea helped build Christendom's universities and centers of excellence. He further underscored a person's call to holiness and service, another climactic notion at the core of Christian self-discovery and personal liberation.

Augustine's political philosophy hinged on a concept of justice that recognized the fundamental rights of the human person, the existence of a natural

law, and the possibility of moral reasoning. Citizens had the right to oppose
unjust laws or any authority that abused power; he saw that in conscience there
is no need to obey unjust laws. "We are not to reckon as right such human laws
as are iniquitous, since even unjust law-givers themselves call a right (*ius*) only
what derives from the fountainhead of justice (*iustitia*) and brand as false the
wrong-headed opinion of those who keep saying that a right (*ius*) is whatever is
advantageous (*utile*) to the one in power."[40] No law, act, or privilege is above the
inalienable "rights of man," which arise from the fact that the human person
is created in the image and likeness of God.

Unlike the Athenian historian Thucydides (460–395 BC), who was an early
Darwinian and Hobbesian without knowing it, Augustine rejected the view
that human nature was corrupted beyond repair. Moreover, Augustine believed that war must be a last resort and "justified only by the injustice of an
aggressor; and that injustice ought to be a source of grief to any good man,
because it is human injustice."[41]

St. Athanasius

St. Athanasius, a gifted scholar, philosopher, and man of letters, emphasized in his writings in the 4th century that people on their own are incapable
of achieving spiritual greatness and peace of mind.[42] The distinguishing characteristic of Christianity is that Jesus Christ was not only a prophet but claimed
to be God. That claim differentiates Christianity from all other religions. Moreover, and critically important to the entire Judeo-Christian dialogue with the
world, there is overwhelming evidence for the historicity of the central events
of the Bible, particularly the claim of the Resurrection of Jesus Christ, and the
peaceful martyrdom of His followers.[43] Even the anti-theists have a hard time
with the evidence for the Resurrection when it is presented convincingly.[44]

Scholars like Athanasius try to convey the idea that the life of Jesus Christ
in the Gospels sought to encourage men and women to see that living a life of
personal sanctity is an achievable goal. By living the Biblical message, people,
with the grace of God, can attain a certain peace of mind in this world without
falling for the traps of utopianism, voluntarism, hedonism, or whatever other
de-humanizing concepts anti-theists throughout history have proposed.

St. Athanasius can serve as an example to those who want to take scholarship seriously. He was open to truth and was a man of principle who did
not back down in the face of evidence, discrimination, or persecution. He
put up a fight against irrational philosophies, took on emperors, and defended
the Judeo-Christian worldview with rational arguments and evidence despite
repeated threats. He promoted policies that pushed Byzantine rulers to respect
the independence of religious authorities and religious freedom. In today's

world, besides a need for leadership, there must be a reasoned opposition to unjust, arbitrary, and de-humanizing behavior as a first step to return society to a semblance of unity and sanity. This process must begin with education and a return of God to the public square.

Monasticism and the Spread of Christianity

Because Christianity is a religion of hope and peace, and fully embraces freedom and independent moral reasoning, it projects optimism. It is also a great treasure that must be shared with others — freely and without coercion, of course. Christianity should never fall into the trap of imposing doctrine, dogma, or codes of conduct, because to do so would be unjust. It can never be a static set of rules and principles that must be observed for salvation. Such an approach is categorically wrong. The Church Fathers recognized the importance of freedom in matters of the soul and tried their best to share with as many people as possible the dynamic vision and joy of the Gospels.

To that end, scores of dedicated missionary-scholars and monks spread the Judeo-Christian message through their personal example and the establishment of schools and centers to carry out their mission of proclaiming the Good News. They focused on extending the Judeo-Christian worldview to peoples throughout the world. There were different approaches to the task of evangelization.

St. Anthony the Great (c. 251–356) was one of the first monks who entirely withdrew from civilization. He settled down in the Egyptian desert to pray for his entire life. He embraced a way of life that few people are called to imitate or follow. His life does show, however, the connection between the tangible and intangible, and the importance of prayer and witness for evangelization. He is considered the father of Christian monasticism. His influence was pivotal in formulating the idea that man might participate in the redemption of the world through asceticism, isolation, and prayer.

St. John Cassian (c. 360–435) brought the Eastern monastic tradition to the Western Roman Empire, where he established a monastery in southern France in the 5th century. Educated in both Greek and Latin, he wrote the *Institutes* and the *Conferences,* which provide first-hand insights into 5th-century monasticism and into educational methods for youth. He influenced both St. Benedict (480–547), founder of the Benedictine Order, and St. Ignatius Loyola (1491–1556), founder of the Society of Jesus, two religious orders that have had a colossal influence on education throughout the world. His belief in the centrality of Christianity helped spread the need for education and build the foundations for universities, art, architecture, and hospitals. Holy men such as St. Benedict, who built Monte Cassino (c. 529) in present-day Italy and devised the Rule of St. Benedict, which is still observed today, did much to keep classical learning alive.

St. Gregory the Great, another distinguished scholar, led the formidable effort to evangelize the non-Christian peoples of Europe. He worked with the Lombards, the Anglo-Saxons, and the French in the late 6th century. St. Gregory extended education and monasticism throughout Europe, but he also encouraged the development of the liturgy, iconography, and sacred music, the latter known as Gregorian chant. He also produced volumes of written material, including letters, sermons, and dialogues that are worthy of the attention of modern-day scholars and educated people.

From what is now England, missionaries evangelized — which should always mean "educated" and not "indoctrinated" — the peoples of the Low Countries, Germany, and many other non-Christian territories in Europe. St. Boniface (672–754), an Anglo-Saxon monk, further extended the Judeo-Christian vision — God, the dignity of the human person, and the ideals of service, equality, liberty, and brotherhood — among the Franks and elsewhere. The goal was to bring about the Kingdom of God and genuine human development even in a world awash in pagan rituals and false gods. The missionaries tried explaining to the tribes in Europe the difference between (a) the personal God of the Bible and their created gods, and (b) charity and mercy, on the one hand, and revenge and naturalistic altruism, on the other.

Surprising Consequences

To the surprise of many anti-theists, saintly men and women in the first millennium put in place the philosophical foundations for today's universities, hospitals, and centers of care. With the establishment of monasteries came increased trade, schools, clinics, and meeting places for a variety of community activities. Towns sprang up, commerce developed, and public services emerged thanks in large part to monasteries. The Judeo-Christian mindset spread not only because of the monks' interest in preserving ancient books, manuscripts, art, and sculpture but because such a mindset made sense and produced results in everyday life.

The monks preserved and promoted education in the secular courts of Europe after the collapse of the Roman Empire.[45] Besides philosophy and theology, they taught biology, astronomy, medicine, and physics in line with Greco-Roman approaches to scholarship.

The great universities of Europe could not have been built by lazy and closed-minded monks who were (according to some of the Wizards) opposed to science and progress. The monks believed in the intelligibility of the universe and in right reason, and were taught to defend their faith with cogent arguments based on the evidence. As John Henry Cardinal Newman (1802–1890) says so eloquently, "We can believe what we choose. We are answerable for what we choose to believe."[46] When anti-theists take a swipe at Christianity and its deep wealth of scholarship, they reveal their own prejudices and blind acceptance of pre-established paradigms, and demonstrate minimal knowledge of history.

Eastern Monks and Expansion

The Eastern monks of the Byzantine Empire, with Constantinople as its center, were as scholarly and energetic as their counterparts in the West. Generally, the Eastern monks put greater accent on mysticism and the faculty of the will than on logic and reason. Beauty, the natural world, personal relationships, and communication were central elements of Eastern education. In the fourth century, St. Basil of Caesarea, like St. Benedict in the West, drafted monastic rules for men who spoke Greek.

Eastern monks between the 6th and 10th centuries not only preserved the ancient learning and writings of the Greek Fathers, but travelled throughout present-day Serbia, Bulgaria, Ukraine, and (Western) Russia to open schools and spread the message of the Gospel. St. Maximus the Confessor (580–662), who lived in Constantinople and died in (present-day) Georgia, serves as one example of the contrast between pagan and Christian views: "Food is not evil, but gluttony is. Childbearing is not evil, but fornication is. Money is not evil, but avarice is. Glory is not evil, but vainglory is. Indeed, there is no evil in existing things, but only in their misuse."[47] For some odd reason, most modern anti-theists can't stand the advice of writers such as St. Maximus, and seem to do everything in their power to discredit their humble messages.

The Enlightenment Trap aims to allure people into thinking that the monks were losers who set back the development of humanity because of their religious beliefs and distain for learning. Wizards who believe that should think again, for science will not prove that God does not exist. Science and Genesis are on the same page regarding the origin of the universe and other cosmological realities.[48]

Regarding the synergies between heaven and earth, Hieromartyr Onuphry Gagaluk, a 19th-century Russian Orthodox monk, described the insights of some of the early monks as follows: "The acquisition of holiness is not the exclusive business of monks, as certain people think. People with families are also called to holiness, as are those in all kinds of professions, who live in the world, since the commandment about perfection and holiness is given not only to monks, but to all people."[49] That is quite a statement, and right in line with Church tradition up to the present day.

By the 7th century, Christian missionaries had also carried the Judeo-Christian vision to the Caucasus and to the Central Asian countries of Uzbekistan, Turkmenistan, Kyrgyzstan, and Kazakhstan along the Silk Road. The missionary work from the Altai Mountains to the Caspian Sea predates Mohammed (late 7th century) and undermines the present-day impression among most peoples of Central Asia that they have always been Muslim. This is a significant historical fact that has been largely ignored.

And so, at the core of the Christian message is that God, who is love and died out of love for each human being, can be approached in prayer and in one's work. Such ideas are absolutely alien to Islam.

Islam

Since the 7th century, Islam has been a powerful and influential force with a history of expansion. At the theological and philosophical levels, it has opposed the concepts of equality, brotherhood, and liberty as understood by the Judeo-Christian tradition. St. John of Damascus (c. 676–749), a Father and Doctor of the Church from Syria, recognized the dangers embedded in radical militant strains of Islam, which appeared on the world scene during his lifetime.[50] He warned against its aggressive elements, especially in relation to women, non-Muslims, and its methods of punishment for transgressions against the laws of God (Sharia Law) as interpreted by Muslim theologians. There has been massive unrest along the borders of the Islamic world with the rest of the world ever since the 7th century. In Islamic theology, the final peace on earth comes when everyone is Muslim, and, this objective, in part, explains its apostolic zeal and expansionist mentality; those who are not Muslim, the historical record confirms, are either tolerated or converted.

As militant Islam seems to be gaining followers in the 21st century, and as Europe continues to ignore its Judeo-Christian heritage, European civilization may be insufficiently prepared intellectually to defend itself and, therefore, may implode from its own self-destructive suicidal tendencies. In 1938, not unlike St. John of Damascus twelve centuries earlier, the English historian Hilaire Belloc (1870–1953) warned his readers, "Millions of modern people ... have forgotten all about Islam. They never come in contact with it. They take for granted that it is decaying, and that, anyway, it is just a foreign religion which will not concern them. It is, as a fact, the most formidable and persistent enemy which our civilization has had, and may at any moment become as large a menace in the future as it has been in the past.... It has always seemed to me possible, and even probable, that there would be a resurrection of Islam and that our sons and grandsons would see the renewal of that tremendous struggle between the Christian culture and what has been for more than a thousand years its greatest opponent."[51] Today, scholars are beginning to take seriously Belloc's words. It seems probable that Europe, by continuing to imbue the ideas of anti-theists and their ideological confreres, the radical multiculturalists will not stand much of a chance against a resurgent Islam and the demands of Sharia law.

Final Observations

Open-minded people need to see through the biased propaganda of some of the Wizards of the Enlightenment who also tend to be aggressive anti-theists, and come to appreciate the fine work and wise counsel of Christianity through the ages. Why not take an interest in the early Christian scholars and study them in order to understand their impact and legacy? They were the forerunners of the great ages of innovation and discovery. Modern society can learn something from the monks. Maybe they can provide a few insights to prevent us from falling irretrievably into the quagmire of bad ideas, as the Romans did (and so many others throughout history).

Today's scholars need to figure out how to communicate the reasonableness and brilliance of the Judeo-Christian worldview to ordinary and not so ordinary people — as John Lennox has[52] — to deflate the factual balderdash and anti-Judeo-Christian mania of the most aggressive anti-theists.

The Church Fathers struggled to explain the mysteries hidden within reality so that humanity — one person at a time — would come to see the reasonableness and hope that the Judeo-Christian vision offers. They attempted to explain the purpose of life, make clear the meaning of truth, and live virtue despite their own failings. They preached the need for personal sanctity in the face of materialism, scheming, and self-abortive narcissism. The Fathers lived in the real world and worked to uncover the secrets of life, confident that God intended human beings to serve others rather than to be served. They proclaimed that faith, when grounded, enlightens; and they never failed to see the link between genuine human development and progress and the Judeo-Christian worldview.[53]

Are not most of the teachings of the early Church Fathers relevant today? People should reflect on the proposition that genuine development depends on the "amount" of love one puts into finding God *in this life* at work, at home, or in the laboratory, and while looking into a microscope or telescope; indeed, the material world reflects that profound love that God has for creation. Despite what most anti-theists say, God, consciousness, and the cosmos are *not* one and the same substance, because God is outside space and time. That is what the Church Fathers understood and believed.

Early Christian scholars preserved, developed, and transmitted the Judeo-Christian worldview by combining the wisdom of the Ancients and the Gospel into a potent and credible message. They understood that perfect equality, freedom, and brotherhood were possible only in the next life; in this life, it was necessary to strive for them and to be virtuous and charitable towards one's neighbor and God, the secret for peace of mind. They taught that ultimate justice comes only in the next life, something which the anti-theists do not offer because there is nothing after death. They intuitively sensed that life was not just a collection of meaningless data points over time in a (Darwinian) game of survival or in a self-defeating (Kantian) world of subjectivism or in a terrifying (Hobbesian) circle of shifting alliances built around intrinsically evil human beings in need of a God-like master, the state. Nor did they use theology to strip religion of intelligibility and undermine human creativity and freedom as an excuse to uphold the omnipotence of God as Muslim theologians have done over the ages. The Church Fathers understood that morality was not the product of reason or logic alone; but it had to be consistent with reason. For them, the existence of a moral ethic (beyond time, space, and constantly shifting situations) and a spirit of service were the keys to genuine human development.

The Church Fathers' vision contrasts with that of the Wizards. Malcolm Muggeridge reminds us of Ambrose and Augustine when he summed up much of the thinking of the anti-theists after being an atheist himself for half a lifetime. "Thus did Western Man decide to abolish himself, creating his own boredom out of his own affluence, his own vulnerability out of his own strength, his own impotence out of his own erotomania, himself blowing the trumpet that brought the walls of his own city tumbling down, and having convinced himself that he was too numerous, labored with pill and scalpel and syringe to make himself fewer. Until at last, having educated himself into imbecility, and polluted and drugged himself into stupefaction, he keeled over — a weary, battered old brontosaurus — and became extinct."[54]

The early Judeo-Christian men of letters did not bring down the Roman Empire or plunge the ancient world into the depths of intellectual gloom and psychological depravity. Men such as Clement of Alexandria, Origen, and Cyril of Jerusalem (c. 313–386) were razor-sharp intellectuals who, with common sense and humility, shed light on the meaning of human nature and the purpose of life. They worked to bridge the disconnect between the world of fiction and the world of facts. Their hope was a product of a confidence anchored in the knowledge that the world *had* to make sense and that God, who is good, had given things a purpose. They intuitively knew that genuine human development was much more than material progress; it was mainly the product of Christian service, smarts, and daring which aimed to improve the living conditions and enjoyment of people on Earth in ways consistent with the nature of a human person.

It may be helpful for the Wizards to reflect on an exchange St. Augustine is said to have had with a child on a beach in North Africa. St. Augustine asked the child, "What are you doing?" The young boy answered, "I'm going to pour the ocean into this hole." "But that is impossible." said Augustine. "The whole ocean will not fit into the hole you have made." In response, the boy, knowing that Augustine himself was trying to figure out the attributes of God, responded, "You cannot fit the attributes of the one uncreated God into your tiny little brain." That exchange made St. Augustine think.

Have the Wizards fallen into the Enlightenment Trap without even knowing it?[55] They seem to believe that they will be able to figure out most, if not all, the problems in the universe with science and mathematics. Sadly, mathematics cannot solve the equation that explains the meaning of "everything" because mathematics cannot explain love or penetrate the spiritual. Why is it that Wizards do not see that Judeo-Christian selfless charity and purpose are beyond the reach of the explanatory powers of mathematics and logic, and, indeed, have a "logic" of their own? Augustine and Muggeridge knew better, and both were skeptics. Christianity, properly understood, is not an enemy of reason; rather it breathes life into reason and science and exposes the interior truths locked "within matter."

The Church Fathers knew that the Biblical message harmonizes with a person's innate tendency to behave in accordance with the natural moral law. They struggled to get the word out that selfless service and hard work for the sake of others (something much more than mere altruism) are more appropriate standards by which to measure genuine human development than government statistics, election results or opinions of the chattering classes. They knew, as most people deep down know, that the age-old utopian promises of the pagans and rationalists lead only to temporary fixes followed by misery and self-destructive doubt.

Contrary to the efforts of the Fathers, and by way of prediction, if the Ten Commandments and the teachings of early Christian scholars are expunged from the public square, despite some remaining pockets of sanity in society, it is highly likely that today's anti-theist ideological cultural elites and multiculturalists will have won a temporary victory over truth, reason, and stability.

Despite Emperor Constantine's official recognition of Christianity in the 4th century, the Church Fathers were not able to arrest the fall of the Roman Empire. They did, however, save and transmit its intellectual and cultural heritage. Fyodr Dostoyevsky, through his art, sought to induce more people to recognize the Judeo-Christian worldview and the wisdom contained in the New

Testament. Consider these words from his *The Brothers Karamazov:* "Above all, don't lie to yourself. The man who lies to himself and listens to his own lie comes to a point that he cannot distinguish the truth within him, or around him, and so loses all respect for himself and for others. And having no respect he ceases to love."[56]

By stirring the Judeo-Christian memory, there is a chance that present-day scholars will reencounter the wisdom of the Church Fathers and turn around what appears to be the collapse of the formerly pan-European Judeo-Christian civilization. The fall of Rome should serve as an example. "As each one has received a gift, use it to serve one another as good stewards of God's varied grace,"[57] for that is the key to genuine human development. There is an urgent need for a big dose of personal sanctity in the middle of the world as advanced by the Church Fathers and the early monks. Personal sanctity must be lived out day-in and day-out because world crises stem from a lack of personal sanctity and a neglect of our Judeo-Christian roots.

---

1.   See Arnold Toynbee, Henri Daniel-Rops, Pitirim Sorokin, Christopher Dawson, and Frederick Copleston for further reading.

2.   Throughout this book, I try to be careful to distinguish between practical "atheists," who can be as kind and thoughtful as anyone else, and radical "know-it-all" and belligerent anti-theists.

3.   St. Augustine, *The Confessions of St. Augustine* (New York: International Collectors Library, n.d.); p. 243 (https://archive.org/stream/confessionsofsta00augu#page/n5/mode/2up/search/tomorrow). In another translation, "For you [God] are infinite and never change. In you, 'today' never comes to an end; and yet our 'today' does come to an end in you, because time, as well as everything else, exists in you. If it did not, it would have no means of passing. And since your years never come to an end, for they are simply 'today' ... you yourself are eternally the same. In your 'today' you will make all that is to exist tomorrow and thereafter, and in your 'today' you have made all that existed yesterday and forever before."

4.   John 8:23 (http://www.usccb.org/bible/john/8).

5.   St. John Paul II (pope), *Sources of Renewal: The Implementation of Vatican II* (New York: Harper and Row, 1980).

6.   St. John Paul II (pope), "Subjectivity and the Irreducible in the Human Being," in Theresa Sandok, OSM, ed., *Karol Wojtyla, Person and Community — Selected Essays* (New York: Peter Lang, 1993). A brief discussion of this book by James Schall is available from *The American Journal of Jurisprudence* 39:1 (1994) (https://academic.oup.com/ajj/article/39/1/499/120905).

7.   Most Wizards cannot seem to figure out that they are as much Biblical literalists (for they always seem to interpret the Bible literally) as the Biblical literalists themselves (who mostly do not). They do not seem to understand that God is a friend of science and that the order and predictability of the universe depend on God, since change is not indepen-

dent of God. Laws just don't pop up out of thin air.

8.   See Edward Gibbon, *The Decline and Fall of the Roman Empire*.

9.   Gibbon considers the period AD 96–192, the Age of the Antonines, as the high point of human history when he says, "If a man were called upon to fix the period in the history of the world during which the condition of the human race was most happy and prosperous, he would, without hesitation, name that which elapsed from the death of Domitian to the accession of Commodus. The vast extent of the Roman Empire was governed by absolute power, under the guidance of virtue and wisdom" (Gibbon, vol. 1, chapter 3) (https://archive.org/stream/historyofdeclinex01gibb#page/96/mode/2up/search/domitian). Roman imperial dynasties numbered seven during the Age of the Antonines, starting with Nerva (AD 96–98) and ending with Commodus (AD 180–92). Gibbon seems to overlook the successive and regular persecution of Christians during the period, including exile and executions. He also seems to admire Machiavelli, believes in the inexorable forward march of progress, and reflects the anti-Christian sentiments of many English historians after the Glorious Revolution of 1688 through the 19th century. The term "Whig History," which is drenched in radical Enlightenment optimism, is often used to describe forward-looking and wishful-thinking historiography.

10.   Arnold J. Toynbee, *A Study of History*, abr. by D.G. Somervell (New York: Oxford University Press, 1987); p. 261.

11.   Pitirim Sorokin, *The Crisis of Our Age* (New York: E.P. Dutton, 1941).

12.   Christopher Dawson, *Religion and the Rise of Western Culture: The Classic Study of Medieval Civilization* (New York: Image Books, 1950); p. 86.

13.   Frederick Copleston, *The History of Philosophy* (1956).

14.   Henri Daniel-Rops, *History of the Church of Christ*, vol. 1, *The Church of the Apostles and Martyrs* (London: J.M. Dent & Sons Ltd, 1960); p. 130.

15.   Demetrius B. Zema, "Foreword" to Augustine, *The City of God* (Washington, D.C.: Catholic University of America Press, 1962); p. xcviii.

16.   St. Augustine, Letter 229 (AD 429).

17.   For an excellent discussion on this topic, see Alexandre Havard, *Virtuous Leadership* (New York: Scepter, 2007).

18.   The pace of uncontrolled immigration into ancient Rome after the 4th century was not dissimilar to what is happening today in the territories of the United Kingdom, France, Germany, and Russia. Unchecked immigration — far beyond the question of legitimate documented migration — unnecessarily dilutes the collective memory of a nation and is a formula for social disorder on a massive scale. If Western Europe has any chance of remaining unified, it seems imperative that the rate of immigration be managed in ways to absorb intelligently the millions of immigrants.

19.   See Bl. Paul VI (pope), *Populorum Progressio* (*On the Development of Peoples*, 1967); Leo XIII (pope), *Rerum Novarum* (*On Labor and Capital*, 1891); St. John XXIII (pope), *Pacem in Terris* (*Peace on Earth*, 1963); Benedict XVI (pope), *Caritas in Veritate* (*In Charity and Truth*, 2009); and Francis (pope), *Lumen Fidei* (*The Light of the Faith*, 2013).

20.   Henri Daniel-Rops, *History of the Church*, vol. 1, p.129.

21.   Galatians 5:13 (http://www.usccb.org/bible/galatians/5).

22.   T.S. Eliot, *On Poetry and Poets* (New York: Farrar, Straus & Cudahy, 1957); pp. 135-48. For a penetrating study of the relationship between religion, politics, and economics see

T.S. Eliot, *Christianity and Culture: The Idea of a Christian Society* AND *Notes towards the Definition of Culture* (San Diego: Harcourt Brace Jovanovich, Publishers, 1976).

23.   Russell Kirk, *The Roots of American Order*, 3rd ed. (Washington, D.C: Regnery Gateway, 1991); p. 116.

24.   Colossians 3:1 (http://www.usccb.org/bible/colossians/3).

25.   St. Ignatius of Antioch (Syria), "On the Epistle to the Romans."

26.   The Greek-speaking School of Alexandria in Egypt and the Latin-speaking School of Carthage in Tunisia stand out as exceptional centers of learning in the 3rd century AD. Besides Alexandria and Carthage, Constantinople, Rome, Antioch, Athens, and a few other notable cities dominated scholarly learning. Carthaginian scholars focused mainly on theology, which was practical in the sense of being about life, as opposed to being speculative.

27.   Benedict XVI (pope), General Audience (March 2007) (http://w2.vatican.va/content/benedict-xvi/en/audiences/2007/documents/hf_ben-xvi_aud_20070321.html).

28.   Philip Schaff, ed., *The Apostolic Fathers with Justin Martyr and Irenaeus* (Grand Rapids, Mich.: Wm. B. Eerdmans Publishing Company, n.d.) (http://www.ccel.org/ccel/schaff/anf01.txt).

29.   Benedict XVI (pope), "St. Justin, Philosopher and Martyr," General Audience, 2007.

30.   For example, Aristotle's theory about perfect concentric heavenly spheres dominating the heavens is the most celebrated case.

31.   See "Dawkins Tells Atheists to 'Mock Religion with Contempt' and Ravi's Response" (https://www.youtube.com/watch?v=51rR4aC9aMg).

32.   See Gideon Rosen and John Lennox, "Making Sense of Suffering" (http://www.johnlennox.org/jresources/make-sense-of-suffering/).

33.   Henri Daniel-Rops, *History of the Church*, vol. 1, p. 344.

34.   The original has not survived. Scholars generally agree that Rufinus (4th century) did not faithfully or accurately translate from the original Greek (3rd century) into Latin.

35.   Henri Daniel-Rops, *History of the Church*, vol. 1, p. 347.

36.   St. John Chrysostom, Homilies on the Ephesians: Homily 21 (http://orthodoxchurchfathers.com/fathers/npnf113/npnf1127.htm#P1406_777874).

37.   St. Augustine, *The Literal Meaning of Genesis*, vol. 1, pp. 42-42; in Ancient Christian Writers, vol. 41), translated and annotated by John Hammond Taylor, S.J. (New York, Paulist Press, 1982) (http://www.resourcemelb.catholic.edu.au/_uploads/rspga/Scripture/Genesis/Augustine.pdf).

38.   Henri Daniel-Rops, *History of the Church of Christ*, vol. 2, *The Church in the Dark Ages* (London: J.M. Dent & Sons Ltd, 1960; p. 14.

39.   St. Augustine, *The City of God* (GardenCity, N.Y.: Image Books, 1958); p. 155.

40.   St Augustine, *City of God*, p. 469.

41.   St Augustine, *City of God*, p. 447.

42.   Peace of mind is an objective that Buddhism, a non-theistic religion, offers to the human person who must seize and take possession of oneself and of the surrounding impersonal forces. It is a philosophy towards which most Wizards gravitate because there is no need to acknowledge the one uncreated God of the universe.

43. Peter Williams, "Things Which Ought to Be Better Known about the Resurrection of Jesus" (lecture, April 2012) (https://www.youtube.com/watch?v=CbBVBUeHXZ4); also, Williams, "New Evidences the Gospels Were Based on Eyewitness Accounts" (lecture, March 2011) (https://www.youtube.com/watch?v=r5Ylt1pBMm8&app=desktop).

44. Listen to Lee Strobel's interesting lecture "The Case for the Resurrection of Christ" (https://www.youtube.com/watch?v=Z5wKYcK_kUs).

45. For example, in 8th-century France, the Frankish king Charlemagne (742–814) asked clerics to determine how to educate his realm.

46. Quotation found at the Newman Society of Ireland (http://newmansociety.ie/we-can-believe-what-we-choose-we-are-answerable-for-what-we-choose-to-believe/).

47. "Three Hundred Sayings of the Ascetics of the Orthodox Church" (Moscow: Orthodox Missionary Society of Venerable Serapion Kozheozersky, 2011) (http://orthodox.cn/patristics/300sayings_en.htm); point 40.

48. John Lennox, *Seven Days That Divide the World: The Beginning according to Genesis and Science* (Grand Rapids, Mich.: Zondervan, 2011) (lecture, http://www.johnlennox.org/jresources/seven-days-that-divide-the-world/).

49. "Three Hundred Sayings," point 46. (http://www.orthodoxchurchquotes.com/category/sayings-from-saints-elders-and-fathers/hieromartyr-onuphry-gagaluk/)

50. See "St. John of Damascus's Critique of Islam" from St. John of Damascus, *Heresies in Epitome: How They Began and Whence They Drew Their Origin* (http://orthodoxinfo.com/general/stjohn_islam.aspx).

51. Hilaire Belloc, *The Great Heresies* (Manassas, Va.: Trinity Communications, 1994) (http://www.ewtn.com/library/HOMELIBR/HERESY4.TXT).

52. Visit his website: http://www.johnlennox.org

53. "Faith is illuminative, not operative; it does not force obedience, though it increases responsibility; it heightens guilt, but it does not prevent sin. The will is the source of action." John Henry Cardinal Newman, *Certain Difficulties Felt by Anglicans in Catholic Teaching Considered,* vol. 1 (New York: Longmans Green and Co., 1895); p. 286 (https://archive.org/stream/certaindifficult01john#page/n5/mode/2up).

54. Malcolm Muggeridge, "The True Crisis in Our Time" (St. Michael Broadcasting, transcript) (https://smbtv.org/index.php/resources-links/muggeridge-true-crisis-audio-transcript).

55. John Lennox and Christopher DiCarlo, *Has Science Made God Irrelevant?* (Toronto: Veritas Forum, March 2017) (https://www.youtube.com/watch?v=L5YDmkAyiO4).

56. Fyodor Dostoyevsky, *The Brothers Karamazov* (New York: Modern Library, Random House, n.d.); p. 48 (https://archive.org/stream/brotherskaramaz00dost#page/n5/mode/2up).

57. 1 Peter 4:10 (http://www.usccb.org/bible/1peter/4).

CHAPTER 4

The Not-So-Dark Ages

That which is the supreme good is supremely the end of all. Now there is but one supreme good, namely God. Therefore all things are directed to the highest good, namely God, as their end.
— Thomas Aquinas, *Summa Contra Gentiles*, Book III, Chapter XVII

Commentators who today talk of the dark ages when faith instead of reason was said to ruthlessly rule, have for their animadversions only the excuse of perfect ignorance. Both Aquinas's intellectual gifts and his religious nature were of a kind that is no longer commonly seen in the Western world.
— David Berlinski, *The Devil's Delusion: Atheism and its Scientific Pretensions*

Always be ready to give an explanation to anyone who asks you for a reason for your hope.
— 1 Peter, Chapter 3, Verse 15

The French scholar Ernest Renan (1823–1892) believed that life during the Middle Ages "was suspended for one thousand years," by which he surely meant that man was uncreative, unadventurous, and bit of a stick. In line with Renan, G.W.F. Hegel (1770–1831), in his *Lectures on the History of Modern Philosophy*, given between 1805 and 1806, told his audience pedantically although humorously that in order to proceed rapidly through his lecture he would skip over the thousand years between the 6th and the 17th centuries. Some 150 years later, their blinkered views are still *au courant* in Paris, London, New York and other intellectual centers.

Similarly, Christopher Hitchens preposterously harkened back to the Middle Ages to illustrate the brutality of Soviet Communism under Joseph Stalin, the mass murderer, as if there were credible parallels. "At one point ... medieval instruments of torture were taken from Russian museums and deployed in the cellars and interrogation pits of Stalin's police. The image is perfect for evoking the choking medieval nightmare of plague-dread, xenophobia, and persecution that enveloped the Soviet Union and destroyed the last remnants of its internationalism."[1] As if the main currents of Medieval philosophy and theology had anything to do with Stalin's megalomania or the depredation of Marxist-Leninist ideology! It sounds like sophistry, since Hitchens was just too smart and well-read to err so badly.

Hitchens' dogmatic views make use of semantics couched in baseless assertions to convince those seeking easy answers to the great questions of life that atheism holds the winning hand. Some Wizards know how to dupe their audience into believing that the Middle Ages were dark ages. Only atheism — the reasonable person's religion — possesses the salvific power to lift human beings above their habitual state of ignorance and boredom. By belittling Christianity with such zealotry, they insult the Judeo-Christian faith tradition and its adherents, among whom are world-class scientists, artists, and statesmen.

The Wizards' poorly thought-through materialistic vision of the universe not only dismisses evidence for the existence of God but reduces the human person to little more than a complex clump of molecules. The process of human development resembles animal husbandry or computer upgrading. Man is a unit of mass and energy devoted to eking out a miserable existence in a hostile and unpredictable world.

Unlike the men and women of the Middle Ages, the Wizards do not seem to understand "that the inalienable worth of a human being transcends his or her degree of [material] development"[2] They cannot see the essential differences between a human being, and say, an animal, a plant, or a computer because ideological materialism has seized the intellectual high ground. As Stanley Jaki, an American philosopher of science, says with typical precision, "De-Christianization means above all the taking of Christ for just another ordinary empirical fact."[3] Because so many people buy into the Wizards' dizzying potpourri of enticing propositions in the hope they will deliver them from a lifetime of pointless striving and boredom, it will not be easy for them to discover the genius of the Middle Ages.

The purpose here is not to demonstrate that the Middle Ages were not a period of great ignorance and violence, or that they were not a time brimming with crude art and unrefined thinking, or even that civilized folk were nowhere to be found. To refute such claims, all one needs to do is read the historical record or visit the medieval cities of Europe. Moreover, contemporary academics such as Joseph Schumpeter (1883–1950), Romano Guardini (1885–1968), and Frederick Copleston (1907–1994), among others,[4] have already written volumes of reliable material documenting that the Middle Ages were a period of inquiry, reason, science, (evidence-based) faith, great art, relative peace, and chivalry.

Rather, my intention is to highlight a few of the outstanding trends and historical figures of the Middle Ages in the hope that readers will recognize the prodigious intellectual contributions to genuine human development that took place during those supposedly lost thousand years. Everyone knows that world history did not pause at the end of the Roman Empire, vegetate during the Middle Ages, and re-emerge again during the Renaissance and the Age of Discovery in the 15th century. The Scholastics of the Middle Ages were largely open-minded and measured academics whose brilliance lay in the enduring reasonableness of their writings, thought, and example.

To dispose of the myth that there was something unnervingly dark about the Middle Ages, it is helpful to revisit some of the great contributions to genuine human development by some of the scholars of the period. "What have we done with this inheritance?" Christopher Dawson (1889–1970) asks. "At least we have *had* it. It has been part of our own flesh and blood and the speech of our common tongue. And the importance of these [Middle Ages] ... is not to be found in the external order they created ... but in the internal change they brought about in the soul of Western man — a change which can never be entirely undone except by the total negation or destruction of Western man himself."[5] It sometimes seems that irrationality has triumphed, that modernity is approaching the "total negation" of reason, history, and biological realities? Or stated differently, has modern Western subjectivism or the voluntarism of the literalist tradition in Islam (the triumph of the will over moral reasoning and the natural order) claimed victory in the battle of ideas? Does not this slavery to relativism explain so much of the violence around us?

This chapter is designed to illustrate the folly of seeking to relegate the Middle Ages to the dustbin of history. Surely if not for the intellectual prowess of the Medieval Scholastics, there would never have been an Enlightenment or a Scientific Revolutions on the scale experienced in Europe from the 16th through the 18th centuries.

Some Background

During the Middle Ages, schoolmasters (generally attached to religious institutions) were academics who loved creativity, welcomed curiosity, and jumped at the possibility of understanding the universe. They were keen to share the truth about humanity and the universe (garnered from experience, reason, and Scripture) with as many people as possible. To ensure effective communication and continuity of their message, they developed an educational system and methodology unrivaled in history. It, of course, did not materialize out of thin air and required fine-tuning and, at times, radical restructuring along the way.

These schoolmasters approached religion holistically (Heaven and Earth in one arena) and embraced science and the scientific method, and encouraged initiative and dialogue as much as any God-loving scientist today. They had confidence in the intelligibility of the universe, the significance of objective morality, and the role of virtue in integral human development. They faced up to the real questions related to the purpose and meaning of life, even at the level of everyday politics, economics, and sociology. Without a doubt, the Middle Ages were not dominated by a cluster of clownish priests, sinister monks, and their obedient sidekicks spinning stories and hiring mind-controllers to keep believers in a mind-numbing trance at the expense of progress; that is the narrative that some Wizards are selling.

To be sure, some Scholastics at times dug in to defend entrenched positions, fixed bayonets, and hesitated to accept new ideas. But most monks then (just as now) welcomed originality and novelty. What is clear is that the great minds of the Middle Ages were pioneers who possessed a scientific outlook towards the world around them because they recognized in the first place that God, the lawgiver, ordered the universe in a way which lent itself to description, testable explanations, and predictability.

The Scholastics differentiated between agent (primary or secondary causes), mechanism (how things work or behave), and laws (that a particular phenomenon always occurs when certain conditions are present), unlike the Wizards who confuse agent, mechanism, and law. Some Wizards shame themselves when they clumsily attempt to indirectly discredit the studious and accomplished friars at the Sorbonne and Oxford by dismissing the Middle Ages.

It is revealing that the Wizards, in order to get their narrative across, have to reduce metaphysics to physics, philosophy to logic, and all of reality to mere matter? This reductionism explains, in part, why Richard Dawkins, for example, suggests that it is inane to ask "why?" in connection with the purpose of life or of the universe in any metaphysical sense.[6] For anti-theists to accept even the possibility that there is only one uncreated God would be a total game-changer, exposing them to the charge of reaching their materialist worldview and other conclusions on the basis of acts of blind faith.

For the sake of clarity, we must understand the Scholastics were not Biblical literalists and they relied on the explanatory power of the evidence before giving assent, unlike nonbelieving scientists who are "science literalists" insofar as they believe that only science can provide real answers to the deepest questions in life. Once again, Stanley Jaki provides context: "There is no intellectual saving grace for those who oppose long geological ages and the exceedingly variegated fossil record with a swearing by the six-day creation story as a literal record of what happened."[7] We must add that there is no saving grace for those who oppose the historicity of the Gospels, or even the record that Christ performed miracles.[8]

The medieval schoolmasters conserved and transmitted the Judeo-Christian legacy for future generations to refine and pass on to others. In developing humanity's treasury of knowledge and experience and uncovering the unknown for the sake of others, they came to grips with the "why" questions. They understood that to remain strictly in the material world was to remain at the dawn of evolutionary history; or they blocked out everything that happened on the sixth day, when, according to Scripture, God created man – a game-changer if ever there was one.[9]

Epistemology and Reasonable Faith

Scholastics from Scotland to Constantinople diligently worked to unravel the mysteries of the universe, to understand the interrelationship between faith and reason, and to disentangle the problem of knowledge and truth. To that end, some Scholastics sided with the Platonic/Augustinian approach to epistemology, metaphysics, and cosmology, while others preferred the Aristotelian/Thomist approach. Neither school rejected the importance of revelation, and both understood the difference between "faith" and "blind faith" and accepted the role of reason in making informed judgments and to support the claims of revelation. To suggest, as the Wizards often do, that a person must pick between religion and science, or faith and reason, is a false choice because faith and reason, at least in the Judeo-Christian tradition, are not only compatible but support each other.

Who can disagree with St. Thomas Aquinas (1225–1274) when he says, "The Truth of our faith becomes a matter of ridicule among the infidels if any Catholic, not gifted with the necessary scientific learning, presents as dogma what scientific scrutiny shows to be false"? Aquinas, like most of his scholastic colleagues, is as enlightened as any Wizard of the Enlightenment, except that Aquinas recognized that the intelligibility of the universe did not come about by chance. As usual, David Berlinski gets to the essence of the matter: "[Aquinas's] life coincided with a period of great brilliance in European art, architecture, law, poetry, philosophy, and theology. Commentators who today talk of the dark ages, when faith instead of reason was said ruthlessly to rule, have for their animadversions only the excuse of perfect ignorance. Both Aquinas's intellectual gifts and his religious nature were of a kind that is no longer commonly seen in the Western world."[10]

Epistemology is that branch of philosophy that deals with the nature and range of knowledge. It mainly tackles two questions: (a) what constitutes certain knowledge? and (b) how is certain knowledge acquired? These questions go to the heart of the debate between faith and reason and help a person assent to truth and act with "right reason." The question *"how does a person come to know what is true?"* is universally accepted as essential in life and development. The Scholastics embraced this challenge as much as any scholar during the Renaissance or the Enlightenment.

The Scholastics were open-minded and followed the facts and evidence wherever they led, an attitude that may come as a surprise to some. For the Scholastics, there was always a healthy tension between "I believe so that I may understand,"[11] and "I understand so that I may believe."[12] What emerged was a profound love of science and Scripture at the same time that nourished the accumulation of knowledge, the university system, and underpinned the quest for truth.[13]

In many ways, Scholasticism was a revolutionary movement in that its approach to learning challenged educational methods based on authority and fixed views of the universe. The Scholastics, to their credit, had a penchant to explain their ideas convincingly, rather than present them as an inert mass in take-it-or-leave-it fashion. For them, the Bible, while it was the inspired word of God, did not have to be taken literally, nor was it the only source of certain knowledge. (This medieval Christian mindset contrasts with a literalist Muslim interpretation of the Koran).

The Scholastics recognized (without fully understanding the interplay between free will and intellect) that "faith alone" and "reason alone" are insufficient to discover and carry out the will of God. Moreover, they saw dogma and the legal system as *guides* to good behavior and not as programs to be mindlessly followed. While the debate between "make up your own mind" versus "do as you're told" continues to play itself out in modern society, the Scholastic tradition emphasized the former over the latter.

One of the real contributions of the Scholastics to the history of ideas was their mostly successful effort to encourage free-thinking and the role of reason in moral reasoning. They promoted research and exploration for the sake of knowledge, social progress, and development. It was the Christian schoolmasters who unleashed the power of reason as a primary means to better understand the rightness or wrongness of personal acts without losing sight of natural-law principles. Pope Benedict XVI sums up a key idea taken up by the Scholastics during the Middle Ages:

The central question at issue ... is this: where is the ethical foundation for political choices to be found? The Catholic tradition maintains that the objective norms governing right action are accessible to reason, prescinding from the content of revelation. According to this understanding, the role of religion in political debate is not so much to supply these norms, as if they could not be known by non-believers — still less to propose concrete political solutions, which would lie altogether outside the competence of religion — but rather to help purify and shed light upon the application of reason to the discovery of objective moral principles. This "corrective" role of religion vis-à-vis reason is not always welcomed, though, partly because distorted forms of religion, such as sectarianism and fundamentalism, can be seen to create serious social problems themselves. And in their turn, these distortions of religion arise when insufficient attention is given to the purifying and structuring role of reason within religion. It is a two-way process. Without the corrective supplied by religion, though, reason too can fall prey to distortions, *as when it is manipulated by ideology, or applied in a partial way that fails to take full account of the dignity of the human person.* Such misuse of reason, after all, was what gave rise to the slave trade in the first place and to many other social evils, not least the totalitarian ideologies of the twentieth century. This is why I would suggest that the world of reason and the world of faith — the world of secular rationality and the world of religious belief — need one another and should not be afraid to enter into a profound and ongoing dialogue, for the good of our civilization [italics added].[14]

Building on the work of the Scholastics, Benedict XVI is urging present-day politicians, economists, and ordinary folk to reflect upon the fact that the truths of faith and the truths of reason both contribute to making sound and reasonable judgments that lead to genuine human development.

Belt of Knowledge

The Scholastics employed their great learning to unlock the secrets of life, nature, and the universe in order to hand them on to future generations. Oxford professor Charles William Previté-Orton notes that "it was the Church and the monks, who preserved the remnants of ancient civilization and Christianity itself with its systematic thought and its ethic."[15] Learning for the Scholastics was more than a career-building exercise or a means of finding personal security in some fortress-monastery along the Rhine or overlooking the Aegean Sea. Josef Pieper rightly said, "Truly to understand scholasticism, we must bear in mind that it was above all an unprecedented process of learning, a scholarly enterprise of enormous proportions that went on for several centuries."[16] They were not just "good Christians," but rather "good and thinking Christians."

The overall approach of Scholasticism in the area of higher education is as relevant today as it was in medieval times. Oxford, Bologna, and the Sorbonne did not come into existence simply to educate the next group of religious hypnotizers to lobotomize the masses or turn into fanatics the privileged and elites. Rather, the schoolmasters educated students about the meaning of life and living. Secondary-school and university education developed to endow young students not only with skills but, most important, with knowledge and culture that would allow them to face the challenges of life wisely, while building intellectual capital necessary for genuine human development.

Studium Generale/Reason

One of the main tasks of the learned men of the Middle Ages was to order, classify, and study extant manuscripts and other source documents that became available after the collapse of the Roman Empire. It was no small undertaking because of the quantity, diversity, and often poor condition of the material. The *studium generale* eventually emerged as the method of education. The object was to develop critical thinking and moral reasoning. Universities came about to teach boys to be virtuous men[17]. As John Henry Cardinal Newman (1801–1890) wrote, "[We are] answerable for what we choose to believe."[18] It is that sense of responsibility before a higher reality – guiding men and women to act in a manner consistent with the laws of nature – that anti-theists deeply resent.

The Scholastics rejected determinism and recognized that naturalistic "altruism" cannot explain acts of selfless charity. Human dignity depends on a person's free ability to make informed decisions on the basis of the available evidence, including that acquired through the natural sciences and experience. The educated person has to have one foot in heaven and another on earth in order to transform the world from within, while serving God and neighbor by dint of reason and hard work.

Boethius, Duns Scotus, More Aquinas, and Ockham

While many of the monks and priests who laid the foundation for and enhanced the quality of education during the Middle Ages have lapsed into obscurity, the names of several continue to shine to this day.

At the end of the Roman Empire, Severinus Boethius (c. 480–524), a layman can take some credit for setting in motion the emerging spirit of the Middle Ages, despite the fact that he was unjustly accused of treason, imprisoned, and executed by the Roman authorities.

As a communicator and promoter of culture, he studied philosophy and produced manuals on mathematics, music, and astronomy. He left behind an astounding trove of written material and served as a generator of good ideas at a time when the world needed clear-eyed men and women with transcendent, moral vision, and who practiced virtue the better to serve God, community, and neighbor.

As a Roman citizen, he was able to identify with non-Romans. As a Christian, he took the time to understand pagans, heretics, and atheists alike. As a layman, he understood and valued clerics. Boethius, perhaps unknowingly, was one of the first to live out the meaning of "unity of life" as embodied in the idea of personal sanctity in the middle of the world — the day-to-day selfless martyrdom of self-sacrifice and self-giving to one's neighbor (whether friend or foe). As a 20th century Catholic leader would say: "A secret, an open secret: these world crises are crises of saints. God wants a handful of men and women 'of his own' in every human activity. And then ... 'the peace of Christ in the kingdom of Christ.'"[19] The *studium generale* was designed to give men and women the tools to become saints in the middle of the world and change society for the better. A desire for service through excellence not only flowed from the struggle to fight against injustices but from the effort to be a saint from one day to the next.

After the fall of Rome, new emerging political dynasties, most notably under the Merovingians (466–751) and later under the Carolingians (752–987), began to consolidate power in what is now France, and, with the assistance of clergymen.[20] While in prison, Boethius wrote *De Consolatione Philosophiae*, a literary masterpiece, which is a thoughtful but philosophically weighty treatise about the meaning of suffering, God's love, and good and evil in light of a person's pilgrimage on Earth and in eternity. These ideas permeate the Judeo-Christian legacy even today.

Earthly goods, Boethius suggested, cannot be ends in themselves. Happiness is not to be exclusively found in wealth, honor, or power. Through the eyes of suffering, *De Consolatione Philosophiae*, in a manner reminiscent of Viktor E. Frankl's account of life in a concentration camp, lays out the meaning of hope in God and his providence in the midst of suffering. "For the first time in my life I saw the truth as it is set into song by so many poets, proclaimed as the final wisdom by so many thinkers. The truth — that Love is the ultimate and highest goal to which man can aspire. Then I grasped the meaning of the greatest secret that human poetry and human thought and belief have to impart: *The salvation of man is through love and in love.*"[21]

The Judeo-Christian message is powerful because it provides meaning in the face of the incomprehensible, shares without expecting payback, and offers truth in the face of doubt. After the collapse of the Roman Empire, secular authorities, whose relationship with the Church was often strained, saw the value in a broad humanistic education as opposed to the narrower "doctrinaire" or technical education that was typical in the days of the Roman Empire and is typical today.

Schools

Two main schools of thought at the time: (1) the Dominican school represented by St. Albert the Great (1200–1280) and St. Thomas Aquinas, and (2) the Franciscan school of St. Bonaventure (1221–1274) and Blessed Duns Scotus (1266–1308).[22]

St. Albert the Great, referred to as the Universal Doctor, maintained that reason alone cannot explain all the truths of revelation, although he aimed to make Aristotle intelligible to others. Albert led the way in formulating the inductive method of reasoning that later scholars such as Francis Bacon (1561–1626) refined significantly. Moreover, his scientific research with flora and fauna was original and earned the acclaim of academics throughout Europe in the 13th century. For Albert, it was critical to search out the causes of observable facts and patterns in nature and not simply accept the ideas of others without questioning.

St. Thomas Aquinas, appointed professor at the University of Paris in 1256, was in a league of his own in terms of intellectual prowess, depth of reasoning, and experience. His crowning achievements are the *Summa Theologiae* (1265–1274) and the *Summa Contra Gentiles* (c. 1270–1273), arguably the greatest explanations of all time of "who man is," "the purpose of life," "the meaning of the universe," "time and eternity," "the existence of God," "man's relationship to God," and "the nature of things — seen and unseen." He also offered proofs for the existence of God. His work was presented in typical Scholastic format: thesis/statement, objection/doubt, and response/ solution. His arguments are generally dismissed by the Wizards, because in their view God does not exist.

Aquinas was an optimist who believed in man's ability to use his intellect in the service of truth and of his fellow man. Reason, he thought, was that unique spiritual quality of a person that ultimately distinguishes humans from animals, plants, and things. More specifically, a person's mind is equipped to seek out truth and to bridge the physical and spiritual worlds. For Aquinas, truth has to be discovered or "earned," i.e., man must work at plumbing the meaning and purpose of life through the application of the intellect. He believed, rightly, that reason and revelation must be consistent, which the Judeo-Christian philosophical-theological tradition accepts, unlike the Muslim tradition, which largely does not.

The Scholastics fused the truths of faith and reason to produce a sense of wonder about life and the universe. That attitude, combined with a spirit of service and desire to "love, serve, and know" God, produced a meteoric rise in the study of the sciences and a fuller acceptance of the scientific method long before the Renaissance. According to Jaki, "Galileo ... acquired his first introduction to non-Aristotelian concepts of inertial and accelerated motion through studies of textbooks introduced in Italy through the Jesuit Collegio Romano."[23] Jaki further shows, drawing on the published research of Fr. Jean Buridan (1295-1363), twice rector of the Sorbonne in the late 14th century, why "it was so easy for Copernicus, Descartes, Kepler, Galileo, and many lesser figures to accept that all bodies on earth shared the earth's motion, rotational as well as orbital."[24] In other words, the Scholastics of the so-called Dark Ages in fact enlightened the world and opened the eyes of later academics, a fact which most anti-theists either dismiss as an exception, or ignore.

The beauty of Christianity is that God does not want to give men and women all the answers to the unsolved mysteries of life and existence, because to do so would mean that a person is no longer free to choose and therefore love in the deepest sense. God is *challenging* humanity to find truth, which is the key to liberation. A Scholastic was smart, nimble, and would have embraced everything about the Enlightenment except for its panoply of ideas that flowed from declaring God dead. The Scholastics were careful not to fall into the Enlightenment Trap because they knew the difference between the one true uncreated God *not of this world* and all the other man-made gods *of this world*.

Aquinas's moral philosophy is grounded in the reasonable Aristotelian assumption that ethics depends on whether or not an act contributes to or detracts from the achievement of a person's *telos*, i.e., his ultimate object or purpose. For Aquinas, a person must be in possession of himself. He must make the effort to develop the moral and intellectual virtues and be open to God's grace in order to elevate himself above the material world. There is nothing deterministic about Aquinas's ethics, since human beings are free and freedom is a necessary component of being a human person.

Aquinas's synthesis of Christian theology and philosophy is a masterpiece of vast proportions in that it provides profound credible answers to the most essential questions about life and living. It is up to human beings, with limited knowledge, to seek truth in a universe that is ordered, subject to laws, and purposeful.

The Scholastics did not have their heads in the sand, as most Wizards would like us to believe. In fact, Aquinas's political sociology, as Joseph Schumpeter mentions, must be seen through the prism of his Judeo-Christian worldview and shows "an individualistic, utilitarian, and (in a sense) rationalist"[25] streak that even the Wizards might envy.

The Scholastics and Economics

In the *Summa Theologiae,* Aquinas says that "the ownership of possessions is not contrary to the natural law but an addition thereto devised by human reason." The words, "devised by human reason" illustrate his confidence in human reason and positive law. Aquinas believed that a person's use of private property or attempt to acquire or exchange goods must at a minimum correspond to God's divine plan, the demands of justice, and the nature of humanity and material things. He believed that government must serve as mediator and honest broker, taking care to administer the common good and advance policies that respect private ownership of property (within limits) as justifiable. It is the responsibility of government to uphold an economic system and a just trading system. (Generally, the Scholastic doctors did not defend political authoritarianism. According to Schumpeter, "The divine right of monarchs, in particular, and the concept of the omnipotent state are creations of the Protestant sponsors of the absolutist tendencies that were to assert themselves in the national states."[26])

For the Scholastics, laws regulating the economic system, i.e., related to investment, finance, and trade, had to be consistent with genuine human development. Politicians had to provide the just means, social structures, and a political environment, anchored in right reason, to properly use, share, and distribute the goods of the Earth. Aquinas would not endorse a political system that rejected private property and yet he would have condemned any policies directed to control or seize resources in a neighboring territory out of greed or a trumped-up or phony appeal to self-defense or national security. Such narratives often hide behind false claims to promote freedom, democracy, fraternal relations or human rights.

The British economist Eric Roll states, "In regard to property, [St. Thomas] did not go back to the unrestricted rights conceded in Roman law, which was beginning to come into its own again. He found in the Aristotelian distinction between the power of acquisition and administration and that of use an important separation of two aspects of property. The former conferred rights on the individual, and Aquinas's arguments in defense of it are those we have already met in Aristotle's attack on Plato; the latter put obligations upon the individual in the interests of the community. Thus not the institution but the manner of using it determined whether it was good or evil."[27] Aquinas was no Hobbesian or Darwinian ideologue. Moreover, he classified wealth "with other imperfections of man's earthly life which were inevitable, but which should be made as good as their nature would permit."[28] Listening to some of the Wizards, one would never guess that ideas such as these could possibly have emerged from the Dark Ages.

Aquinas regarded trade as a necessity of life to maintain one's family and country — a recognition of the dignity of the human person and family unit. The profit realized from a trade transaction would be a reward for labor where the exchange should reflect a "just price." He did much to dispel the notion, held by some earlier Christian thinkers, that trade was somehow marginally bad. Aquinas, for example, would have urged farmers to grow more of one product in order to sell or to barter for something else, as long as traders and exchange merchants had good motives, a clear conscience, and observed the norms of justice in light of the common good.

With regard to the theoretical basis for valuation, Aquinas and St. Albert the Great seem to have adopted the concept of labor-cost or a labor theory of value, which in significant ways stands to this day. Their achievements, as well as those of Duns Scotus and Richard of Middleton (1249–1306), another English Scholastic, contributed greatly to economic thought which, as with the Scholastics' contributions to the development of science, would seem unlikely accomplishments for simple monks and friars.[29]

The Scholastics, unlike those who support godless utilitarianism and moral relativism in economics, refined humanity's understanding of justice in light of human nature, the common good, and ends of governance. In term of public policy, special care had to be taken when deciding issues related to taxation, pricing, exchange rates, accounting policies, and regulations.[30]

Duns Scotus must be credited for having related "just price" to "cost," i.e., to the producers' or to traders' expenditure of money and effort (*expensae et labores*). He discovered the condition of competitive equilibrium that came to be known in the 19th century as the "Law of Cost."[31] The economists of the Enlightenment period gained much from the Scholastics. When applied to the work of the Scholastics in economics and political theory, the term "Dark Ages," again, is a complete misnomer.

William of Ockham (1285–1347), the English Franciscan friar, professor at Oxford University, laid some of the groundwork for the skepticism of the Enlightenment in that his epistemology rested on the inability to differentiate between infused knowledge and knowledge derived by the senses. Some of his ideas also point to the lasting influence of the Scholastics in other fields and show their diversity of views and open-mindedness. Ockham is credited with some lasting ideas, such as "When two competing theories make the same predictions, the one that is simpler is the better." For academics and scientists testing hypotheses, Ockham's insights have also served to push science and philosophy forward.[32] It is good to be skeptical like the Scholastics, but not so skeptical that truth evaporates into a bottomless pit of moral relativism.

Other Scholastics and the Spaniards

Aquinas, Albert the Great, Duns Scotus, and Ockham as well as many other scholars, such as Roger Bacon (1214–1292), were influential in formulating and garnering support for the scientific method and the development of science, philosophy, the arts, literature, and education. Along with St. Bonaventure, one of the great Franciscan academics of the age, they debated the most fundamental issues affecting human knowledge, morality, behavior, public policy, and economics. St. Bonaventure's philosophy and theology are linked to the mystical tradition as articulated by St. Augustine, St. Bernard, and many of the Eastern Fathers.

The late Scholastics, who must also be recognized for their contributions to economics as well, include the great Jesuits, such as Leonardus Lessius (1554–1623), Luis de Molina (1535–1600), and Juan de Lugo (1583–1660). As Diego Alonso-Lasheras has noted: "It is within their systems of moral theology and law that economics gained definite if not separate existence, and it is they who come nearer than does any other group to having been the 'founders' of scientific economics."[33] The contributions of these 16th-century scholars anticipated the marginal-utility theory that was later developed mainly by Carl Menger (1840–1921) and the 19th-century Austrian school of economics. The Austrian school ultimately challenged the classical school of economics developed by Adam Smith (1723–1790) and David Ricardo (1772–1823). The Scholastics participated in this debate from the beginning.

Economic theory benefited over the centuries from the original work done by other Iberian Scholastics, who include the Dominicans Francisco de Vitoria (1492–1546), Domingo de Soto (1494–1560), Juan de Medina (1490–1547), Martin de Azpilcueta (1491–1586), Diego de Covarrubias (1512–1577), and Tomas de Mercado (1525–1575).

St. Antoninus (1389–1459), the Dominican friar and bishop of Florence, represented the typical learned master of the late Middle Ages with a flair for both scholarship and art. He encouraged Fra Angelico (1395–1455) to paint the astounding frescos in the Priory of San Marco. St. Antoninus is, as Schumpeter says, "the first man to whom it is possible to ascribe a comprehensive vision of the economic process in all its major aspects."[34] That is quite an achievement for an age many persist in calling "dark." St. Antoninus also shared the view of other Scholastic scholars that cost was only one factor in determining the exchange value (or price) of something. He introduced the concept of *complacibilitas*, or the degree of pleasure that one can derive from a thing, into the determination of value.

Islamic Scholarship and Development

The influence of Islamic philosophy and theology on the development of thought in the Muslim world and in Judeo-Christian Europe was significant and can be divided broadly into two main periods — pre– and post–13th century.

Islamic scholars were well acquainted with the science and philosophy of the Ancient world, and their contributions went beyond the mere translation of manuscripts. It was Muslim scholars such as Ahmad ibn Hanbal (780–855), Al-Farabi (872–951), Abu 'Ali al-Husayn ibn 'Abd Allah ibn Sina or Avicenna (980–1037), Abu Hamid Muhammad ibn Muhammad al-Ghazali (c. 1058–1111), 'Abu l-Walid Muhammad bin 'Ahmad Ibn Rushd or Averroes (1126–1198), and many others who, individually, either embraced or rejected many works of classical scholarship.

We must go back in time to get a sense of the major ideas running through Islamic scholarship (especially in its more extreme manifestations) that have influenced the mindset of the majority of the Muslim faithful from Afghanistan through the Middle East to North Africa (excluding the mindset of the majority of the peoples of the Central Asian republics of the former Soviet Union).

Since the 14th century, as Robert Reilly shows, the Ash'arite school of theology has been the most influential in Muslim society. It sees the relationship between God and man, and the meaning of knowledge and reason as radically different from the Mu'tazilites (Shafii) school of theology. Violence between the followers of these schools spills out into the streets of Cairo, Istanbul, and Teheran on a regular basis. To understand the difference between these schools is to get a sense of the internal struggle within Islam that is raging today. It also helps understand why the spirit of the Scientific Revolution and the Renaissance did not develop in Muslim-dominated lands in the same way as it did in Europe during the same period in history, despite being in continuous contact.

The Ash'arites (a form of Wahhabism) discourage free-thinking (the Hellenistic tradition of philosophy) and reject the possibility of moral reasoning as means to acquire certain knowledge and to guide moral behavior. They see God (who acts in the world) as omnipotent and omniscient *and, therefore, the only actor in the world,* i.e., the first, efficient, and final cause of everything at one and the same time. This idea stifles creativity and initiative. A person's actions are essentially an extension of the will of God, thus neutralizing independent thought (freedom) and moral reasoning. That attitude obliterates creative thinking and accepts the supremacy of the will, and, thus, negates the existence of a stable order in nature.

When analyzed closely, Ash'arite philosophy undermines the appetite of a person for independent thought and, thus, retards societal development. The incentive to innovate disappears. Progress, which requires a spirit of curiosity and an acceptance of science (which is predicated on a firm belief in the intelligibility and regularity of the laws of nature), stalls. By implication, human freedom becomes meaningless because it is directed by the will of God at all times. In order to solve the question of good and evil, right and wrong, Ash'arite philosophers invoke the need to obey (with blind faith) revelation (its literal interpretation), which is embodied in the Koran and Sharia Law. Do not such ideas lead to intellectual paralysis, an unquestioning "herd mentality," and an inability to judge the rightness or wrongness of an act (because God is the source and agent of all actions)? This mentality lives on today throughout much of the Muslim world.

As Robert Reilly showed in *The Closing of the Muslim Mind: How Intellectual Suicide Created the Modern Islamist Crisis,* "Many wonder why democracy did not develop indigenously in the Muslim world and ask whether it can still develop today. The answer is that, so long as the Ash'arite (or Hanbalite) world is regnant, democratic development cannot succeed for the simple reason that this view posits the primacy of power over the primacy of reason. Those who might contend that Ash'arism is already irrelevant in the Middle East then need to provide some other explanation for its dysfunctional character. I do not assert that Ash'arism is a living force in the sense that people consciously seek solutions to the problems of Islam in the modern world through it.... Rather, it functions as an embedded dead weight that inhibits the reasonable search for such solutions. Even worse, it is Hanbalism,[35] which al-Ash'ari originally rose to defend, that is gaining traction today in the form of Wahhabism, which is even more inimical to the primacy of reason than Ash'arism."[36] Since the obligation to act morally comes from Sharia (and the Koran), with reason playing no role, moral philosophy as a guide to human behavior is meaningless. And the primacy of power (over reason) dominates the language and actions of its adherents, who are all too prone to see radical, militant Islam as the future.[38]

In contrast to the Ash'arites, the Mu'tazilite (or Shafii) school of philosophy recognizes the importance of reason in making moral judgments (following in the footsteps of Plato and Aristotle). According to the Mu'tazilites, a person can come to know what is morally good and evil, just and unjust through the use of reason, i.e., the human intellect or the mind can function *independently* of God's omnipotence and directive powers. Law (jurisprudence) serves as a guide for moral behavior (and human freedom remains intact) rather than an object of obedience. Moreover, since the world is intelligible, the Mu'tazilites thought that there is no shame in using science to uncover the laws of nature. Personal initiative and creativity are not seen as private matters but rather good traits that dignify the human person. This Mu'tazilite mindset amongst Muslim theologians and philosophers today has largely remained dormant, if not disappeared.

Other Features of Islam

One of the core principles of Islamic theology is the principle of inequality that also undermines fraternity (and mutual understanding) at the most fundamental levels. By the will of God, it is believed, men are superior to women, and Muslims are superior to non-Muslims. While these hierarchical structures are anathema to modern democratic societies, ironically, they are not to ideological multiculturalism and ecumenism.

Unfortunately, these ideas, along with a kind of fatalism and blind faith in the dictates of Sharia Law (and its authoritative interpretations by religious scholars[40]), are deeply rooted in certain segments of Islamic society, especially among those less exposed to Western thinking and the Hellenistic world. Jaki: "Muslim mystics decried the notion of scientific law (as formulated by Aristotle) as blasphemous and irrational, depriving as it does the Creator of his freedom. The intellectuals (philosophers) glorified the *a priori*, necessary validity of those laws. Neither position was conducive to that progress which science was to represent."[39] Does not this intellectual legacy produce indifference and inaction towards establishing education systems?

More about Ash'arites Versus Mu'tazilites

Up until the close of the 13th century, Islamic scholarship was not overtly anti-learning, anti-science, or anti-freedom but rather drew from Greco-Roman philosophy. This pre–13th-century openness to science ended surprisingly (even tragically) with the triumph of the Islamic Ash'arite school of philosophy over that of the Mu'tazilites. Unlike the view of the Greek philosophers, the Ash'arites, as noted above, believed that God was the first and only cause of everything, which tended to eliminate freedom, the notion that the universe is intelligible, and the role of reason in moral judgments. Since God is all-powerful and all-knowing, and unconstrained in any way, only revelation and strict obedience to the law can show a person what is good or evil; the intellect is irrelevant. With this mindset, if the will destroys the intellect (reason), do not truth and moral reasoning disappear?

In this philosophical battle between Muslim academics, a few scholars deserve particular mention. Avicenna (not an adherent to Ash'aritism) was a native from Bukhara, in present-day Uzbekistan, and a region at various times under Persian influence. As a great philosopher, man of science, and mathematician, he is perhaps best known for his astronomical tables and medical treatises. His *Canon* of medical science was considered the principal authoritative work for medical schools, both in Europe and North Africa, through much of the Renaissance. His commentaries on Aristotle's works include his two great encyclopedias, *Al Schefa* and *Al Nadja.*

Averroes, an Andalusian Muslim scholar who enthusiastically dove into Hellenistic science and philosophy, tried to counter the Ash'arites' negation of human freedom. His works include the *Commentaries* and *The Book of the Healing of the Soul.* Aquinas in his writings paid Averroes a great complement by calling him "the Commentator." Averroes's work mainly consisted of his attempt to reconcile the various interpretations of the Koran with Aristotelian philosophy and epistemology — a task that became impossible with the victory of the Ash'arites over the Mu'tazilites.

Al-Ghazali, on the other hand, was perhaps the leading Muslim theologian-philosopher who undermined the Islamic world's profound interest (up to then) in science and reason. With his ascendency, he dominated scholarly efforts from Spain to Persia, including endeavors of scientists to uncover the workings and mysteries of the universe. He and his followers encouraged a less-than-mild form of intellectual defeatism. In his manuscript entitled *The Incoherence of the Philosophers,* he undermined the thought of Abd al-Jabbar (935–1025) and other adherents to the Mu'tazilite or Shafii school of philosophy. By accepting Al-Ghazali's views (the denial of free will denied, the belittling of enquiry, and the reduction of the predictive laws of nature to the will of God), the Islamic world was dealt a body blow from which it has not yet been able to recover.

Averroes was unable to accomplish in the Muslim world what Aquinas and Moses Maimonides had achieved vis-à-vis the Judeo-Christian mind. In other words, while Al-Ghazali prevented science from entering the mosque, Aquinas and Maimonides carried science, with confidence and hope, into the cathedral and synagogue, respectively.

And so, the Islamic world, by embracing Al-Ghazali's ideas, stagnated and, thus, did not develop modern social and economic policies or an attitude towards science comparable to that in Europe. Indeed, change itself was a problem. Under the Ash'arites, the relationship between human beings (and classes of persons) depended on the law, which supported the inequality of persons and beliefs. People were "rated" by religion (Muslim or non-Muslim) and biology (man or woman).

Since "no obligations flow from reason, but from the Sharia,"[40] there is no moral philosophy. For all practical purposes, then, Al-Ghazali and his followers fathered ideas that have led to the intellectual suicide of the Islamic nation-state and to the modern Islamist crisis.[41] While these Asha'rite ideas never penetrated into Western Europe in any meaningful way, they appear to be gaining momentum in the post-modern era given their importance of the "will" over "intellect" or voluntarism.

In contrast, the Scholastics and the Mu'tazilites (in the main) saw no contradiction between revelation and reason, and embraced human freedom and its pivotal role in the story about human progress. One could hear Aquinas say, "Scientists and philosophers and all you people out there: Listen up! Go out into the deep and see and touch and smell the world around you. Measure and weigh the visible. Gather evidence, look into the heavens and look into the depths of molecules. Go beyond description and make sense of nature and of its order and harmony and movements and draw conclusions. Convince yourselves. Moreover, it is wrong to think that there is no freedom because God 'controls' everything and because there are no secondary causes in nature. Discover those secondary causes; discover the governing laws of nature that hold true and that are predictive. Have no fear. Revelation, Hellenic thought, and the institutional Church support science, discovery, and human freedom."

Are Wizards such as Victor Stenger and Hitchens incapable of seeing the fundamental differences between Scholasticism and Islam's dominant Ash'arite philosophy, which degrades science, material progress and freedom? Academics today should drop their anti-Judeo-Christian tub-thumping and denounce the anti-rationalist anti-progressive strains of religious extremism with roots in the scholarship of academics such as Muhammad ibn Abd al-Wahhabi and Al-Ghazali.

Mosheh ben Maimon

Moses Maimonides or Mosheh ben Maimon (1135–1204), a Sephardic Jewish philosopher and an Old Testament expert, is universally known for his insights into philosophy, law, and ethics. He showed a stunning ability to fuse Aristotelian logic and metaphysics with the Talmud and Hebraic religious teachings. His principal work was *The Guide for the Perplexed*, wherein he argued that the Jewish faith is not inconsistent with philosophy and science.

Maimonides insisted that the findings of science could be harmonious with revelation, since God and reason were not incompatible. Revelation has a broader meaning than "believing in something without evidence." Maimonides' attempt to unify Aristotelian and Old Testament thinking further encouraged Jewish scholars over the centuries to look into a microscope or telescope without feeling like they were violating religious laws. He rejected the eternity-of-the-universe argument in favor of the proof-from-motion argument for the existence of God. Like many Christian Scholastics, Jewish scholars have had nothing to fear in pursuing science and philosophy with an open mind, unlike the general emphasis of Islamic studies on a blind acceptance of revelation, its interpretation by Muslim scholars, and Sharia Law, especially since the 14th century.

Chivalry

No commentary of the Middle Ages would be complete without mentioning the rise and development of chivalry, as exemplified in the Orders of Knighthood. The concept of *noblesse oblige* took root in the Middle Ages throughout the territories of Christendom, including the Slavic nations. Chivalry is much more than being courteous and kind and likeable. It is much more than a watered-down form of Darwinian altruism.[42] It is not just opening doors for women or helping old ladies cross the street. At its core, chivalry merges Christian living — in the broadest sense — with Christian faith. Chivalry is the on-going process within a person's consciousness — heart, mind, and body — of setting self-imposed limitations on one's behavior for the sake or good of others in recognition of the dignity of the human person.

Chivalry is a powerful reminder of what distinguishes a human being from beasts. It represents a concrete effort to respond to a higher calling and uphold the dignity of the human person. Chivalry cannot be reduced to a cynical means to curry favor and ensure survival, which would be the explanation of the materialist who sees survival or advantage as the only motivator.

Chivalry is vital to what it is to be a gentleman; it is not the exclusive privilege of one social class. The concept of chivalry, however inconsistently lived, is directly linked to the maturing of the Judeo-Christian mindset. It should be the hallmark of statecraft in politics and social relations.

Geoffroi de Charny (1306–1356) tried to capture the qualities and spirit of the knights and of knighthood in his book *Livre de Chevalerie*, written circa 1351. It is a somewhat formal outline of chivalry and yet draws out its main ideas.

Part of the chivalrous spirit of the age was reflected in the extensive, albeit still primitive, network of hospitals that sprang up all over Europe during the Middle Ages. Hospitals at the time were largely designed to care for patients' material *and spiritual* needs. They were focused more on *caring* than *curing* — an attitude that rests on the assumption of the dignity of each human person.

In the eastern reaches of Christendom, the Slavonic knights assumed a stature of epic proportions and are still idealized in present-day Russia, Ukraine, and Belarus as examples of men who defended the sacred lands of Kievan Rus against all enemies, including the Turks and Mongols. Eulogized in epic stories called *bylinas*, their chivalric traditions go back more than a 1,000 years and, just as in Western Europe, pagan mythology was merging with the Judeo-Christian worldview.[43] Their stories are all expressed in stunningly beautiful ancient Slavonic languages.

Some Thoughts about Byzantium

Byzantium immensely influenced the development of the Judeo-Christian mindset and was an integral part of the making of the pan-European civilization. According to most historians, the Byzantine Empire during the Middle Ages existed at least from the middle of the 5th century to the fall of Constantinople (1453) at the hands of the Ottoman Turks. This thousand year history has largely been overlooked by Western historians, partly because of the lack of scholars who know Greek and the Slavic languages, the relative paucity of manuscripts owing to destruction, and the somewhat reclusive nature of Eastern scholars.

Following the collapse of the Roman Empire, Greek replaced Latin in the East as of the 6th or 7th century. The Byzantine Emperor and the Orthodox Patriarch lived in Constantinople. Hagia Sophia, the Patriarch's residence, was one of the greatest churches in all of Christendom and remains a commanding symbol for all of the Orthodox Slavic and non-Slavic nations to this day. The University of Constantinople was founded in the 5th century, and throughout the Middle Ages, scholarship flourished in Byzantium. Eastern scholars, after the 8th century, continued to play a significant role in preserving Greco-Roman culture.

It would be impossible here to provide an in-depth review of the intellectual prowess of Eastern scholars. Nevertheless, just as their counterparts in the Western Roman Empire, the monks and priests of Byzantium did much more than pray. Their achievements in various fields are remarkable. Men such as Isidore of Miletus (442–537), scientist and mathematician, and Anthemius of Tralles (474–534), professor of geometry, were the architects of the dome of Hagia Sophia; and Michael Psellos (1018–1096) was a prominent historian and philosopher. St. Cyril (827–869) and his brother St. Methodius (815–885), the Apostles to the Slavs, whomPope John Paul II named as patron saints of Europe in 1980, devised the Cyrillic alphabet to facilitate the spread of Christianity in the Slavic lands.

While the Western Church focused on preserving and spreading Judeo-Christian culture to its frontier regions, such as present-day Scandinavia, Scotland, Germany, Poland, Hungary, and the Baltics, the Eastern Church concentrated on the lands north and east of the Black Sea. By the 10th century, present-day Russia, Ukraine, Serbia, and Bulgaria had become Christian.[44] Up to the fall of Constantinople in the 15th century, much of the spiritual care of Christians throughout the Middle East and the Caucasus, was the responsibility of Constantinople, although it increasingly ceded authority to the West because of continuous conflict with the Ottomans.[45]

The inquisitive medieval mind urged explorers and geographers to discover the world. Cartography was not some initiative that started in the 16th century; it pre-dates the Renaissance. Bearing in mind technological differences, medieval cartographers probably knew more about Planet Earth then than scientists in the 20th century knew about the Milky Way, which is to say that attitudes towards discovery of the unknown were similar then and now. And any educated or observant person during the Middle Ages, especially the Scholastics, recognized that the Earth was not flat, since its shadow on the Moon is curved during a lunar eclipse.

Who's the Literalist?

It is hard to escape the conclusion that the Wizards have more in common with Biblical-literalists (in their reading of the Bible) than with the Scholastics, who were open-minded and recognized the difference between metaphor and analogy. Ironically, the Wizards seem to take the Bible literally, despite the contempt in which they hold Biblical-literalists. The Scholastics, by contrast, did not promote Biblical-literalism, and believed that God is not a literalist.[46]

Aquinas would have agreed with the Big Bang theory after having reviewed the evidence and understood its reasonableness. He analyzed concepts such as infinity, eternity, and time in light of all available information (including revelation). He would not have rejected the argument, for example, that man descended from apes, as long as man's human nature was not reduced to materiality.

Most Wizards push the idea that there seems to be a negative correlation between intelligence and religiosity; in other words, the more intelligent a person, the less likely he is to be religious (which is by definition a good thing). And in a debate about the existence of God at Oxford in 2012, Peter Millican seemed to poke fun at John Lennox and others present for their evidence-based defense of God.[47] But we ask, do not most of the anti-theist Wizards call into question their own rationality when they fail to put forth credible evidence for their atheism? On what basis, other than blind faith (as Atkins seems to confirm in a discussion with Lennox) or a knee-jerk disdain for philosophy, does their atheism rest?[48]

Other Fables and Exaggerations about the Middle Ages

It is sad that medieval monks and schoolmasters are regularly lambasted by the anti-theists. Jean-Baptiste Moliere (1622–1673), the French playwright, revealed his prejudices towards the Judeo-Christian worldview when he wrote of "the bland taste of Gothic monuments. They represent the heinous monstrosities of ignorant centuries." The tradition of criticizing Judeo-Christian symbols and ideas is well documented in history and continues to this day but is false and misleading.

Can anyone in his right mind seriously call the works of medieval architects such as James of St. George (1230–1309), Henry Yeverley (1320–1400), or Pierre de Montreuil (c. 1200–1266), the man behind the Abbey of Saint German-des-pres and Notre Dame de Paris, intellectually incompetent because of their Judeo-Christian worldview or because they lived in the Middle Ages? It would be disingenuous to think that medieval architects who designed the cathedral of Durham in the 12th century and that of Cologne in the 13th century were second-rate when compared to modern-day architects, simply because they believed in God.

Daniel-Rops writes that the Middle Ages were "an era which bequeathed to us the Royal Porch at Chartres, the façades of Amiens and Rheims, the windows of La Sainte Chapelle, and the frescoes of Giotto; which begot the mystical St. Bernard and St. Bonaventure, the *Summa Theologica* of St. Thomas, and the prophetic works of Roger Bacon and of Dante; which saw the birth of those religious and secular institutions which were to serve as bases for posterity. Only the ages of Pericles, Augustus, and Le Roi Soleil can rival in creative energy the period which elapsed from the death of Louis VII of France to that of his great-grandson St. Louis, from the election of Innocent II to that of Pope St. Celestine."[49] Is it not obvious that the Middle Ages were not a period of decline as they are often portrayed by many of the Wizards of the Enlightenment? And yet, to this day, many people repeat the catchy phrase of Ruth H. Green, a leading skeptic in the 20th century: "There was a time when religion ruled the world. It is known as the Dark Ages."[50]

Literature, Conflict, and Witches

Literature during the Middle Ages was not unrefined, as many anti-theists have suggested. There were plenty of great books that helped preserve and transmit the Judeo-Christian historical legacy. For example, *The Divine Comedy* of Dante Alighieri (1265–1321), written in the Tuscan dialect, encapsulates the Judeo-Christian worldview of the afterlife and much of Scholastic philosophy and the science of the day.

In England, Ireland, Scotland, and Wales, there is a long tradition of medieval literature that is written both in the vernacular languages and in Latin, Ireland possessing perhaps the richest and most diversified literary tradition among the Nordic regions in the early Middle Ages. Other great works of the period include the *Canterbury Tales,* by Geoffrey Chaucer (1386–1400), and the *Decameron,* by Giovanni Boccaccio (1313–1375).

Over the past 350 years, however, volumes of literature against the so-called Dark Ages have been written that is fictional but often presented as factual and historical. Because of the gross generalizations and excellent narrative, monks and other religious folk have been portrayed as sleazy and stupid. Take, for example, Matthew Gregory Lewis's powerful 1796 book, *The Monk,* as an example of anti-religious literature designed to mock and belittle. It is a garish yarn set in the Middle Ages about scandalous monks, treacherous clerics, and creepy nuns. Yes, serious abuses of all sorts existed (but they were not representative of the mast majority of religious folk). *The Monk* represents a type of (gratuitious) anti-religious Gothic literature in England designed to undercut the credibility of the Judeo-Christian community.

French and German Gothic literature of the same genre also publicized the negative aspects of the Middle Ages, as if the men and women religious at the time were more immoral, hypocritical, and irrational than the current scandals and sexcapades in and around Hollywood, which, incidentally, regularly entertains us with anti-Christian nonsense. For anti-theists to harp on the sins of some wayward monks would be like condemning anthropology, evolutionary theory, and even science, because certain scientists in 1912 *deliberately* forged the Piltdown Man to advance their interests and ideas about human evolution. The forgery stood for more than 40 years. An honest scholar should not condemn Scholasticism and the Middle Ages because of a few wayward clerics. Likewise, no one should condemn science because of some deceitful scientists (such as those who believe in alien life without a stitch of evidence).

Men such as Renan, Hegel, and Hitchens expressed disdain towards the Middle Ages because of their general derision of religion and the Judeo-Christian worldview. They trumpeted the negative "big news" items, such as renegade monks, the Spanish Inquisition, or the sacking of Constantinople (1204),[51] as if those aberrations are representative of Christianity throughout the centuries. There is no need to defend the Inquisition (or torture); it was unequivocally a misguided Christian affair carried out by a minority of errant religious authorities who misread the meaning of freedom and tolerance.

To put matters into context, during the entire 350 years of the Spanish Inquisition about 3,000 people were put to death; that is 3,000 too many, and such actions should never be justified or repeated. Compare this with the 6,000,000 (or 6 million) Jews killed by the Nazi regime during its brief lifespan, or the 60 million done to death in the Soviet Gulag (estimated death tolls vary but were in the tens of millions).

An interesting indicator shedding light on the Middle Ages is the *relative* state of peace that prevailed in Europe during the period. It would seem that large-scale wars and mass killings in medieval Europe were much rarer than in modern times. Not even the Hundred Years' War (1337–1453) can be compared with the Nazis' 900-day siege of Leningrad or the dropping nuclear bombs on Japan or firebombing Dresden less than 75 years ago.

It is claimed that the Middle Ages were a brutal and uncivilized age compared with the supposed humaneness of later eras. Surely no historian would dispute the fact that the total casualty figures from all *European* military conflicts over nearly 800 years from the 6th to the 14th century did not begin to approach the number killed in warfare in any given century from the Enlightenment to the present day. Or that the combined casualty figures from the ten biggest modern-era battles, including the First Battle of the Marne (1914), the Somme (1916), Verdun (1916), Leningrad (1941-44), and Stalingrad (1941), and the bombings of Tokyo, Dresden, Hiroshima, and Nagasaki (1945) exceeded the total of all casualties from all *intra-European* wars during the Middle Ages. As Fyodr Dostoyevsky (1821–1881) sums up eloquently in *The Brothers Karamazov*, "If there is no God, anything is permitted."

Closing Remarks

The Middle Ages were full of life and at the cutting edge of philosophy, science, architecture, economics, music, and literary arts. It was a time of exploration and of great expectations. It was a time of relative intra-European tranquility, except along the geographic frontiers of Christendom. The great schoolmasters understood that there could not be any contradiction between matters of Christian revelation and reason. They saw that the workings of the universe were intelligible and that God, not chance, made that possible.

The Scholastics prepared men and women not only to be good but to be good for the sake of others. They encouraged students and colleagues to go out into the deep and discover the world through serious learning, travel, dialogue, and mathematics. They defended the study of science, economics, politics, medicine, and much more, and progress in those and other fields remains a testament to their hard work and ingenuity, which were by-products of a lively and balanced Judeo-Christian mindset unafraid of the truth and in love with it.

They demanded free debate, sought predictability in the laws of nature, and recognized that people have a purpose or end beyond survival and procreation. They believed in the natural moral law and tried to live by it, just as we must live by the laws of nature or suffer the consequences if we do not. Genuine human development was seen not as an accidental offshoot of random, unguided evolutionary processes, but rather as an expression of the mind of God in the universe not inconsistent with reason and science. And the men and women of the Middle Ages believed in Christ because He loves us and rose from the dead.[52]

The Church welcomed science and scientists into its universities and schools. It did not oppress, hassle, clamp down on, torture, gut, or burn scientists, as some have intimated. On the contrary, Aquinas, Albert, Bacon, Ockham and many others lived a privileged life and were toasted and revered.[53]

The Scholastics did not fall into the Enlightenment Trap of believing that the only source and guarantor of truth is science. They did not buy into materialism, because to do so is irrational. A kind of self-inflicted and real "Dark Ages," however, in fact appeared much later, and exists to this day. It became manifest when scientists began to claim, as Jaki says, that "[Christ's] miracles are the kind of empirical facts over which science claims exclusive competence. The exact measure to which the rise and growth of empirical method contributed to the de-Christianization of the Western world may never be settled but the measure was not negligible."[54] If science is the source and guarantor of truth, then historical singularities or facts of history (which are not repeatable or testable by science) would simply not be subject to verification, and, therefore, of uncertain validity and quite possibly untrue. History would then be meaningless.

Humanity should heed the words of Cardinal Newman, not because he was a clergyman but rather because what he said remains robustly reasonable and in line with the majority of the work of the Scholastics: "I want a laity, not arrogant, not rash in speech, not disputatious, but men who know their religion, who enter into it, who know just where they stand, who know what they hold and what they do not, who know their creed so well that they can give an account of it, who know so much of history that they can defend it."[55] The Scholastics did not fear ideas, accepted the rigors of the laws of nature, and were in a love affair with innovation and a spirit of discovery for the sake of others, which is why the Judeo-Christian worldview stimulated science and education in ways that atheism, Buddhism, Hinduism, Islam, and pantheism never did.

The Middle Ages were not dark, dangerous, and dreary. Exploration, innovation, and curiosity were as much a part of the Middle Ages as they were in later periods in history. The spirit of the men who landed on the Moon is not unlike the spirit of the men of the late Middle Ages who sailed over the horizon in rickety ships to discover the secrets of the unknown world. Marco Polo (1254–1324) was a great explorer not because he fled from the boredom of the Middle Ages, but rather precisely because his Judeo-Christian roots developed within him an adventurous spirit, a desire to see the world and get to the bottom of the mysteries of the universe (and perhaps to make a name for himself as well and have a good time doing it).

And so, while the Wizards' confidence in unlocking the mysteries of the natural world is praiseworthy, it is foolish for anyone to mock the very Judeo-Christian worldview that inspired and continues to inspire a spirit of service that led not only to scientific research but to great art, literature, and genuine human development.

Unless one entirely denies the historical record of the Middle Ages, the Scholastics, building on the past and on their own genius, with the encouragement of the solid and reasonable ideas of sound clerics and the Church, laid the groundwork for the Renaissance and the Enlightenment. Unlike many of the Wizards (and unlike the mindset of many Muslim theologians today), the Scholastics took very seriously the Petrine injunction in the New Testament: "*Always be ready to give an explanation to anyone who asks you for a reason for your hope.*"[56]

---

1.   Christopher Hitchens, "Pictures from an Inquisition," *The Atlantic*, December 2003 (https://www.theatlantic.com/magazine/archive/2003/12/pictures-from-an-inquisition/302838/).

2.   Francis (pope), *Laudato Si' (On Care for Our Common Home)*, (encyclical letter; Vatican Press, 2015); point 136 (http://w2.vatican.va/content/francesco/en/encyclicals/documents/papa-francesco_20150524_enciclica-laudato-si.html).

3.   Stanley L. Jaki, *The Savior of Science* (Edinburgh: Scottish Academic Press, 1990); p.4.

4.   See also the works of Jacob Burckhardt (1818–1897), Charles William Previté-Orton (1877–1947), Arnold Toynbee (1889–1975), Christopher Dawson (1889–1970), Henri Daniel-Rops (1901–1965), and Josef Pieper (1904–1997). Focusing on the 7th to 10th centuries is Emmet Scott, *A Guide to the Phantom Dark Ages* (Sanford, N.C.: Algora Pub-

lishing, 2014).

5. Christopher Dawson, *Religion and the Rise of Western Culture: The Classic Study of Medieval Civilization* (NewYork: Image Books, 1950); p. 224.

6. Richard Dawkins explains why he believes that certain questions are not meaningful in his discussion with Paula Kirby (Eden Court Theatre, Inverness; April 2008) (https://www.youtube.com/watch?v=LSZ_fsG5uMg).

7. Stanley L. Jaki, "Monkeys and Machine-Guns: Evolution, Darwinism and Christianity," *Chronicles,* August 1986.

8. See John Lennox, "Miracles: Is Belief in the Supernatural Irrational?" (Veritas Forum, March 2012) (https://www.youtube.com/watch?time_continue=9&v=2Kz4OgX-sN1w).

9. "Then God said: Let the earth bring forth every kind of living creature: tame animals, crawling things, and every kind of wild animal. And so it happened: God made every kind of wild animal, every kind of tame animal, and every kind of thing that crawls on the ground. God saw that it was good. Then God said: Let us make human beings in our image, after our likeness." (Genesis 1:24-26).

10. David Berlinski, *The Devil's Delusion: Atheism and Scientific Pretensions* (New York: Basic Books, 2009); p. 65 (vedicilluminations.com/downloads/Intelligent-Design/the-devils-delusion-atheism-and-its-scientific-pretensions-david-berlinski.pdf).

11. "Credo ut intelligam."

12. "Intelligo ut credam."

13. The Scholastics produced such milestones as: (a) a clear development in man's understanding that revelation (God's communication with mankind) and reason (man's powers of mind to logically think, understand, and form judgments, especially in science and natural philosophy) cannot be contradictory, but rather reinforce each other at all times; (b) culture is not static but rather advances or recedes over time from generation to generation and that Judeo-Christian culture must be preserved and transmitted for there to be integral human development; and (c) reality is the basis of truth, i.e., that truth is not relative, subjective, or self-referencing.

14. Benedict XVI (pope), (adddress, September 2010 [italics added]) (http://w2.vatican.va/content/benedict-xvi/en/speeches/2010/september/documents/hf_ben-xvi_spe_20100917_societa-civile.html).

15. C.W. Previté-Orton, *The Shorter Cambridge Medieval History,* vol. 1 (NewYork: Cambridge University Press, 1982): p. 283.

16. Josef Pieper, *Scholasticism: Personalities and Problems of Medieval Philosophy* (New York: McGraw–Hill, 1964); p. 23.

17. For an excellent discussion on this topic, see Paul Shrimpton, *The "Making of Men": The* Idea *and Reality of Newman's University in Oxford and Dublin* (Leominster, England: Gracewing Publishing, 2014).

18. Wilfred Ward, *The Life of John Henry Cardinal Newman,* vol. 1, *The King William Street Lectures* (New York: Longmans, Green, and Co., 1912); Newman, Letter to Mrs. Froude, June 27, 1848, note 5; p. 243.

19. Josemaria Escrivá, *The Way* (New York: Scepter Press, 1983); point 301.

20. Alcuin of York (735–804) was the brainpower behind the Carolingian Renaissance

at the end of the 8th century that brought together the best minds in Europe to lay the foundations of present-day France. He developed the liberal arts. His influence stretched from Spain to Scotland and from Germany to Italy. As a cleric and the abbot of Tours, he was representative of the great scholars and schoolmasters of the Middle Ages.

21.   See Viktor Frankl, *Man's Search for Meaning* (New York: Beacon Press, 1992); pp. 48-49.

22.   See Frederick Copleston, *History of Philosophy*, vol. 2, *Medieval Philosophy* (New York: Image Books, 1993); pp. 202–434. For a charming biography of St. Thomas Aquinas see G.K. Chesterton, *St.Thomas Aquinas: "The Dumb Ox"* (New York: Image Books, 1956).

23.   Jaki, *Savior of Science*, pp. 87-88.

24.   Jaki, *Savior of Science*, p. 50.

25.   Joseph A. Schumpeter, *History of Economic Analysis*, revised/expanded ed. (New York: Oxford University Press, 1963); p. 92.

26.   Schumpeter, *History*, p. 92.

27.   Eric Roll, *A History of Economic Thought* (London: Faber and Faber Ltd., 1938); p. 45.

28.   Roll, *History*, p. 45.

29.   Schumpter, *History*, p. 93.

30.   In the case where no normal competitive price existed, Aquinas recognized, as coming within his concept of just price, the element of the subjective value of an object to the seller and not to the buyer. The distinction is important for the treatment of interest by the later Scholastics.

31.   Schumpeter, *History*, p. 93.

32.   Hume may have picked up on some of Ockham's ideas. Ockham's moral ethics is somewhat confusing in that it is not clear whether the goodness or badness of an act (and the overall normative structure) depends on man's mere acceptance of the will of God or on man's exercise of human reason in the light or presence of God's will. The challenge for the thinking man throughout history has been to figure out to what extent morality depends on right reason and personal freedom and to what extent it depends on his need to conform his own will to the eternal (unchanging) will of God, which is expressed in the form of commands. Islam chose the latter. The Judeo-Christian tradition chose the former. Is God's will always acting in the world in a way that incapacitates free will?

33.   Diego Lasheras, *Luis de Molina's De Iustitia et Jure as Virtue in an Economic Context* (Leiden: Brill, 2011); p. 222.

34.   Schumpeter, *History*, p. 95.

35.   The Hanbali school represents an orthodox Sunni Islamic school of theology (jurisprudence) that reflects the thinking of Ahmad ibn Hanbal (d. 855), an Iraqi scholar. In the 19th century (and up to the present day), the Islamic academic Muhammad ibn Abd al-Wahhabi (whence Wahhabism) and the House of Saud supported the movement and its dissemination around the world (and still do).

36.   Robert R. Reilly, *The Closing of the Muslim Mind: How Intellectual Suicide Created the Modern Islamic Crisis* (Wilmington, Del.: Intercollegiate Studies Institute, 2010), pp. 128-29.

37.   The leaders of radical militant Islam today are not just a bunch of thugs or other-

wise victims of discrimination who want justice; they are steeped in Ashar'ite thinking.

38. The interpreters of Mohammedan revelation.

39. Jaki, *Savior of Science*, p. 43.

40. Robert R. Reilly, "The Pope and the Prophet," CatholiCity, October 8, 2009 (repr. from *Crisis* magazine, November 2006) (https://www.catholicity.com/commentary/rreilly/00178.html).

41. Reilly, *Closing of the Muslim Mind*.

42. A definitive literary treatment of courtly love and chivalry may be found in the first chapter of C.S. Lewis, *The Allegory of Love: A Study in Medieval Tradition* (Oxford: Oxford University Press, 1936). It is worth adding that the chilvalric code also served to keep unruly knights from running amok.

43. In the 12th century the warrior culture of the Nordic peoples merged with the idea of a fair fight with Christian ideals and virtues.

44. Under the influence of the Byzantine Empire, most Slavonic languages, except Polish, Czech, Slovak, and Slovenian, had adopted the Cyrillic alphabet.

45. While not related to the Ottomans of today, the collapse and genocide of Christian communities in the Middle East is unprecedented, except when compared with the Armenian genocide during World War I in Anatolia. Historians will not have a difficult time in determining the cause of the current tragedy.

46. Richard Dawkins seems to take what is written in the Bible literally. That presumably is why he recommends that children read the Bible in his article "Why I Want All Our Children to Read the King James Bible," *The Guardian,* May 19, 2012. Is it really possible to fit God (who is infinite) into the human mind (finite)? (https://www.theguardian.com/science/2012/may/19/richard-dawkins-king-james-bible).

47. Lennox is brilliant in his debate with Millican and others ("Belief in God," 2013) (https://www.youtube.com/watch?v=XZlXcQtrmIQ).

48. See "Duelling Professors — John Lennox and Peter Atkin" (Big Questions, 2012) (https://www.youtube.com/watch?v=5gMS7WTHnho).

49. Henri Daniel-Rops, *History of the Church of Christ*, vol. 3, *Cathedral and Crusade: Studies in the Medieval Church, 1050–1350* (New York: E.P. Dutton & Co. Inc., 1961); p. 3.

50. Ruth Hurmence Green, *The Born Again Skeptic's Guide to the Bible* (Madison, Wisc.: Freedom from Religion Foundation, 1979).

51. In fact, in recent years, Pope St. John Paul II, formally apologized to the Greek Orthodox Church. In 2004, the Ecumenical Patriarch of Constantinople, Bartholomew I, accepted the apology.

52. Lee Strobel, *The Case for Christ: A Journalist's Personal Investigation of the Evidence for Christ* (Grand Rapids, Mich.: Zondervan, 1998).

53. The Church honored academics Walter Burley, Anthemisu of Tralles, Thierry of Chartres, John Philoponus, Paul of Aegina, Venerable Bede, Rabanus Maurus, Thomas Bradwardine, Pope Sylvester II, Albrecht of Saxony, Abulcasis, Constantine the African, John Peckham, Robert Grosseteste, John Sacrobosco, Theodoric Borgognoni, William Salceto, Richard of Wallingford, Guy de Chauliac, and Nicole Oresme.

54. Jaki, *Savior of Science*, p. 4.

55.   As quoted in Benedict XVI (pope), Homily at the Beatification Mass for John Henry Cardinal Newman, September 2010.

56.   1 Peter 3:15 (http://www.usccb.org/bible/1peter/3).

CHAPTER 5

The Renaissance: God Everywhere

Humanism was a real historical movement, but it was never a philosophy or a religion. It belongs to the sphere of education, not to that of theology or metaphysics. No doubt it involved certain moral values, but so does any educational tradition. Therefore, it is wiser not to define humanism in terms of philosophical theories or even of moral doctrines, but to limit ourselves to the proposition that humanism is a tradition of culture and founded on the study of humane letters.

— Christopher Dawson, *Christianity and the Humanist Tradition*

The creative prowess of the Renaissance was not a result of "getting rid of God" or of ignoring the great ideas, chivalric traditions, humane letters, and pious attitudes of the Middle Ages; rather the splendid achievements of the Renaissance represent in the main a continuation of the legacy of the Judeo-Christian worldview and approach to education, which fundamentally rested on the centrality of human dignity, the beauty and intelligibility of the universe, the celebration of a spirit of innovation, a love of curiosity and freedom, and the importance of service towards society and other people. For anti-theists or anyone else, for that matter, to imply that the Renaissance was a mostly secular event is like suggesting that the sun revolves around the earth.

It is likely that the Florentine painter and sculptor Michelangelo (1475–1564), the Polish scientist Nicolaus Copernicus (1473–1543), and the English Cardinal St. John Fisher (1459–1535) each enjoyed the same unwavering conviction of his own ability to understand the meaning of life, living, and the universe without feeling compelled to declare theism nonsense. Likewise, the Russian engraver Ivan Fyodorov (1525–1583), the English playwright William Shakespeare (1564–1616), and the Genoese explorer Christopher Columbus (1451–1506) would have agreed with the proposition that genuine human development can best be built on the fundamental Judeo-Christian idea of the dignity of the human person. They knew (deep down) that their innovative spirit, desire to excel, and achievements did not depend on some irrational need to reject their Judeo-Christian heritage, as many present-day anti-theists argue, but to embrace it more fully.

The Renaissance Christian humanists possessed a healthy self-confidence that allowed them to "push the envelope" of knowledge and performance while respecting the demands of objective truth, the natural moral law, and the physical laws of nature. They were driven to discover God in their work and surroundings. The Judeo-Christian worldview inspired the thinkers and artists of the Renaissance; it undergirds their propensity to celebrate life, think expansively, and live dangerously without taking leave of reality or denying the existence of the one, uncreated God of the universe. "For humanism also appeals to man as man. It seeks to liberate the universal qualities of human nature from the narrow limitations of blood and soil and class and to create a common language and a common culture in which men can realize their common humanity."[1] And should anyone have forgotten, Christian humanism has zero tolerance for racism, bigotry, xenophobia, cultural superiority, or belittlement of others.

Some Background

The epoch of the Renaissance was marked by the partial breakdown of Christendom including revolts against the unity of the Christian Church, beginning in earnest with John Wycliffe in the late 14th century and Jan Hus in the early 15th century. These "protestantizing" movements were followed by the emergence of semi-mystical groups (displaying elements of godless pantheism or sorcery), and then by Martin Luther, Huldrych Zwingli, John Calvin, and Henry VIII. We shall not dwell on the Reformation here, except to remind our readers that spiritual disunity among brothers and sisters is never good or productive. Nor shall we address the view that fratricide is inevitable, except to assert that it *is* avoidable.

The common people of the Renaissance sensed that the attainment of happiness and, ultimately, eternal salvation was as much in their own hands, as free agents with intellect and will, as it was in the hands of the Christian institutions that guided them in this life. Those two attitudes, in part drawn from efforts to clean up much of the waywardness within the ecclesiastical structures of the time, fueled the Judeo-Christian humanist spirit of the Renaissance and brought out the genius in the human person across the pan-European landscape, which includes the nations of the Orthodox world.

The Renaissance's new receptiveness to the wonders and mysteries of the world can best be explained by a desire to understand God and nature better and to discover new ways to serve others. That required people to explore their inner souls and find novel ways of expression. In some cases, academics had to come down from the rarefied sanctuary of logic and theology and experience ordinary reality to understand what "personhood" meant. The Renaissance humanists managed to delve into the material conditions of life as no one had ever done before, even as they preserved the insights about human nature and personhood garnered from early Christianity and the Middle Ages.

More Background

According to Christopher Dawson, absent the achievements of the Roman Empire, early Christian scholars and the Scholastics, there would never have been an identity strong enough to create a lasting pan-European civilization: "The beginnings of Western culture are to be found in the new spiritual community which arose from the ruins of the Roman Empire owing to the conversion of the Northern barbarians to the Christian faith. The Christian Church inherited the traditions of the Empire. It came to the barbarians as the bearer of a higher civilization, endowed with the prestige of Roman law and the authority of the Roman name. The breakdown of the political organization of the Roman Empire had left a great void that no barbarian king or general could fill, and this void was filled by the Church as the teacher and law-giver of the new peoples. The Latin Fathers — Ambrose, Augustine, Leo and Gregory — were in a real sense the fathers of Western culture, since it was only in so far as the different peoples of the West were incorporated in the spiritual community of Christendom that they acquired a common culture. It is this, above all, that distinguishes the Western development from that of other world civilizations." [2]

The rapid development in art, architecture, and literature, particularly during the 15th and 16th centuries, can be traced not only to the innate human aspiration for personal self-expression but to a Judeo-Christian spirit that actively encourages personal perfection and service towards others. In this sense, the University of Oxford's motto, *Dominus illuminatio mea* (the Lord is my Light), constitutes wise counsel regarding the link between faith and reason, and its relationship to personal development. This inscription, and many others of the time, was seen not only as a key to unlocking the wisdom of ancient philosophy but delving into knowledge itself, i.e., a master key to gain a better understanding of the nature of persons and the meaning of equality, brotherhood, and freedom.

Lest anyone forget, Christian humanists and their Scholastic predecessors, far from being intellectually arid and closed-minded, were in a love affair with the universe (visible and invisible), precisely because the human person was seeking to do well by God and neighbor. And for the most insightful of the Scholastics, "feelings" and the senses were as much a part of being human as reason and logic. (And this acceptance of reason as compatible with revelation and the intelligibility of the universe is at the core of the profound difference between the Judeo-Christian and Islamic philosophical-theological mindsets.)

The human quest for truth bore similar characteristics during the medieval period and the Renaissance. A spirit of enterprise, a sporting approach was just as important to navigating the high seas as for self-discovery. The growing spirit of exploration, which would open the Americas, Africa and East Asia, was seen as a good thing, despite the nattering of naysayers, adherents of old ways of doing things, and stick-in-the-mud clerics who were prone to look askance at change. But the Church as an institution at no time penalized people for being inquisitive or curious.

Shedding Aristotelian Apriorism

The beginning of the end of *apriorism* occurred in the early 14the century, at the height of the so-called Dark Ages. Its undoing was the work of priests.

During the Renaissance, both Christians and non-Christians were still under the impression that Aristotle's longstanding fixed idea about the movement of celestial bodies was the last word on the subject. Acceptance of Aristotle's universals handicapped the development of science for more than 1,500 years until clever scientists such as Copernicus, Johannes Kepler, and Galileo Galilei disseminated the ideas of some of the Scholastics who saw the folly of Aristotle's intellectual blunder. In time, science and art came more and more to be understood as different stories from the same book of reality, each bearing the stamp of God on its binding. But it must be clear that Aristotle's mistake, and that of subsequent generations of scientists and philosophers up to the 16th century, did not arise because of their belief in God but rather because they were simply wrong.

Michelangelo saw the difference between divine and natural law, as well as respected the physical laws of nature and that "things" had a purpose. He thus could say that "the true work of art is but a shadow of the divine perfection." Leonardo da Vinci (1452–1519) and his great contemporaries, among them St. Thomas More (1478-1535) and Desiderius Erasmus (1466-1536), studied Aristotle, Plato, Cicero, and the Dominican and Franciscan Scholastics of the Middle Ages. They believed in the one, uncreated God of the universe, and saw that civilizations depended on respecting natural law, transcendent values and moral reasoning anchored in the eternal wisdom of a loving God.

Atheism and pantheism, which are virtually one and the same thing, did not have the impact on Renaissance thinking that they had in ancient Greece and are having today. In the 16th century, nearly every thinking person accepted that God was not just one among many other gods in the world, but the unique God of creation, outside of time and space, and always beyond the reach of those inclined to try to measure or find that which has no material properties. As a result, Renaissance thinkers had nothing to fear in speaking publicly about God or theorizing about the physical universe, because philosophy, theology, science, and art were seen as compatible with religion. Renaissance thinkers, artists, and scientists drank from the same Hellenized Judeo-Christian source as the Scholastics.

There is no specific date for the start of the Renaissance. It developed organically from historical antecedents that reflected the truth of Joseph Schumpeter's dictum that "historical developments are always continuous.[3]" Christopher Dawson amplified the point. He said the Renaissance "had its roots deep in the past and ... had been developing for centuries in the Mediterranean world before it achieved its full expression in fifteenth-century Italy."[4] It is clear that the Renaissance did not spontaneously materialize after a few *avant-garde* Italian scholars unearthed the long-lost beauty of Antiquity and reintroduced the classics into university curricula. It is more accurate to say that Christian humanism *was* the spirit behind the Renaissance and that it was, therefore, much more than a simple rebirth of pre-Christian pantheistic spiritualism.

Dawson again brings the full story into focus: "Taken in its widest sense education is simply the process by which the new members of a community are initiated into its way of life and thought from the simplest elements of behavior up to the highest tradition of spiritual wisdom. Christian education is therefore an initiation into the Christian way of life and thought, and for one thousand two hundred years, more or less, the peoples of Europe have been submitted to this influence. The process has been intensive at some points, superficial at others, but taking it as a whole it may be said that nowhere else in the history of mankind can we see such a mighty stream of intellectual and moral effort directed through so many channels to a single end. However incomplete its success may have been, there is no doubt that it changed the world, and no one has any right to talk of the history of Western civilization unless he has done his best to understand its aims and its methods."[5]

A Christian humanist, in some ways, was a super-charged Scholastic with a lay mentality and a Medieval education who "de-mythologized" St. John of the Cross (1547–1591) and St. Teresa of Avila (1515–1582), all the while embracing a generalist's education that included reading the classics and studying the works of Augustine and Tertullian. The Renaissance was an attempt to bring God more fully into the middle of everyday life.

As such, the men and women of the Renaissance cherished the imagination as a means to uncover and express the beauty of God and of the natural world. They made great advancements in understanding that human development was about the whole person, and that a certain level of interior peace of mind could be attained not only in heaven but on earth without buying into utopian fairytales or magic. Leonardo da Vinci, it would seem, was the embodiment of a scientist, artist, and man of God who saw no opposition between (evidence-based) faith and reason.

Peace of Mind amid Crisis

During the Renaissance, the struggle between the temporal and spiritual carried on unabatedly. As always, life had its share of crises and suffering. Kings and popes feuded while princes and bishops angled for power and influence. Moreover, the wounds inflicted by the Hundred Years' War (1337–1453), the Great Western Schism (1378–1418), and the Black Plague (1347–1349) had not yet healed. To further complicate the political landscape, Ottoman armies were marching into Central Europe and controlled the eastern Mediterranean, despite their expulsion in 1492 from the Iberian Peninsula with the Reconquista, and their staggering defeat at Malta in 1565.[6] Additionally, such issues as the Investiture Controversy, simony, and the arguments over the role of the legal system in the regulation of the civil and ecclesiastical worlds had no easy solutions at the time.

But as long as fundamental principles and the underlying Judeo-Christian spirit of service, however tattered, prevailed, there remained a unity of vision that encouraged reconciliation and allowed for diversity of expression and personal freedom. As a result, a shared Judeo-Christian worldview and a common understanding of the meanings of virtue, freedom, justice, and rational behavior guided public discourse and public policy. Despite problems and disappointments along the way, men such as Roger Bacon (1214–1294), Bl. Dun Scotus (1266–1308), Galileo (1564–1642), Michelangelo, Kepler (1571–1630), and Copernicus remained faithful to truth, i.e., to reality. They did not embrace the philosophical errors of the anti-theists of the time who managed in later centuries to bamboozle such notables as Baron d'Holback (1723–1789), Denis Diderot (1713–1789), and David Hume (1711–1776).

To the chagrin of most Wizards, scholars such as Galileo did not get lost in a world of skepticism or embrace atheism or pantheism as a precondition for creative thinking. While some scholars rightly disliked ecclesiastical overreach and the inertia of orthodox thinking, the Christian humanist, not unlike scholars during the Middle Ages, knew that God welcomed innovation, mathematics, and artistic expression. There was no need for Galileo, for example, to make an "act of unfaith" — an act of the will to *not* believe in God — in order to engage in science. It has been shown many times that science and Christianity are entirely compatible, and yet many Wizards continue to push the opposite view.

The Renaissance emphasized emotion over formal logic or compliance with external rules and obligations, as was more often done during the Middle Ages. One might say that the Renaissance was a movement to transform the world from within while remaining faithful to the laws of physics and the natural moral law. In support of this view, G.K. Chesterton, when explaining Shakespeare's brilliance, says, "The Renaissance was, as much as anything, a revolt from the logic of the Middle Ages. We speak of the Renaissance as the birth of rationalism; it was in many ways the birth of irrationalism. It is true that the medieval School-men, who had produced the finest logic that the world has ever seen, had in later years produced more logic than the world can ever be expected to stand. They had loaded and lumbered up the world with libraries of mere logic; and some effort was bound to be made to free it from such endless chains of deduction. Therefore, there was in the Renaissance a wild touch of revolt, not against religion but against reason.... When all is said, there is something a little sinister in the number of mad people in Shakespeare. We say that he uses his fools to brighten the dark background of tragedy; I think he sometimes uses them to darken it."[7] Yes, the Renaissance mutinied against reason but not against religion — and that is what is important.

The Renaissance produced a more settled and mature understanding of a person's need for inner self-expression and freedom. It brought to life Scholastic learning while eschewing the trappings of quietism, atheism, voluntarism and rationalism. During the Renaissance, scholars with a Judeo-Christian outlook understood that a desire for freedom had to be compatible with virtue and balance. With such an outlook, artistic expression matured, and artists added a third dimension – depth – to painting, which expanded beyond the predominant taciturn and aloof two-dimensional works of medieval artists into moving expressions of real life and feeling. Compare, for example, the works of Hildegard of Bingen (1098–1179) and Michelangelo (1475–1564). By adding depth and perspective to works of art, the Renaissance invigorated the innately imaginative heart of the human person.

Science and Galileo

Science and the humanities progressed, not because man exiled God from the public square, but rather because men such as Michelangelo, Leonardo, and Galileo had nothing to fear from God and the ecclesiastical authorities of the period. Of course, there is the "Galileo Affair," which is one of those grossly overblown events in history which anti-theists love to fling in the faces of the Judeo-Christian mainstream to discredit religion, and, in particular, Christianity.[8] It is worth taking a closer look at this event because most of the Wizards point to it, repeatedly, as an example of Christianity's opposition to science and, ultimately, to truth itself.

Galileo was a brilliant scientist of the late Renaissance. He captured what it meant to push forward new ideas and question old assumptions. But Galileo was a difficult personality, who, by most accounts, had a chip on his shoulder towards his peers. His personality accounts for a large part of the story. If he was condemned by the ecclesiastical authorities, it is because he tried to do theology when he should have stuck to science. In a sense, he confused miracles and magic. He nonetheless was right when he said that "the Bible shows the way to go to heaven, not the way the heavens go"[9] but that only stated the obvious, which nearly everyone already knew.

Is it not unreasonable for anti-theists, militant critics of religion, to use this largely isolated event to accuse the Church of threatening science when one of their heroes, Galileo, was in fact the first president of the newly created Pontifical Academy of Sciences of the Catholic Church established in 1603? In his article *The Galileo Saga*, Atila S. Guimaraes explains, "What is happening is simple. These critics distort the condemnation [of Galileo's theology] by interpreting it as an attack on the scientific method, and science in general. They conveniently overlook the fact that the condemnation decree was made against the philosophic and exegetical implications of Galileo's heliocentric theory. Instead, they loudly proclaim that Galileo was unjustly condemned for applying scientific knowledge to the exegesis of Holy Scripture. They conclude his condemnation was unjust since it would be legitimate to apply scientific criteria to alter traditional Catholic exegesis, and even the meaning of revelation. The specious basis of these conclusions drawn from the Galileo saga arises from the confused boundaries between the fields of science, philosophy, and theology at the beginning of the seventeenth century."[10]

The way most anti-theists drone on about the "Galileo Affair" shows their lack of academic seriousness and paucity of ideas regarding the true spirit of the Renaissance, the differences between philosophy, theology, and science, and the larger sweep of history. And so, while it is well-known that many Wizards use the "Galileo Affair" in their on-going effort to undermine Judeo-Christianity and obscure the clear evidence of the Church's devotion to the pursuit of scientific truth, the truth about the Galileo affair is more nuanced than they let on, and deserves to be widely broadcast.

Humanists, except for the few who embraced necromancy, saw God as beyond space and time as well as omniscient and ubiquitous. Listen to Stanley Jaki discussing Galileo: "Any geometrical order in the universe could, so argued [Galileo] in the *Dialogue,* be confidently taken for an insight into the plan of the universe set by God Himself. That the plan was throughout geometrical or mathematical was not something to be learned from Archimedes, 'divine,' as he was called by Galileo. Whether they liked to admit it or not, the men of science of the Renaissance owed much to the medieval tradition where one of the most often quoted scriptural phrases was the one in the Book of Wisdom (11:20) according to which God disposed everything in measure, number and weight. No dictum of Archimedes had ever approached in emphasis that phrase which formed Judeo-Christian perception with an efficiency still to be fathomed."[11] In other words, in the Bible, thousands of years ago and well before the Greek philosophers put pen to paper, so to speak, God invited men and women to study and understand the laws of nature. In fact, the first taxonomy is mentioned in the Book of Genesis, as John Lennox insightfully points out.[12]

A godless Renaissance did not give us masterpieces such as Copernicus's *De Revolutionibus Orbium Celestium* and Kepler's *Astronomia Nova* and *Harmonices Mundi.* Those accomplishments and many others[13] came about, in no small measure, thanks to the Judeo-Christian openness to research, its embrace of Hellenistic philosophy, a recognition of the compatibility of faith and reason, and the intellectual breakthroughs of the Scholastics.

Prejudice on Both Sides

During the Renaissance, as always, there were instances of grave prejudice towards new ideas that clashed with orthodox thinking as in any age. There is no doubt that historical biases negatively impacted the credibility of ecclesiastical authorities in the eyes of skeptics. But the story cuts both ways. Stanley Jaki, a historian of science, when referring to Copernicus and to the debate about celestial motion, comments insightfully about the dogmatism of science and rationalism: "If heliocentrism was to be saved and with it the future of science, it was to be saved not so much from the grasp of fallible churchmen, who in the long run could and did learn their lesson. Heliocentrism was to be saved rather from the hold of the pontiffs of a secularist counter-church ready to hide their obscurantism under a cloak that symbolized an infallibility falsely attributed to science."[14] Jaki's assessment is spot-on. While scolding churchmen, he more severely rebukes anti-theists and the present-day Wizards who are more doctrinaire and pontifical than any of the churchmen of the 16th century.

Growth in Expression

For the men and women of the Renaissance, progress was possible without having to choose between God and man, faith and reason, or the supernatural and the natural. In this sense, most priests and monks were happy to work with laypersons simply for the sake of making life more pleasant for everyone, rather than for the sake of efficiency or material compensation. To acquire a spirit of generosity was the goal, and as such spurred on the development of the arts, sciences, jurisprudence, and humanities.

Interestingly, an attitude of independent thinking was particularly present in England and Scotland, given their exceptional traditions of individual initiative and free-thinking. These qualities helped propel a spirit of enterprise and curiosity that released an unprecedented impetus to discover the unknown. In contrast, Islamic theology and philosophy, after the victory of the Ash'arites, utterly failed to support science and the creative energies of academics in the Islamic world. Islamic scholars focused mainly on jurisprudence, having centuries earlier rejected the bases for moral reasoning and science, i.e., the link between reason and freedom.

The Renaissance's freewheeling approach to life is visible in Raphael (1483–1520), Titian (1488–1576), Ferdinand Magellan (1480–1521), Johannes Gutenberg (1398–1468), Prince Henry the Navigator (1354–1460), Erasmus (1466–1536), Donatello (1386–1466), St. Thomas More (1478–1535), and many others. These artists and scholars teach us that it is possible to think outside the box and be creative while at the same time possess a Judeo-Christian mindset. In other words, to advance along the road of integral human development, the human person must work within the bounds of reality, i.e., in line with the laws of nature and the natural (moral) law, without forgetting that respect for human dignity and personal freedom is the glue that holds societies and nations together. For without God, anything is possible, and chance explains everything and nothing, which only points to the irrationality and fecklessness of the Wizards' blind faith in anti-theism.

Pico della Mirandola and Others

Renaissance humanists recognized that a wise person accepts self-imposed limits to personal behavior because human nature, reason, experience, and good sense demand it, but there were some exceptions. Pico della Mirandola (1463–1494), in his *Oration on the Dignity of Man* (1486) likened man to an angel, a risky notion when taken literally: "If, however, you see a philosopher, judging and distinguishing all things according to the rule of reason, him shall you hold in veneration, for he is a creature of heaven and not of earth; if, finally, a pure contemplator, unmindful of the body, wholly withdrawn into the inner chambers of the mind, here indeed is neither a creature on earth nor a heavenly creature, but some higher divinity, clothed with human flesh."[15] This language suggests that human beings, having godlike qualities, might indeed be able to live freely and equitably without the guidance of an objective moral order, since reason is sufficient. Dawson is correct when he says that elements of "the Renaissance ideology also had a religious aspect since it was inspired by the Christian ideal of the dignity of human nature and the greatness of every individual soul — ideals which were constantly reiterated by Renaissance thinkers from Pico della Mirandola to Campanella."[16] One must be careful, however, not to go too far in raising the status of human beings to the level of an angel, for such thinking is de-humanizing.

The Renaissance, it must be admitted, saw the reemergence and strengthening of certain currents of spiritualistic and pantheistic thought (often cleverly disguised as consistent with Christian philosophy). A decadent form of Scholasticism combined with the intellectual weakness of some priests and bishops facilitated the emergence of ideas that tried to highjack and redefine the meaning of Christian humanism and education in the minds of ordinary people. And so, while human beings have a smattering of godlike qualities, we are not gods, which, going back to the beginning, is the mistake that Adam and Eve made.

After Aquinas, despite the great clarity of his writing about God, human nature, and morality, there began a period of extensive intellectual disagreement over the introduction from various sources of profoundly erroneous intellectual approaches (e.g., nominalism, voluntarism, and several forms of false mysticism). At the same time, some clergymen and other educators had a hard time coming to grips with the onslaught of erroneous ideas due to poor formation, physical hardships, the devastations of the plagues, political chicanery, power plays directed against them, and even irreligiosity. As a result, Christian humanism and education developed in a less than fully adequate philosophical framework, opening the door to false gods and phony messianisms.

And yet, despite the ascendency of irrational atheistic thinking, Dawson points out that "we should note that there is no justification here for the popular notion that the Renaissance was an irreligious neo-pagan movement."[17]

Let us not forget that the purer and more non-Christian variations of Neo-platonic universals that arose anew around the Platonic Academy of Florence, founded in the mid 15th century by Cosimo de Medici, were not representative of genuine Christian humanism during the Renaissance. De Medici enlisted the support of Gemistus Pletho (d. 1450) and his Gnostic allies to make their philosophy and worldview attractive to academic and common folk alike.

The most significant figures of this Neo-platonic view of life were Marsilius Ficinus (1433–1499) and Pico della Mirandola. Their ideas are more vibrant today than they were during the Renaissance.

Different currents of spiritualistic and pantheistic atheism

Marsilius Ficinus, Italian scholar and priest, introduced a version of the *Corpus Hermeticum*, a type of Gnostic text from Egypt that attributed divine status to the occult sciences and the pantheistic view of being. Into this brew he added his own Platonic and Neo-platonic conceptions. Humanity was conceived of as "one man" linked to the whole of the universe through its occult forces of movement and development. These views reduced God to a force that could supposedly be "tapped into" to produce the peace of mind required to achieve moral perfection.

Nicholas of Cusa (1401–1464) was preoccupied with the question of how to reconcile many seemingly contradictory positions among scholars. His basic proposal was that scholars had to work with contradictions as aspects of the one universal truth, which is a god in whom all opposites are reconciled. Thus, he opposed definitive statements of particular truths.

Michel Eyquem de Montaigne (1533–1592) epitomized the skeptic given his motto, "What do I know?" He espoused a radical toleration of all religions because all were fantasies of the imagination anyway; he argued that dogmatism is what keeps most people from being able to appreciate the richness of life. The study of "self" is where the richness of existence lies. These ideas are akin to those of the Wizards and their pantheist allies, and have gained considerable traction today.

More Pico

Pico della Mirandola espoused a similar pantheistic belief, which he promoted under the mantra of Christian Platonism and Neo-platonism, and a boundless exaltation of humanity. Elements of the Renaissance's spirit of self-reliance and self-awareness often led to self-adoration and self-exaltation. Attitudes of self-absorption tend to produce unhealthy individualism rooted in an exaggerated sense of self-importance and moral relativism. Pico's famous panegyric to humanity uses language that sounds reasonable but is really pseudo-Christian:

> We have given you, Oh Adam; no visage proper to yourself, nor any endowment properly your own, in order that whatever place, whatever form, whatever gifts you may, with premeditation, select, these same you may have and possess

through your own judgment and decision. The nature of all other creatures is defined and restricted within laws which We have laid down; you, by contrast, impeded by no such restrictions, may, by your own free will, to whose custody We have assigned you, trace for yourself the lineaments of your own nature. I have placed you at the very center of the world, so that from that vantage point you may with greater ease glance round about you on all that the world contains. We have made you a creature neither of heaven nor of earth, neither mortal nor immortal, in order that you may, as the free and proud shaper of your own being, fashion yourself in the form you may prefer. It will be in your power to descend to the lower, brutish forms of life; you will be able, through your own decision, to rise again to the superior orders whose life is divine.[18]

Notwithstanding an exaggerated spiritualism akin to Neo-platonism, the clear majority of men and women of the Renaissance never embraced atheism or its many philosophical subsets. In contrast to some of the well-known thinkers of the period such as Ficinus, Nicholas of Cusa, and Pico, most Renaissance artists and thinkers cultivated a fully positive humanism; that is the real story of the Renaissance. The tragedy today is that this story has been muffled or distorted by those who see Christian humanism as de-formative because God is somehow in the picture.

To get a further sense of Judeo-Christian humanism, one might read the works of Cardinal St. Cajetan (1468–1528), Francis of Ferrara (1468–1528), Francis de Victoria (c. 1483–1546), Melchior Cano (1509?–1560), Dominic de Soto (1494–1560, Dominic Banez (1528–1604), and the great academics such as St. John Fisher (1459–1535), John Colet (c. 1467–1519), and Thomas Linacre (c. 1460–1524). These scholars fed the Renaissance and later generations; their faith did not hinder their accomplishments but rather made them possible.

Clash of Other Ideas

Notwithstanding isolated cases, we need to get beyond the idea that Christianity discourages progress. During the Renaissance, a newfound confidence in self, and in life, helped to cultivate an unapologetic expression of the hidden Judeo-Christian life-force that is embedded within the human consciousness and nature. Less hindered by self-doubt, which usually stemmed from the inappropriate paternalism of some misguided educators, men and women of the Renaissance gazed more confidently into a telescope to discover the truths of life and the universe, or to work as never before with a chisel and hammer to unlock the magic found in a block of lifeless marble.

It is fair to say that the greatness of Renaissance Christian humanism stemmed from an interest in maintaining an on-going dialogue between God and man, and faith and reason. [19] That dynamic attitude stands in contrast to the views of today's radical Wizards, who believe in humanity's capacity to dominate nature and bring about a kind of unending material progress *without* the need for God while, many of them, worshipping at the altar of pantheism, voluntarism, reason, mathematics, and/or technology.

Some argue that it was a godless secular Renaissance and the Copernican revolution that launched the Scientific Revolution by releasing a pent-up spirit of optimism and creativity that religion had bottled up. They further surmised that once the riddle of the universe was cracked, so the argument goes, the Wizards would quickly master its workings to bring about some kind of permanent peace and relief from the pains of earthly existence.

In contrast, humanists with a Christian outlook were never so confident that they could discard God and Judeo-Christian culture to achieve a lasting peace of mind. That is why Kepler, astronomer and mathematician and avowed Christian, for example, was buried in the Cathedral Basilica of the Assumption of the Blessed Virgin Mary in Regensburg, Germany, whereas Voltaire and Jean-Jacques Rousseau, champions of radical Enlightenment thinking, were entombed in the Panthéon, the cathedral to atheism and pantheism, in Paris.

Liberal Education

The purpose of education during the Renaissance was largely an outgrowth of the Medieval educational experience. Italian Renaissance scholars popularized the Greek idea of a liberal education, or *paideia*, which included the study of the Greco-Roman classics from Socrates (438–338 BC), Plato (429–347 BC), and Cicero (106–43 BC) to Quintilian (AD 35–100), Tacitus (AD 56–117), and Aulus Gellius (AD 125–180). The study of their works and those of others became an essential part of a gentleman's education, representing a balanced and attractive development of mind and body, or the education of a "man for all seasons."

As some Wizards speak nonsense about the inadequacy and built-in biases of a liberal Christian education, let them and other modern skeptics ponder Dawson's words:

> It is true that Christianity is not bound up with any particular race or culture. It is neither of the East or of the West, but has a universal mission to the human race as a whole.

Nevertheless, it is precisely in this universality that the natural bond and affinity between Christianity and humanism is to be found. For humanism also appeals to man as man. It seeks to liberate the universal qualities of human nature from the narrow limitations of blood and soil and class and to create a common language and a common culture in which men can realize their common humanity. Humanism is an attempt to overcome the curse of Babel which divides mankind into a mass of warring tribes hermetically sealed against one another by their mutual incomprehensibility. If this only means that humanism is attempting to build a new tower of Babel — a city of Man founded on pride and self-will in ignorance and contempt of God — then no doubt humanism is anti-Christian. But this is not the only kind of humanism. As man needs God and nature requires grace for its own perfecting, so humane culture is the natural foundation and preparation for spiritual culture. Thus, Christian humanism is as indispensable to the Christian way of life as Christian ethics and a Christian sociology. Humanism and Divinity are as complementary to one another in the order of culture, as are Nature and Grace in the order of being.[20]

Critics of Judeo-Christian humanism unabashedly assert that education during the Middle Ages emphasized the dour and dull aspects of life rather than stimulated a mindset that rejected authority and moral reasoning anchored in natural law. This view distorts the profoundly optimistic and positive message of Christianity throughout Europe at the time. Life was viewed as a dazzling adventure full of exciting challenges and delightful earthly surprises along the way, since God, human beings, and the universe are good in themselves.

This externally positive attitude towards life and living contrasted with some of the harsh post-Reformation dogmas of those Reformers who believed in the complete corruption of human nature. It is that pessimistic, mostly Protestant, view which the Wizards may be erroneously attributing to all of Christianity.

The Italian city-states of Florence, Rome, Venice, Verona, and Siena, along with other independent courts such as Ferrara and Urbino, propelled the Renaissance forward in every aspect of human endeavor. From Florentines such as Filippo Brunelleschi (1377–1446), Michelangelo (1475-1564) Andrea del Sarto (1488–1531) and Benvenuto Cellini (1500–1571) to Venetians such as Carpaccio (c. 1465–1525), Gentile Bellini (c. 1429–1507), and Tintoretto

(1518–1594), to Veronese such as Corregio (1489–1534) to Urbinati such as Raphael (1483-1520), Italy's creative genius seemed to tower over all others at the time.

Humanist educators strove to teach students the meaning and purpose of life and to convey the importance of virtue, virtuous living, and critical thinking. As John Henry Cardinal Newman was to write centuries later, "The view taken of a University ... is the following: that it is a place of teaching of universal knowledge. This implies that its object is, on the one hand, intellectual, not moral; and, on the other, that it is the diffusion and extension of knowledge rather than the advancement. If its object were scientific and philosophical discovery, I do not see why a university should have students; if religious [i.e., strictly theological] training, I do not see how it can be the seat of literature and science."[21] This states as a good summation of Christian humanism.

Likewise, the university was designed to defend the integrity of the moral life with solid arguments and evidence. Students were taught to think independently, since genuine moral reasoning was attainable. "The aim of natural science," said Albert the Great in the 13th century, "is not simply to accept the statements of others, but to investigate the causes that are at work in nature." To rely exclusively on the authority of others for answers was increasingly discouraged during the Renaissance. And so, following the educational legacy of early Christianity and the Middle Ages, the Renaissance also produced a great variety of masters, such as Albrecht Durer (1472–1528), Lucas Cranach the Elder (1472–1553), the Danube School, Hans Holbein (1497–1543), Albrecht Altdorfer (1480–1538), and the Little Masters, as well as More, Fisher, Erasmus, and Johannes Murmellius (c. 1480–1517).[22]

In the field of education and apologetics, current Church authorities, including Popes, rely on the treasure trove of ideas and wise advice provided to humanity over the past two millennia. Take, for example, the Encyclical Letter of Pope Pius XI of 1929:

> The scope and aim of Christian education as here described, appears to the worldly as an abstraction, or rather as something that cannot be attained without the suppression or dwarfing of the natural faculties, and without a renunciation of the activities of the present life, and hence inimical to social life and temporal prosperity, and contrary to all progress in letters, arts and sciences, and all the other elements of civilization. To a like objection raised by the ignorance and the prejudice of even cultured pagans of a former day, and repeated with greater frequency and insistence

in modern times, Tertullian has replied as follows: We are not strangers to life. We are fully aware of the gratitude we owe to God, our Lord and Creator. We reject none of the fruits of His handiwork; we only abstain from their immoderate or unlawful use. We are living in the world with you; we do not shun your forum, your markets, your baths, your shops, your factories, your stables, your places of business and traffic. We take shop with you and we serve in your armies; we are farmers and merchants with you; we interchange skilled labor and display our works in public for your service. How we can seem unprofitable to you with whom we live and of whom we are, I know not.[23]

One senses a unity of life where one may live in the world and yet touch the supernatural. Work, as long as it is upright and noble, may be turned into prayer in so far as it is done for the benefit of others and as a means to love, serve, and know God.

An Educational Anomaly

Without a doubt, school masters across Europe have applied educational methods differently, even while having common objectives. Their approaches have depended on differing cultural, philosophical, and personal attitudes about the human person and the role of institutions in the learning process. Some Wizards and their anti-theist boosters, unfairly and unhelpfully, focus on those Judeo-Christian approaches to education that are unrepresentative of its broad-minded and generally balanced approach. Their querulous criticism of Christian humanism reveals an unscientific partisanship detrimental to their own case. Just as the anti-theists see the one, uncreated God of the universe as just one more god among many others, so they see all monotheistic religions as inventions of the mind. They tend to rank religions from bad to worse, just as one might rank viruses.[24] And, presumably, just as some viruses are more harmful to children and society, so are some religions.

Most Wizards, therefore, see Christian humanism as an oxymoron, and, somehow, seem to equate the Judeo-Christian approach to education in the sciences with that of Christian literalists. Because of their blinkered view of Christian humanism, anti-theists must maintain that humanism should be de-Christianized and reflect only a non-religious, secular way of thinking centered on reason and human agency without God. For the Wizards, Christianity simply corrupts learning and the process of integral human development, and therefore should be left as a form of private personal amusement.

The Wizards correctly reject educational methods that have relied more on authority than on critical thinking and self-discovery because such methods, in their view, *always* clash with the spirit of creativity. As a case in point, many educators from countries bordering the Mediterranean, while brilliant, baroque, and unremittingly tough-minded in their dogmatism, have tended to adhere to certain authoritarian teaching methods — often elitist — that set them apart from other educators in the pan-European space at the time. Such an approach to education — which is not the Judeo-Christian approach — rubs many people the wrong way, and rightly so.

Iberia

There can be little doubt that Iberia is complicated and unique: from the 8th to the 16th centuries it continued to bear the traces of 800 years of Islamic rule, and was marked by a continuing, militant Reconquista mentality, a drive to conquer the New World for God and gold, a fiery determination to counter the Protestant Reformation, and a misplaced type of educational snobbery towards common people. This powerful mix of missionary-like passions and a bare-knuckled approach to education[25] can be very off-putting, especially to those who cannot stand authority or paternalism no matter what form they take. Those with authoritarian tendencies often argue that the purpose of education is to avoid the problem of autonomous moral reasoning and free-thinking because independent thought is a very risky proposition. This corporatist spirit and elitist approach to education, so strong in in Iberia after the Renaissance, has presented the anti-theists an easy target.[26]

Schoolmasters who believed in "top-down" schooling have tended to follow standards that delivered or transferred information (and doctrine) to students. The goal of teaching was to "instruct," rather than to "guide" students towards virtue and the good. For information to be credible, its source — the one propagating it (usually an elder or eminent scholar) — had to possess authority. Creativity, originality, and personal initiative were generally not encouraged. In place of allowing autonomous thought and independent study ("punching above one's weight"), a paternalistic attitude towards students slowed the development of entrepreneurship, science, and creative thinking. It has been this isolated but institutionalized bias on the part of narrow-minded educators that has attracted the attention of the Wizards and worked against the historical record showing Christian humanism's love affair with initiative and personal autonomy.

Genuine Christian humanism embraces independent thought and moral reasoning and welcomes guidance over prescription or memorization. It does not see human nature as entirely corrupted but rather as the stuff of great spiritual and material progress. Moreover, it embraces a positive attitude towards creativity and recognizes the interplay between intellect, will, and grace.[27] The Wizards need to understand that Christian humanism in education welcomes exploration and independence.

Whenever the Wizards claim that Christians are anti–free-thinking, they should visit the libraries of European universities, beginning with the Pontifical Academy of Sciences dating back to the Renaissance.[28]

The role of the East

The Fall of Constantinople in 1453 to Ottoman armies was a catastrophic event for Christendom, Byzantium, and the Eastern Orthodox Church.[29] In the early 15th century, the last remnants of the Roman Empire in the East consisted of variegated enclaves of rivalries between the Venetian and Genoese territories in parts of present-day Greece, the Knights of St. John in Rhodes, the independent Kingdom of Cyprus, and certain territories of Byzantium consisting of Constantinople and the Peloponnesus. By 1430, all of Thessaloniki in present-day Greece had succumbed to Ottoman control.[30] These events required that Russia and Ukraine would have to carry the banner of Eastern Orthodox Christianity.

The threat of Ottoman rule in the 15th century encouraged a wave of Byzantine scholars to migrate north to Muscovy and Novgorod (Russia) and west to Italy. These migrations enriched Moscow and Rome and subsequently helped build and enrich Christian humanism, introducing an Eastern flavor to scholarship that was rooted in ancient Constantinople, Athens, Ephesus, Antioch, and Jerusalem.

Some of the more interesting figures from the period included John Cardinal Bessarion (1395–1472), the Latin Patriarch of Constantinople; the philosopher John Argyropoulos (1415–1487), of the university of Florence; the Platonist, humanist, and scholar Demetrius Chalcondyles (1424–1511); and Emmanuel Chrysoloras (1355–1415), a Greek literary scholar resident in Florence. The painter El Greco (1541–1614), Doménikos Theotokópoulos, who worked in Spain, hailed from the island of Crete.

Alexander Solzhenitsyn warned of the dangers of a secularized and de-Christianized humanism hostile to God:

> But as long as we wake up every morning under a peaceful
> sun, we must lead an everyday life. Yet there is a disaster that
> is already very much with us. I am referring to the calamity of
> an autonomous, irreligious humanistic consciousness.
>
> It has made man the measure of all things on earth —

imperfect man, who is never free of pride, self-interest, envy, vanity, and dozens of other defects. We are now paying for the mistakes that were not properly appraised at the beginning of the journey. On the way from the Renaissance to our days we have enriched our experience, but we have lost the concept of a Supreme Complete Entity, which used to restrain our passions and our irresponsibility.

We have placed too much hope in politics and social reforms, only to find out that we were being deprived of our most precious possession: our spiritual life. It is trampled by the party mob in the East, by the commercial one in the West. This is the essence of the crisis: the split in the world is less terrifying than the similarity of the disease afflicting its main sections.[31]

At some profound level, the response of the men and women of the Renaissance to Solzhenitsyn's speech at Harvard would not only have been understanding but positive, unlike the American elite who greeted his address with howls and imprecations. For all practical purposes, his Judeo-Christian–inspired humanism was trapped between the secular humanism of a godless Soviet Russia and a no-longer god-fearing capitalist America.

Statecraft

Renaissance scholars developed new insights into economics, politics, and international relations within a commonly accepted Judeo-Christian framework and a basic sense of the common good. Many of the theorists of the Renaissance went on to advise kings and their courts. They included Niccolo Perotti (1429–1480), Marsilio Ficino (1433–1499), John Doget (c.1434–1501), Cosimo de'Medici (1389–1464), Gerard Groote (1340–1384), Sigismund von Herberstein (1486–1566), Bartolome de las Casas (1484–1566), Philipp Melanchthon (1497–1560), and Michel de Montaigne (1533–1592). Bartolome de las Casas, for example, wrote treatises in defense of the Indian populations of the Americas. His work was seminal and reflected a keen understanding of the dignity of all human beings.

But not all was agreeable. The state was increasingly viewed as a vehicle to direct, rather than guide. Of particular note are the views of Niccolò Machiavelli (1469–1527), which solidified in the modern mind the idea that "evil is politically more significant, more substantial, more real than good,"[32] and therefore that evil is always present in larger doses than is good. In his basic work, *The Prince* (1513), he proposed a new political atheism. The State

— the Prince — is the highest authority, not subordinated to any extrinsic moral authority such as natural law. The wise prince must do whatever is necessary to achieve and maintain power and control. The prince must always appear (give the impression) as honest and religious, and embody many of the noblest leadership virtues while not hesitating to act ruthlessly, hypocritically, and/or deceptively to achieve his goals, irrespective of the consequences. Evil, he asserted, is often the best path to attaining a "good."

Machiavelli was probably the first person (after Thucydides) to deal systematically with the issue of war and peace. In *The Art of War* (1521), he provided practical advice on warfare and politics. Moreover, in *The Discourses* (1531), he, as an ideological pragmatist, argued that *any* action is justified to preserve political supremacy. Loyalty, discipline, and citizenship were but tools for the retention of power and the success of the city-state. John Hallowell notes, "For Machiavelli the only values that really matter are those of greatness, power, and fame. In this sense Machiavelli is truly typical of the Renaissance and truly modern. Here are laid the foundations of Realpolitik or 'power politics.' Such a conception is made possible only by divorcing politics from its foundation in metaphysics and ethics."[33] While basically agreeing with Hallowell, I would refine his statement that Machiavelli's thinking was not "truly typical" of the Renaissance but rather of modern times. Although the actions of political leaders were often as morally questionable then as they are now, a Judeo-Christian moral sense of right and wrong, good and evil, still permeated the political landscape during the Renaissance. Despite the abuse of power and corruption, moral relativism and voluntarism were broadly seen, unlike today, as unbefitting a statesman and detrimental to the dignity of the human person and the common good.

When taken to an extreme, Machiavellian Realpolitik becomes a tool with which to manage an inevitable, Darwinian struggle over resources between deadly competitors. Statecraft is reduced to vapid political moralism,[34] a system of controls, national security paranoia, the use of force, and a series of endless tactical moves in a contest of high-stakes political chess where there are only winners and losers.

If we wish to reintroduce God into the world of affairs – political, commercial and otherwise -- John Henry Cardinal Newman, gives us something to think about:

> I say, let us take "useful" to mean, not what is simply
> good, but what tends to good, or is the instrument of good;
> and in this sense also, Gentlemen, I will show you how a
> liberal education is truly and fully a useful, though it be not
> a professional, education. "Good" indeed means one thing,

and "useful" means another; but I lay it down as a principle, which will save us a great deal of anxiety, that, though the useful is not always good, the good is always useful. Good is not only good, but reproductive of good; this is one of its attributes; nothing is excellent, beautiful, perfect, desirable for its own sake, but it overflows, and spreads the likeness of itself all around it. Good is prolific; it is not only good to the eye, but to the taste; it not only attracts us, but it communicates itself; it excites first our admiration and love, then our desire and our gratitude, and that, in proportion to its intenseness and fulness in particular instances. A great good will impart great good. If then the intellect is so excellent a portion of us, and its cultivation so excellent, it is not only beautiful, perfect, admirable, and noble in itself, but in a true and high sense it must be useful to the possessor and to all around him; not useful in any low, mechanical, mercantile sense, but as diffusing good, or as a blessing, or a gift, or power, or a treasure, first to the owner, then through him to the world. I say then, if a liberal education be good, it must necessarily be useful too.[35]

In some ways, the Renaissance was a sort of liberation in that it reflected the good impulses of men and women who wanted to seek and find God amid the struggles and uncertainty of everyday life. In this sense, the Renaissance wanted to convey the idea that God is hidden in the activities of everyday life. Science could be made holy. Art could be divinized. Politics could be sanctified. Men and women wanted to discover joy in the midst of everyday life. Any noble work could be done to serve others. It was that kind of humanism which is imbued with the Judeo-Christian worldview, which the Renaissance, in particular, brought to life.

---

1.   Christopher Dawson, "Christianity and the Humanist Tradition," *The Dublin Review* (Winter 1952) (https://www.ewtn.com/library/HOMELIBR/DAWCHT.TXT).

2.   Christopher Dawson, *Religion and the Rise of Western Culture: The Classic Study of Medieval Civilization* (New York: Image Books, 1950) (https://archive.org/details/DawsonReligionAndTheRiseOfWesternCulture).

3.   Joseph A. Schumpeter, *History of Economic Analysis,* revised/expanded ed. (New York: Oxford University Press, 1963); p. 379.

4.   See Christopher Dawson, *The Dividing of Christendom* (New York: Sheed & Ward,

1965); pp. 64-65.

5.   Christopher Dawson, *Understanding Europe* (New York: Sheed & Ward, 1952), p. 242.

6.   For a profound view on Islam and its challenges to the modern world, see James V. Schall, S.J., "Belloc on the 'Apparently Unconvertible' Religion" (Vital Speeches of the Day, April 1, 2003); pp. 375-82 (http://www.catholicculture.org/culture/library/view.cfm?recnum=3437).

7.   Dale Ahlquist, ed., *The Soul of Wit: G.K. Chesterton on William Shakespeare* (New York: Dover Publications. Inc., 2012); p. 25.

8.   Regarding the Galileo affair, I would refer you to Pope St. John Paul II's address in October 1992 to the Plenary Session of the Academy of Sciences, where the whole issue is laid out and put to rest (http://bertie.ccsu.edu/naturesci/cosmology/galileopope.html).

9.   Galileo Galilei, *Letters* (Torino, Einaudi, 1978); pp. 128-35; cited in Edoardo Aldo Cerrato, C.O., "How to go to Heaven, and not how the heavens go" (http://www.oratoriosanfilippo.org/galileo-baronio-english.pdf). This article provides an excellent overview of the controversy and helps clarify the age-old misunderstanding between science and Scripture. Galileo also apparently said, "Mathematics is the language with which God has written the universe."

10.   Atila Guimaraes, "The Galilio Saga," *Social Justice Review* (January/February 1998): p. 25. See also Ronald L.Numbers, ed., *Galileo Goes to Jail and Other Myths about Science and Religion* (Cambridge, Mass.: Harvard University Press, 2009).

11.   Stanley L. Jaki, *The Savior of Science* (Edinburgh: Scottish Academic Press, 1990); pp. 87-88.

12.   See John Lennox, "Seven Days That Divide the World" (lecture, January 31, 2013) (https://www.youtube.com/watch?v=0FmO2XKMe6g).

13.   See, for example, Isaac Newton, *Principia Mathematica* (1687), during the Enlightenment. If nothing else, Newton's work stands in thunderous contradiction to the idea that there was ever a clean break between evidence-based belief and science.

14.   Jaki, *Savior of Science,* pp. 85-86.

15.   Giovanni Pico della Mirandola, *Oration on the Dignity of Man,* A. Robert Caponigri, trans. (Chicago: Henry Regnery Co. 1956); pp. 10-11 (http://www.andallthat.co.uk/uploads/2/3/8/9/2389220/pico_-_oration_on_the_dignity_of_man.pdf).

16.   Dawson, *Dividing of Christendom,* pp. 45-46. Pico della Mirandola (1463–1494) was a Neoplatonist philosopher; Tommaso Campanella (1568–1644) was a child prodigy who earned his fame, primarily, as the utopian poet who wrote *The City of the Sun,* an allegory of a utopian communist society.

17.   Christopher Dawson, *The Crisis of Western Education* (Washington, D.C.: Catholic University of America Press, 2010). p. 19.

18.   Pico, *Oration,* pp. 7-8.

19.   The idea of stewardship of natural resources is particularly strong in the Eastern Orthodox Christian world, perhaps, because of a general absence of the Protestant ethic of success, a suspicious attitude towards unruly competition, and the continuing tradition of mysticism, which focuses more on caring for creation than on dominating it.

20.   Christopher Dawson, "Christianity and the Humanist Tradition," *The Dublin Review*

(Winter 1952) (https://www.ewtn.com/library/HOMELIBR/DAWCHT.TXT).

21.	John Henry Newman, *The Idea of the University* (London: Longmans, Green, and Co., 1886); p. ix (https://archive.org/stream/a677122900newmuoft#page/n5/mode/2up).

22.	The spirit of the Renaissance in Iberia was brilliant in many areas. The best examples of Spanish Renaissance personality include the Cathedral in Granada, the façade of the University in Salamanca, the church of San Salvador in Ubeda, the Palace of Charles V in Granada, and the Monastery of El Escorial, as well as the works of El Greco (El Entierro del Conde Orgaz), Alonso Berruguete (1488–1561), Juan de Juanes (c. 1507–1579), Tomas Luis de Vitoria (1548–1611), and Cervantes, whose Don Quixote is recognized as the best representative of Spanish Renaissance literature.

In Portugal, there are fine examples of Renaissance religious and secular architecture which include the Chapel of Nossa Senhora da Conceição (1530s), the Mercy Church of Santarem (1560s), the Cathedral of Leiria (1550s), the manor houses such as La Quinta de Bacalhoa (1530–1550), the Ribeira Palace (early 16th century), and the magnificent Casa de Bicos in Lisbon (c. 1525). Great ideas produce great architecture and not the other way around.

While some of the intellectual and emotional characteristics of the Italian Renaissance penetrated Northern Europe, there are significant differences in the arts which mainly reflect local conditions and styles. In France, examples of creative thinking abound. This creativity can be seen in the Château d'Amboise (c. 1495) in the Loire Valley, one of the first examples of outstanding French Renaissance architectural design. In 1508, the François brothers designed the Cloître de Saint-Martin in Tours as well. Other great examples of Judeo-Christian inspired artwork are the Chateau de Blois (1515–1524) and the Chateau Chambord (1519–1535) as well as the decorations of the Chateau de Fontainebleau (1528–1547). There is little that can compare in the world of painting to some of the Dutch Renaissance masters such as Jan van Eyck (1390–1441), Rogier van der Weyden (1400–1464), Gerard David (1455–1523), Hans Memling (1433–1494), Hugo van der Goes (1440–1482), and Pieter Bruegel (1525–1569) the Elder.

23.	Pius XI (pope), "Divini Illius Magistri" (encyclical letter; December 31, 1929) (w2. vatican.va/content/pius-xi/en/encyclicals/documents/hf_p-xi_enc_31121929_divini-il-lius-magistri.html).

24.	Thus Dawkins: "It's tempting to say all religions are bad, and I do say all religions are bad, but it's a worse temptation to say all religions are equally bad because they're not.... If you look at the actual impact that different religions have on the world, it's quite apparent that at present the most evil religion in the world has to be Islam." (speech; quoted in Sarah Knapton, "Richard Dawkins: Religious Education Is Crucial for British Schoolchildren," *Telegraph,* June 11, 2017 (http://www.telegraph.co.uk/science/2017/06/11/richard-dawkins-religious-education-crucial-british-schoolchildren/).

25.	It is such a spirit that is reflected in so much of Iberian art, literature, architecture, scholarship, and education even to this day.

26.	If my view is correct, the long presence of the Islamic mindset in Iberia helps explain the general absence of innovation, creativity, and grass-roots level independent thought in the sciences and engineering until the early 20th century. Fortunately, these attitudes towards learning (and personal expression) have partially ceded in recent years to educational approaches that more amply accept the value of personal moral reasoning, independent thought, and creative thinking.

27.	England has enjoyed a great penchant for dialogue and exchange of ideas. Historically, people have tended to assume personal responsibility for property and decision making related to moral questions.

28.   For additional insights, see Scott Hahn and Benjamin Wiker, *Answering the New Atheism: Dismantling Dawkins' Case against God* (Steubenville, Ohio: Emmaus Road Publishing, 2008); p. 76.

29.   In the coming intellectual debate with ideological Muslim scholars of the 21st century, the Wizards of the Enlightenment should ally themselves with those of us who hold the Judeo-Christian worldview. Many do not seem to understand the perils of radical militant Islam, which, in some quarters, remains locked in an anti-intellectual dogmatism destructive of reason and inimical to development. "There is in Islam a paradox which is perhaps a permanent menace. The great creed born in the desert creates a kind of ecstasy out of the very emptiness of its own land, and even, one may say, out of the emptiness of its own theology. It affirms, with no little sublimity, something that is not merely the singleness but rather the solitude of God. There is the same extreme simplification in the solitary figure of the Prophet; and yet this isolation perpetually reacts into its own opposite. A void is made in the heart of Islam which has to be filled up again and again by a mere repetition of the revolution that founded it. There are no sacraments; the only thing that can happen is a sort of apocalypse, as unique as the end of the world; so the apocalypse can only be repeated and the world end again and again. There are no priests; and yet this equality can only breed a multitude of lawless prophets almost as numerous as priests. The very dogma that there is only one Mahomet produces an endless procession of Mahomets. Of these the mightiest in modern times was the man whose name was Ahmed, and whose more famous title was the Mahdi; and his more ferocious successor Abdullahi, who was generally known as the Khalifa. These great fanatics, or great creators of fanaticism, succeeded in making a militarism almost as famous and formidable as that of the Turkish Empire on whose frontiers it hovered, and in spreading a reign of terror such as can seldom be organized except by civilization." G.K. Chesterton, *Lord Kitchener* (London: Field & Queen [Horace Cox], Ltd., 1917); pp 4-5 (http://gutenberg.net.au/ebooks09/0900751h.html).

30.   "When people talk as if the Crusades were nothing more than an aggressive raid against Islam, they seem to forget in the strangest way that Islam itself was only an aggressive raid against the old and ordered civilization in these parts. I do not say it in mere hostility to the religion of Mahomet; I am fully conscious of many values and virtues in it; but certainly, it was Islam that was the invasion and Christendom that was the thing invaded." G.K. Chesterton, *The New Jerusalem* (New York: George H. Doran Company, 1921); p. 17 (http://www.gutenberg.org/ebooks/13468).

31.   Alexandr Solzhenitsyn, "A World Split Apart" (commencement speech; Harvard University, June 8, 1978) (http://www.americanrhetoric.com/speeches/ alexandersolzhenitsynharvard.htm).

32.   Albert Manent, *An Intellectual History of Liberalism* (Princeton, N.J.: Princeton University Press, 1995); p. 13.

33.   John H. Hallowell, *Main Currents in Modern Political Thought* (New York: Henry Holt & Company, 1950); p. 60.

34.   "Political moralism, as we have lived it and are still living it, does not open the way to regeneration, and even more, also blocks it. The same is true, consequently, also for a Christianity and a theology that reduces the heart of Jesus' message, the "kingdom of God," to the "values of the kingdom," identifying these values with the great key words of political moralism, and proclaiming them, at the same time, as a synthesis of the religions." Joseph Cardinal Ratzinger, "On Europe's Crisis of Culture" (homily, April 1, 2005) (https://www.catholiceducation.org/en/culture/catholic-contributions/cardinal-

ratzinger-on-europe-s-crisis-of-culture.html).

35.   Newman, *Idea of the University*, pp. 163-64 (https://archive.org/stream/ a677122900newmuoft#page/n5/mode/2up).

CHAPTER 6

The Protestant Reformation and Some Observations

I have a new commandment to give you, that you are to love one another; that your love for one another is to be like the love I have borne you. The mark by which all men will know you for my disciples will be the love you bear one another.

— John 13: 34-35

To be deep in history is to cease to be a Protestant.

— Bl. John Henry Cardinal Newman, *The Essay on the Development of Christian Doctrine* (1845)

Peace is the work of justice indirectly, in so far as justice removes the obstacles to peace; but it is the work of charity (love) directly, since charity, according to its very notion, causes peace.

— St. Thomas Aquinas

The Reformers, at no time, lost sight of God, notwithstanding outliers who declared their atheism. Rather, the movement in the 16th century to reform the Church was a call to reexamine certain elements of medieval scholarship and address the practices and preaching of both scholar and clergy concerning the relationships between God, man, society, and the institutions guiding man through life. In some not yet fully understood mysterious way, as Jacques Maritain suggests, "[the] Reformation unbridled the human self in the spiritual and religious order, as the Renaissance (I mean the hidden spirit of the Renaissance) unbridled the human self in the order of natural and sensible activities."[1] At no time, however, did the prevailing mood of the age dismiss the Judeo-Christian worldview or its fundamental principles, which were central in supporting the cause of genuine human development and the making of a pan-European civilization.

That there was a need to reform much of the ecclesiastical world and the emergent political order in Europe in the early 16th century is undeniable. It is regrettable, however, that the efforts of the Reformers — both Catholic and Protestant — eventually struck at the heart of European unity in the process of trying to clean up the wayward drift of some clerics (and practices) in the Church within a disturbingly semi-Pelagian[2] setting.

Adding to the problems in society related to the human condition, some Scholastic theologians, in atypical fashion, publicly embroiled themselves in futile but high-profile arguments over philosophical minutiae of little or no use to the common man or cleric. As a result, the entire profession and the (Catholic) Church (of Rome) suffered from the false impression that theology was mostly useless, when in fact the work of the Scholastics and of many of the Reformers, such as Desiderius Erasmus (1466–1536), St. Thomas More (1478–1535), and Lefèvre d'Étaples (1455–1536), was generally centered and insightful; commentary never shed its purpose to guide and teach in light of reason and a natural order that reflected the mind of God. John Calvin (1509–1564) and, particularly, Martin Luther (1483–1546), on the other hand, assumed a more combative stance against the institutional Church and its teachings, unable to differentiate the message from the messenger. (Luther, in fact, endorsed a more personal and literalist, even voluntaristic, approach to the interpretation of scripture, not unlike the attitude assumed by Islamic theologians some 400 years earlier. But that is a different story needing additional research.)

Background

The reform movement in 16th-century Europe initially represented a necessary re-thinking about the Church's role in society and the ways and means by which a person might find greater peace of mind in this life while experiencing the fruits of personal development. To that end, the Reformers started by wanting to clarify aspects of the Church's apologetics and restore the confidence of the faithful in the ecclesiastical authorities of the day.

Within the multi-layered drama for reform, the original inspiration behind the Reformation, as the French theologian Louis Bouyer convincingly argues, "[started] from positive, orthodox, traditional principles, never abandoning them entirely, and periodically returning to them."[3]

However flawed their efforts, the vast majority of Reformers never questioned the validity of natural law as a basis for morality and saw revelation as a starting point from which to guide free persons in a free society. In this sense, the relationship between reason and revelation remained largely intact. Indeed, there was *no* serious attempt to push, as is done today in the public forum, atheism. In other words, atheism never got any serious traction at the time. At a minimum, academics accepted the proposition that genuine human development, including the ideas of freedom, fraternity, and equality, was only possible when man accepted God, scripture, reason and natural law which informed the intellect and guided human behavior.

In the 16th century, a real sense of permanent truths was front and center in the minds of academics and ordinary folk; the task was to get their heads around these truths. Truth was not seen as subjective nor did it embrace an open-mindedness so expansive that, as Ven. Fulton Sheen correctly said, when it is indifferent "to right and wrong, [all] eventually ends in a hatred of what is right."[4]

To address conventional theological thinking and certain clerical practices, the Reformers engaged in a healthy exchange of ideas, until differences got personal and issues were tagged as Catholic or Protestant. These divisions did cause Christians to lose interest in religion, God, and the Judeo-Christian faith tradition, and made holding Christendom together more difficult. There arose a legitimate trauma because of the severe bickering that also advanced the cause of those who wanted to undermine the influence of the institutional Church, particularly in the political arena.

Unlike the Wizards today, neither the Reformers nor academics in the 16th century embraced philosophical materialism or naturalism. They did not raise science to the status of a god or replace "the grace of God" with the omnipotent faculty of "reason." Nor did they swap the "Books of the Bible" with the "Books of Nature," because they recognized that the Bible and the natural world equally sprang from the mind of God (which does not mean all at once). Anti-theism, the trademark of most of the Wizards, was not the trademark of the Reformers.

In order to establish clarity about the clash of ideas during the Reformation, and in the interest of not getting bogged down in the mass of theological and historical issues of the age, I bring to your attention two award-winning films: Robert Bolt's 1966 *A Man for All Seasons,* and Gabriel Axel's 1987 *Babette's Feast.* Each film, in its own marvelous way, captures some of the high drama and different approaches to life that took root, in part, within western European society as a consequence of the Reformation.[5]

Whatever the controversies of the age, the Reformers believed, with rare exceptions, in the existence of one, undivided God, universal transcendental values, the possibility of independent moral reasoning, and the natural moral law. They believed not only because everyone else believed, but because it made sense to believe in the existence of transcendent laws of nature. And that belief, both philosophical and theological, is the basis upon which to advance genuine human development and build civilizations.

Some Salient Issues

The most important theological issues confronting the Reformers were the need to clarify the role of free will, grace, and the Church in a person's life, especially in view of the immortality of the soul. Some of the early Reformers wanted the Church to reemphasize the preeminence of grace in personal sanctification. They saw that self-sacrifice, virtuous behavior, moral excellence, and good works *on their own* are not sufficient for salvation. Other Reformers reemphasized that Christ is the Savior of each human being — not the clever teacher, rabble-rouser, or slick magician of the anti-theists' imagination.

That there were deep divisions and problems during the 16th century is undeniable, but at no time would the Reformers ridicule God and Christ as today's anti-theists do. Most Reformers believed that God's love sanctifies us, i.e., we don't sanctify ourselves. It is not the purpose of this chapter to focus on the well-known problems of nepotism, the selling of church offices, the selling of indulgences, or priestly absenteeism from pastoral duties within the Church at the time. Neither shall it discuss the Great Western Schism (1378–1418), the issue of church and state relations, the destruction of the monasteries, or the persecution of Catholics and Protestants by each other.

Moreover, among the salient issues which needed to be addressed in the movement for genuine reform, the Reformers focused on the abuses of clergymen and the inadequacies of the institutional Church, which included: (1) the accumulation of wealth and misuse of power in the hands of bishops; (2) simony, or the appointment of unqualified and uncalled men to the clergy on the basis of connections, power, or wealth; (3) the misuse of indulgences; (4) the neglect of the canonical norms for episcopal visitations and diocesan synods; and (5) the low standard of clerical education.[6]

While the nations within the pan-European landscape from Russia to Portugal were often in conflict, their core Judeo-Christian identity and culture remained intact. At the time, the elites then, unlike their counterparts today, acknowledged that moral good and evil existed and that the ability to exercise one's freedom was not the same as the full freedom of a son or daughter of God. The Reformers intuitively recognized that Christianity served as a break against war; it was not the cause of war.

Conflict and political intrigue were used, of course, as tools to effect change and seize power, and had nothing directly to do with Christianity although Christians were conflicted and sinful. Some Reformers used the princes to their advantage; some princes and bishops used the Reformers; and both Reformers and princes used the crown, while commoners and ordinary folk were typically and unceremoniously trampled underfoot in the struggle for power. Surely, do not conflict and intrigue spring more from a defective human nature, moral relativism and hubris than from Christian charity, timeless moral standards and humility?

To lay the blame for division and discord on Christianity, as many anti-theists do, is irresponsible and reveals a stunning inability to understand reality, which is, of course, a-political, a-moral, and a-religious. Does anyone seriously believe that the Gospel's Sermon on the Mount or its broader emphasis on peace encourages warfare more than godless ideologies, the Darwinian evolutionary survival-of-the-fittest imperative, or Hobbes's vision of the Leviathan (or Islam's voluntarism)?

For the purpose of clarity, it is instructive to list the Beatitudes to understand the focus of the Gospel message: "Blessed are the poor in spirit: for theirs is the kingdom of heaven; Blessed are the meek: for they shall possess the land; Blessed are they who mourn: for they shall be comforted; Blessed are they that hunger and thirst after justice: for they shall have their fill; Blessed are the merciful: for they shall obtain mercy; Blessed are the clean of heart: for they shall see God; Blessed are the peacemakers: for they shall be called the children of God; Blessed are they that suffer persecution for justice' sake: for theirs is the kingdom of heaven."[7] To live the Beatitudes does not mean surrendering to sloth or indifference or cowering before some god of wrath, or, most important, acting as an unreasonable fanatic; and, yet, is not that the narrative of many of the Wizards and at the core of the Enlightenment Trap?

A religion that encourages its faithful to "turn the other cheek" and love their neighbors may be naïve, but it is not violent. Asked about the greatest of the commandments, Jesus says, "You shall love the Lord your God with all your heart, with all your soul, and with all your mind. This is the greatest and the first commandment. The second is like it: You shall love your neighbor as yourself. The whole law and the prophets depend on these two commandments."[8] Does that sound violent?

There is no doubt that violence and skullduggery have regularly been carried out by Christians who have used their Christianity for selfish unchristian ends; but the same tendency to violence and skullduggery applies as much to skeptics, atheists, Muslims, Buddhists, and animists. And just as many scientists have used the cloak of science to justify their atheism, many former believers use religion to cloak their irreligiosity. No one should be surprised that tendencies towards dishonesty, selfishness, and treachery are embedded in human nature; such tendencies are not simply a product of an evolutionary process gone astray over millions of years. There is no credible evidence that shows that Christianity and genuine Christian living intrinsically intensify the inclination to deceive, double-deal, be perfidious, or cause war. But is not that what we are told by some of the enlightened?

Other Issues of Importance

In 1545, the Church of Rome, with the backing of some of its secular allies, convoked the Council of Trent. Its purpose was to analyze and understand where the Church's apologetics and teaching methods had gone wrong and how it might better articulate its theological positions and canon law to guide the faithful in the face of inadequate structures and a slew of abuses.

In the eyes of many Reformers, at a very practical level, education and pastoral care of persons needed to morph from an approach more focused on simple instruction to providing a more robust guidance in the use of one's freedom; that ment discerning in different ways the intelligibility of scripture. Other Reformers sought to deemphasize, even eliminate, the role of intermediaries, especially institutional ones, to make more intelligible revelation and facilitate the quest for personal holiness and salvation. In such an atmosphere, the Church made every effort to offer the wherewithal to help the faithful understand scripture, find their vocation and freely live in the service of others.

Bl. John Henry Cardinal Newman (1801–1890) insightfully points out one of the deficiencies in Christian apologetics, which has turned people off, to wit, a somewhat heavy-handed teaching style and focus on matters other than the person of Christ: "I would say this then: that a system of doctrine has risen up during the last three centuries, in which faith or spiritual-mindedness is contemplated and rested on as the end of religion instead of Christ. I do not mean to say that Christ is not mentioned as the Author of all good, but that stress is laid rather on the believing than on the Object of belief, on the comfort and persuasiveness of the doctrine rather than on the doctrine itself. And in this way religion is made to consist in contemplating ourselves instead of Christ; not simply in looking to Christ; but in ascertaining that we look to Christ, not in His Divinity and Atonement, but in our conversion and our faith in those truths."[9] If only the anti-theists would take the time to understand Newman's point, they might reassess their militant anti-Christian positions. In the first instance, it is the person of Christ, and not all the surrounding noise, which is most important in the life of the Christian. To avoid contact with the person of Christ is to miss the entire point of Christianity, the cross, redemption, resurrection, and salvation. C.S. Lewis explains the mysterious beauty of Christianity: "[The Christian] does not think God will love us because we are good, but that God will make us good because He loves us; just as the roof of a greenhouse does not attract the sun because it is bright, but becomes bright because the sun shines on it."[10] These concepts emphasize the need for voluntary cooperation with a loving God, who is willing to take the risk of giving us freedom. To imitate Christ is to love neighbor as self, which, more than anything else, explains a Christian's drive to put love before hate and peace before conflict in the interest of peace.

Politics, Ambition, and Power

During the 16th century, continental Europe was ruled by several major royal families, including the Hapsburgs in Spain and the Holy Roman Empire, the Valois in France, and Tudors in England. Italy was divided into city-states and greatly influenced by the papacy, which wielded extensive political and economic power. The so-called religious wars included the Schmalkaldic War (1546–1547), the German Peasants' War (1524–1525), the Swiss Confederacy Wars (1529–1531, also known as the Kappel Wars), the Eighty Years' War (1568–1648) in the Netherlands, the French Wars (1562–1598), and the Thirty Years' War (1618–1648).

Patronage and bloodlines dominated the political landscape. After a series of marriages and royal subterfuge, Charles I of Spain (1500–1558) became Emperor Charles V of Germany, the Low Countries, Burgundy, and the northern territories of Italy. This event resulted in a consolidation of power that facilitated new alliances and threatened others; it brought out the best and worst in dynastic rivalries, politics and human nature.

The radical elements of the German Reformation basically arose from the political corruption of some of the clergy, Luther's revolt against reason, the exaltation of the passions over sound moral reasoning, and the polarization of Christianity by princes who used religion as an excuse to seize and maintain power.[11] Msgr. Philip Hughes (1895–1967) was spot on when he summarized the situation in Europe at the time: "And in nothing was this chronic infidelity to the Christian moral law more mischievous than when the great men — the nobles, the kings, and the highly placed churchmen — would definitely flaunt their insubordination or, even more wickedly, strive to make the spiritual power a means to advance their own personal designs."[12]

Many German princes, to impede Hapsburg and papal political meddling, formed the anti-Hapsburg Schmalkaldic League, and joined forces with Francis I of France (1494–1547) and other anti-Catholic leaders. Similarly, the French formed expedient alliances with the Ottomans at different times during the 16th century to counterbalance the ambitions of rival royal families and other interests. What shortsightedness and stupidity.

The fighting in Europe at the time had little to do with Christianity and more to do with an ingrained and disordered desire for power, control, prestige, and security. Pride, greed, lust, envy, gluttony, wrath, and sloth played a larger role in bringing about disunity than the clear Christian message of peace, forgiveness, temperance, charity, cheerfulness, patience, kindness, and humility. Any deviation from that message should not be attributed to Christianity but rather to wayward Christians.

Shifting Alliances and Clashes

Alliances regularly shifted — which suggests the nonideological and mostly a-religious nature of intra-European conflicts. To illustrate the turbulence in continental Europe at the time, the Spanish at one time or another were allied with the English and the Papal States against the French, the Venetians, and the Ottomans. At other times, the same players shifted allegiances in the best Realpolitik tradition, irrespective of religious confession. The Italian Wars (1494–1559), which had little to do with religion, were typical of the period.

To illustrate the mess further, in the German Peasants' War of 1524–1525, Luther took the side of the princes under the banner of authority and order! And in 1525, after years of skirmishes, Hapsburg forces defeated the French at the Battle of Pavia in Northern Italy. Between 1526 and 1530, the League of Cognac (France, the Papacy, England, and various Italian city-states) joined forces as a counterweight to Spain and the Holy Roman Empire (without the support of the Papal States.) In 1527, Charles V's armies sacked Rome and neutralized the papal armies. In 1535, Francis I attacked but failed to conquer Milan. In the 1540s, the French and the Ottomans seized Nice, while the English, along with the Spanish, invaded northern France. These conflicts reflect the predominately irreligious nature of the unrest of the 16th century as hundreds of other smaller battles were taking place throughout Europe in Poland, the present-day Baltic states, the Republic of Venice, the Kingdom of Naples, Portugal, Savoy, Genoa, Milan, Brandenburg-Prussia, Denmark, Sweden, and, of course, along the entire border with the Ottoman Empire and Central Asia. Just as Christianity was not the cause of conflicts in Europe in the 16th century, it did not cause the collapse of the Roman Empire. Conflict was rather the result of the absence of a properly formed Christian conscience and mindset.

The Ottomans

While Francis I aligned with the Ottomans, Sultan Suleiman I (1494–1566) was advancing against Vienna and other German- and Slavic-speaking territories in Central and Eastern Europe. While the Christian message of peace towards non-Christians is clear, the same cannot be said of Islam where non-Muslims are concerned, according to many scholars and Muslim theologians. For Christianity, peace is a result of an internal struggle with oneself and not the consequence of conquest and subjugation of others.

In the east, Belgrade and the island of Rhodes fell to the Ottomans in

1521 and 1522 respectively. In 1526, Suleiman's forces defeated the armies of the Kingdom of Hungary at the Battle of Mohacs, and in 1529 the Ottomans almost overran Vienna. Ottoman forces were turned back eventually in the Mediterranean with their failure to capture Malta in 1565 and at the naval engagements at the Battle of Lepanto in 1571. The Venetians ceded Cyprus to the Ottomans in 1570.[13]

The Thirty Years' War

There was nothing particularly shocking about the 16th century's matrix of alliances, the unprincipled behavior of powerbrokers, the unjust social structures,[14] or the abuse of political power. The Treaty of Westphalia (1648), already more than 100 years into the Reformation, ended the Thirty Years' War (1618–1648), which is forever characterized as the end of the wars of religion. Ironically, if the Thirty Years' Wars represents the worst of the so-called religious wars, radical anti-theists, who always seem to blame conflict on religion, might want to change their narrative in view of the barbarism of the 20th century, which atheism undoubtedly facilitated as it embraces, theoretically, a culture of violence and death in the name of equality, peace and stability.

The litany of conflicts and intrigue during the period of the Reformation came about either because of the actions of irreligious people who claimed to be religious or because of people who only embraced the trappings of religion. Today the Wizards misunderstand or ignore the main principles of Christianity.

Exaggerated Claims?

I, of course, beg to differ with the well-known anti-theist Sam Harris, who unabashedly asks "When will we realize that the concessions we have made to faith in our political discourse have prevented us from even speaking about, much less uprooting, the most prolific source of violence in our history?"[15] He suggests that violence stems from various religious-like thinking.[16] It might be news to Harris, but the conflicts in Europe in the 16th century, as in most periods in history, had less to do with Christianity as a religion than with human nature, irreligiosity, and a disregard for God and the dignity of the human person.

What must be clear is that Christianity should never be used as a justification for war (beyond legitimate self-defense), irrespective of the actions or statements of its representatives — whether pope or patriarch — to the humblest of the faithful. As Rabbi Alan Lurie has expertly said,

In his hilarious analysis of The 10 Commandments, George Carlin said to loud applause, "More people have been killed in the name of God than for any other reason," and many take this idea as an historical fact. When I hear someone state that religion has caused most wars, though, I will often ask the person to name these wars. The response is typically, "Come on! The Crusades, The Inquisition, Northern Ireland, the Middle East, 9/11. Need I name more?"

Well, yes, we do need to name more, because while clearly there were wars that had religion as the prime cause, an objective look at history reveals that those killed in the name of religion have, in fact, been a tiny fraction in the bloody history of human conflict. In their recently published book, *Encyclopedia of Wars,* authors Charles Phillips and Alan Axelrod document the history of recorded warfare, and from their list of 1763 wars only 123 have been classified to involve a religious cause, accounting for less than 7 percent of all wars and less than 2 percent of all people killed in warfare. While, for example, it is estimated that approximately one to three million people were tragically killed in the Crusades, and perhaps 3,000 in the Inquisition, nearly 35 million soldiers and civilians died in the senseless, and secular, slaughter of World War 1 alone.

History simply does not support the hypothesis that religion is the major cause of conflict. The wars of the ancient world were rarely, if ever, based on religion. These wars were for territorial conquest, to control borders, secure trade routes, or respond to an internal challenge to political authority. In fact, the ancient conquerors, whether Egyptian, Babylonian, Persian, Greek, or Roman, openly welcomed the religious beliefs of those they conquered, and often added the new gods to their own pantheon.

Medieval and Renaissance wars were also typically about control and wealth as city-states vied for power, often with the support, but rarely instigation, of the Church. And the Mongol Asian rampage, which is thought to have killed nearly 30 million people, had no religious component whatsoever.

Most modern wars, including the Napoleonic Campaign, the American Revolution, the French Revolution, the American Civil War, World War I, the Russia Revolution,

World War II, and the conflicts in Korea and Vietnam, were not religious in nature or cause. While religious groups have been specifically targeted (most notably in World War II), to claim that religion was the cause is to blame the victim and to misunderstand the perpetrators' motives, which were nationalistic and ethnic, not religious.[17]

But When Guilty, Forgiveness

And yet, whenever uninformed, weak, and overzealous religious folk have used religion as a reason to advance their own interests or any interests that do not respect the dignity of human life, it is necessary to admit culpability and follow Pope St. John Paul II's example: "We [Catholics] are asking pardon for the divisions among Christians, for the use of violence that some have committed in the service of truth, and for attitudes of mistrust and hostility assumed towards followers of other religions."[18] Forgiveness and mercy are keynote virtues of Christianity because Christians aim to help others rather than criticize or dominate. In modern-day politics, just as in everyday life, charity and forgiveness must be cornerstones of our actions and relations with others.

Some Goals of the Anti-Theists' Agenda

What is important to realize is that many Wizards use the Reformation (and the earlier Schism in the 11th century between Rome and Constantinople) as well as wars and conflicts as means to sow disunity and doubt within the ranks of those who hold to the Judeo-Christian worldview and its principles. They continue to attack Christianity as the cause of violence with but scant historical evidence.

Whenever Wizards excoriate essential passages of the Bible (particularly Genesis and the Gospels)[19] and Christian education, they reveal their prejudices and knee-jerk anti-theism. Anti-theism attempts in every way possible to replace the God of Abraham with the gods of science and skepticism while bludgeoning religion, particularly the Judeo-Christian tradition, as the source of naïveté and irrationality.

There can be little doubt that most Wizards want to see the pan-European landscape stripped of its Judeo-Christian identity and converted into a functional association of deracinated political entities whose economic and political interests are managed by a universal central government in which Judeo-Christian principles play no role in building up society. The way things are going, the Wizards will produce a society dominated by agnostic high priests and thought police, as portrayed in George Orwell's novels *Animal*

Farm and *Nineteen Eighty-Four*. In order to achieve their objectives, one of their immediate goals is to repeat the slogan "no religions, no wars", knowing that a such platitude in a de-Christianized world is an easy sell.

The Reformation, no doubt, contributed to the breakdown of European unity. But contrary to the claims of many of theWizards, no credible historian would lay blame for disunity and conflict within European civilization mostly at the feet of Christianity.[20] Rather, the main explanation for conflict in Europe at the time, just as today, lies with folk who used human weaknesses, official corruption, aggressive forms of nationalism, and divide-and-conquer strategies against the unity of a pan-European civilization to advance personal and political agendas devoid of God.

Glory to God in the Highest

Christianity encourages its followers to give "glory to God in the highest, and on earth, good will towards men,"[21] so it should never be the case that Christianity is the cause of war, especially between brothers in Christ. Since Genesis, the ideal of brotherhood has rarely been upheld in practice; that is not the fault of Christianity, but rather consequence of its absence. As further explained in the Gospel, "For though we live in the world, we do not wage war as the world does. The weapons we fight with are not the weapons of the world. On the contrary, they have divine power to demolish strongholds. We demolish arguments and every pretension that sets itself up against the knowledge of God, and we take captive every thought to make it obedient to Christ."[22] Ambition, jealousy, greed, injustice, impatience, vanity, weakness, envy, fear, lust for power, and arrogance are the main causes of war, not Christianity. Christians should never be fanatics. If they are, they have forgotten their Christianity, which would then make them unchristian.

Most of the Reformers recognized that God loves people; he does not merely tolerate them, much less torture them. Christianity gives meaning to life; its absence gives way to randomness, unpredictability, and absurdity. Freedom enables us to participate in the redemptive work of salvation. Service towards one's neighbor opens the door to belief in God. Despair turns to hope, and foes and competitors are seen in a more tolerant light. Economics becomes a means for achieving integral human development. Leisure becomes a manifestation of culture rather than an excuse for self-indulgence and killing time. The Judeo-Christian worldview represents hope in a world in need of hope. How can a Christian's hope, imbued with the love for others, learning, and science, be worse than the Wizards' world of chance and brute survival, where the only surcease from pain and uncertainty lies in tranquilizers and death?

Conclusion

Let me underscore my point again. Christianity, properly understood, is never the source of disunity or a principal cause of irrational behavior or war, although that is precisely what many Wizards want us to believe.[23]

War is venomous to the genuine Christian mentality because it is dehumanizing and the antithesis of charity and love, the highest of virtues. As St. Paul says, "Charity is patient, is kind; charity feels no envy; charity is never perverse or proud, never insolent; does not claim its rights, cannot be provoked, does not brood over injury; takes no pleasure in wrong-doing, but rejoices at the victory of truth; sustains, believes, hopes, endures, to the last.... Meanwhile, faith, hope, and charity persist, all three; but the greatest of them all is charity."[24]

There is an urgent need today to deepen our understanding of the Judeo-Christian tradition and properly reflect on the history of the Reformation, the purpose of the Reformers and the so-called wars of religion.[25] The 16th century was a turbulent time in world history, as indeed is our own. Despite rejecting some of the sacraments, the Reformers did not abandon God, transcendental values, natural law and a rock-solid acceptance of the dignity of the human person, notwithstanding exceptions among the ranks of scholars and theologians at the time. Rather, the movement in the 16th century to reform the Church heralded a need to reexamine certain elements of medieval scholarship and address deficiencies in our understanding of God, humanity, society, and the institutional Church. We could do worse than to be guided by the "Commandment of Love" at the core of Christianity: "I give you a new commandment: love one another. As I have loved you, so you also should love one another. This is how all will know that you are my disciples, if you have love for one another."[26]

1.　Jacques Maritain, *Three Reformers: Luther, Descartes, Rousseau* (New York: Charles Scribner's Sons, 1929 [repr. London: Sheed & Ward, 1944]); p. 14 (https://archive.org/stream/in.ernet.dli.2015.151667/2015.151667.Three-Reformers-Luther-descartes-rousseau)

2.　Pelagius (c. 360–418), a monk who lived many years in Rome, came from England, Ireland, or Scotland — it is not clear. Pelagianism denied Original Sin and claimed that personal sin and the wickedness of man was essentially a result of Adam and Eve's scandalous behavior and disobedience. Their sinfulness was passed on as a result of their bad example to future generations. Not unlike the Greek Stoics, Pelagius believed that will power and virtue could overcome personal sin. The role of Christ and the Church was to teach good doctrine and guide persons to salvation through good example. There was no need for grace. A person could cut his own path without the help of God's grace. Permutations of Pelagius's ideas remain very much alive today.

3.   Louis Bouyer, *The Spirit and Forms of Protestantism* (Princeton, N.J.: Scepter Press, 2001); p. 32.

4.   Ven. Fulton J. Sheen, *The Life of Christ* (New York: McGraw Hill, 1958); p. 57.

5.   *A Man for All Seasons* captures the high drama of Henry VIII's (fruitless) efforts to bend Sir Thomas More to his will over the matter of his (Henry's) divorce and marriage to Anne Bolyen, while *Babette's Feast* illustrates the different approaches to life and culture that took root in various parts of Europe depending on whether they were Catholic or Protestant. I am quite certain that Henri Daniel-Rops, John H. Hollowell, and Christopher Dawson, the Rev. Dr. John Lingard (1771–1851), Hilaire Belloc (1870–1953), Ernst Troeltsch (1865–1923), Msgr. Philip Hughes (1895–1967), Arnold L. Toynbee (1889–1975), R.H. Tawney (1880–1962), Jacob C. Burckhardt (1818–1897), Etienne Gilson (1884–1978), Pitirim Sorokin (1889–1968), Jacques Maritain (1882–1973), Sir Herbert Butterfield (1900–1979), Fredrick Copleston (1907–1994), Paul B. Johnson (b. 1928), and Max Webber (1864–1920) would have acknowledged the historical insights of these films.

6.   See Christopher Dawson, *The Dividing of Christendom* (New York: Sheed & Ward, 1965); pp. 64-65.

7.   Matthew 5:3-12 (http://www.usccb.org/bible/matthew/5).

8.   Matthew 22:36-40 (http://www.usccb.org/bible/matthew/22).

9.   John Henry Newman, "Lecture 13: On Preaching the Gospel," in *Lectures on the Doctrine of Justification* (London: Longmans, Green, and Co., 1908 (http://www.newman-reader.org/works/justification/lecture13.html).

10.   C.S. Lewis, *Mere Christianity* (New York: Macmillan Company, 1952); p. 26 (https://canavox.com/wp-content/uploads/2017/06/Mere-Christianity-Lewis.pdf).

11.   Maritain, *Three Reformers.*

12.   Philip Hughes, *A Popular History of the Reformation* (New York; Image Books, 1960) p. 12.

13.   The Ottoman Empire was fundamentally expansionist until it ran out of steam towards the end of the 19th century. To give an idea, note the following conflicts: Ottoman-Habsburg wars (1571–1718), Ottoman-Venetian War (1537–1540), Ottoman-Portuguese War (1538–1557), Russo-Turkish War (1568–1570), Ottoman-Portuguese War (1580–1589), Polish-Ottoman War (1620–1621), Austro-Turkish War (1663–1664), Polish-Ottoman War (1672–1676), Russo-Turkish War (1676–1681), Great Turkish War (1683–1699), Ottoman-Venetian War (1716–1718), Austro-Turkish War (1714–1718), Ottoman-Persian War (1743–1746), Russo-Turkish War (1787–1792), and Austro-Turkish War (1787–1791). There are scores of other conflicts with the Ottoman Empire up to the 1920s.

14.   The miserable socio-economic conditions of the ordinary person, who suffered at the hands of a largely unprincipled gentry in alliance with landowners, princes, and even bishops, complicated the political and religious landscape of the 16th century. The violent revolt of the peasantry in 1517, which the Holy Roman Emperor was not able to control, neither by suppressing its causes nor by resolving the abuses that led to the rebellion, was less religiously motivated than politically and economically. Moreover, during the period, many temporal authorities targeted Church properties for expropriation and destruction, which also militated against an atmosphere of dialogue and ecclesial reform.

15.   Sam Harris, *The End of Faith: Religion, Terror, and the Future of Reason* (New York: W.W. Norton & Company, 2004); p. 27.

16.   Harris, *End of Faith*, pp. 26–28.

17.   Alan Lurie (rabbi), "Is Religion the Cause of Most Wars?" *Huffington Post*, June 10, 2012) (https://www.huffingtonpost.com/rabbi-alan-lurie/is-religion-the-cause-of-_b_1400766.html).

18.   St. John Paul II (pope), "Day of Pardon" (homily, March 12, 2000).

19.   "The Bible may, indeed does, contain a warrant for trafficking in humans, for ethnic cleansing, for slavery, for bride-price, and for indiscriminate massacre, but we are not bound by any of it because it was put together by crude, uncultured human mammals." Hitchens, *God Is Not Great*, p. 36.

20.   See Charles Phillips and Alan Axelrod, eds., *Encyclopedia of Wars*, 3 vols. (New York: Facts on File, 2004). Also, to reinforce the essential point of this chapter, "In 5 millennia worth of wars — 1,763 total — only 123 (or about 7 percent) were religious in nature (according to author Vox Day in the book *The Irrational Atheist*). If you remove the 66 wars waged in the name of Islam, it cuts the number down to a little more than 3 percent. A second scholarly source, edited by Gordon Martel (*The Encyclopedia of War* [Hoboken, N.J.: Wiley-Blackwell, 2007]), confirms this data, concluding that only 6 percent of the wars listed in its pages can be labelled religious wars. Thirdly, William Cavanaugh's book, *The Myth of Religious Violence* (Oxford: Oxford University Press, 2009), exposes the "wars of religion" claim. And finally, a recent report (2014) from the Institute of Economics and Peace further debunks this myth" (Brett Kunkle, "Is Religion the Cause of Most Wars?" [Stand to Reason, 2016]) (https://www.str.org/blog/is-religion-the-cause-of-most-wars).

      In those few cases where a war can be properly attributed in some measure to religious zeal, rather than blame the Judeo-Christian tradition, it is useful to remember the dictum "abusus no tollit usus" — the misuse of a thing is no argument against its proper use.

21.   Luke 2:14 (http://www.usccb.org/bible/luke/2).

22.   2 Corinthians 10:3-5 (http://www.usccb.org/bible/2corinthians/10).

23.   To understand more clearly Islam's vision to bring "peace" to the world, which is an approach completely alien to the Judeo-Christian vision and which is akin to a "war of religion" against infidels (non-Muslims), see Fr. James V. Schall, *On Islam: a Chronological Record, 2002-2018*, (San Francisco: Ignatius, 2018).

24.   1 Corinthians 13:4, from *The New Testament of Our Lord and Savior Jesus Christ: A Translation from the Latin Vulgate*, by Ronald A. Knox (http://catholicbible.online/side_by_side/NT/1_Cor/ch_13).

25.   Our Eastern Orthodox brothers could be very helpful in unlocking some of the insights of the Fathers, given their long history of scholarship. Newman's words are thought provoking: "To be deep in history is to cease to be a Protestant."

26.   John 13:34-35 (http://www.usccb.org/bible/john/13).

CHAPTER 7

The Enlightenment: Darker Than Commonly Understood

[The modern Enlightenment philosophies, considered as a whole] are characterized by the fact that they are positivist and, therefore, anti-metaphysical, so much so that, in the end, God cannot have any place in them. They are based on the self-limitation of rational positivism, which can be applied in the technical realm, but which when it is generalized, entails instead a mutilation of man. It succeeds in having man no longer admit any moral claim beyond his calculations and, as we saw, the concept of freedom, which at first glance would seem to extend in an unlimited manner, in the end leads to the self-destruction of freedom.
     — Joseph Cardinal Ratzinger, *On Europe's Crisis of Culture*[1]

There is not really any courage at all in attacking hoary or antiquated things, any more than in offering to fight one's grandmother. The really courageous man is he who defies tyrannies young as the morning and superstitions fresh as the first flowers. The only true free-thinker is he whose intellect is as much free from the future as from the past.
     — G.K. Chesterton, *What's Wrong with the World?*

The dominant ideas of the Enlightenment represent a brilliant and much-needed attempt to moderate the despair of age-old pessimists and the exuberance of optimists. But many of the savants of the Enlightenment, in putting their faith in perpetual progress, moral relativism, and the ever-expanding powers of the intellect, ended up blinded by their own brashness and optimism. The ideas of these men need to be put into plain words so as to expose their folly. Their fringe positions — not the brilliance of the Enlightenment as represented by men such as Sir Isaac Newton (1642–1727) — have in the past hundred years seized the high ground in debates over metaphysics, cosmology, and epistemology. Moreover, scientific enquiry, a mere tool, has become something of a panacea.

At its best, the Enlightenment was about bringing to life the evangelical aspirations of liberty, equality, and fraternity in a manner consistent with the nature of being, the dignity of man, and the limitations of science. At its worst, however, it and its radical proponents tried to fast-track the process of human development but failed miserably because they forgot that God exists. The more radical ideas of the Enlightenment are the mistaken notions that people themselves are the masters of the universe and that they are capable of establishing paradise on Earth. Those ideas have produced a number of philosophically toxic ideas, some with predictable and destructive consequences for humanity, despite the elegance of the arguments in their defense. That is what the modern world needs to understand. That is what we need to learn from history.

It is probably not too far off the mark to say that the Enlightenment's extreme positions were not just a bit nutty, but literally crazy and self-destructive. When the mind is sharpened to the exclusion of everything else, reality and practicality go out the window and the differences between realistic and unrealistic goals become blurred. Impossible objectives are proclaimed to be within reach. Wishful thinking and political idealism generate madness and dreadful ideologies. Tragically, it is those radical ideas of the Enlightenment that much of the modern world has fallen in love with. As Philip Trower noted, "The Enlightenment simply took over Christianity's linear view of history, removed God, and placed the 'kingdom of heaven' inside, instead of outside, of time. It is in this sense that we can call the religion of perpetual progress a Christian heresy."[2]

Since the time of the French Revolution, man, in love with abstractions and the scientific method, has tried to transform politics from an art to a science, an impossible undertaking because political science does not deal with animals, robots, or computers, but rather with free human beings whose dignity is higher than that of all other beings (with body and soul). People have come to view their existence on Earth as a scramble for survival and security in a world where might makes right. That, in part, explains why many modern politicians embrace the illusory (and phony) concept of a new world order. To achieve their aims, they welcome transnationalism, ideological multiculturalism, globalism, techno-genetic manipulation of human beings, and advanced methods of psychiatric treatment.

One of the clear consequences of having accepted radical Enlightenment beliefs is that the scientific method has been elevated to the status of an Olympian god. There is nothing earth-shattering about the scientific method. It is in fact a product of pre-Enlightenment thinking dating back to the Ancients (rudimentary observation and testing) and further developed by the scholarly monks of the Middle Ages. Since the Enlightenment, the scientific method is held by many academics to be the *only* way to discern the truths of being and nature. While the methodology is itself robust within its domain, it excludes all that is not subject to the physical laws of nature by confining certitude to that which can be measured. In that way it was possible to bottle up God as a conjuration of religion along with everything else that flows from transcendence (and the invisible world) and to cast it away into some far-off and meaningless magical kingdom suitable for the weak and deranged.

Many of the 21st-century Wizards of the Enlightenment believe they are saviors of the world and constitute an untouchable priestly class. They enjoy the patronage and protection of leading think tanks, universities, ecclesiastical authorities, opinion leaders, and even, in some cases, governments. Their works are often inspired by Jean-Jacques Rousseau's *Social Contract* (1762), Johann Gottlieb Fichte's *Speeches to the German Nation* (1808), Karl Marx's *Das Kapital* (completed 1894), George Sorel's *Illusions of Progress* (1908), and Thomas Paine's *Rights of Man* (1791) and *The Age of Reason* (1793)[3] as well as the writings of Friedrich Nietzsche, Charles Darwin, and G.W.F. Hegel.

Large numbers of educators and politicians today have swallowed the Wizards' messianic ideas without even knowing it. Hope is consumed by pessimism. Many of our Wizards (those who embrace the extreme positions of the Enlightenment as the only approach to human development) treat humanity and society as purely advanced chemical or biological objects, absent any transcendent qualities. People (the elite excepted, of course) are seen as so many cogs in a wheel. They have certain physical and psychological needs that can and must be managed or re-programmed, like plants in a greenhouse. A mechanistic outlook towards the management of society ignores the natural law and the fundamental dignity of the human person (without which, as we already know, there can be no genuine, sustainable human development).

The Wizards have focused on simultaneously attaining a developmental state in which equality and liberty perfectly co-exist. Most Wizards don't understand that equality and freedom are mutually exclusive, that the classless, regulated, pain-free, and liberated society of their dreams leads only to de-humanization and dystopia.

That is what Philip Trower had in mind when he stated that "liberalism, secularism or secular-humanism, socialism, communism are merely the new faith's [the Enlightenment's] main denominations. Their adherents may differ about how the final goal is to be reached (is the principal instrument of salvation to be politics, revolution, social engineering, improved education, extra productivity, mind manipulation, or genetic tinkering?) and about which of the ingredients of happiness matter most (liberty, equality, fraternity, human rights, an abundant cash flow, or sexual license?). But they are at one as regards the new message of salvation itself: paradise in this world, brought about mainly or entirely by human effort."[4] Today these radical Enlightenment sects employ the antics of a virulent and warped secularism, "Judeo-Christian" in name only, to obtain a global reach into areas where language, ethnicity, and culture have no bearing on the propagation of their march toward global liberation. The Enlightenment radicals see the common-sense values and institutions of the Judeo-Christian worldview as their primary enemy. Moral ethics is nothing but a set of regulations designed to inhibit progress and dumb-down people. They must deny any link between the dignity of the human person and genuine human development.

Most anti-theists are hostile to any ideas or to any person or institution that puts forth views contrary to their own. Denis Diderot (1713–1784), the leader of the French Encyclopedists, represented both the intensity and extremism of the Enlightenment's fanatical wing when he is alleged to have said, "Men will never be free until the last king is strangled with the entrails of the last priest." It is precisely that uncompromising messianic-like "death to all who don't agree with us" attitude that is so troublesome. In fact, anyone who does not agree with their views is in a state of "grave sin" and instantly becomes an enemy. Voltaire is clear: "Every man of sense, every good man ought to hold the Christian sect in horror."[5]

Conceived to satisfy the deepest longings of the human soul, the Enlightenment claimed to have identified the sources of evil in the world and then tried to minimize them, if not eliminate them entirely, for the good of everyone. To that end, anti-theists encouraged people to declare independence from the historical forces of bondage, which had produced bored, unthinking, and unfulfilled men and women. Such independence only complicated matters because it made it impossible to rule a society in need of enlightened governance. Against the backdrop of René Descartes's systematic skepticism (1598–1650), Ludwig Feuerbach's anthropological [i.e., proto-materialist] interpretation of religious phenomena (1804–1872), and Hegel's idea of uninterrupted progress through the clash of ideas (1770–1831), Nietzsche (1844–1900) titillated elites with his doctrine of "the will to power" and his concept of the "superman." In a dog-eat-dog world, salvation could be achieved only by the direct intervention of enlightened "supermen and women."

The Wizards' success can be explained, in part, by their claim — which is a verbal stunt — that "thinking" is better than "not thinking" and "wanting to find out" is better than "indifference," as if ignorance and a lack of curiosity were the norm prior to the Enlightenment and the Scientific Revolution. For them, the discovery of truth (as they understood it) was exhilarating, because it led to the liberation of the downtrodden from all manner of bad things

— from repressive familial, educational, religious, hereditary, and communal conventions. Genuine human development meant freedom from all forms of manipulation, ignorance, and personal weakness (rather than fidelity to the nature and purpose of things). The by-product of such liberation movements, so they argued, is self-realization and self-mastery, which translated into a balanced, progressive political system guided by the elites but devoted to the good of the common man.

Embedded in radical Enlightenment thinking is the possibility of personal redemption from humanity's self-inflicted hell on Earth. It is that possibility of redemption and liberation, through reason and science, which makes the Enlightenment Trap so alluring. As Pope Benedict XVI said, "In fact, the principle is now valid, according to which man's capacity is measured by his action. What one knows how to do, may also be done. There no longer exists a knowing how to do separated from a being able to do, because it would be against freedom, which is the absolute supreme value. But man knows how to do many things and knows increasingly how to do more things; and if this knowing how to do does not find its measure in a moral norm, it becomes, as we can already see, a power of destruction."[6]

The ability of people to justify a socio-political paradigm that leads to a genuine hell on Earth is not the monopoly of any single political, economic, social, or ethnic group. Rather, insane social engineering spans the political spectrum and finds a home in those godless political philosophies that violate basic norms of common sense or the dignity of the human person. G.K. Chesterton wrote, "All sane men can see that sanity is some kind of equilibrium; that one may be mad and eat too much, or mad and eat too little. Some moderns have indeed appeared with vague versions of progress and evolution that seek to destroy the ... balance of Aristotle. They seem to suggest that we are meant to starve progressively, or to go on eating larger and larger breakfasts every morning forever. But the great truism of the [balance] remains for all thinking men, and these people have not upset any balance except their own.... [The] real question is how that balance can be kept."[7] Fortunately, Judeo-Christian academics, guided by Hellenistic philosophy, managed to define what constitutes sanity.

During the Middle Ages, an attempt at sanity in social relations was reflected in chivalry, where the practice of virtue reached beyond Earth into Heaven and gave purpose to suffering and joy to life. The chivalric code elevated humanity and mitigated fear by seeing suffering as a meaningful event. It allowed people to perform the important Christian task of affirming others, thus acknowledging their dignity. Unfortunately, most Wizards see chivalry as a quaint custom of a bygone day and age, and little more than an expression of good manners. The Enlightenment Trap is replete with half-truths that appeal exclusively to humanity's inner desire to excel or look good without the need for God, eternal truths, or a purpose beyond self-preservation, implicitly denying that virtuous acts are possible and can be selfless.

The Enlightenment Trap proclaims that human ingenuity, free of historical and cultural baggage, can remove the cobwebs that inhibit clear thinking and show the way to a near-angelic mastery over the laws of nature. It offers (in the future) a pain-free world filled with physical and intellectual comforts as if in a magical kingdom. C.S. Lewis identified a flaw in the Wizards' thinking: "If you look for truth, you may find comfort in the end: if you look for comfort you will not get either comfort or truth — only soft soap and wishful thinking to begin with and, in the end, despair."[8] This helps us understand why the Wizards never stop trying to explain away the existence of the one uncreated God of life and the universe.

The Wizards' high-minded ideas are often as alluring as a Hollywood film. Their zeal to save humankind from one ailment or another, expressed in happy talk, is very sophisticated, but, C. S. Lewis warns, conceals hidden dangers: "Of all tyrannies, a tyranny sincerely exercised for the good of its victims may be the most oppressive. It would be better to live under robber barons than under omnipotent moral busybodies. The robber baron's cruelty may sometimes sleep, his cupidity may at some point be satiated; but those who torment us for our own good will torment us without end for they do so with the approval of their own conscience."[9] It is crucial for educators and statesmen to recognize the danger of this type of thinking, especially given humanity's inclination (even with the flimsiest of causes) to invoke national security, national interests, or sovereign rights in the name of liberty, equality, and fraternity.

There are many reasons why the Enlightenment Trap is so hard to perceive. It postulates that evil and sin are basically external to us and that it is possible for us (the elites) to tame the universe by eliminating sin (i.e., imperfections in or mismanagement of nature) and by believing in the curative properties of science and man's ability to manage life in every respect. Science, the Wizards claim, can replace religion. The British Museum of Natural History (1873–1881) in London is built in an architectural style meant to emulate a cathedral, and thus suggests that science is a suitable substitute for religion.

At the level of psychology, the Enlightenment radicals proclaimed that humanity could not emerge from centuries of spiritual exploitation and subhuman treatment without courageously facing the evils enslaving humankind. It was argued that humanity's existing conventions, institutions, and structures preyed upon people to keep them docile and stupid. Those structures and psychological instruments of manipulation had to be overthrown or reengineered: that was the job of the "inspired" anti-theists of the Enlightenment. Charles Dickens, in *A Tale of Two Cities*, summed it up eloquently: "Liberty, equality, fraternity, or death; — the last, much the easiest to bestow, O Guillotine!"[10] The radical Renaissance man was egotistical; the radical Enlightenment man was egomaniacal. One can reason with the former; it is almost impossible to reason with the latter.

In their quest to remove religious belief (that is intellectually grounded) from man's consciousness, the Wizards argue that to believe in anything other than that which is confirmed by science is ill-advised if not downright idiotic. There is no need for people to rely on the transcendental principles of natural law or divine revelation to advance towards integral human development. To support their worldview, the Wizards declare religion, particularly Christianity, bogus.

In *Mere Christianity*, C.S. Lewis addresses the core of the problem: "If Christianity is true why are not all Christians obviously nicer than all non-Christians? What lies behind that question is partly something very reasonable.... The reasonable part is this. If conversion to Christianity makes no improvement in a man's outward actions ... then I think we must suspect that his 'conversion' was largely imaginary.... Fine feelings, new insights, greater interest in 'religion' mean nothing unless they make our actual behavior better; just as in an illness 'feeling better' is not much good if the thermometer shows that your temperature is still going up. In that sense the outer world is quite right to judge Christianity by its results.... When we Christians behave badly, or fail to behave well, we are making Christianity unbelievable to the outside world.... Our careless lives set the outer world talking; and we give them grounds for talking in a way that throws doubt on the truth of Christianity itself."[11] Christopher Hitchens and others are not wrong in questioning those who hypocritically hold the Judeo-Christian worldview; hypocrites should be challenged. But the Wizards are dead wrong when they dismiss the entire Judeo-Christian worldview without offering serious counter-arguments or point to the existence of suffering as proof of atheism.

What must be clear is that to believe in the Judeo-Christian worldview (the existence of God and natural moral law) is reasonable, as opposed to blindly believing in the elixirs of materialism, naturalism, relativism, and chance. The radical men of the Enlightenment are wrong to hide behind the myth that only science, atheism, and agnosticism are compatible. There is plenty of evidence for the existence of God; there is no evidence for atheism. It is invalid to argue that since one cannot measure, see, or smell God, therefore God does not exist. That the "Invisible Man" is invisible does not mean he does not exist. Such an argument is only an excuse to avoid submitting oneself to the demands of one's nature or reality.

The Spread of the Enlightenment

It is important to keep in mind that the Enlightenment was a broad and creative movement. Among its exponents, some hostile to the Judeo-Christian worldview, others quite friendly to it, are Descartes, John Locke (1632–1704), Carl von Linnaeus (1707–1778), Rousseau (1712–1778), Alexander Hamilton (1755–1804), Thomas Jefferson (1743–1826), Johann Wolfgang von Goethe (1749–1832), and Wilhelm von Humboldt (1767–1835).[12]

The Enlightenment planted deep roots across geographical boundaries while producing great insights into science and technology and pulling off a staggering transformation in modern thinking about time and space. We owe a great deal to those men and women for their discoveries, creativity, and acumen. The Enlightenment itself was a period of great achievements in human history especially when the ideas of its radical wing are stripped away. When fanatical ideas such as "perpetual progress" are given free rein, the result is such enormities as the desecration of Notre Dame de Paris by revolutionaries in 1793 and their converting it into a temple of the Cult of Reason.

Twenty-first-century civilization is plagued by radical Enlightenment thinking and has fallen into the Enlightenment Trap with grave consequences for world peace, stability, and genuine human development. Immanuel Kant (1724–1804), a quintessential man of the Enlightenment, eloquently captured the period's enthusiasm and faith in the march towards liberation and equality when he wrote, "Enlightenment is man's release from his self-incurred tutelage. Tutelage is man's inability to make use of his understanding without direction from another. Self-incurred is this tutelage when its cause lies not in lack of reason but in lack of resolution and courage to use it without direction from another. *Sapere aude!* 'Have courage to use your own reason!' — that is the motto of enlightenment."[13] Kant, in fact, *transcendentalizes* subjectivism and individualism, reducing good and evil, or moral behavior, to personal choices and self-referencing moral ethics. His definition of the Enlightenment belittles critical thinking, redefines human nature, and exalts will power.

The ideology of the Enlightenment Wizards has an alarming simplicity and hope in the future. Its prophetic message is drenched in Biblical lingo that is messianic, salvific, and redemptive. It assigns transcendence to reason and feelings, while it accords godlike status to mathematics and rejects teleology (i.e., the explanation of phenomena by the purpose they serve) as a sound philosophical principle. In other words, it replaces purpose with randomness, confuses virtues with circus tricks, and is incapable of understanding that adversity and tears have meaning. Through the lens of the Enlightenment, reasonableness is reduced to sentiment, certitude is restricted to measurement, trust is folly, and belief is demeaning. Enlightenment ideology is reckless and hubristic in its ambition to eliminate evil by manipulating the laws of nature, reengineering society, and revamping the culture.

Christopher Hitchens, the most articulate of the Wizards, voiced his call for a New Enlightenment in 2006:

> Above all, we are in need of a renewed Enlightenment, which will base itself on the proposition that the proper study of mankind is man and woman. This Enlightenment will not need to depend, like its predecessors, on the heroic breakthroughs of a few gifted and exceptionally courageous people. It is within the compass of the average person. The study of literature and poetry, both for its own sake and for the eternal ethical questions with which it deals, can now easily depose the scrutiny of sacred texts that have been found to be corrupt and confected. The pursuit of unfettered scientific inquiry, and the availability of new findings to masses of people by electronic means, will revolutionize our concepts of research and development. Very importantly, the divorce between the sexual life and fear, and the sexual life and disease, and the sexual life and tyranny, can now at last be attempted, on the sole condition that we banish all religions from the discourse. And all this and more is, for the first time in our history, within the reach if not the grasp of everyone. However, only the most naïve Utopian can believe that this new humane civilization will develop, like some dream of "progress," in a straight line. We have first to transcend our prehistory and escape the gnarled hands that reach out to drag us back to the catacombs and the reeking altars and the guilty pleasures of subjection and abjection. "Know yourself," said the Greeks, gently suggesting the consolations of philosophy. To clear the mind for this project, it has become necessary to know the enemy, and to prepare to fight it.[14]

Setting aside his hubris and brashness, Hitchens's claims are alarming. Does not his desire to "transcend our prehistory" reflect radical Enlightenment thinking in its purest form? Does not his screed amount to a call for a "new man"? His use of the sacred language of the Judeo-Christian lexicon notwithstanding, does Hitchens really think that sex anywhere, anytime, with consent will lead to genuine human development? At the end of the day, how does transcending evil and history produce an enlightened man?

Hitchens and so many others like him fail to grasp that it is impossible to eliminate suffering or the human conscience without destroying human freedom. Despite his insistence, Hitchens's liberality in all areas of human behavior (anything goes as long as no one suffers unwillingly) is an expression of a narrow Cartesian interpretation of human behavior.

Radical Enlightenment thinking afflicts a wide spectrum including right and left political parties, pessimists and optimists, religious and nonreligious alike. No one is immune from falling into the Enlightenment Trap.

Most Wizards of the Enlightenment such as Hitchens, Jean-Baptiste le Rond d'Alembert (1717–1783), Voltaire, Nicolas de Condorcet (1743–1794), Baron d'Holbach (1723–1789), and Diderot, the godfather of the radicals, replaced the miracle-worker of Galilee with the would-be miracle-workers of "enlightened despotism," no doubt without even knowing it. They did not recognize that a socio-political system of governance, to be successful, must apply principles consistent with the nature of man. C.S. Lewis says, "Progress means getting nearer to the place where you want to be. And if you have taken a wrong turning, then to go forward does not get you any nearer. If you are on the wrong road, progress means doing an about-turn and walking back to the right road; and in that case the man who turns back soonest is the most progressive man."[15]

Intellectual Advance

There is no doubt that the Cartesian Revolution of the 17th century was influential in certain philosophical circles looking to find contradictions between science, philosophy, and theology. But its influence was felt also among those who embraced the Judeo-Christian worldview.

The works of Nicolaus Copernicus (1473–1543), Johannes Kepler (1571–1630), Galileo Galilei (1564–1642), Descartes, Newton, and many others energized the thinkers of the 17th and 18th centuries by helping to reinforce positive attitudes towards inquiry, discovery, and inquisitiveness. Serious men founded national scientific societies and associations throughout Europe, including the Royal Society in London, the Académie Royale des Sciences in Paris, the Akademie der Wissenschaften in Berlin, the Academia Scientiarum Imperialis in St. Petersburg, and Kungliga Vetenskapsakademien in Stockholm. During the Enlightenment, the emphasis on research and experimentation shifted from a study of people as spiritual, moral, and physical beings to a study of humanity as physical specimens with psychological needs and measureable responses to ideas and stimuli. The spiritual side of humanity was deemphasized, and the question of human purpose was ceded to mathematics, and of "human will and foresight to immutable and inflexible mechanical order."[16] At this point, however, science had not yet come to be dominated by atheists and agnostics.

By contrast, the Pontifical Academy of Sciences in Rome, with its origins in the Accademia Dei Lincei (1603) predating others in northern Europe, has always focused on a broad understanding of the universe; unlike most other academies of science, it never lost its emphasis on the spiritual and ethical components of the human person. Its holistic approach to humanity and science is more appropriate to understanding the origins and purpose of humanity and the universe than the approach taken by many of the one-dimensional secular European academies during the same period.

With the dawn of the 17th century, the pace of inventions and discoveries in the natural and physical sciences was unprecedented. This revolutionary spirit of intellectual entrepreneurship was surely impressive to behold as it gained momentum and adherents throughout most of Europe. The period's achievements were many and none was accidental; each new accomplishment sustained subsequent discoveries.

Allow us to list a few of the inventions from the period that were earth-shattering in nature. With few exceptions, they were rooted in the curiosity, inventiveness, quest for discovery, and inquisitiveness that were part and parcel of the Judeo-Christian tradition. From the late 17th to the mid 19th century, a series of inventions transformed life and the world economy: Hans Lippershey (1570–1619) invented the first refracting telescope, William Oughtred (1574–1660) the slide rule, Giovanni Branca (1571–1645) the steam turbine, Blaise Pascal (1623–1662) the adding machine, Evangelista Torricelli (1608–1647) the barometer, Gottfried Wilhelm Leibniz (1646–1716) the calculating machine, Gabriel Fahrenheit (1686–1736) the first mercury thermometer, John Harrison (1693–1776) the navigational clock for longitude, Benjamin Franklin the first bifocals, John Fitch (1743–1798) the steamboat, John Barber (1734–1793) the gas turbine, William Murdoch (1754–1839) gas lighting, Eli Whitney (1765–1825) the cotton gin, and Alessandro Volta (1745–1827) the battery.[17]

In 1927, the Big Bang, a reasonable cosmological model about the origins of the universe, was first proposed by Fr. Georges Lemaître (1894–1966), a Catholic priest. Lemaître's theory presents a terrible problem for atheists and agnostics: whatever went bang was matter, and it had to come from somewhere. His theory demolished the notion that the universe has no creator by asserting implicitly that it is impossible to get something from nothing. Where did the matter that went bang come from?

Humanity's hunger to uncover, to understand, and to manage the wonders of the universe is a bedrock characteristic of the human spirit that cannot be explained simply by a need for self-preservation or comfort. The dramatic mushrooming in curiosity and inventiveness in Europe was mainly due to the evolution, development, and acceptance of the Judeo-Christian intellectual legacy of openness to discovery and to the recognition that freedom and theology are as compatible as freedom and mathematics.

There really can be no doubt that Europe was the epicenter of creative thinking and speculation from the time of the Ancients through the Middle Ages, the Renaissance, and the Enlightenment. (There were periods of speculative brilliance in parts of the Muslim world and Central Asia from the 9th to the 12th century with men such as Abu al-Rayhan al-Biruni [973–1048] and Abu Ali Sina [Avicenna, ca. 980–1037].[18]) It bears repeating that the Middle Ages solidified the intellectual underpinnings of the Enlightenment, which subsequently gained momentum in the 17th century, and then expanded across Europe after the French Revolution to reach across the world. Unfortunately, Rousseau's fanatical ideology and dogmatic positions became the dominant ideas of the Enlightenment because of his brilliant ability to frame an argument, his resort to Christian symbolism, and his facility for expressing his ideas with great precision.

As the Enlightenment became more radical, it increasingly rejected history and objective moral ethics. Fringe ideas latched onto anti-theism and scientism and simultaneously moved to undermine any established conventions or institutions. Joseph Schumpeter (1883–1950) comments, "A wave of religious, political, and economic criticism that was pathetically uncritical of its own dogmatic standards swept over the intellectual centers of Europe."[19] One of the Enlightenment's new gods was Reason "but bound by the truths of Nature as revealed by the methods of scientific empiricism."[20] John Hallowell hits the nail on the head when he says, "It was not that the eighteenth century substituted reason for faith, as some suppose, but that it exchanged one kind of faith for another, a faith in the methods of scientific empiricism for those of theology…. The eighteenth century, however, did not begin by repudiating the tenets of orthodox Christianity but by converting them into a 'reasonable' religion acceptable to minds enlightened by the new science."[21] For Hallowell, Enlightenment radicalism is a species of religious fanaticism presenting itself as the quintessence of truth, virtue, peace, freedom, and brotherhood.

Any informed adherent of Judeo-Christianity would agree with Galileo: "[Man] does not feel obliged to believe that the same God who has endowed us with sense, reason, and intellect has intended us to forgo their use."[22]

The Enlightenment (wisely) questioned authority (which does not mean that they stood in opposition to it), especially when it felt those claims rested on superstition. Confronting superstition is not an unreasonable thing to do, but in so doing the fanatical wing of the Enlightenment began to discredit and undermine some of the major philosophical and theological foundations of the Judeo-Christian universe of ideas, especially in the area of faith and morals. In this connection, much of the work of the French Philosophes and Encyclopedists, while often superb, reached the wrong conclusions about Christianity, not least because their attachment to science and mathematics impelled them to create imaginary (nonexistent) worlds. The idea of perpetual progress was enthroned, goodness was reduced to mechanical efficiency, and material outcomes and moral ethics became personal rather than universal.[23]

Political Philosophy and Economics

Academic specialization in the social and physical sciences and philosophy is fully compatible with belief in God. As most of the greatest thinkers and inventors of the Enlightenment were God-fearing men and women and not atheists, the Wizards have no business claiming (as they often do) to have monopoly on reason.

Enlightenment academics were rarely atheists and agnostics. They drew inspiration not only from such writers as Francis Bacon (1561–1626), Hugo Grotius (1583–1645), and Descartes, but from the Scholastics and the Church Fathers. In the behavioral sciences and moral ethics, academics during the Enlightenment redoubled their efforts in epistemology (i.e., the investigation of what distinguishes justified belief from opinion). In this sense, Bacon's empiricism (in many respects, the forerunner of modern-day skepticism) as well as Descartes's rationalism challenged scholars to question *old* (which is not to say erroneous) ways of thinking. Unfortunately, some radical Enlightenment scholars such as Hume cast doubt on the natural law and belief in God because they got their epistemology wrong. Hobbes's social-contract theory combined with Hume's skepticism and Jeremy Bentham's (1748–1832) simplistic utilitarianism weakened the credibility of natural-law ethics in the mind of the public. Many Enlightenment philosophers also picked up on Grotius's declaration that natural law derived from the nature of humanity itself rather than from a higher source (as Plato suggested and Judeo-Christian scholarly work had confirmed).[24]

John Locke is of particular interest to Anglo-American scholars because of his influence on the Founding Fathers. He started from the premise that Biblical revelation and law both originated in God and for that reason could not be contradictory. For Locke, human nature possessed two qualities:

reasonableness and tolerance. Contrary to Hobbes, he believed that the individual in the state of nature had intrinsic rights and that civil powers should be limited to the protection of those rights.[25] Locke saw moral law as a necessary set of rules, exhibiting the will of a higher authority. His essay *The Reasonableness of Christianity* (1695) underscored his belief in God, the reasonableness of man, and the importance of the Judeo-Christian heritage in understanding the nature and purpose of man. Revelation confirms what reason could discover for itself but had not in fact done so.[26]

Locke believed that "the prime duty of a Government is not to defend the Christian faith but to secure the rights of private property, 'for the sake of which men enter into society.' Thus, as Lord Acton says, the English Revolution substituted 'for the Divine Right of Kings the divine right of Freeholders.' For two centuries and more England was to be the Paradise of the Man of Property."[27] Locke helped the Anglo-American world understand the meaning of "inalienable rights" as used in the U.S. Declaration of Independence.

The emergence of economics as a science pre-dates the Enlightenment and was initially to a large extent a product of priestly scholarship during the late Middle Ages. There can be little doubt that Adam Smith learned much from the Scholastics (concerning, for example, value theory, free markets, wages, and trade). In his 1776 book *The Wealth of Nations,* Smith advocated economic freedom as a remedy for the outmoded policies of mercantilism. He used philosophical concepts not only to discredit the theories of the mercantilists but also and primarily to establish the basic principles of a "natural" and rational economic order where the individual reigns supreme.[28] One must be careful to see that the idea of the supremacy of the person does not morph into an ideological libertarianism.

Smith emphasized individual self-interest, the division of labor, exchange, and competition. His theory asserts that individual self-interest leads to the collective welfare of all, which arises from a natural identity of interests.[29] The problems of greed and utilitarian self-interest are addressed by borrowing Hume's concepts of benevolence and mutual sympathies. Smith argues that "there exists a guiding hand of Providence which endowed human nature with certain propensities that led men to take actions, moral decisions, the consequences of which were favorable for social order and harmony and, as a result, conducive to human welfare and happiness."[30] The idea of a self-regulating economy is a colossal contribution to economic theory. The problem, however, is that the definition of a successful system tends to ignore the dignity of the human person and the fundamental nature of man.[31]

Since markets are regulated automatically "invisible hand," as it were, man's role is to limit the damage when they malfunction. How? By tweaking the economy. Thankfully, Smith is an optimist; other, more pessimistic economists dump norm upon norm on free agents because of their perceived inability to exercise right judgement day after day. Smith, however, believed in the fitness of ordinary men and women to judge rightly. With such thinking, economics, politics, and ethics are essentially autonomous of each other (at least in theory). Smith, in effect, "transcendentalizes" markets — i.e., glorifies them — thus providing cover (if not justification) for predatory forms of capitalism in the name of efficiency, productivity, and the wealth of nations.

Jeremy Bentham followed Adam Smith and became the preeminent exponent of epistemologically and morally incoherent *laissez-faire* economic utilitarianism. Utility becomes the ultimate arbiter of a transaction's moral value — good, bad or indifferent.[32] He was deeply influenced by Helvétius (an agnostic), who believed in the natural equality of intelligences and in the power of education to mold human beings (rather as one would housebreak a pet).

Bentham stood firmly behind the idea that "in business life, as such, intelligent pursuit by each individual of the greatest financial gain for himself could be made to harmonize with the greatest general growth of the wealth or prosperity of all men collectively."[33] He extended this principle not only to economic life but to all of life and all aspects of human happiness. Arthur Schopenhauer (1788–1860) sums it up thus: "English Utilitarians talk about happiness, but they mean money."[34] We must be careful not to identify Christian salvation with material success.

By abandoning the connection between human behavior and natural law, Bentham dreamed up his *calculus of pleasure,* according to which, simply put, pleasure and pain are the measures of good and evil. And in a trice, moral and ethical complexity was reduced to a simple formula. Reason and law became the sole basis upon which to regulate all aspects of society in a fair and equitable manner. Bentham ended his story by saying the foundation of ethics is the principle of utility, "the object of which is to tear the fabric of felicity by the hands of reason and law."[35] He tried to demonstrate that just as God had it all figured out, now humanity has it all figured out. It had become possible to replace natural law with human calculations based on a supposedly scientific understanding of human nature.

While some Enlightenment thinkers produced incredibly valuable works in multiple fields, others generated materials downright hostile to the dignity of the human person and detrimental genuine human development. Most of the contributors to the *Encyclopedie* professed a vague rationalist deism that denied the existence of one, uncreated, personal God. As I've written elsewhere, "an insipid Deism, which had already revealed certain traits of positivism, gradually turned into agnosticism, if not outright atheism."[36] Radical materialism left no room for an external (not to mention personal) deity. Holbach, in one of his popular works, *Systeme de la Nature*, slammed Christianity and rejected the very ideas of God, freedom, and immortality as understood in the Judeo-Christian tradition. Likewise, Helvétius, in discrediting Christianity in *De l'homme* and *De l'esprit*, was influential in Christopher Hitchens's later rejection of God and Christianity.

Perhaps the most powerful tactic of the radical Enlightenment thinkers is their skillful use of religious concepts within a materialist vision of reality. Christopher Dawson puts it well: "The French Enlightenment was, in fact, the last of the great European heresies, and its appeal to Reason was in itself an act of faith which admitted of no criticism. Even materialists, like Helvétius and Holbach, shared the Deist belief in the transcendence of Reason and the inevitability of intellectual and moral progress, though there was nothing in their premises to warrant such assumptions."[37]

The Reign of Terror in 1793 confirmed the ascendency of the moral relativism and secular materialism, and politicized justice, which led to the slaughter of innocent people in the name of liberty, equality, and fraternity, and is still doing so today.[38] Our elites often fail to perceive the dangers of utopian, godless ideologies. Albert Einstein understood the perils of succumbing to materialist slogans and feel-good bromides: "The ideals which have always shone before me and filled me with the joy of living are goodness, beauty, and truth. To make a goal of comfort or happiness has never appealed to me; a system of ethics built on this basis would be sufficient only for a herd of cattle."[39]

It would be irresponsible and stupid to claim that the Enlightenment amounted to nothing more than an affront to Christianity. That is why, according to Robert Barron, "John Henry Newman, faced with the onslaught of a fierce rationalist critique of Christianity, blithely utilized the work of David Hume and John Locke in his own articulation of religious epistemology."[40]

Overzealous Moralizing and Casuistry

Attempts by moral theologians to catalogue all possible sins (an extreme form of casuistry) are an offshoot of Enlightenment thinking and are as patronizing as Napoleon's attempt to regulate human behavior with his eponymous Code. Casuistry is the attempt to tailor moral norms to a person's capacity to live them, rather than to foment a person's moral growth so as to become capable of the norms; the upshot of casuistry is that, in the end, very little is actually asked of the human person, and as a result there is no real conversion. The systematic effort to index the good or evil in human behavior usually backfires. Overzealous, moralizing clerics sought to "educate" students on how to think and behave in order to be saved. Such an approach goes against human dignity and can degenerate into moral absolutism and theocracy.

Once again, let us turn to C.S. Lewis: "I fully embrace the maxim ... that 'all power corrupts.' I would go further. The loftier the pretensions of the power, the more meddlesome, inhuman, and oppressive it will be. Theocracy is the worst of all possible governments. All political power is at best a necessary evil: but it is least evil when its sanctions are most modest and commonplace, when it claims no more than to be useful or convenient and sets itself strictly limited objectives. Anything transcendental or spiritual, or even anything very strongly ethical, in its pretensions is dangerous and encourages it to meddle with our private lives. Let the shoemaker stick to his last. Thus, the Renaissance doctrine of Divine Right is for me a corruption of monarchy; Rousseau's General Will, of democracy; racial mysticisms, of nationality. And Theocracy, I admit and even insist, is the worst corruption of all."[41] While it is indispensable to hear the voices of genuinely holy men and women, overzealous moralizing by theologians is not helpful because it negates human freedom and dignity.

Governance, Democracy, and Jean-Jacques Rousseau

Since the Enlightenment, the belief has become widespread that democracy is the best political system, and the one most likely to bring about liberty, equality, and fraternity. What does that mean? First, it is important to distinguish between theoretical and practical forms of democracy. In either form, however, a just democratic political system falls apart when its leaders reject the Judeo-Christian worldview and sacrifice the dignity of the human person as they impose — violently if necessary — the sacrosanct values of the French Revolution.

Clearly Rousseau — not Voltaire or Robespierre — was, as Dawson says, "the spiritual father of the makers of the [post-Enlightenment] new age, and the source of that spirit of revolutionary idealism that finds expression not only in liberalism but in socialism and anarchism as well."[42] His *Social Contract* was, as French historian Pierre Gaxotte has written, "the total alienation of all the rights of each individual in order to place them in the hands of the community."[43]

Rousseau turned the idea of speculative democracy into a workable political ideal. It is bewildering the number of intellectuals he has intoxicated with his shaman-like wizardry. His masterful writing skills empowered men such as Nietzsche and Marx to justify a state with unlimited powers. In his widely read book *Emile*, Rousseau explains that man once lived in a state of natural innocence where there were no conditioning factors such as obligations, duties, obedience, or commands. He goes on to say that malice enters the heart of a child through the family, society, and the educational system, and upholds personal experience as the purest form of education. By the same token, any anxiety or sense of being repressed had to be eliminated. In *What's Wrong with the World?* G.K. Chesterton may be thinking of Rousseau when he writes, "Most modern freedom is at root fear. It is not so much that we are too bold to endure rules; it is rather that we are too timid to endure responsibilities."[44]

Not unlike a high priest or Wizard of the Enlightenment, Rousseau needed an excuse to preserve his personal rights, to do whatever he wanted, and dispense with burdensome duties and responsibilities that were not dictated by the state in the name of true democracy or material human development. Freedom emerged, he argued, from man's unification with the mind of the state. A transcendent natural law had no place in his harmonious theoretical earthly Garden of Eden. Rousseau was a utopian steeped in Judeo-Christian verbiage but who could not distinguish between one uncreated God and the interior gods of his own imagining.

Arnold Toynbee in his introduction to Dawson's book *The Gods of Revolution* writes, "The [French] Revolution's supreme paradox was that, in the act of deposing the traditional Christian 'Establishment,' it opened the way for an atavistic return to a pre-Christian religion: the worship of collective human power which had been the religion of the pagan Roman Empire and of the Greek city-states which the Roman Empire had incorporated. This worship of human power is about ninety percent of the religion of about ninety percent of the present generation of mankind. Shall we succeed in shaking it off? And, if we remained slaved to it, whither will it lead us?"[45]

It is hard to escape the conclusion that Rousseau concocted *The Social Contract* to justify the conflict within himself between human freedom and responsibility and *his* personal need to identify with some external standard, which was the collective will of "the people." He did not believe in Original Sin and thought that education, surroundings, and upbringing were enough to form people in the virtues and behavior appropriate to a democracy. He was less interested in inculcating the politics of a free, self-governing people than in that of a managerial, regulatory system in which people were cogs in the machinery of social uplift, which meant seeing to it that they held the right opinions and behaved in acceptable ways. For that reason, he made politics into a kind of religion and sought to enlist the educational establishment and the press in the cause of re-educating people.

The result is a political system rooted in moralism rather than morality. God gets pushed aside, and humanity enshrined in his place. Consequently, modern political economy aims less at the self-realization of the individual — the authentic aim of systems rooted in Judeo-Christian values —— than at the imposition on people — violently if necessary — of preconceived ideological constructs in the bogus expectation that this will result in their moral and material uplift.

Joseph Cardinal Ratzinger (later Pope Benedict XVI) gives us food for thought: "Political moralism, as we have lived it and are still living it, does not open the way to regeneration, and even more, also blocks it. The same is true, consequently, also for a Christianity and a theology that reduces the heart of Jesus' message, the 'kingdom of God,' to the 'values of the kingdom,' identifying these values with the great key words of political moralism, and proclaiming them, at the same time, as a synthesis of the religions."[46] Moralism then is the adulation of certain principles or values in a utopian context. It thwarts genuine human development because it acts against human freedom and dignity. When God is taken out of the picture, any enormity can be justified.

As the high priests of the Enlightenment, Rousseau and his followers behaved like closed-minded clerics whose fanaticism and narrow-mindedness belied their inability to see beyond their own noses. As Christopher W. Mitchell has pointed out, "There is always the danger that those who think alike should gravitate together into *coteries* where they will henceforth encounter opposition only in the emasculated form of rumor that the outsiders say thus and thus. The absent are easily refuted, complacent dogmatism thrives, and differences of opinion are embittered by group hostility. Each group hears not the best, but the worst, that the other groups can say."[47] The blindness of the radical men of the Enlightenment was made worse by their need for mutual approval in the face of unreal claims. As is the case with any small group of like-minded men and women whose ideas are inbred, they felt compelled to create a forum for discussion and mutual support. It is the only way that their fictitious, unreal world could remain afloat. It seems Rousseau was able to infect modern people with his imaginary intellectual construct.

Why were Rousseau's ideas so alluring? He claimed freedom was made possible when a sufficient number of individuals identified their will with that of "the people." The will of "the people" usually was the will of a tight-knit political class claiming to represent the community or nation. In Rousseauian terminology, the leader who embodies the General Will of the body politic was invested with sovereignty.

Rousseau's key idea rests on the assumption that to benefit from communal living, people have to relinquish a part of their freedom in order to secure it. What he misconstrues is that people must align their freedom with objective reality (not ideological pseudo-reality) if they wish to secure their freedom. A problem arises when individuals do not accept the general will. In that case, coercion to one degree or another — including state violence — may be used to enforce compliance.

I quote at length from Philip Trower's book *The Catholic Church and the Counter-Faith: A Study of the Roots of Modern Secularism, Relativism and De-Christianization* (2006):

> *The basic principles of theoretical democracy (as opposed to common sense democracy) are that there exists such a thing as "the people,"* an aggregate of equal units all having the same needs, thoughts and will; that together they are the source of truth, right and the power to command obedience; that the people should rule, either directly by intervening day to day in the details of government, with no decision being taken without their knowledge and consent, or in the sense that the rulers are merely their mouthpieces. For a man to have to submit to an authority other than his own is an affront to his dignity and a limitation of his humanity.
>
> There is a close connection between Rousseau's idea of democracy and Luther's concept of the Church as a people acting together directly under the inspiration of the Holy Spirit [or of a transcendent force]. Rousseau's difficulty was that, in leaving out the Holy Spirit, he could not explain why the people should always be of one mind and will. Hence his second famous idea.
>
> By what right can the collective mind and will compel the individuals, absolutely free by birth, who make up the people, to obey its authority and laws? Because of the social contract. Having freely (in the person of his remote ancestors?) entered into the contract, the free individual remains his own master because the collective mind and will are now his mind and will. Can he withdraw from the contract? No. It is for keeps. Those who disagree with the collective mind and will are no longer a part of the people. They have become severed limbs, enemies of the people. The people is . ... the majority? Those with the right ideas? Here theoretical democracy becomes evasive.
>
> The theory of social contract is an attempt to explain the origin of society and political authority without God; to

show why men and women who are assumed to be subject to no one but themselves should accept laws manifestly coming from outside them, and not always to their liking. It is assumed that social living is artificial, not natural.[48]

It bears repeating that most modern politicians, despite their optimism about the perfectibility of man and the efficacy of government activism, fail to grasp the fundamental impossibility of achieving liberty and equality simultaneously. It is modern man's utopian belief that the impossible can become possible — government can eliminate the differences between men and women, allow children to determine their own gender, reverse weather patterns, et cetera — that is undermining freedoms around the world. An egalitarian order cannot exist without destroying distinction, merit, and quality. When politicians lose sight of people — with all their strengths and weaknesses, virtues and failings — freedom suffers.

C. S. Lewis: "God created things which had free will. That means creatures which can go either wrong or right. Some people think they can imagine a creature which was free but had no possibility of going wrong; I cannot. If a thing is free to be good, it is also free to be bad. And free will is what has made evil possible. Why, then, did God give them free will? Because free will, though it makes evil possible, is also the only thing that makes possible any love or goodness or joy worth having."[49]

History has shown that when utopian systems are imposed on people, the uncooperative wind up being liquidated. The history of the 20th century through our own day is full of such mass violence. It starts with Orwell's Commandment that "All animals are equal." Over time, the Commandment becomes "All animals are equal, but some animals are more equal than others." That is when the atrocities begin in the name of the common good.

Equality cannot be imposed on people. No amount of social engineering, wishful thinking, or psychological manipulation will produce the desired result. Academics and development organizations continue to push for the impossible. No matter how hard some international financial institutions, the United Nations, the European Commission, or well-heeled NGOs might try to impose gender equality, for example, the fact remains that a man is not a woman and a woman is not a man, although both are human beings. Moreover, Rousseau's theoretical democracy cannot come about without doing violence to people.

In plain words, Trower points out the current state of affairs in the West:

[Today], theoretical democracy is widely seen as the ideal.

This is why we have so many well-intentioned liberals seeking to realize the principles of theoretical democracy within the framework of our common-sense democracies until they crack at the seams. Such liberals feel guiltily that the will of the majority ought somehow to make wrong things right, even if it doesn't; that the people ought to rule, even if they can't; and that liberty and equality ought to be maximized even if the attempt is going to burst the seams of democracy. The breakdown of parliamentary democracies in Europe in the 1920s and 1930s was partly attributable to this cause. [50]

Similarly, Aleksandr Solzhenitsyn said, "Many new countries have in recent years suffered a fiasco just after introducing democracy; yet despite such evidence, the same period has seen an elevation of democracy from a particular state structure into a sort of universal principle of human existence, almost a cult."[51] When democracy achieves cult status, it can easily become as intolerant as the Wizards claim organized religion is. Solzhenitsyn continues, "Respect for the individual represents a broader principle than democracy and it is a principle that must be ensured without fail. But this need not necessarily be rendered only by means of a parliamentary system."[52] The danger for Anglo-American democracy is the threat of its radicalization and its conversion into an ideology.

According to Rousseau, failure to identify with his General Will was tantamount to a lack of personal freedom and thus a form of enslavement. In such cases, the whole body politic, including enlightened politicians, lawyers, and the media, has to compel unruly or noncompliant persons to bend to the will of the godlike, infallible, supreme, and unassailable sovereign power. Multiculturalism, consumerism, and hedonism are some of the weapons used by Rousseau's modern heirs to pacify the masses and create a trouble-free consensus in society. Political correctness is a tool for mass intellectual suicide, since it aims to silence free will and differing opinions.

In the 21st century, free speech in the United States and Western Europe is heavily monitored. Severe penalties apply to anyone who doesn't toe the line. Any views based on inconvenient truths are simply not tolerated. Our "enlightened" leaders discredit and hush up anyone with an opinion different from theirs and try to legitimize their actions by invoking democracy. Just as dissidents in the Soviet Union were often sent to psychiatric wards for expressing a view contrary to party orthodoxy, dissidents in the United States and Europe may someday be forced into isolation and treated as opponents of the ruling regime.

Oswald Spengler (1880–1936) described one aspect of the Wizards' approach in his perceptive book *The Decline of the West* (1918): "To-day we live so cowed under the bombardment of this intellectual artillery [i.e., the media] that hardly anyone can attain to the inward detachment that is required for a clear view of the monstrous drama. The will-to-power operating under a pure democratic disguise has finished off its masterpiece so well that the object's sense of freedom is actually flattered by the most thorough-going enslavement that has ever existed."[53]

With the eclipse of communism and other utopian systems as viable post-Enlightenment political systems, democracy in its "progressive," atheistic configuration is increasingly a vehicle for delivering man and society from earthly imperfections, irrespective of a people's historical or cultural realities, and is akin to ideological and religious fanaticism. Here again is Rousseau:

> As soon as this multitude (i.e., the people) is so united in one body, it is impossible to offend against one of the members without attacking the body, and still more to offend against the body without the members resenting it. Duty and interest therefore equally oblige the two contracting parties to give each other help; and the same men should seek to combine, in their double capacity, all the advantages dependent upon that capacity.
>
> ... In order then that the social compact may not be an empty formula, it tacitly includes the undertaking, which alone can give force to the rest, that whoever refuses to obey the general will shall be compelled to do so by the whole body. This means nothing less than that he will be forced to be free; for this is the condition which, by giving each citizen to his country, secures him against all personal dependence. In this lies the key to the working of the political machine; this alone legitimizes civil undertakings, which, without it, would be absurd, tyrannical, and liable to the most frightful abuses.[54]

Rousseau presents us with a philosophy for democracy disguised as freedom where force and scheming are legitimate and indeed necessary tools to establish the ideal society. Some of his followers down the centuries have employed methods akin to those of the jihadi mujahideen (or fanatics of the Inquisition) to save men's souls in the name of a noble cause. Rousseau's brilliance attracted the praise of such men as Kant, Friedrich Schiller (1759–

1805), Percy Bysshe Shelley (1792–1822), and John Stuart Mill (1806–1873).

Rousseau and many of his soulmates inspired the debate between Edmund Burke (*Reflections on the French Revolution,* 1790) and Thomas Paine (*The Rights of Man,* 1791). Both men had an enormous influence on the American political mind along with the brilliant work of the Founding Fathers. It has become increasingly clear during the opening years of the 21st century that the practical and wiser American democratic political tradition is in a life-and-death struggle against the proponents of messianic, revolutionary democracy. It explains the growing encroachment of Washington on families and education, and its efforts (violent if necessary) to export radical non-Judeo-Christian Western "values" to the rest of the world. Money and resources are but means to these ends. The assault on freedom in Europe, America, and increasingly around the world is a signal that they are drifting into authoritarianism.

"Common-sense democracies [*ed.,* as in the United States and France today] have now taken over from theoretical democracy the notion that [*ed.,* popular] sovereignty (the right to command obedience) comes from 'the people' or the majority vote, not from God," writes Jonathan Trower. "In so far as they accept this principle, first passed into law by the French constituent assembly in June 1789, modern states have moved from a Christian foundation to an atheist-humanist foundation. We can therefore see the French Revolution as incorporating three not two revolutions: a political revolution, a social revolution and a metaphysical revolution, as the transference of power from God to Demos has been called."[55]

When people confuse reality with conceptual constructs and see evil as arising exclusively from external factors such as the environment, institutions, surroundings, or long-standing communal structures, they have boxed themselves into a corner. The difference between the Gospel and the radical Enlightenment ideology is that the Judeo-Christian tradition sees reform as beginning from within the person with the help of God rather than beginning outside of man with the help of government and media.

The disinclination of modern man to admit his limitations has its main roots in the Enlightenment's tendency to disregard the dignity of the human person, and in its uninterest in genuine human development as it cheerfully went about constructing earthly paradises at various times and in various places. Hitler and Stalin also entertained utopian visions and led their nations and the world to disaster. And so, will anyone who tries to fashion the world into a state of theoretical perfection through atheistic scientism, or ideologized democratism, capitalism, communism, socialism, national socialism, liberal globalism, religion-based theocracy, or any other political system be spared the ignominy of failure and the self-destruction of society itself? There can be no genuine human development without a recognition of the dignity of the human person.

President Dwight D. Eisenhower, an extraordinary leader, warned America and the world of the possible rise of a military-industrial complex, disguised as democracy, which could endanger our core dignity as human beings:

> [The] conjunction of an immense military establishment and a large arms industry is new in the American experience. The total influence — economic, political, even spiritual — is felt in every city, every statehouse, every office of the federal government. We recognize the imperative need for this development. Yet we must not fail to comprehend its grave implications. Our toil, resources, and livelihood are all involved; so is the very structure of our society. In the councils of government, we must guard against the acquisition of unwarranted influence, whether sought or unsought, by the military-industrial complex. The potential for the disastrous rise of misplaced power exists, and will persist. We must never let the weight of this combination endanger our liberties or democratic processes. We should take nothing for granted. Only an alert and knowledgeable citizenry can compel the proper meshing of the huge industrial and military machinery of defense with our peaceful methods and goals so that security and liberty may prosper together.[56]

Eisenhower's warning reflects an awareness of the depredations — real and potential — of the Wizards' vision of perpetual progress and earthly redemption. As this philosophical paradigm (pre-programmed to feed upon the goodness of ordinary citizens) aims to control society at the expense of freedom itself, one can only wonder what is the point of equality and brotherhood if there is no freedom?

G.K. Chesterton wrote, "There is less difference than many suppose between the ideal Socialist system, in which the big businesses are run by the State, and the present Capitalist system, in which the State is run by the big businesses. Communism is the form of Capitalism in which all workers have an equal wage. Capitalism is that form of Communism in which the organizing officials have a very large salary."[57]

Over time, the weapons of the radicals of the Enlightenment have changed but their aims have essentially remained the same: to give the impression that they can create paradise on Earth in the not-too-distant future irrespective of social costs, violations of human rights, and the disruption of ordinary life. Let me be absolutely clear: most of the Wizards of the Enlightenment have bought into godless techno-utopian phantasies that have scant purchase on reality. Angry, fanatical Wizards will stop at nothing to achieve their aims, including the intellectual neutralization or belittlement of those who stand in their way.

The Wizards' philosophy appeals to a person's ego by offering liberation through reason and science. It is an absurd proposition because Judeo-Christianity already passionately embraces reason and science. In fact, therefore, there is no need to choose. As such, there is no need to make an "act of unfaith" to gain one's freedom, as many Wizards propose, because men and women are already free.

Some Wizards continue to foment the illusion that freedom and utopia are just around the corner. We could do worse than to listen to the sage words of Jesus of Nazareth: "Indeed the time is coming when anyone who kills you will think he is doing a holy service to God."[58]

In conclusion, Pope Benedict XVI, when he was still Joseph Cardinal Ratzinger, made this proposal in one of his most brilliant lectures, "On Europe's Crisis of Culture" (2005):

> At the time of the Enlightenment there was an attempt to understand and define the essential moral norms, saying that they would be valid "etsi Deus non daretur," even in the case that God did not exist.... [T]he attempt, carried to the extreme, to manage human affairs disdaining God completely leads us increasingly to the edge of the abyss, to man's ever greater isolation from reality. We must reverse the axiom of the Enlightenment and say: Even one who does not succeed in finding the way of accepting God, should, nevertheless, seek to live and to direct his life "veluti si Deus daretur," as if God existed. This is the advice Pascal gave to his friends who did not believe. In this way, no one is limited in his freedom, but all our affairs find the support and criterion of which they are in urgent need.
>
> Above all, that of which we are in need at this moment in history are men who, through an enlightened and lived faith, render God credible in this world. The negative testimony of Christians who speak about God and live against him, has darkened God's image and opened the door to disbelief. We need men who have their gaze directed to God, to understand true humanity. We need men whose intellects are enlightened

by the light of God, and whose hearts God opens, so that their intellects can speak to the intellects of others, and so that their hearts are able to open up to the hearts of others.[59]

Why does Pope Benedict encourage us to embrace the Judeo-Christian understanding of God and man, and to live accordingly? I would suggest this answer: so as to permit all of reality, that which is visible and that which is not — life, sanctity, truth, wisdom, the hereafter, et cetera — to open up before us. For we are all seekers after the truth — are we not?

---

1.   Joseph Cardinal Ratzinger, "On Europe's Crisis of Culture" (lecture, April 2005) (https://www. catholiceducation.org/en/culture/catholic-contributions/cardinal-ratzinger-on-europe-s-crisis-of- culture.html).

2.   Philip Trower, *The Catholic Church and the Counter-Faith: A Study of the Roots of Modern Secularism, Relativism and De-Christianization* (Oxford: Family Publications, 2006); p. 31.

3.   The latter writings are milder and less virulent forms of dogmatic Enlightenment thinking. Nonetheless, they inspired much of America's current Girondist-like "spread-the-democratic- revolution" approach to foreign policy.

4.   Trower, *Catholic Church and Counter-Faith*, p. 31.

5.   Arthur Cushman McGiffert, *Protestant Thought before Kant* (New York: Charles Scribner's Sons, 1911); p. 244.

6.   Ratzinger, "On Europe's Crisis of Culture."

7.   G.K. Chesterton, *Orthodoxy* ((New York: Dodd, Mead & Co., 1908); p. 63 (http://www.ccel.org/ccel/chesterton/orthodoxy.html).

8.   C.S. Lewis, *Mere Christianity* (New York: Macmillan Company, 1952); p. 25 (https://canavox.com/wp-content/uploads/2017/06/Mere-Christianity-Lewis.pdf).

9.   C.S. Lewis, *God in the Dock*, Walter Hooper, ed. (Grand Rapids, Mich.: William B. Eerdmans Publishing Company, 1970); p. 292. (Also C.S. Lewis, "The Humanitarian Theory of Punishment," Issues in Religion and Psychotherapy, 13, no. 1 (1987) (http://scholarsarchive.byu.edu/cgi/viewcontent.cgi?article=1271&context=irp) .

10.   Charles Dickens (Intro. and Notes by Richard Maxwell), "The Wood-Sawyer," in *A Tale of Two Cities* (1859; London: Penguin Books, 2003); p. 285.

11.   Lewis, *Mere Christianity*, page 161.

12.   I would like particularly to mention the contributions of Princess Yekaterina Romanovna Vorontsova-Dashkova to the development of Russia and to the country's modernization. In 1782, she was the first woman to head the Imperial Academy of Arts and Sciences in Russia. In the following year, she was appointed as Director of the Russian Academy that produced the Dictionary of the Russian Language and, in 1784, she was made a member of the Swedish Royal Academy of Sciences. These were enormous accomplishments and a tribute to the Enlightenment.

13.   Immanuel Kant, *On History* (Indianapolis: Bobbs-Merrill Educational Publishing,

1963), pp. 3-4.

14.   Christopher Hitchens, *God Is Not Great: How Religion Poisons Everything* (New York: Twelve Books, 2007); p. 283.

15.   Lewis, *Mere Christinaity*, p. 22.

16.   John Herman Randall Jr., *The Making of the Modern Mind* (New York: Houghton Mifflin, 1926); p. 227.

17.   James Gregory (1638–1675) fashioned the first reflecting telescope. In 1670, Dom Pierre Pérignon (1638–1715) produced champagne at the Benedictine Abbey of Hautvillers. In 1675, Christian Huygens (1629–1695) built the first pocket watch. In 1679, Denis Papin (1647–1712) crafted the pressure cooker. In 1767, Joseph Priestley (1733–1804) fashioned soda water. In 1774, Georges-Louis Le Sage (1724–1803) completed the electric telegraph. In 1742, Anders Celsius (1701-1744) developed the Celsius thermometer. In 1795, Nicolas Appert (1749–1841) developed the jar for food. In 1796, Edward Jenner (1749–1823) discovered the smallpox vaccination. In 1674, Antonie van Leeuwenhoek (1632–1723) saw bacteria with a microscope. In 1698, Thomas Savery (1650–1715) crafted the steam pump. In 1784, Andrew Meikle (1719–1811) industrialized the threshing machine. In 1769, James Watt (1736–1819) assembled the steam engine. In 1775, Alexander Cumming (1731–1814) produced the flush toilet.

18.   As stated earlier, it is likely that the triumphant philosophy of Al-Ghazali (1058–1111), rather than that of Averroes (1126–1198), won the philosophical debate among Islamic thinkers in North Africa and Iberia, leaving Spain with a predominately anti-scientific mentality and delaying the introduction and spirit of the Enlightenment in Iberia. Averroes, whose ideas were more in line with classical Aquino-Aristotelian philosophy, the Church Fathers, and common sense, never recovered as a philosopher in the Islamic world. While this hypothesis needs further validation, it does seem likely that the Caliphate in Iberia and subsequently the Spanish Crown into the 20th century were reluctant to encourage imaginative and original thinking. The only exception to be realized was in Spain's hard-nosed aggressiveness (and inflexibility) in missionary or military matters. The deep imprint Al-Ghazali and Islam left on the Iberian soul remains at the core of the modern Spanish mind and explains the suspicious attitude of certain Spaniards towards the broader positive spirit of the Enlightenment.

19.   Joseph A. Schumpeter (Intro. by Mark Perlman), *History of Economic Analysis* (1954; repr.; London: Routledge, 1997); p. 118.

20.   Schumpeter, p. 122.

21.   John H. Hallowell, *Main Current in Modern Political Thought* (New York: Henry Holt, 1950); pp. 119-20.

22.   Galileo Galilei, Letter to Grand Duchess Christina (1615) (http://www.inters.org/galilei-madame-christina-Lorraine).

23.   The effects of the Enlightenment were felt as much in the public square as in the royal courts of the day. Many European monarchs used ideas from the Enlightenment to justify their authority and validate their political and social agendas, and some of them were heavily prejudiced against Judeo-Christianity. Of all the European monarchs of the 18th century, Frederick II of Prussia (1712–1786) was most culpable for the spread of anti-Christian ideas during the Enlightenment. Other monarchs such as Carlos III of Spain (1716–1788), Joseph II of the Holy Roman Empire (1741–1790), Catherine II of Russia (1729–1796), Louis XVI of France (1754–1793), and Joseph I of Portugal (1714–1777) took defiant pleasure in the ideas of enlightened despotism, since they did

not want to be held accountable to a world order beyond their personal control.

24.   The writings of men such as Spinoza and Richard Simon (1638–1712) impressed a highly skeptical European intellectual mindset molded during the Protestant Reformation and the Renaissance. Spinoza's skepticism and Simon's "higher criticism" attacked Sacred Scriptures as a means to lower their status as authoritative sources of moral ethics.

25.   "For Thomas Hobbes, for example, the state of nature was characterized as a 'war of all against all' in which life was 'nasty, brutish and short.' For Rousseau, the state of nature far from being a fearful existence was an idyllic one. For Locke, the state of nature was neither idyllic nor fearful." See Hollowell, *Main Currents*, p. 103.

26.   Hallowell, *Main Currents*, p. 121.

27.   Christopher Dawson, *Progress and Religion* (New York: Image Books, 1960); p. 151.

28.   Alberto M. Piedra, *Natural Law: The Foundation of an Orderly Economic System* (Lanham, Maryland: Lexington Books, 2004); p. 55.

29.   Piedra, *Natural Law*, p. 60.

30.   Piedra, *Natural Law*, p. 60.

31.   See Wilhelm Roepke, *La crisis social de nuestro tempo* (Madrid: Biblioteca de la Ciencia Economica, 1956); p. 65.

32.   Roepke, *La crisis*, p. 120.

33.   Overton H. Taylor, *A History of Economic Thought* (New York: McGraw Hill Company, Inc., 1960); p. 119.

34.   Taylor, *History*, p. 120.

35.   Jeremy Bentham, *An Introduction to the Principles of Morals and Legislation* (Oxford: 1869); pp. 17ff., as quoted by Hollowell, *Main Currents*, p. 209).

36.   Piedra, *Natural Law*, p. 16.

37.   Dawson, *Progress and Religion*, p. 154.

38.   With reference to the principle of equality, Edmund Burke had this to say: "France, when she let loose the reins of regal authority, doubled the license, of a ferocious dissoluteness in manners, and of an insolent irreligion in opinions and practices; and has extended through all ranks of life, as if she were communicating some privilege, or laying open some secluded benefit, all the unhappy corruptions that usually were the disease of wealth and power. This is one of the new principles of equality in France." See Edmund Burke, *Reflections on the Revolution in France* (Garden City: Dolphin Books, 1961); p. 50. For a criticism of Burke's analysis of the French Revolution see Thomas Paine, *The Rights of Man* (New York: Dolphin Books, 1961).

39.   Albert Einstein, *Einstein on Politics: His Private Thoughts and Stands on Nationalism, Zionism, War, Peace, and the Bomb,* David E. Rowe and Robert Schulmann, eds. (Princeton, N.J.: Princeton University Press, 2013); p. 227.

40.   Robert Barron, *Catholicism: A Journey to the Heart of the Faith* (New York, Image Books, 2011); p. 159.

41.   C.S. Lewis, *The World's Last Night* (New York: Houghton Mifflin Harcourt, 2002); p. 40.

42.   Christopher Dawson (Intro. by Arnold Toynbee), *The Gods of Revolution* (London: Sidgwick & Jackson, 1972); p. 36.

43. "Despotisme de la Liberté, dogmatisme de la Raison, c'estee que les révolution-naires appelaient le régime qu'ils avaient fondé. Camisole de force, tyrannie, enfer, op-pression: c'estee que les historiens les plus impartiaux le qualifient au jour d'hui. Disons plus simplement que c'est le règne de l'aliénation totale de chaque individu avec tousses droits, a la communauté,' selon l'exacte formule de Rousseau. Quant à ceux qui object-eraient que les révolutionnaires ne sont point la communauté, Saint-Just leur répondra que la Volonté Générale n'est point la volonté du plus grand nombre, mais la volonté des purs, charges d'éclairer la nation sur ses véritables désires et son véritable bonheur." See Pierre Gaxotte, *La Révolution Française* (Paris: Fayard, 1970); pp. 367-68.

44. G.K. Chesterton, *What's Wrong with the World?* (Lawrence, Kans.: Digireads Publishing, 2004); p. 67.

45. Dawson, *Gods of Revolution*, p. xi.

46. Ratzinger, "Crisis of Culture."

47. C.S. Lewis, from an article published in *Socratic Digest* 1:2-4; as quoted in Christopher W. Mitchell, "University Battles: C.S. Lewis and the Oxford University Socratic Club," in Angus Menuge, ed., *C.S. Lewis: Lightbearer in the Shadow Lands* (Wheaton, Ill.: Crossway Books, 1997).

48. Trower, *Catholic Church and Counter-Faith*, pp. 45-46.

49. C.S. Lewis, *Mere Christianity*, page 37.

50. Trower, *Catholic Church and Counter-Faith*, p. 47.

51. Aleksandr Solzhenitsyn, *Rebuilding Russia: Reflections and Tentative Proposals* (New York: Farrar, Straus and Giroux, Inc, 1991); p. 63.

52. Solzhenitsyn, *Rebuilding Russia*, p. 64.

53. Oswald Spengler, *The Decline of the West*, Charles F. Akinson, trans. (1923; repr. New York: Alfred A. Knopf Publisher, 1928); p. 461.

54. Jean-Jacques Rousseau, *The Social Contract*, book I (http://www.constitution.org/jjr/socon_01.htm).

55. Trower, *Catholic Church and Counter-Faith*, p. 47.

56. Dwight D. Eisenhower, "Farewell Address to the Nation," 1961 (http://mcadams.posc.mu.edu/ike.htm).

57. In Dale Ahlquist, *The Complete Thinker: The Marvelous Mind of G.K. Chesterton* (San Francisco: Ignatius Press, 2012); p. 165.

58. John 16:2 (http://www.usccb.org/bible/john/16).

59. Ratzinger, "On Europe's Crisis of Culture."

EPILOGUE

The False Prophet will have a religion without a cross. A religion without a world to come. A religion to destroy religions. There will be a counterfeit church. Christ's Church will be one. And the False Prophet will create the other. The false church will be worldly, ecumenical, and global. It will be a loose federation of churches. And religions forming some type of global association. A world parliament of churches. It will be emptied of all divine content and will be the mystical body of the Antichrist. The mystical body on earth today will have its Judas Iscariot and he will be the false prophet. Satan will recruit him from among our bishops.

— Ven. Fulton Sheen, *Communism and the Conscience of the West*

Over a half century ago, while I was still a child, I recall hearing a number of old people offer the following explanation for the great disasters that had befallen Russia: "Men have forgotten God; that's why all this has happened." Since then I have spent well-nigh 50 years working on the history of our revolution; in the process, I have read hundreds of books, collected hundreds of personal testimonies, and have already contributed eight volumes of my own toward the effort of clearing away the rubble left by that upheaval. But if I were asked today to formulate as concisely as possible the main cause of the ruinous revolution that swallowed up some 60 million of our people, I could not put it more accurately than to repeat: "Men have forgotten God; that's why all this has happened."

— Aleksandr Solzhenitsyn, *Voices from the Gulag*

There is a growing need for clarity in a world inundated by moral relativism, voluntarism and a destructive anti-theist narrative designed to undercut not only the Judeo-Christian worldview and legacy but sanity itself. In a global village filled with half-truths, lies, and failed utopian projects, it is high time the world's elites woke up from their self-induced stupor and ditched their infatuation with half-baked unworkable ideologies of liberation, equality, and brotherhood, which are pitched as salvific but invariably are divorced from

232

truth and reality.

In their quest to master the universe, the Wizards tirelessly hawk an aimless self-referencing moral ethos that is anti-developmental because it is self-centered and hostile to any external authority. They speak of human beings as statistics and commodities and see them through the prism of an unending struggle for survival, where hope is replaced by power and threats appear around every corner. Life ends in death after years of struggle to survive in a dog-eat-dog environment in which human nature is revealed to be "nasty, brutish and short." Such is everyone's fate.

Does not Nietzsche also see such a world when he says, "Hope in reality is the worst of all evils because it prolongs the torments of man"? By implication, human beings need to create their own reality in a godless world of random events, or else be left to suffer the indignity of being counted among the weak and unproductive.

Is it not time to come to our senses and see the narrative of the anti-theists as irrational and dangerous because it aims to create alternative worlds on this side of death? Hasn't the world had enough of social engineering? What will it take to get man to realize that the path to genuine interior peace and liberation must pass through the mind and heart of the Creator of human beings, God, and not through the "will to power" or the dawn of a "new man?"[1]

What will the Wizards think of next? Some propose imbuing society, through neural networks, with "universal consciousness" to replace God. The next fad will surely be the attempt to merge human physiology and psychology with technology, an effort that is doomed to fail.

Present-day utopians speak of new emergent faiths and capabilities that will be able to free humanity from the bonds of human existence. This vision rests on the false optimism that advanced nanotechnology, mathematics, and artificial intelligence will bring about a fresh state of "cyberconsciousness," somehow introducing humanity to life without death. Such thinking is absolute poppycock and dangerous stuff because the human person and God are reduced to data points and information. The one uncreated God of the universe is not a man-made straw man to be knocked down at will or used, but rather the God of the universe, who precedes space, energy, gravity, and time.

To achieve their objectives, the radical Wizards try to lure us into making an "act of unfaith," an act of disbelief in God, so that human beings contaminated with religion will shake off their delusional tolerance of suffering caused by their irrational belief in the transcendental. But is not their own ideological materialism an act of blind faith? John Lennox sums it all up nicely: "I don't have faith to be an atheist."[2]

The historical record and the testimony of millions undermine the predominant storyline of the anti-theists. They poke fun at Judeo-Christian humanism as if it has caused today's societal schizophrenia and inhibited the pursuit of happiness. Ravi Zacharias is right when he says: "I have news for [atheists] — news to the contrary. The reality is that the emptiness that results from the loss of the transcendent is stark and devastating, philosophically and existentially. Indeed, the denial of an objective moral law, based on the compulsion to deny the existence of God, results ultimately in the denial of evil itself."[3]

The anti-theists' belief in perpetual progress and in their ability to eventually deliver human beings from the inconveniences of life reveals the sorry state of their philosophy. Such beliefs are disingenuous because they promise, through the acquisition of power and knowledge, the impossible dream of personal liberation from "whatever," when in fact their utopian visions bring an endless stream of doubt and despair. The 20th century stands as testimony to the failure of the godless ideologies and pie-in-the-sky panaceas put forth by anti-theists and their publicists. Malcolm Muggeridge sheds light on the narcissism of many modern thinkers: "[Pascal] was the first and perhaps is still the most effective voice to be raised in warning of the consequences of the enthronement of the human ego in contradistinction to [God and] the cross, symbolizing the ego's immolation. How beautiful it all seemed at the time of the Enlightenment, that man triumphant would bring to pass that earthly paradise whose groves of academe would ensure the realization forever of peace, plenty, and beatitude in practice. But what a nightmare of wars, famines, and folly was to result therefrom."[4]

Our challenge today is to reassess who we are as human beings and rediscover the dignity of the human person and the power of selfless service without which there is no integral human development but only the vicious cycle of rise and fall, progress and decline. The sanity of societies and nations depends on recognizing that we are not alone in this universe but rather are sons and daughters of a loving God. Such a view is profane to the Wizards because it requires a certain degree of subordination to an external authority.

Throughout this book, I have celebrated the accomplishments of Nobel Prize-winning scientists who recognized that there is no contradiction between science, on the one hand, and belief in God, Christian humanism, and the Gospel message, on the other. Is it really wise to remain silent as the narrative of the anti-theists takes hold of human consciousness? Is not the proposition that it is reasonable to think that chance and the theory of evolution explain the origin of the universe better than God absurd? And is it not silly to buy the claim that "something" can come from "nothing,"[5] or that the wizardry of science is the basis for the idea of perpetual progress?

It may be helpful to ponder the simple but penetrating words of C.S. Lewis: "Consequently atheism turns out to be too simple. If the whole universe has no meaning, we should never have found out that it has no meaning: just as, if there were no light in the universe and therefore no creatures with eyes, we should never know it was dark. Dark would be without meaning."[6]

Let there be no mistake. Having given the praiseworthy efforts of the Enlightenment a bad name, the radical anti-theists have been busily engineering a cultural revolution directed against the Judeo-Christian legacy and institutions. As Aleksandr Solzhenitsyn so poignantly noted in 1978 at Harvard University, it is imperative to learn from our past mistakes or else suffer a fate similar to that of other godless utopians and naïve dreamers: "It would be retrogression to attach oneself today to the ossified formulas of the [radical] Enlightenment. Social dogmatism leaves us completely helpless in front of the trials of our times. Even if we are spared destruction by war, our lives will have to change if we want to save life from self-destruction. We cannot avoid revising the fundamental definitions of human life and human society. Is it true that man is above everything? Is there no Superior Spirit above him? Is it right that man's life and society's activities have to be determined by material expansion in the first place? Is it permissible to promote such expansion to the detriment of our spiritual integrity?"[7]

The Wizards, armed with better tools, seek to blur the differences between man and animal in both theory, and, it would seem, practice. To achieve their ends, they argue that religion must be turned into a philosophical and psychological "experience" with no need of a deity to ensure societal development. And make no mistake; it is the Biblical message which is their greatest enemy, as shown by the amount of energy and number of words spent on trying to discredit Judeo-Christian–inspired philosophy and education.

Furthermore, it is almost certain that some of the Wizards will increasingly and more passionately target not just radical Islam but Islam itself as it wakes up and moves away from its dominant Ash'arite philosophic moorings, which have held in check (for a sizeable portion of the Muslim scholarship) moral reasoning, equality, free-thinking, and other enlightened ideas and practices. Fortunately, it is increasingly the vision of Islamic scholars that there is a need for reform[10] within Islamic thinking,[11] especially in theology.

On the other hand, there are those academics in the West who may indeed embrace Islam because of its philosophical kinship to ideological relativism, as Fr. Schall points out: "The case of Islam falls under this general consideration as an example of a religious theory that cannot, in principle, maintain the logic of science and simultaneously be consistent with itself."[8] Not unexpectedly, with a bit of reflection, Fr. Schall goes on to say that "What is remarkable, however, is that Islam and modern secular science and politics may well be intellectually closer to each other than either is to classical philosophy and Christian revelation. This philosophic closeness is what the Regensburg lecture was about. The two-truth theory in Islam meant that Allah could change his mind, and hence reality, on any question so that nothing in reality was stable. Hence, it could not be examined by reason. Truth could be contradictory; otherwise, Allah's power was said to be 'limited'. In the West, in a logical development that led from Scotus to Hume, once any trace of order in nature was removed, the human mind could make reality into whatever it wanted it to be. Both positions held that nothing necessary or stable could be found in God, man or nature. The divine mind of Allah and the human mind of the relativist scientist ironically were identical."[9]

If there were some way to delete from memory the entirety of the Judeo-Christian historical record, without causing serious blowback, there is little doubt that some of the anti-theists would do it without hesitation. Is that not what is afoot today? For example, the just-completed "House of European History" in Brussels (reported to have cost more than US$60 million), contains only a sprinkling of curiosities about the history and impact of the Judeo-Christian heritage on European civilization in the 21st century.

Given this situation, courageous political leadership must convey the idea that integral human development starts with a recognition of God and of the eternal truths about the human person. To that end, there is a need to clearly explain that the Judeo-Christian concepts of equality, fraternity, and liberty do not mean radical egalitarianism, multiculturalism, and libertarianism. As Benedict XVI has written, "Natural law is, definitively, the only valid bulwark against the arbitrary power or the deception of ideological manipulation. The knowledge of this law inscribed on the heart of man increases with the progress of the moral conscience."[12] Moreover, we might want to reflect on Solzhenitsyn's suggestion: "It is time in the West to defend not so much human rights as human obligations."[13]

These world's crises are crises of men and women who have not tasted the joy of venturing beyond the confines of the Wizards' materialist world and who cannot accept that the unknown is not as risky and scary as they think. We call upon free-thinkers to open their minds and see the divine in the ordinary things around us. Wizards may decide to ignore the evidence about the existence of God, but they can no longer play dumb in the face of the scientific evidence. Antony Flew, perhaps the most prominent atheist in the Anglo-Saxon world until his awakening in 2008, hits the nail on the head: "we have all the evidence we need in our immediate experience, and that only a deliberate refusal to 'look' is responsible for atheism of any variety."[14]

Benedict XVI offers us words to reflect upon: "Love is not dependence but a gift that makes us live. The freedom of a human being is the freedom of a limited being, and therefore is itself limited. We can possess it only as a shared freedom, in the communion of freedom: only if we live in the right way, with one another and for one another, can freedom develop. We live in the right way if we live in accordance with the truth of our being, and that is, in accordance with God's will. For God's will is not a law for the human being imposed from the outside and that constrains him, but the intrinsic measure of his nature, a measure that is engraved within him and makes him the image of God, hence, a free creature. If we live in opposition to love and against the truth — in opposition to God — then we destroy one another and destroy the world. Then we do not find life but act in the interests of death."[15]

Let us plumb the depths of our being and transcend the limits imposed by time, space, and transient circumstances. Let us enter into dialogue with those, including the Wizards, who, perhaps through no fault of their own, no longer see the difference between liberation and conquest because they reject any mention of God, and thus fail to see the immense panorama of the Judeo-Christian worldview's message of love and hope in truth. No matter what is said or done, we hold the winning hand.

---

1.   Benedict XVI (pope), "Religious Freedom, the Path to Peace" (message, January 2011) (http://w2.vatican.va/content/benedict-xvi/en/messages/peace/documents/hf_ben-xvi_mes_20101208_xliv-world-day-peace.html).

2.   John Lennox, "I Don't Have Enough Faith to Be an Atheist" (2014) (http://www.johnlennox.org/jresources/i-dont-have-enough-faith-to-be-an-atheist/).

3.   Ravi Zacharias, "God's Dupes?" (August 2008) (https://www.ligonier.org/learn/articles/gods-dupes/).

4.   Malcolm Muggeridge, *The End of Christendom* (Grand Rapids: W.B. Eerdmans, 1980); p. 9.

5.   Moreover, the anti-theists must differentiate between agency and mechanism, since evolution does not cause anything but only describes how something might change over time.

6.   C.S. Lewis, *Mere Christianity* (New York: Macmillan Company, 1952); p. 26 (https://canavox.com/wp-content/uploads/2017/06/Mere-Christianity-Lewis.pdf).

7.   Alexandr Solzhenitsyn, "A World Split Apart" (commencement speech, Harvard University, June 8, 1978) (http://www.americanrhetoric.com/speeches/alexandersolzhenitsynharvard.htm).

8.   James V. Schall, S.J, *On Islam: A Chronological Record, 2002 – 2018*, (San Francisco, Ignatius, 2018); p.71

9.   James V. Schall, S.J, *On Islam: A Chronological Record, 2002 – 2018*, (San Francisco,

Ignatius, 2018); p.94-95. See Regensburg Address: Benedict XVI (pope), "Faith, Reason and the University: Memories and Reflections" (Lecture, Aula Magna of the University of Regensburg, Germany, September 2006) (http://w2.vatican.va/content/benedict-xvi/en/speeches/2006/september/documents/hf_ben-xvi_spe_20060912_university-regensburg.html)

10.   Stephen Ulph and Patrick Sookhdeo, eds., *Reforming Islam: Progressive Voices from the Arab Muslim World* (McLean, Va.: The Westminster Institute, 2014).

11.   Robert R. Reilly, *The Closing of the Muslim Mind: How Intellectual Suicide Created the Modern Islamic Crisis* (Wilmington, Del.: Intercollegiate Studies Institute, 2010).

12.   Benedict XVI (pope), "On Natural Moral Law" (address, February 2007) (https://w2.vatican.va/content/benedict-xvi/en/speeches/2007/february/documents/hf_ben-xvi_spe_20070212_pul.html).

13.   Solzhenitsyn, "World Split Apart."

14.   Antony Flew and Roy Abraham Varghese, *There Is No a God: How the World's Most Notorious Atheist Changed His Mind* (New York: HarperCollins, 2008); p. 163.

15.   Benedict XVI (pope) (homily, December 2005) (https://w2.vatican.va/content/benedict-xvi/en/homilies/2005/documents/hf_ben-xvi_hom_20051208_anniv-vat-council.html).

Appendix I

The Natural Law and Freedom

The relationship between the natural moral law and civil law presupposes the existent and permanent truth of the natural moral law — in its basic concept and normative content.[1] The question then is how and to what extent the absolutes of the true moral law as naturally intelligible impinge upon that aspect of societal life that requires the governance of public authority and its duty of promoting what is called the political common good without falling into political moralism and utopianism. What are the ultimate criteria for the free decisions involved in all the activity of the human person in view of genuine human development and the final perfection of each and every individual person?

Positions of ontological[2] relativism (especially those that are overtly atheistic, such as the radical ontologies that deny human freedom or the existence of the one uncreated God of the universe), or positions of false absolute ontologies (whether materialistic, spiritualistic, or animistic) lead to notions of the political order and civil law that leave no room for the true natural law position. The critical error of such ontological positions is that they cannot lead to anything but increasing chaos or totalitarianism — or, perhaps better said, cannot but go from covert totalitarianism (manifest in the intolerant exclusion of the voice of the natural moral law) to increasing moral and civic chaos and, finally, to overt and brutal totalitarianism (as evidenced in the 20th century).

How does the truth of the natural law translate into civil law and public policy? On the one hand, there is a need to know what principles of the natural law must be explicitly defended and become part of the legal system for the sake of guidance and what limitations exist for the application of other principles. By having that clear, jurists and politicians will be better able to articulate fundamental principles, overcoming the mostly false fears of the

Wizards who reject them (a) as a reaction against what are considered unjust impositions or arbitrary limitations of freedom proposed in the name of the natural law,[3] or (b) out of fear that any reference to a higher law will undermine the sound and immediate normativity of the established order, intelligibly contained in the *existing* body of written law.

Most Wizards fear that the proponents of a jurisprudence based on true natural moral-law principles will establish through both its negative and positive absolutes all the criteria for judging right and wrong human action, both on the personal and on the interpersonal or societal levels. The idea of permanence is what they fear. The natural moral law establishes, for example, the right and duty that each person has to contribute to the material, moral, and spiritual good of each other human being, to what is generally called the "common good." The truth of that good of others is their integral perfection as minimally enabled and protected by the negative absolutes of the natural law.[4]

Moreover, the true moral law, in clarifying and fostering genuine human development (i.e., the social nature of the human person), defines and defends the obligatory reality of public authority and civil law that is necessary in order to respond to that social reality. It acknowledges and defends what is generally called the "political common good," an aspect of the ultimate common good understood in its full ontological reality. The political common good is related more to the conditions enabling the true good of everyone ("the common good") than to that good itself. Thus, it is by the moral law itself that we seek a definition of the valid scope and content of civil law and find the elements for judging what constitutes necessary and legitimate civil law and public policy according to God's plan.

Key Elements of a Morally Valid Notion of Public Authority, Civil Law, and Public Policy

Prudence (the habit of right practical moral judgment and decision) cannot exist in the void of ontological relativism or within the framework of fundamental error about the human person and the purpose of life. The points that will follow are based on the truth as naturally intelligible along with the moral principles embedded in the nature of things and especially the human person, discoverable in the sincere use of a person's intelligence in its natural functioning.

The duties of the political order, public authority, and civil law are not to be confused with useful maneuvering in a utilitarian sense.[5] The natural moral law and the truths about God, the universe, and the human person on which it is founded grounds and guides the notion of civil law. It is specifically the truth about the person as social by nature — and therefore the truth that the individual person is essentially related to his fellow humans in the quest for mutual perfection through service and integral human development — that gives rise to the notion of the common good in general, that is, the notion of that ultimate good of each and every human being which it is an obligation on the part of each person to foster. More specifically still, it is the truth about a person's social nature and the moral obligations which derive from it that validates and gives the meaning and limits to the truths of public authority, civil law, and the "political common good." Any attempt to develop a political theory — and therefore a notion of public authority, civil law, and the political common good — that rejects the relevance of the nature of the human person, purpose, and the true moral law derived from it is doomed to failure; or rather, it will doom to indignity the people involved in its implementation.

Political authority and the broad political entity that functions under it — that is, the state — exist both historically and conceptually as a derivative of the truth of the human person, families, groupings of families, and institutions of work, education, and religious worship — what we call "civil society." It exists therefore to serve them and to enhance the fulfillment of the purposes of each entity and person in their mutual interrelationships, in view of a person's and society's integral human development. There is no true notion of political authority and its instruments that is not morally bounded by the duty to serve the ontological and moral good of those entities and especially their participants, and to coordinate with other political authorities or states so that that goal might be carried out in the best of ways.[6]

The concepts of the common good and the political common good are related as end and means. It is important to distinguish the two distinct concepts independently of the terminology used, since those terms are frequently used quite differently. In fact, what will be defined below as the political common good is most frequently called simply the "common good."

Of critical importance is to know the end of man and therefore the end which all of society and all its entities, including public authority and its activity, must serve. The end of humankind is integral human development, a bodily, moral, spiritual perfection for the glory of God and in the love of God that will continue after death and eternally. This perfection of the individual is inextricably linked to a person's work and love for the perfection of others, reaching out at least in intention to everyone. The ultimate good that the individual person must seek — and this precisely in imitation of God — is the ultimate happiness of all human beings in eternity; it is what the political common good of each state and of all states exists to enable. The Judeo-Christian worldview, unlike the worldview of some Wizards, condemns any political ideology that removes God from the public square or that aims to "lobotomize" human beings, so to speak — to keep them in some state of bliss out of ignorance.

This notion of the common good is the ultimate moral criterion for progress and development for all individual and societal functioning, despite human failings and personal sin. Statecraft exists to facilitate genuine human development by advancing and defending the political common good, while recognizing the evils of trying to bring about political utopias of one sort or another on this side of death. The true perfection of the human person is a question of free and responsible living according to the truth of existence and reality. It is not the function of political authority to define or to impose that truth, but to carry out a key role in maintaining the conditions of authentic freedom, peace, order, and justice such that individual people — who are the only protagonists of perfection — will be enabled to help themselves and others to that final perfection, which, contrary to the Wizards' narrative, is not of this world. Thus, the political common good can be defined as the totality of societal conditions that enable the people of a nation to reach their final ontological, moral, and spiritual perfection, which is to say, reach their integral human development. This notion of adequate societal conditions involves defending what is called an objective ethical or moral minimum in all relationships and activities, without which it would be difficult to speak of enabling human development, ultimately an ethical, moral, or spiritual reality.

At the same time, however, it is precisely the minimum which constitutes the political common good, since no created entity, neither political authority nor religious authority, is capable of specifying — in legal norms — the maximum which constitutes integral development. Thus, a main content of the political common good is the adequate protection of all the fundamental moral rights of the human person as civil rights; since authentic rights exist for the exercise of virtue and duty, the political common good involves the legal demand of the performance of some duties, specifically those that are necessary to maintain the political common good, thus guaranteeing realistically the minimum conditions of freedom (including religious freedom), justice, peace, and opportunity for all.

Minimums and Defense of Primordial Freedoms

The truth about the one uncreated God of the universe and the truth about the natural moral law that is intrinsically related to that universe are naturally intelligible. Like other naturally intelligible truths, however, they may not be known or accepted by particular people at any given time. Because of the nature of the human person as a being who can reach his perfection only by free acceptance of the truth of reality and free action according to it, *never is it proper to impose the truth.*

Right Reason and God

The truth about God and therefore the ultimate motivation for human action is an especially important and delicate matter: that the fullness of the truth about God and about the nature of the perfection or development of the human person is related to the intelligent acceptance through reason and faith of the voice of God. Reason can be right only when it "captures" the true nature and purpose of being. In this connection, while all historical religions have some beliefs and practices that do correspond to the specific demands of natural intelligibility, they also have some beliefs and practices that do not correspond to specific demands of natural intelligibility; some have beliefs and practices that are objectively contrary to some natural truths but not clearly offensive to human dignity or to the public peace.

The duty of public authority is to deal with that state of affairs as it exists, as a matter of primordial importance and of ultimate care and refinement. More specifically, its duty is to defend the essential right of personal freedom *in the search for religious truth.* It does so by establishing as law the freedom of every citizen not to be coerced externally, whether positively or negatively, especially not by public authority — but also not by other persons or entities of society — in matters of ultimate belief and motivation, religious practice in correspondence to certain beliefs, religious speech, and enrollment of members, all within certain qualifications determined by the political common good and, specifically, respecting the primordial rights of parents to educate their children according to their religious convictions.

This is not a policy corresponding to the notion of a so-called necessary toleration of evil by public authority but rather to the obligatory defense of the primordial freedom of the individual person in the search of ultimate truth, a defense of the core element of the dignity of the human person. The establishment of the civil right to religious freedom is central to the political common good that public authority must in part create and maintain.

The qualifying limits on religious freedom of particular persons and religious groups are all related to the ethical minimum of the fundamental rights and duties defined by other principles of the natural moral law, particularly those related to public order and peace. Thus they are related to external actions and not to interior beliefs.

Some Guidelines for the Common Good

There are therefore some restrictions on religious worship, on religious speech and enrolling, restrictions that do not go against the protection of religious freedom but rather defend it:

1. Public authority must prohibit — whether advanced in the name of religion or any other name — human sacrifice, torture, murder, conquest, subjugation, or attempts to establish earthly utopias in the name of national security, equality, fraternity, or liberty as directly contrary to specific fundamental principles of the natural moral law, solidarity, and subsidiarity, and thus to the dignity of the human person and immediate public order and peace.

2. Public authority must have a positive attitude to religion and the particular religious traditions of the people it is obliged to serve. It would be a cause of deep disorder and an attack on public peace for a government to undertake a project of undoing long-standing peaceful public traditions in the name of religious freedom unless one or another of those traditions were proven to be objectively against the religious freedom of others. Thus, for example, with regard to the United States, it would be wrong for public authority to try to eliminate long-standing public customs and traditions related to the Judeo-Christian tradition and as embodied in the Constitution. It is not that the customs are absolute but rather that they respond to a long-standing sociological dynamic and the general good of the people, and are not objectively offensive to anyone's legitimate religious freedom, or, thus, to public peace and order.

3. Public authority should not prohibit, whether in public or nonpublic functions, religious speech or any other speech that is minimally respectful of the truth. Otherwise, the only speech that would be permitted would be expressions of positions denying the ultimate truth, thus promoting a political order dominated by the ideologies antithetical to genuine human development. Involved here, of course, would be the very definition of what constitutes religious speech.

4. No particular religious tradition or political ideology may demand that public authority impose its particular traditions beyond what is naturally intelligible on people of other religious traditions or of no religion; public policies affecting everyone need to be based on arguments of natural intelligibility (which is not limited to the truths of science). It is, however, against the political common good for public authority to permit the development of a cultural or legal dynamic in which the naturally intelligible truth of reality and the moral law would be excluded from public discourse and institutions

in the name of a false notion of religious freedom (or of any utopian wishful thinking or political moralism), which would make the only parameters of public discourse and decision-making atheism and its relativistic and pragmatic normativity.

5. As regards enrollment in religions, public authority may properly regulate only what objectively goes against clear acts of deceit, fraud, and brainwashing of the young and the weak, which effectively are often related to acts that are properly prohibited in general, that is, are crimes in themselves unrelated to religious legislation. Any religion that would seek enrollment on the basis of such acts would have to be restricted in the same way as individual persons or other institutions seeking other objectives.

Legitimate National Sovereignty

The political common good of a nation must be related to the political common good of all nations and finally to the ultimate common good of humanity. Thus:

1. Relationships between nations must be governed by the natural moral law, which is one for all nations. Any notion of national sovereignty that excludes the governance of the universal concepts of morality in the relations between nations is entirely false.

2. The proper view of public authority and the political common good of a nation means the maintenance of the conditions whereby all citizens and entities of the nation can fulfill freely their duties towards their neighbors and fellow citizens. The political common good of a nation will not have been reached if statesmen or other public authorities cancel or make difficult the relations of their citizens and entities with other peoples towards fostering good everywhere.

3. Modern economics and communications which tend to unify the peoples of the world and make the notion of a culturally differentiated national political common good artificial and detrimental to the nation that invokes it should not undo the notion of the good of national entities with full political protection or authority. The notion of a one-world political common good with a one-world political authority is dangerous because of the concentration of power that it entails and because of the almost certain impossibility of creating and maintaining one homogeneous political common good without the use of force or de-humanizing strategies.[7]

Limits of Civil Law

The concept, basic content, and limits of civil law have as their basic and only purpose the establishment and maintenance of the conditions for genuine human development. The moral legitimacy of what the civil law regulates is determined by whether or not it effectively accomplishes that purpose.

Thus, civil law or regulation that would establish legal rights to do intrinsically moral evil as defined by the natural moral law — and thus that impedes a legal defense against those evils by individual citizens and families or the various entities of civil society — would be against the political common good or genuine human development. To repeat: the fundamental normativity for political authority and civil law are the negative absolutes of the natural moral law. The first obligation of political authority and civil law is to do no harm, by refusing to legitimize intrinsically evil actions.

Common sense dictates that "one must therefore reject the thesis, characteristic of teleological and proportionalist theories, which holds that it is impossible to qualify as morally evil according to its species — its object — the deliberate choice of certain kinds of behavior, or specific acts, apart from a consideration of the intention for which the choice is made or the totality of the foreseeable consequences of that act for all persons concerned."[8]

On the positive side, civil law — in order to maintain in place the conditions for integral human development — must defend the moral rights of all its citizens and encourage the fulfillment of their moral duties. In maintaining or promoting the political common good, political authorities must be careful not to try to do too much, either in prohibiting evil or in encouraging good. Otherwise, they undermine the main elements that encourage responsible freedom and local decision-making and thus the best conditions enabling everyone to do good.

In general, civil law and the political common good that it must maintain and promote apply to external actions alone and only those that affect in some clear way the fundamental rights of others. The rights of others are not only those related to physical life and health or only to property but, in a special way, are those related to family integrity, the very foundation of societal order. A person's right to essential information and the truth, the right to not be deceived, especially by political authority, is essential as well for integral human development.

Moral Evil: Prohibiting without Approving but without Impeding

We turn now to the concept and limits of legislative "tolerance of moral evil."

1. The moral law, i.e., the natural moral law, clarifies for everyone what actions are evil and, especially clearly, what actions are intrinsically evil. Thus, the topic of tolerance of evil is not abstract or arbitrary with regard to what constitutes moral evils.

2. The tolerance involved here is "permitting without approving but without impeding."

3. The tolerance of evil should not be confused with what must be respected, e.g., respect for morally legitimate options and differences of people, even for their adoption of beliefs and ways of action known objectively to be erroneous, especially when they are religious beliefs and practices, within certain limits that do not impede genuine human development.

4. The moral question here is not the extent to which individual persons must or must not tolerate evil actions in the lives of the people they associate with and encounter; it is the question of what political authority can, must, or cannot permit. The question of an individual is often an exclusively moral question with no direct dimension of civil law or political common good.

5. Public authority and civil law must not try to prohibit all moral evil. We refer to some intrinsically immoral actions that threaten the fundamental rights and duties of others and the basic peace and order of society. Within those matters there can be situations when political authority can judge it opportune or even obligatory not to establish a prohibitive law or a specific enforcement because of the strong probability or certainty that by attempting to regulate the matter there would result a greater evil for the public order and peace, or there would be an impediment to a greater good. For a decision to be morally valid, however, the situation must not be handled in such a way that it can be construed (especially legally) to legitimize or facilitate the evil actions.

Solidarity, Subsidiarity, and Just Law

The principles of solidarity and subsidiarity are principal norms for the proper ordering of society. They are universal moral principles that must govern simultaneously in all situations. Thus, an action of solidarity must always respect the principle of subsidiarity and vice versa.

The universal moral principle of solidarity (or unity while maintaining diversity and individuality) clarifies for every person's conscience the moral duty of that person and that of all the institutions of society towards integral human development and thus toward the good of human unity and collaboration.

Political authority and civil law have a special though not exclusive part to play in defending this principle and fostering its fulfillment. Civil law must defend the fundamental rights of each and all by which they are enabled to contribute to solidarity; it must also take care that the fundamental needs, especially of the weak and the disadvantaged, are satisfied. These objectives do not and cannot justify, however, a policy of utopian ideological egalitarianism or a quest for it, but rather a caring for fundamental rights and needs; the goal of equalization cannot be intrusive or artificially imposed. The actions by public authority fostering solidarity must also be consonant with the principle of subsidiarity and thus not be first and foremost actions through public structures, which would preempt the rights and duties of individuals, families, local bodies, churches, and others to be the agents of this work of solidarity.

The principle of subsidiarity is a moral principle that prohibits the political authority to carry out directly the functions of solidarity that can be carried out adequately by individuals, families, or the many nonpublic institutions of society at the local level. If public authority were to ignore this principle, it would be acting directly against the political common good and the ultimate common good, which rest fundamentally on the freedom and responsibility of individuals, families, and others in carrying out their particular purposes in solidarity with the rest. The principle of subsidiarity is critical for genuine human development.[9]

What are considered just and unjust laws must follow upon the correct notions of justice and injustice and the situations or conditions that give rise to them. Many situations that are called unjust are not so, strictly speaking. Instead, they are situations of differences of peoples' circumstances, talents, or opportunities that are neither good nor bad, morally speaking, but rather the reality of the temporal conditions that those people can and must responsibly handle in view of their perfection and that of others.

Human laws (whether civil or ecclesiastical) are by their nature imperfect in the sense that they are incapable of articulating fully the good to be done and the evil to be avoided for all subjects in all circumstances. For that reason, human law incorporates the legal realities of dispensation. Imperfection must not, however, be the basis for introducing arbitrariness into the law or its interpretation, or for calling all law unjust to some degree. It is the nature of human law that it cannot give direction for all good or prohibit all evil.

Civil laws are just and to be obeyed if they do a reasonable job of mandating aspects of objective good and discourage the objective evil within the purview of the political common good and the objective of genuine human development.

Political Authority, Statecraft, and Constitutionalism

Any valid notion of political authority must be founded in or refer to the natural moral law, which the Constitution of the United States does clearly and amply.

There are some notions of constitutionalism that serve as the basis for political authority and law, but that lack a true moral foundation and therefore are inadequate.

Perhaps, most generally, constitutionalism is said to be the definition of any political order with a body of known law — whether based in a common-law tradition or a written constitution — which governs not only the citizens but the political authority, such that governance is by rule of law rather than decree of authority. The simple notion of rule by law does not in itself establish a morally legitimate political order; the law of the rule must be in conformity with the natural moral law; the reference to a social pact (such as that of Rousseau) is not a sufficient moral foundation. For example, the Supreme Court of the United States, the Court of Cassation of France, or the Saikō-Saibansho in Japan should not be enabled to override the inalienable and fundamental principles of natural law that are embedded in human nature. Augustine states the matter thus: "A law that is unjust is considered no law at all."[10] Individual freedom, social contracts, or the "will of the people" cannot override natural-law principles. "In today's ethics and philosophy of law, petitions of juridical positivism (i.e., the law is only what the legislator says) are widespread. As a result, legislation often becomes only a compromise between different interests: seeking to transform private interests or wishes into laws that conflict with the duties deriving from the social responsibility."[11]

The term "constitutionalism" is also used to describe most modern democratic nation-states in which there are a division of the powers of political authority, periodic elections of rulers, and the determination of most of the laws by majority vote within a framework established by a written constitution. This conception tends to put exaggerated emphasis on the good of procedure over substance. It has tended to unravel in critical moral matters directly impinging on the common good when procedures are abused in the name of especially pressing needs artificially constructed by those in positions of power. A constitutionalism that puts the emphasis on procedure without grounding the substance of the law in the true moral law becomes the instrument of those who are expert in procedures and their manipulation.

Lastly, there is a constitutionalism that seeks rule by statute that arises from the legislative power in its clear straightforward meaning, without interpretations that make reference to constitutional questions or political or philosophical theories, which are assumed to have been the basis for the legislative act. The plain language of the statute is said to incorporate all the necessary interpretation; if it is not clear, it is to be ruled null and void. While that theory might be reasonable if there were common-sense acceptance of the fundamental ontological and moral truths of reality by citizens and legislators, that is precisely *not* the case today; the basis for agreement on plain language and interpretation is at present nonexistent. Decisions often default to power or arbitrariness, hardly the basis for legitimate governance.

It is not logical to expect any merely procedural system to guarantee a political arrangement that will serve genuine human development. There are too many powerful forces — as all of history shows — that undo the spontaneous good use of procedures by the majority of people to do good. Fundamental substantial goods must be defined, protected, and fostered, and that can be done only by having a body of law (at a minimum without overreach) that is written and interpreted according to the essential ontological and moral truths of reality and human existence.

The natural law applies as much to men and women in India and Japan as to those in Nigeria and Paraguay, irrespective of race, color, creed, or language, precisely because natural law is embedded in human nature.

---

1.   The Ten Commandments reflect natural moral law (and divine wisdom) within the Judeo-Christian tradition, and are consistent with reason and the Greek philosophical tradition.

2.   Ontology is the branch of metaphysics dealing with the nature of being, existence, becoming, and reality itself. It deals with which beings exist or may exist and in what manner they may be grouped or subdivided as per relationships or likenesses.

3.   The natural law itself cannot demand the imposition of unjust limitations on human freedom. By its very nature, natural law is coherent with reason.

4.   For example, a given person will not be fulfilling his/her obligation with respect to the common good by being indifferent to a cultural environment of atheism and sexual immorality; the natural law demands that the individual seek to change that environment within realistic possibilities through educational and other formative efforts, especially toward the young, or concerning political action, protest, et cetera.

5.   Utilitarianism, as set out by the English philosophers Jeremy Bentham and John Stuart Mill, is a consequentialist system of moral ethics. According to their views, a person should always act in such a way that his/her actions produce the greatest possible balance of good over evil — an unreasonable position because "good" is defined as "what suits a person best," all else being irrelevant. Utilitarian philosophers start from the premise that the goodness of an act is measured by the amount of gratification or security it produces. They would reject the view that there are intrinsically evil acts that can never be justified

independently of their consequences. In a sense, selfishness becomes one of the highest of virtues.

6. Political authority is a moral authority under God, a structure of the order of creation which is focused on establishing and maintaining the temporal conditions that are necessary to facilitate the perfecting work of each and every human being and aiming at final completion and happiness in eternal life.

7. Proponents of a unipolar world order usually base their international political agenda on the subordination of other peoples.

8. St. John Paul II (pope), "The Splendor of Truth: Regarding Certain Fundamental Question of the Church's Moral Teaching" (encyclical letter, August 1993) (http://w2.vatican.va/content/john-paul-ii/en/encyclicals/documents/hf_jp-ii_enc_06081993_veritatis-splendor.html).

9. Recent Anglo-American liberal state ideology and socialism have tried to deny the principle of subsidiarity at least in practice. They both have promoted concentrations of power among certain elites (public and private) who have sought to set out structures and laws against the innate rights and duties of local communities, their families, and other local entities. This tendency toward centralized governance has gained momentum in recent years.

10. St. Augustine (quoted in St. Thomas Aquinas, *Summa Theologiae,* Q. 96).

11. Benedict XVI (pope), "On Natural Moral Law" (address, February 2007) (https://w2.vatican.va/content/benedict-xvi/en/speeches/2007/february/documents/hf_ben-xvi_spe_20070212_pul.html).

APPENDIX II

Descartes: Two Views

René Descartes (1596–1650) was a brilliant mathematician whose achievements include the invention of coordinate geometry (called "Cartesian geometry" in his honor) and analytical geometry. Proposing to describe the universe in mathematical terms and describing material phenomena in basic mechanistic ways, he laid groundwork for the mathematical approach to much of modern natural science. His reaction against the influential animistic and magical theories of the time served as the basis for an important body of his work.

Descartes is generally called the first modern philosopher because of the attribution to him of helping to bring about the Copernican shift from seeking knowledge through sense contact with objects outside the mind to seeking knowledge through a form of subjective certainty about the ideas found in the mind. It is asserted that he was the father, or culprit, of all the modern subjectivist/relativist positions that have dominated intellectual history over the last four and a half centuries. What follows is a more or less standard presentation of his teaching, which I consider invalid because of the initial denial of sense knowledge and what I assert to be an illegitimate move from an idea in the mind to reality outside the mind:

1. He proposed to doubt the reality/truth of everything generally known (his methodological doubt) on the basis of the unreliability of all traditions and sense data.

2. That done, and thus with no certain reality coming to him from outside his mind, he asked whether there was some indisputable certainty he could base further thought upon. He was overpowered by the realization that his very thinking, feeling, and other mental acts brought spontaneously to his consciousness the conviction of his existence.

He found it indisputable that moment by moment his thinking implied that he existed.

3. From this insight, Descartes derived what he called "clear and distinct ideas," which followed from his initial certainty, to fundamental statements of reality. For example, he said that he had the clear and distinct idea of a necessary substratum in himself for his activity of constant thinking, i.e., his substantial soul, and therefore it had to exist. Similarly, he asserted the existence outside himself, and as completely distinct from himself, of the Infinite one God, who created and sustains his soul and its activity, because he (Descartes) had a clear and distinct idea of the necessary existence of such a being in the inner experience of his own finiteness. Finally, on this same fundamental level, he affirmed the existence of all things outside himself that his senses perceive because the God who he now knows exists is good, is honest, cannot deceive, and guarantees their existence and the reliability of his senses.

A considerable number of authors do not agree with the standard portrayal of Descartes as a complete subjectivist, and do not agree that the devastating subjectivism and relativism of the following centuries come substantially from him. Those authors give the following contrary interpretation, which they say is important so that we are not ignorant of where the essential problems lay:

1. Descartes's initial methodological doubt corresponded to a full confrontation with the dominant skepticism of his time about normal sense knowledge, traditions, et cetera. He was seeking to create a path to certainty for the skeptic, to give an answer to that skepticism.

2. What he says about thinking and the certainty of existing in the moment of thinking is indisputable.

3. To talk about going from the known activity of thinking to assert the existence of a substantial source for the continuity of that activity is not a subjectivist whim but objective logic: in traditional treatises of the metaphysics of man, we say that it is philosophically certain that the spiritual activity of a human being implies that the human life-principle or soul must be spiritual. Perhaps one could logically ask whether the source of a person's activity is within the person or outside, being perhaps a kind of collective life-principle acting from a distance rather than one contained in and operating as an individual life-principle. But since we agree that there is no indication whatsoever of a collective life-principle for anyone, we can concede that Descartes had every reason to conclude that he had an individual sub-

stantial life-principle.

4. Descartes's proof for the existence of God should not be discarded as completely ungrounded in objective thinking. The acknowledgement by him of his finiteness, and therefore the impossibility that his soul alone explains the certainty of his mental acts, lead him to say that the existence of his Creator and the Sustainer and Guide of his activity is a clear and distinct idea that is true. It is not much different from the third way of St. Thomas. At least, one has to say it is not an essentially subjectivist argument.

That there are weaknesses in Descartes's philosophy is incontrovertible, and that his approach is vulnerable to being abused is historical, but it is important not to ignore that the essential cause of the horrendous mistakes of thinking and of decision-making in modern times is a voluntaristic choice to oppose God and His will and therefore to arbitrarily build systems that block access to the true God and His law. The source of truly subjectivistic and relativistic systems of the modern world are the many pantheistic and materialistic atheists of the Renaissance whom Descartes was seeking to counter, along with Baruch Spinoza (1632–1677) and countless other later atheistic rationalists and empiricists.

Lastly, it should be understood that a main context for Descartes's erroneous philosophical conception of the relation between the human person's body and soul was the horrendous intellectual milieu of pantheistic atheism positing a soul in all matter exposed to esoteric, magical forces; that was a supposed scientific view of the prior couple of centuries, and it was still dominant in his time. He was himself initially drawn into that milieu and conception but he rebelled against it, and sought to show that there were no such forces at work, that bodies responded basically to mechanical laws. (Obviously, he did not have much knowledge of physical, biological, and chemical laws.) It is a mistake to attribute to him many erroneous approaches to the body based on his "dualism"; the source of those mistakes is the choice to oppose God and the natural moral law.

While Descartes was essentially a philosopher, he did a lot of experimental work, seeking data to confirm some of the hypotheses he had formulated. He did not always accept experimental data from others against his hypotheses, but it is not correct to say that he simply proposed assertions from his head. He was not a rationalist in the philosophical sense of erroneously trying to derive reality from thoughts in the mind.

ABOUT THE AUTHOR

Alberto Martinez Piedra

Alberto M. Piedra, Professor Emeritus and former Donald E. Bently Professor of Political Economy at The Institute of World Politics, was U.S. Ambassador to Guatemala 1984-1987. He holds three earned doctorates: Doctor in Law, University of Havana (1951); Doctor in Political Economy, University of Madrid (1957); and Ph.D. in Economics, Georgetown University (1962). At Catholic University of America, he was chairman of the Department of Economics and Business (1989-1995) and director of the Latin American Institute (1965-1982). He has published widely in fields ranging from economics to intellectual history.

27107702R00141

Made in the USA
Columbia, SC
19 September 2018